MY INSTANT FAMILY

From Single to Wife and Mother... Just Like That

GINA M. IACIOFANO

DEDICATION:

This is dedicated to Carol, my twin and best friend, who has heard every word, thought, and idea about this book. Carol, thank you for always listening and being my cheering squad. I love you.

To my loving family, who may not always know what I am writing and working on — I thank you for your love.

CHAPTER ONE

My name is Ken. Well, actually it is Kennedy Rose Jackson. I am thirty-nine years old. I have never been married. I do not have any kids; however, I love them more than anything in the world. I have a twin sister, Jamie Daisy Jackson and an older brother, Parker Dean Jackson. We lovingly call our brother Park.

Our mother didn't know she was having twins when we were born. Jamie my best friend, was born first and eight minutes later I was born. We have never been competitive like you hear that some twins are. Not us. Jamie has always been the singer and dancer of the two of us. I am the runner. In high school, Jamie was a cheerleader; while I was on the soccer team, softball team, basketball team, and I ran track.

Parker being three years older than us was wrapping up his high school career as we were just starting. He went on to college and played football. We were his biggest fans when we were kids.

Our parents kept on us about getting our schoolwork done. "You want to be productive every single day of your life," dad would say from the time that we started school. We had separate rooms. Usually parents like to put their twins together or keep them together. Our parents allowed us to be individuals from the start. Our childhood house was huge as far as houses go. It was an older house that at one time had been the town's only hotel so to speak. It was more like a bed and breakfast. There were ten bedrooms each with their own bathroom. There was a conference room or our homework room as we called it. There are a total of four conference rooms, there is a theater room, a library, and a game room as well that are all on the first floor. The kitchen was huge, and the dining room was a grand state room. Plus on the second floor in the front of the house, there is an apartment which is a four bedroom three and half bathroom with a fully furnished kitchen, dining and living rooms.

We have kept the house. The Jackson Estate as it is lovingly known as and always has been. I still live there. Parker and his wife Addison work here. We are in the process of turning it back into a B & B with our parents' consent.

The Jackson Estate is a residence in Florida. Our parents bought the land around the property when we were all young and growing up. "We want to keep it the old Florida way," our mother would say. Therefore, we now have just under a thousand acres. There are tennis courts, basketball courts, a quarter mile track, an Olympic size swimming pool, and we are in processes of building a gym and adding kiddy pools, and an in ground hot tub; with possibly a lazy river pool.

I went to school for architecture. So though my parents gave me the blue prints to our house and property, I had to go and draft it up myself. It's something I always did. I was always drawing up maps of things. Scaling things out. Working through beyond what was there.

"Ken, are you listening?" Addison asked.
"What?"
"We need to build a playground for kids."
"Yeah, I know."
"When Parker and I bring the kids here, they have nowhere to play?"
"They have a million places to play, Addison."
"But they need a proper playground."
"I'll draw something up tonight."

Drawing something up was much much more than that for me. It was actually sketching something up, yes, but it was also making a model and seeing how it would work and where it would work. Knowing my sister-in-law, she would want it in plain sight. This in her eyes as a chef would be right out the kitchen windows. Out the kitchen windows is an elaborate garden that I constructed when I was ten and our parents left it there, so it is still here today. The property is huge. There is a place for a playground or play area for children. It is just not going to be where Addison wants it.

Ten years ago, our uncle purchased a lot of horses with nowhere in the world to put them, so our father being the good and kind brother had the old run-down barn rebuilt, so we have livestock on the property as well. Also when he did it, he had everything upgraded and four more stables added as well. There is WiFi and phone service in the barn.

Park has three boys and two girls. They range from ten to two years old. I love them. They are fun to be with. The oldest is Michael, then there is Kate, Carter, Tyson, and Beth is the baby. Michael is into sports: karate, judo, soccer, lacrosse, and swimming. Kate is a music bug. She is always working on arranging music, singing, and composing. She is almost ten and is determined that she will be famous before she is twelve. Carter loves the horses and the animals. He is seven and has a wickedly funny sense of humor. Tyson is four and Beth is two. They are two little characters. They are into everything but nothing at the same time. They come with Addison and Park almost every day. They run around the house, they get lost in the yard and on the property. They always come in crying or fighting and always dirty.

Like I stated before, I live on the property. I stay in my childhood bedroom, which I decorated even as a young child. Our parents were into white and off whites. While my sister, brother and I were into color. Vibrant colors. Our rooms were never white. Every summer starting when Jamie and I were eight, we would strip the paint off the walls and start again. She's always been into the purple range of the color spectrum. Me. Well, that was another story. My room has been just about every color under the sun excluding the yellow ranges. Yellow isn't my favorite color. Not that I hate it, it's just not for me. Park's room was brown, tan, black for about three years, and then he went into the blues on the color wheel. It's fun to be creative. And that's something I've always been.

"Ken?" Park said for…well I don't know how many times he said my name. "Kenny!"

I looked at him.

"What the hell! I said your name like ten times."

"Sorry. I'm just lost in thought."

"Did you speak to mom and dad about building on to the house yet?"

"No." *I don't need their permission. This is my house. It is MY house.*

"Ken!"

"It's not just something you can talk to them about over the phone. I'm going to go down and see them."

"Wait! What? How long will you be gone? They are hours away."

"They are in the Keys, Park. It's not that far. Besides, we aren't open for business just yet."

"Don't I know it."

"Don't be a jerk."

"Listen I told my friend that he could have his wedding here."

"When?"

"At the end of the month."

"I'm not setting up for his wedding."

"I didn't ask you to."

"This is my place until we open. You have to discuss your plans with me before you can give your friend the ok to have a wedding at my house."

"Kenny, this is all of ours."

"No, it's not. You and Addison have your own home that you go home to every night."

"I'll call mom and ask her."

"Be my guest," I said to him.

He fished his cell out of his pocket and called mom. She answered on the third ring. "Hello, Parker."

"Hi, mom."

"What can I help you with?"

"I'm at our old house. Whose house it is now?"

"It's Ken's," mom said. "She bought your father and me out, so therefore, it belongs solely to her."

He breathed out hard.

"I know that she is going to open it as a B & B, but it will always be her house until she sells it."

"Fine. How are you and dad doing?"

"We are great. We are going to take the boat out this afternoon and do a little fishing."

"Sounds like fun."

"What are you all up to?"

"You know. Working. The kids. Married life," he said.

"Well, always take the time to enjoy it."

"Yes, I will."

They kept the conversation short. They kind of had to because the toddlers came into the house yelling at each other.

"NO!"

"YES!"

"NO!"

"YES!" Tyson said. "You're not nice."

"I am too."

"Are not."

"I have to go," Park said. "Love you." He hung up the phone just as Beth smacked Tyson hard on the arm. He in turn turned and grabbed her arm and bit her. Then the screaming crying began.

I walked into the room not seeing my brother, and I first lifted Beth up. I examined the bite mark. No blood. No broken skin. I sat her on the couch. "Two minutes," I said to her. Then I lifted Tyson up, he was holding his arm. He had a vibrant red mark on his fair skin. I rubbed the spot. However, I sat him in a chair as well. "Four minutes."

"But she started it."

"Tyson, you are older. Not saying that you should know better, but you should. Four minutes."

"Yes, Aunt Ken," he said. He sat in the chair that I put him. I knew that Beth had gotten up and ran into the kitchen to see her mom.

"Aunt Ken put me in time out," she stated.

"Are you supposed to be there now?"

"Yes."

"Then go be there."

"But I'm hungry."

"And you will still be hungry in two minutes when time out is over. Now go," Addison said.

"Yes, mommy," she said and came back into the living room. She sat on the couch where I put her.

"Tyson, you can go play," I said to him.

He got up from his chair without saying anything. He left the room where I was in with Beth, who was on the couch playing with her shoes. I timed two minutes. "You can get up now," I said to her. "Remember that there are rules in the house."

"Ok," she said with an angelic smile and then ran into the kitchen. Addison made the two of them lunch.

I was busy in my own world. Addison touched my shoulder. I jumped. "I didn't mean to startle you. I made something new for lunch. I want you to try it."

"Ok. Thank you."

Addison found Parker. "She jumped again when I touched her."

"She's ok," he said. "Something smells delicious."

We were all in the kitchen now. The two kids were sitting at the small table eating together nicely. I sat next to Addison. "What is it? It smells magnificent."

"Thank you," she said.

"I think it's chicken," Tyson said.

"You think everything is chicken," I said to him.

"I'm done. Can I go play?"

"Not just yet," Addison said.

He sat there. I got up and took a coloring book off the far counter. I reached for the crayons and put it down on the table.

"Thank you," Addison said. "So I'm not going to tell you what I made. I want to you take a bite and tell me what you taste."

"Ok," Parker and I said together.

The smell was out of this world. Tyson was right. It was chicken in a pesto sauce with risotto. It had an amazing taste.

"Thank you," I said. "This is delicious."

"We would need to work out a schedule of when the kitchen will be up and running for the customers," Addison said.

"Well, it's a B & B," I said. "So what do you think? Breakfast and lunch?"

"We'd have to serve dinner too," Jamie said coming into the house.

I stood up and went to my sister. We wrapped our arms around each other. It was a hug that could have lasted forever.

"Hi," we said together. "How are you?"

"I've missed you," I said to her.

"I've missed you too."

"How was the tour?"

"Oh, my god, it was great," she said.

I had gone to several of her shows. I would go to all of them if time allowed me to.

"Hey, Park. Hi, Addison."

"Hi, Jamie. It's good to see you."

"Can you stay tonight?" I asked her.

"Yes, of course," she said. "This tour is over."

Parker hugged Jamie. I found myself touching her constantly. Her hand, her shoulder, her hair. Just something that was her.

"Have you seen mom and dad?" Parker asked.

"Yep. I spent the last couple days with them. My last concert was in Key West. What a bunch of drunken assholes," Jamie said with a laugh in her voice. "How are the kids?"

"They are good," Addison said.

Jamie hugged Beth and Tyson. Jamie came and stood behind me. She was touching my shoulder, my back and my hair. She bent and kissed me on the back of the head. "I've missed you," she said to me.

"So where was the tour?"

"It was a nationwide tour," Jamie said to Addison. "All forty-eight states, plus Hawaii and Alaska."

"Did you see whales?"

"I did," she said to Tyson.

"Were they big?"

"Big doesn't even describe what they are."

I wanted to be greedy and tell my brother and sister-in-law to leave so that I could have quality time with my sister. Addison sensed something. "We should go. The kids will be home from school soon. They need help with their homework. We will see you on Friday," Addison said.

After they left, Jamie and I helped ourselves to more of Addison's cooking. "Jesus, this is good," Jamie said.

"Can I give you another hug?"

"Oh my god yes," Jamie said.

We hugged again.

"So tell me, Ken, what is new with you?"

"As you know, I'm turning this into a B & B. Parker wants to control everything. Same old shit," I said with a smile. "What is new with you?"

"I met someone," she said.

"Oh, wow, that's great."

"Um yeah," she said. "Can I tell you a secret?"

"Of course," I said. "But I think I already know."

"What do you know?"

"You are pregnant," I said.

"How in the hell did you know that?"

"I dreamt it."

"When?"

"About three weeks ago."

"That's when I found out," Jamie said.

"Congratulations."

"Thank you."

"Did you tell mom and dad?"

"No. Not yet."

"Why not?"

"I wanted you to know first," she said.

CHAPTER TWO

That night we stayed up all night catching up. She told me all about her new boyfriend. "He's the one," she said. "Not just because he got me pregnant, but because… Well, it's hard to put into words."

"Does he treat you right?"

"Like I'm a princess. It's so satisfying. He's wonderful."

"What does he do?"

"He's an entrepreneur. He makes things," she said with a smile on her face.

I smiled back at her.

"Tell me. Is there anyone in your life right now?"

"No."

"Ken," she whined. "Why not?"

"I'm busy."

"You still like living here?"

"Yes, I do," I said.

At five in the morning, work started for me. I had to go feed, brush, and walk the horses. When I was done, I mucked their stables, replaced the hay, made sure there was water in their buckets, and I moved on to the next thing. The pool. I swept it and added chemicals. By this time it was six and I wasn't even close to being done with the yard work.

Parker and Addison pulled up with the kids. Tyson and Beth came running towards me. I hugged them both.

"What are you doing?" Beth asked.

"I'm cleaning up."

"But why?"

"Because it needs to be done," I said.

"Ok. Bye," she said and ran into the house. You have to love her spirit. I looked at Tyson. "What's wrong, buddy?"

"Daddy says I have to start school soon."

"Yes, you do, but you know what?"

"What?"

"You will do great at school."

"Yeah, I guess."

"Come on. Let's go check the courts."

"What are we checking for?"

"Standing water."

"What's that?"

"Standing water is when there is a puddle that never dries up."

"I know where those are," he said. "I'll show you."

"Ok," I said.

He took my hand and pulled me to the track. Sure enough there was a puddle that would recede, but it never dries up.

"What do we do for that?"

"I'm not sure. Is there anymore puddles like this?"

"Yes."

"Where?"

"I'll show you," he said again and took my hand. Tyson led me to the behind the barn. I let go of his hand and he went splashing right into the puddle. However, this was more than a puddle. It was like a kiddie pool full to the tippy top. Tyson is only four, so when he jumped into it, he was more than waste deep in water.

"Come out of there please." He did. "Let's go get your daddy." I carried him to the house. "Park?"

"Why is so wet?" Addison asked. "Did you go in the swimming pool again?"

"No."

"Don't lie to me."

"He's not lying to you. He didn't. We were looking for standing water, and Tyson here found a deep pool of standing water."

"Where is it?" Parker asked.

"Behind the barn."

He got on the phone and called someone to come out and see it. Within the hour all the standing water sites on the property were being addressed. The guy that came out, Jamie and I had gone to high school with.

"Hey, Ken, can I get a glass of water?"

"Sure, Dean," I said.

"What are you up to these days?"

"Working."

"What do you do again?"

"I'm an architect."

"Yeah, that's how I always remember you." I looked at him with the glass of water in my hand. "Always building something or drawing structures. Do you remember being in Mr. Greens' class."

I handed him the water glass. "Yeah, I had Mr. Greens for three years of high school. Why?"

"You remember that construction project that we were given."

"Yeah," I said.

"Everyone was mad at you because your design won."

"No, everyone was mad because I was the only girl in his class, and I won."

"Aunt Ken?"

I turned to Carter standing behind me. "Hi. When did you get here?"

"I got in trouble in school yesterday."

I scooped my seven-year-old nephew up in my arms. "What on earth did you do?"

"My teacher said I lied repeatedly."

"Lied about what?"

"About that structure on the playground at school," he said.

"What about it?"

"I said that I know the person who built it."

"Which you do," I said to him.

"I told my teacher and my classmates that my aunt built it."

This is the structure that Dean had just brought up.

"I was sent home for the next three days because I wouldn't write that I lied to my teacher and classmates one hundred times."

"But you didn't lie," Dean said.

"Come. Let's go straighten this out," I said to Carter. "Dean, are you coming?"

"No. I have to get back to work fixing your problems here with the standing water."

"Will you be here when I get back?"

"I should be."

I went and found Addison. "Carter was suspended from school for three days because he told the truth, but his teacher is a jackass who didn't want to believe him? And you are ok with this?"

"No, I'm not ok with this, but I have no clue what he apparently lied about."

"I told you," Carter said. "The structure on the playground. It's a Florida panther and an alligator dancing. I said that Aunt Ken built it and my teacher said that I lied."

"Please can I deal with this?"

"Yes, Ken," she said.

"Thank you. I'll see you in a little while."

"While you are there, can you get the other two from school?"

"Sure. And will stop for…"

"No, ice cream on the way the back," Addison said.

"Ok," I said.

"Ken, I mean it."

I kissed her on the cheek and stole a piece of ham off the cutting board. As we were getting in the car, Tyson came racing over.

"He never walks."

"No, he doesn't," I replied.

"Can I come?"

"Sure," I said. "But you have to promise me that you will be good."

"I prowmiss," he said. I lifted him into the car seat. I made sure both boys were buckled in and we were off.

Within ten minutes we were at the elementary school. Tyson in those ten minutes that it took to get there had fallen asleep. I took him out of the car seat and lifted him to my shoulder. I took Carter by the hand and we walked into the school.

"Ken Jackson, what can we do for you?" the office lady asked as we walked in.

"Apparently, Carter has been sent home for the next few days because his teacher said he lied to her and the class."

"What did you lie about?" the office lady asked him.

"I didn't lie. My Aunt Ken built the structure on the playground."

"Yes, she did. I remember when it happened. Let's me see if I can Mrs. Evert to come to the office."

"Thank you," I said.

She was on her planning period, so she was able to come to the office. She walked in seeing Carter sitting there on one of the chairs. "What is this about?"

"Mrs. Evert, please come into the principal's office with Carter and his Aunt Ken."

"Your parents named you Ken?"

"Kennedy," I said. "But I have been called Ken since I was this one's age," I said pointing to Tyson. We went into the office. Surprisingly it still smelled the same. It smelled like fresh paint and dried up old crayons. I put Tyson down on the small couch in the office.

"Carter, who did you bring with you today?"

"This is my Aunt Ken," he said with a smile.

"Now please tell me what this is all about," he said.

"Mrs. Evert said I can't return to class for three days because I wouldn't write one hundred times that I lied to her and the class about the structure on the playground."

"Mrs. Evert, first off, I know that you are a new teacher here to our school. You cannot tell the students that they can't come back for three days without notifying someone in the office. And yes, he is telling the truth. Kennedy Jackson designed, structured, and built that playground. Kennedy is Carter's aunt."

She took a breath. "I just thought he was lying. When I instructed him to write one hundred times that he lied to me and his classmates, he became defiant and said no he wouldn't do it."

"Why should I have to do it, if I wasn't lying?" Carter said.

"Carter, you have a point, but you have to do what your teachers tell you to do."

"But I wasn't wrong. Mrs. Evert asked if anyone knew who built the structure of the panther and alligator dancing on the playground and I said that my Aunt Ken did. She did. I'm not lying. I didn't lie."

"I want him out of my class," Mrs. Evert said.

"What?" Carter, the principal, and I asked all together.

"I won't stand to be made fun of by a seven year old little brat."

Carter, who was sitting in an armed chair, pulled his feet up on the seat and put his head on his knees and started to cry. "I'm not a brat. I do everything she tells me to do," he cried. "I stand in the corner when Mason throws things across the room. I walk at the end of the line even though I should be in the middle because Pepper pushed me and said I pushed her."

"No. No. I don't want him in my class anymore," she said.

"Carter, please go sit with Joanne in the front office."

"Yes, sir," he said. "Should I take Tyson?"

"No," I said.

He got up and walked out of the room. He went to Joanne, the office lady and sat in her lap and cried. She tried to comfort him.

"Mrs. Evert, it is too late in the school year to transfer Carter from your class. After all he is in your advanced second grade class. To transfer him now, would mean to be putting him in regular second grade and at this point that is not fair to young Carter, who has not been in my office or in front of me in the last four years of his schooling."

"Can I ask something?"

"Yes, of course."

"You put my nephew in the corner? Have you sent a note home to his parents?"

"No. I deal with the children the way I see fit."

"Are we done here?" I asked. "If this is going to continue, Carter will be home schooled for the rest of the school year."

"Well, maybe that is best for him. I don't want him in my class another day," she said.

"I need to make a phone call," I said. "Can I leave him here for a minute?" I said pointing to Tyson.

"Yes, that's fine, Ken."

I called Addison. "We have a situation here at the school. Mrs. Evert doesn't want Carter in her class anymore. He innocently embarrassed her in front of the class."

"What the hell are we going to do, Ken? He needs to be in school. Parker and I both work."

"I know you do. What if I teach him till the end of the school year?"

"I can't ask you to do that."

"You didn't ask me. I'm asking you if you will let me teach him until the end of the year?"

"Let me talk to Parker."

Parker agreed. With Addison on the phone, I withdrew Carter from school.

"Am I in trouble?"

"Why would you be in trouble?"

"I'm not going to school until next fall."

"No, you aren't going here for school till next fall, but you will be going to school."

"Where?"

"At my house," I said.

"Who is going to teach me?"

"Me," I said. I looked at Joanne. "I'm taking Kate and Michael home early today."

"Michael is on field trip to the art museum," Carter said. "And Kate has music as her special today, so she wouldn't want to miss that."

"Ok. I'll be back at two," I said. "Thank you, Joanne."

We left the school with Carter's books and the work that he would need to complete before the end of the school year. I could see that he was sad.

"What time will I start school every day?"

"Hmm," I said. "Eight. Like always."

"Are mommy and daddy mad at me?"

"No, they are not. Now where would you like to go for lunch?"

His smile was more than an answer. We went to a rustic restaurant that also had a gift shop in it. Tyson finally woke up when we pulled into the parking lot of the restaurant. I got him out of his car seat.

"I'm starving."

"I imagine that you are. You didn't have breakfast this morning," I said to him.

We went in and the boys knew the rules. We eat first and shop before we leave. Tyson ordered pancakes. Carter and I ordered the breaded steak with macaroni and cheese and dumplings for lunch. I let Tyson try a dumpling.

"Nope. Don't like it," he said. We laughed at him. "We are done. Can we go in the shop now?"

"I need a few minutes and then yes we can."

My phone rang. I looked at it. "Hello."

"When are you coming back?" Dean asked.

"I'm picking up the kids from school at two and then I'll be home. Why?"

"I have another job, so I can't stay and wait for you."

"Oh, it's ok. Things got a little out of hand at the school today, so I need to get things set up for tomorrow."

Carter started to fidget. "What's up, buddy?"

"There's a field trip tomorrow for my class."

"Where are you going?"

"To the space station."

"What time is that at?"

"Nine o'clock."

"And you will be there," I said. "Don't worry about anything, Carter. It's going to all work out. I promise."

"Can we go in the store now?" Tyson asked.

"Yes. And then we have to go pick up your brother and sister."

"I like when we get them," Tyson said. I smiled at his comment.

I came back to the phone. "Sorry."

"No, it's ok. You have your hands full right now. I'll call you later."

"Thank you, Dean."

I paid the bill for lunch. The boys were having fun looking at everything. I already told them that they could each pick something. Tyson picked a man with a parachute on his back. Carter picked a science kit volcano.

"Can we do this?"

"If we don't do it today, we will do it either tomorrow or the next day."

I went back to the school to meet Kate and Michael. They both were excited to see me. Kate announced as she got in the car, "Carter was kicked out of school."

"I was not," he said.

Michael looked at his little brother. "Dude, you are seven and you got kicked out of school."

"Stop teasing your brother please. He didn't get kicked out of school. His teacher has issues with him and doesn't want him in her class anymore, so a decision had to be made of where he would go."

"So what was decided?" Michael asked.

"I'm going to home school him starting tomorrow," I said.

"Wow," Kate said. "So when you start third grade next year, you will be able to teach the class," she said.

"Thank you, Kate," I said.

"But wait," Michael said. "He has a field trip tomorrow to the space center."

"And he's not going to miss it. I'm going to take him."

"Can we come?" Kate asked.

"Well, it's not your field trip, but how about this. Tomorrow while we are there, I'll buy the tickets for us to go and then I'll take you there."

"Me too?" Tyson asked.

"Maybe," I said.

He was ok with that. "Ice cream!" he said getting so excited when I pulled into the parking lot where the ice cream shop is. We all got out of the car and went in. Tyson picked a Captain America blue ice cream, which he asked for on a cone. Kate picked coffee ice cream on a cone as well. Michael picked a chocolate brownie with dark chocolate ice cream. Carter picked cinnamon ice cream in a cup with the cone on the side. When they were done, we got into the car and went back to the house.

Addison and Parker took Carter into the conference room and caressed him and made sure that he knew that they weren't mad at him. I sat Tyson down at the table next to me and pulled out the coloring book and crayons. I gave him directions of what to color with what crayon. "And you have to stay in the lines," I said to him. "Can you do that?"

"I can do that."

"I don't know," I said. "Let's see."

He sat there for the next half hour trying to color neatly. Michael asked if he could play on the computer and I said he could. Kate sat at the far end of the table with her knees and feet tucked under her and she was diligently working on something.

"Kate, do you need help?"

"No, Aunt Ken. I need more sheet music. Can I print some?"

"No. I got this for you," I said. I went to my office and came back with a journal for her. When she opened it up, she jumped up and hugged me. "Thank you, Aunt Ken," she said. "Thank you, so much."

I sat at the table next to Tyson again. I took out paper and drew a rough sketch of the backyard. I added a playground area. When Addison came back into the kitchen, I showed it to her.

"That would be good," she said.

"I'll get in touch with some of the guys I work with at the studio and see what we can do to get this done soon."

"Thanks," she said. "Carter is going to stay here tonight with you. You have to leave for the space center at or around six in the morning. Here are all the details. After visiting the space center, he has to write a paper on things that he saw."

"Ok. Are you coming here tomorrow?" I asked her.

"No. I came today because I can't come tomorrow. Kate has a music recital tomorrow at the retirement home. And Tyson needs new shoes."

"You should have told me. I would have taken him today."

"Thanks," she said. She got the kids ready to go home. "Dinner is in the oven. It is all cooked, so it is just staying warm in there."

"Thank you."

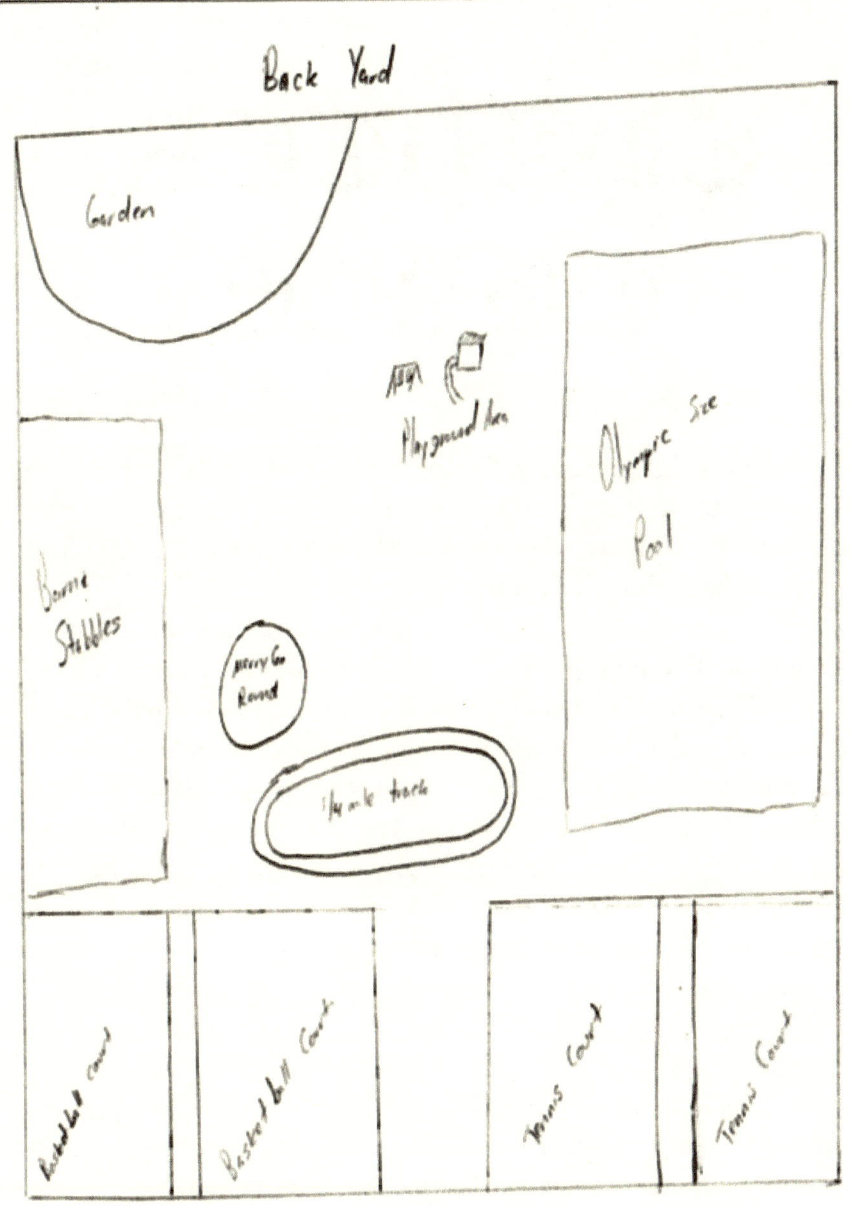
Back Yard
Garden
Playground Area
Olympic Size Pool
Barne Stables
Merry Go Round
Go Kart track
Basketball Court
Basketball Court
Tennis Court
Tennis Court

CHAPTER THREE

That night before putting Carter to bed in my room with me, he showered, and we laid his clothes out that Addison had left for him to wear tomorrow. However, it was his school uniform, which he didn't have to wear anymore this school year.

"I'll be right back," I said to him. I went downstairs and into what will soon be the gift shop when the B & B opens. I had ordered a lot of random things for the shop including polo shirts for kids. I pulled open the box and grabbed the first shirt on top. It was a collared shirt with a little dinosaur on it. Then I remembered that I also got ones with rockets on them. So I grabbed one of those too. Then I went back upstairs. When I got back in the room, Carter was sleeping. I set the shirts over the chair in the room, covered him, and went to my bed. My bedroom door opened a crack. "Are you still awake?" Jamie asked.

"Yeah."

"Can I come in?"

"Sure."

She came in and sat on my bed with me. "I heard what your new endeavor is going to be. That's great. Tomorrow, I'm going to go surprise Katie Bell and meet her and her class at the retirement home."

"Wow. That's so great."

In the morning, Carter and I work up at five. He was so excited. I showered and got dressed. He got dressed. I got his backpack and put pencils and a notebook in it. Then we went downstairs. I grabbed my phone and charger and a camera. I also had a backpack. I put not only the camera in the bag with film, but also my tablet.

"We can either have breakfast here at the house or we can stop on the way."

"Stop on the way," he said. "I'm so excited."

"I know you are."

We went and got into the car that Parker filled with gas last night for me. Carter sat in the middle.

"Why don't you try to get some sleep?"

"No," he said. "I don't want to miss anything. How long does it take to get there?"

"About two hours."

His excitement had him jumping around in the middle of the backseat.

"Do you want to watch a movie?"

"Yeah," he said.

I set up my tablet for him and let him pick the movie. He made the movie loud so that I could hear it too. With him occupied in the backseat, I pulled out of the driveway and started our journey. We got there sooner than I thought we would. We left the house at six and we were in the area at seven thirty.

"I'm hungry," he stated.

"As am I. Where do you want to go?"

"Do you really have to ask?"

He loved going to this restaurant that is a chain, so we went there. He ordered French toast with sausage. I ordered pancakes with grits and bacon.

"What is that?" he asked.

"What is what?"

"That. In the bowl," he said pointing.

"It's grits. Do you want to try it?"

"Yes," he said.

I gave him a spoonful. When the waitress came by, he asked for an order of grits. When they came, he added a little sugar to them, and he ate them. When we were done, I paid the bill and we left. We drove to Kennedy Space Center.

"Everything is so big," Carter said.

"It has to be,"

An air-conditioned bus pulled up behind us. Carter said that that was the bus from school. I paid for parking and we continued to a space. We got out of the car. I put my tablet back in my backpack. Carter took his backpack and we walked to the entrance, where his whole second grade class and Mrs. Evert stood. Carter stood tall next to me.

"What is he doing here?"

"His parents paid for this trip, so he's not missing it," I said to Mrs. Evert.

"Hi, Carter," a little girl with bright blond hair said.

"Hi, Pepper," he replied.

"Who is this with you?"

"This is my Aunt Ken," he said.

"Kenny," I told him.

"My Aunt Kenny," he said with a smile.

"Kenny is a boy's name," a boy with a mop of brown hair on his head said.

"Her name is Kennedy."

"Like the Space Center," Pepper said.

"Yep, just like the Space Center," Carter answered.

We had our bags checked and then we were allowed inside. Mrs. Evert gathered her class and chaperons. "As you know, we arrived at nine and we have to be back on the bus at two," she said. "Please stay with your assigned groups. Everyone has been partnered up."

"What about Carter?" Pepper asked.

"He is no longer in our class or school. So whoever was partnered with him will have to just join another group."

That is planning ahead and accordingly I thought. I took hold of Carter's hand.

"What time can we stay till?"

"Till it closes," I said.

"That's at six tonight."

"Well, then we should get started so that we don't miss anything," I said.

He beamed and jumped up and down.

I did a little exploring myself last night to see what the main attractions are and things that we shouldn't miss. If we are planning to see and do everything, the whole day would take about eight hours. We did the bus tour first. Where his class stayed in the building doing their tour. Because I fueled him up on breakfast, I knew that we should be good until at least eleven or so. Then we would stop and have lunch and keep on going.

"Can we go into the gift shop?"

"Yes, of course."

"Do I have budget?"

"Yes."

"What is my budget?"

"One hundred dollars," I said.

A small yay escaped from him. He climbed on my lap during the bus tour. I thought for sure he would fall asleep, but he didn't. The tour was an hour long and it deeply held his interest. When that was over, we located a map and guide and set up for our next adventure. The day had escaped us. He said he was hungry at one forty-five. We went to lunch there. Carter was happy. After lunch, we went into the gift shop. He explored everything in there. In the end, he picked a sweatshirt and sweatpants, a stuffed monkey, and space kit. By five o'clock, he was starting to slowly fade.

"Do you want to go home yet?"

"No. Please can we stay?"

"Yes."

By five thirty, I had both backpacks on my back and I was carrying him. He was fighting sleep so badly at this point.

"Carter, we will come back."

"You said we could stay till they closed."

"Your right. I did."

Ten minutes later, he was fast asleep on my shoulder. For a seven-year old, he wasn't too heavy. Having to lug around two backpacks and now a sleeping child was a little bit heavy. I made the trek out to the car. I put the backpacks in the trunk of the car and then put Carter in the car. I put him in Tyson's car seat because he was sleeping. I buckled him into the car seat and then I got into the car. He slept the whole way home. It had taken us an hour and half to get there; however, it took us over two hours to get home. When I pulled into the driveway, Addison's car was there. She came out of the house all excited. "How was… when did he fall asleep?"

"At almost six," I said.

"He stayed awake all day?"

"He did."

"Did he nap in the car on the way there?"

"No. He watched a movie on my tablet and by the time it ended we got there. We went for breakfast and then met his class there."

"What time did his class stay till?"

"Till a little after two. They had to find Pepper before they could leave."

"Yeah, she's a handful."

"She has the ultimate crush on Carter."

"What?" Addison asked.

"Yes, I'm telling you. The ultimate crush. She was supposed to stay with her group; however, every time I turned around, she was with us. She kissed our Carter goodbye before they left."

"On the cheek?"

"Nope. She kissed him on the lips."

"Did he kiss her back?"

"Yeah," I said with a chuckle.

The whole time we were talking, we had gotten everything from the car. I'd gotten Carter out of the car seat and had him in my arms. We went into the house. Addison put the backpacks in the conference room off the kitchen. I put Carter down on the oversized couch. I put a blanket over him. He curled up on the couch and continued to sleep.

"Thank you for taking him."

"Oh, it was my pleasure. Thank you for giving me the experience."

"Yeah, you're welcome," she said. "Now were you serious about teaching him from home?"

"Yes, I was. Why?"

"It's a big responsibility."

"I'm aware of that. I want to do this for you and Park. It's only for the next three months anyway. I'm great with this."

"What time do you want him here?"

"Addison, you come every morning at or by seven thirty anyway, so no special trips are needed. I'll start with him when you get here."

That night, I sat down and worked out a schedule for Carter and I. Each subject gets the devoted time of at least forty-five minutes. We would start at or about eight and the schedule looked like this: Spelling and vocabulary first thing, followed by reading, then math, then a history lesson, followed by science, and his newest thing would be starting to learn a language. I picked sign language for us to learn together. I set the conference room in stations. On the big table in the back of the room, I put coloring books and crayons out. Two to three times a week, I worked with Tyson with his coloring. He had just missed the cut off for the preschool starter class, so while his brothers and sister were in school and he was here at the house with us every day, I'd sit him down and make him do a little work. Plus, I would read to him for about a half hour to an hour every day too.

CHAPTER FOUR

The first day of home schooling; Addison had to go into the restaurant that she actually worked at and got paid from. Parker too had to work, but he dropped Carter off with me. Tyson and Beth were going to the day care that they paid for, but rarely used.

"So how is this going to work?" Carter asked.

"We are going to start with spelling words and vocabulary and writing and we will move on from there."

"Do I have to work till two o'clock like in school?"

"Let's not put a time length on this yet ok. Let's just get started."

I sat with him and went over his spelling and vocabulary words for about twenty minutes. "Now I want to you write the spelling words down. Write it spelled out three times and then put it in a sentence for each word. When you are done with that, I want to write the vocabulary word down once and write a sentence for each word. You have to write nicely, or I'll make you write it again ok."

"Ok," he said.

While he worked on that, I went on the computer and checked in with my guys at the studio. We were in midst of a project and I was to be called if anything too demanding came up, but I had a great crew. Jenny called my phone.

"Hey, just have a question about the roof?"

"Tell me where we are at?"

"We are finishing the outer structure. We are doing fine with it. It's just the round room in the front. How do you want to that roof? Dillion was thinking flat."

"No, it's going to be a waffle cone made of all glass. Remember it's a sunroof."

"Ok, got it. When are you going to come see it?"

"Tomorrow. I need to do the inspections. The only thing, I will have my nephew Carter with me. I am home schooling him for my brother and sister-in-law."

"Which one is that? The ten-year-old?"

"No. The ten-year-old is Michael. Carter is the seven-year-old. He had an issue in school, so I told them I would be more than happy to help them out."

"Sounds like work."

"No," I said. "Well, yeah, it is, but no. This was a great decision. If you need anything else call me. I'm here. I have to go. We are moving on to lesson two."

Next, we worked on math. Carter was quick and pretty accurate with math. Though the lesson time on the paper and in the book said forty-five minutes, we were through with it in a half hour. After that was history.

"I know what to do for this. I read the chapter, answer the questions, go online, and take the test. It takes about an hour or a little longer. I do the same for science."

"Ok, but before you begin that lets break for a snack and some exercise."

"Ok," he said.

"Let's go feed the horses."

He got up from the table and pushed his chair in and came out with me to feed the horses. "Don't we have to clean their stales?"

"Nope. I already did it," I said.

"When do you sleep?"

"When I'm tired." He laughed. We fed the horses and then we went for a run around the track. It was more of a chase. We had had fun outside for about an hour. Then we went in and I made us lunch. We ate our lunch outside on the wrap around porch. When we were done, I cleaned up and he went back into our classroom and read science first and did all the work for that and set the computer up to take the test. "You have to supervise this," he said.

"I'm coming."

I sat right behind him and watched as he blew through the science test. At the end, he printed the test with his answers and then he printed his score. "Yes, I got a 98," he said.

"Why didn't get a one hundred?"

"Because I got number nineteen wrong."

"And what does number nineteen say?"

"Stanley is mixing and matching test tubes. He has to pour three drops of blue in everyone, followed by two drops of red, followed by a drop of green. What colors of the rainbow will Stanley end up with?"

"Ok, so this a multiple question problem, right?"

"Yeah."

"So let's do it and see. I have paint, so we can try it outside."

We went back outside. We did just like the problem said. And we mixed it up. We got black, white and yellow."

"How did we get yellow?" Carter asked.

"Here watch again. See when you mix all three colors together it makes black because there is no light showing. When the colors are showing, it makes white and we get yellow when the green and red are mixed together."

"Awesome," he said. "Thank you."

"You're welcome."

We went back into the house and back into our classroom. He did his history lesson, and again I supervised the test. He got a hundred percent on it.

"Now what?" he asked. "Are we done for the day?"

"Almost," I said. "I need you to write a paper on our field trip."

"Ok," he said.

He changed tables. First, he took blank paper and drew a picture of a rocket. Then he started his paper.

April 28, 2017 Trip to The Space Center By: Carter Jackson Age: 7

Yesterday, my Aunt Ken took me on my school trip to the Kennedy Space Center. I was supposed to go with my second-grade class on the field trip, but my teacher Mrs. Evert doesn't want me in her class anymore. She said I lied about a sculpture at the school on the playground. She asked who designed it and I told her that it was my Aunt Ken. She said I lied, but I didn't. And then she said that she doesn't want me in her class anymore.

So Aunt Ken, who is home schooling me now, took me on the field trip. We left real early in the morning, and we had time to stop for breakfast at my favorite place. I loved it.

Then we went to the Kennedy Space Center. Everything is huge and it was a little scary, but I had my Aunt Ken with me, so I wasn't scared for long. We went on a bus tour, and we saw everything that is there. We had such a fun time. We got to stay till they closed. We saw the space outfits, and rockets, and we got to pretend that we were in the space shuttle taking off. We got to go on a ride too, and crawl through small spaces.

Getting to spend the day on a field trip with my aunt was like finding a treasure that I'll have forever. I hope we can do it again and have more adventures. Thank you for such a great time.

When he was done, he left it on the table. I was on a phone call for another work issue. Carter came and stood in front of me. "Hold on one second please," I said to the person on the other end of the call. I looked at Carter. "Did you finish?"

"Yes."

"Great. Go put your shoes on please."

He ran and found his shoes and put them on. I wrapped up my call, which wasn't anything important. Just one of the guys complaining about another guy's work ethics. Something I'd have to address tomorrow.

"Are we going somewhere?"

"Yes."

"Where?"

"I'm taking you to the bookstore."

"Yay!" he said jumping up and down.

"I'm very proud of you," I said to him as I pulled him into a hug. "I love you."

"I love you," he said.

I took him to the bookstore and let him pick whatever book he wanted. Before I paid for it, I took him to a table and sat him down. "Ok, so you picked a book. Now here's the deal. We are going to reading this book together starting tomorrow and when we are all done, you are going to write a report on the book."

"Ok," he said.

A lady came over with her young child. "How old is your son?"

"He is seven."

"Isn't that book a little too advanced for him?"

"No," I said. "We think he will be able to read it and comprehend it."

"How come he isn't in school?"

"He is. Come honey, it's time to go," I said.

Jamie was picking Michael and Kate up from school today and we were going to meet at the ice cream shop when she was done. She shot me a text message: *on my way to get Michael. Katie Bell is with me. Can't wait to tell you all about her concert. SYS*

I paid for the book. He picked the Wind and the Willow. After that, we went to the ice cream store. Jamie pulled in minutes after I did. She came in and joined us with Michael and Kate. We all had ice cream as we listened to Kate tell us about her field trip to the retirement home.

"So are we bringing the kids to Park or to Addison?" Jamie asked.

"I don't know. I haven't heard from them all day."

"How was your fun day with Aunt Ken?" Kate asked Carter.

"We worked," he said.

"On what? Playing?" she asked.

"No, she had me doing schoolwork for most of the day."

"What?"

"He's not on vacation, Kate," I said. "He's being home schooled so that he will join his class in the fall where he should be."

"I want to be home schooled," she said.

"Think of all the things that you will be giving up," Jamie said. "No more music classes with Mr. Singer."

"But I love music."

"We know you do," Michael said.

"I'll talk to your parents about arranging a day where I can have the two of you on a school day, so you will see what Carter will be doing for the next three months."

"Really?" Michael said. "You will do that?"

"Sure," I said.

The following week, I had all three kids for two days. They had spent the night on Sunday. Monday morning, Kate thought that I would let them sleep in, but I didn't. I woke them up at six thirty, which was their normal time to get up for school. "Teeth brushed, get dressed for school, and come downstairs for breakfast in ten minutes," I said. They did what they were told. When they came downstairs, breakfast was on the table.

"Please eat you breakfast. Your school day starts in twenty-five minutes," I said.

"Why couldn't we sleep in today?" Kate asked.

"The same reason your brother doesn't get to sleep in on a school day. It's a school day," I said. "When you are done eating, please come into the conference room off the kitchen."

Kate looked at Michael. "I think she's serious, Katie," he said.

They ate their breakfast and put their dishes in the dish washer. Then the three of them came into the conference room. Carter sat down at his stationed area and started working right away.

"Michael, pick a table not close to your brother please. And Kate, you are over here," I said pointing to the table closest to my desk. "Carter has explained to me about your history and science lessons that you read the chapter, do the book work, and then go on the computer to take the test."

"We also do that for math and reading too," Michael said.

"I'm here if you need my help. We will have a break at eleven."

Cater was good. He started with science and then went to history because they were the longest for him do. Kate didn't start right away. Michael started up immediately. I watched Kate sitting there trying my patience.

"Kate, can I talk to you for a minute?" She got up from the table and I took her in the kitchen. 'Please tell me what you are doing?"

"I'm thinking," she said.

"And I'm thinking that I have a barn that needs to be cleaned and mucked. You have a choice right now. You can either go in there with your brothers and work on schoolwork, or you can go out to the barn and sweep out the stables. It's your choice. The day is wasting away though."

"Why can't we do fun things? Like a field trip?"

"Because it's a school day. I'm home schooling your brother because your mom and dad are too busy for it. We can have fun and we will have fun when your schoolwork is finished."

Kate, who was usually good, stormed out of the house. I went out and met her and marched her right into the barn, where the men who worked for me to help with the barn were starting to get their day started.

"Hi, fellows," I said. "You all know my niece Kate. She will be doing work with you all for the next hour. She is to muck out two stalls and then sweep them for the new hay. If she gives you any trouble, please call my cell and I'll come right back." I left her with the men.

I went back to the house. Both boys were still working. Carter put his book work and science test and results on my desk. He sat down and started his next assignment. Michael finished with his first assignment and test and put it next to Carter's on the desk. Then he sat back down and worked on math. Both boys blew through their math assignments.

"It's time for a break," I said.

Michael looked up at the clock. It was only ten. But he got up with Carter and they came with me. "I want you both to run around the track for the next fifteen minutes." They didn't answer me. They ran out there. They started their laps together. I went into the barn to check on Princess Katie Bell. She was sweeping out a stall. "How are things going?"

"Good," she said.

"Are you ready to come in and do some schoolwork?"

"Yes."

"Go take a shower and when you are dressed meet us in the kitchen please."

"Yes, Aunt Ken."

She put the broom down and went to the house. She stopped halfway and came running back to the barn. "Is anyone in the house?"

"Yes. Aunt Jamie is in the house."

She turned and ran to the house. She went upstairs and showered. I timed the boys for another five minutes and then called them over. We went back into the house. I fixed lunch for the five of us. Jamie was finally present downstairs. "Where is Katie Bell?"

"She's taking a shower and getting dressed."

"You let her sleep in this morning?"

"Nope," Carter said with a smile. "She had to work in the barn this morning."

"Well, Aunt Ken means business," Jamie said. "There is a time to play and have fun, but only after your work is done."

"That's what daddy says," Michael said.

"Well, that's the way we learned it," Jamie said. "It's not that your daddy or Aunt Ken is being hard on you. It's the way we were brought up."

"Jamie, are you eating with us?"

"Yeah," she said. "But why are you doing that?"

"The kids need to eat."

"I already cooked."

"What did you make?"

"My specialty," she said.

"Where is it?"

"It's staying warm in the oven."

Jamie's specialty was grilled cheese hotdogs. Kate came in the kitchen all clean and smelling so good. "I'm really hungry," she said.

"Before you eat," Jamie began, "You owe Aunt Ken an apology."

"Jamie, no. That's not necessary," I said.

"Bullshit, it's not necessary. We all know the rules. School always comes first. Fun and games and music comes second."

"Can I call my mom?" Kate asked.

"Yes, of course."

Kate called Addison and started to cry. "Can you come get me? It's not fun here anymore. I want to go back to school. I want to come home."

"Honey, I'm working, and your dad is out of town for the next couple days. Let me speak to Aunt Ken."

Kate gave me the phone. "What the hell is going on there?"

"Hi, Addison," I said.

"Are the kids behaving?"

"The boys are."

"Kate is not behaving?"

"No, she's not."

"Put her back on the phone please."

"Yep," I said.

"Mom," Kate said.

"What is this I'm hearing that you aren't behaving? If I get another phone call, you are grounded for the next month. Do I make myself clear?"

"Yes, mommy."

When Kate hung up the phone, she went into the conference room and started her schoolwork. I brought her lunch into the conference room.

"What did your mom say?"

"That she's going to ground me for a month if I don't do what you say."

"Kate, I want this to be fun for you, but its school. And it's not going to be all day like your school day. And I have some fun stuff scheduled, so I need for you and your brothers to get as much work done this morning, so we can go do what we are going to do."

"What if we don't finish stuff?"

"You can work on it when we get back."

"Ok."

"When are we leaving?"

"Boys! Come in here please." They came into the room and sat down at their tables. "Ok, I need for you to work on school assignments for the next hour and half and then we are going to go somewhere."

"Ok," they said.

Kate ate her grilled cheese hotdog and then went back to her lessons. The boys worked on their lessons. I went to go see if Jamie wanted to go with us.

"Hey, I'm going to take the kids to an art museum in about an hour. Do you want to go with us?"

"Sure."

I went back into the conference room, where I worked with the three of them. When we were done with the lesson, I had them tidy up their tables and then we got ready to go. Jamie had made brownies, so we took those with us. The five of us got into the car, and we were off to the museum. Because one of my friend's ran the museum, we didn't have to pay to get in.

"Ok, I'm sending the three of you on a mission. Carter, you have to find a picture that has shapes and colors. First, you have to write down what you see and then I want you go beyond that and tell me what's not in the picture."

"Cool!" he said.

"Kate, I want you to take Aunt Jamie and see if you can find five ballerinas. I just want you to write where they are from. And Mr. Michael," he smiled. "My little sports buff. I want you to find five pictures that are sports related and write down what you see."

The four of them walked off leaving me alone. I went and found Connie. "Hey, how are you?" she asked.

"Busy as hell," I said.

"What are you up to these days?"

"Working, trying to get the B & B up and running, and now I home school Carter, my seven-year-old nephew."

"Why that is so special," she said with a smile.

"He's in advanced second grade."

"My daughter is in that class. Carter is your nephew?"

"Yep."

"Pepper talks about him constantly."

"Well, then I guess you know that Mrs. Evert didn't want him in her class anymore and if he was sent to the normal second grade class, he'd be so far ahead that he wouldn't be able to do anything in the class. So now I'm home schooling him."

"That must be hard?"

"Not really. I gathered everything that we need to finish the school year, and Addy or Park brings him to the house in the morning after dropping Michael and Kate off at school. We work for about four hours or a little more on schoolwork and then I take him to do something fun."

"Fun is going to run out in a few weeks after you've done everything with him."

"No, maybe not."

"And why do you have the other two home from school today?"

"Addison had to work in the restaurant and Parker is out of town, so they are staying with me for a few days."

"You look good," Connie said. "You're losing weight. Are you stressing on the B & B?"

"No. I'm good," I said. I looked at my watch. "I've got to run and see what the kids are up to. Thank you so much for today."

"Anytime."

I walked into the lobby area of the museum. Carter came running over. I scooped him up in my arms and kissed him. When I put him down, he hugged me. Jamie came over with Kate, so now we were just waiting for Michael. Ten minutes later he joined us. "Let's go for ice cream and then we need to go home ok."

"Ok," they said together.

When we got home, without being told, the three of them went into the conference room and got right back to work on their assignments. With Jamie in the house, I went out to the barn and worked a bit. Jamie came out about a half hour later. "Hey, would you mind if my friend Lennox Nolan came over?"

"What are you? Five?"

"It's not my house anymore," she said. "It's yours. So I will always ask you first."

"Is this the fiancé?"

"Yeah," she said with a smile that pierced her face.

"Yes, of course," I said.

"Oh, I'm making dinner."

"Great. Thank you."

"Don't you have workers to do this?"

"I do, but it's a distraction from what I'm supposed to be doing."

"And what's that?"

"Finalizing the last…"

"AUNT KEN!" Kate yelled.

I dropped the shovel that I was using and raced to the house. Jamie was seconds behind me. We ran into the backdoor. Carter's nose was bleeding. "It's ok," I said. "It's ok. Don't panic. Panicking only makes you bleed more. It's ok," I said again. He was prone to nose bleeds. I lifted him and sat him on the countertop. I got a clean dish towel and held it to his nose. He was crying. "I'm going to take him to the hospital," I said.

Jamie stayed in the house with Kate and Michael. I got one of the guys that lived on the property to drive us, so I could hold Carter. When we got to the hospital, I jumped out of the car with him and raced inside. They took him in a room leaving me holding the bloody towel in the hallway. I called Addison. "Not to let you worry or make you worry, but I'm in the hospital with Carter. His nose is bleeding again."

"I'll come," she said.

Within twenty minutes, Addison was there with Carter. I sat in the waiting area. Addison came and sat with me. "They are doing a procedure to him right now," she said.

"Is he ok?"

"Yeah, he's fine. Did everything work out with Katie today?"

"Yeah, it did. Sorry it got to that."

"It's not your fault. To you, the kids know that it's all fun and games, so when it's a little different, Katie has little melt downs. Why don't you go home? I'll bring him to your house when he's released."

"If it's ok, I'd like to stay."

"Sure, "she said.

He was released at midnight. There was no sense in Addison driving out to the house to bring him there to sleep over and then have to turn around and drive the fifteen miles in the opposite direction. Addison kissed Carter good night. "I'll see you tomorrow evening. I love you, little bear," she said to him.

"I love you too, mommy."

When we got to the car, I put him in. I buckled him in and then got in the car. I drove to the house. When we got there, I knew he was sleeping. I pulled the car into the garage and then got out. I lifted him into my arms and went into the house. The house was extremely quiet. I carried him upstairs and put him to bed. Then I went to go check on Kate and Michael. Michael was sleeping soundly in the room that he and Kate were sharing. Kate wasn't in the room. I checked to see if she was in with Jamie, but she wasn't. I went downstairs and found her still awake working on schoolwork. "What are you doing?" She looked up. "It's after midnight," I said. "Come on. Let's go to bed."

"I'm really sorry."

"I know you are, Kate. Come on. You can leave everything like it is."

She got up from the table. I put my arm around her, and we walked upstairs together. "Can I sleep with you tonight?" she asked.

"Yeah," I said. We went into my room. Carter was sleeping on one side of my king size bed. Kate looked at her little brother. Then she looked at me. "He's fine," I said reading her expression. "The doctors did a procedure on him that will most likely stop the bleeding." Kate climbed into my bed. She got comfortable and within a minute she was sound asleep. I changed my clothes and then got into bed.

Day two of home schooling all three kids went a hell of a lot smoother. First, I let the kids sleep in. They woke up at eight. I was already up, dressed, had attended to the horses, and did the morning work outside. I cooked breakfast for them and now just waited for them to come downstairs. Michael came in first. "How come you let us sleep in?"

"I needed to get some work done before working with you guys today," I said.

"Oh," he said. "I'll go get Kate and Carter."

"If Carter is still sleeping, let him sleep please."

"He's awake," Michael said. "He was taking a bath when I came downstairs."

Kate was in with Jamie this morning. Though I love having my sister here, she's a distraction for Kate, which is why I had so much trouble with her. I'm usually the fun cool aunt and then Jamie comes back into town for a few weeks or for god knows how long – never too long, and Kate constantly wants to be with her. I'm not jealous of that. My sister is cool, and I too want to spend as much time as I can with her.

Kate came downstairs. "Hi," she said and came and gave me a hug.

"Good morning."

Michael returned downstairs. I put their breakfast on the table for them. Carter came downstairs last.

"How are you today?" I asked him.

"I'm good," he said.

"Well, we are going to take it easy today."

"What? Why?" he asked.

"Because of the procedure that you had last night. You have to take it easy today."

"But what does that mean?"

I lifted him on the countertop. "That means we are staying here today and after all three of you finish your schoolwork, we will watch movies and have Katie Bell perform for us."

A smile like I had not seen in a long time lit up her entire face. "After schoolwork is done," she said.

"Yes."

Jamie and her friend came downstairs. I turned my back to try to hide my aggravation. This is my house until the B & B opens, yet they don't respect that.

"Wow!" he said. "You two look alike."

Really? Maybe because we are identical twins stupid.

"Do you have rhyming names?"

Please tell me what the fuck would rhyme with Jamie?

"No," I said turning back around. "I'm Ken?"

"Your parents gave you a boy's name?"

"Ah no," I said. "It's short for first name."

He smiled. "Yeah, I know. Jamie told me that already," he said.

Oh, boy. She picked another dumb ass guy. And she's not only going to marry him, but she's going to reproduce with him. FABULOUS!

"I'm sorry. Who are you?"

"Lennox Nolan," he said. "It's nice to meet you."

"Nice to meet you too," I said. "Congratulations is in order."

"Thank you. So are you into the music industry too?"

"No..."

"Aunt Ken is an architect," Michael chimed in.

"Really?"

I nodded my head. "Yeah," I said.

"What have you done?"

"Um. Too much to say anything," I said. "Guys please finish your breakfast, so we can start our school day."

"Yeah," he said. "Jamie was telling me about that. So you are homeschooling all three of them?"

"Just for yesterday and today for Kate and Michael. I'm homeschooling Carter till the end of the school year."

"That's got to help your brother out a bit," he said.

"Yes, it does," I said.

The three kids finished their breakfast; they rinsed their dishes and then put them into the dishwasher. After that, they excused them form the room to get started on their day.

That night when Addison came to get them, Kate and Michael were done with the school week's work and it was only Tuesday. Addison thanked me for keeping the kids.

"Tomorrow do I get Tyler back?"

"Yes, you will have Carter and Tyler. I have to take Beth to the doctor and then I have parent-teacher conferences at the school."

"Are you meeting with Mrs. Evert too?"

"I am," she said.

"Oh, I can't wait to hear all about that."

"Ken, thank you again for keeping the kids."

"No problem. I had fun with them."

"What did you do today with them?"

"After their work was done, we watched movies," I said.

Carter came into the kitchen. "Can I stay another night?"

"No, not tonight," Addison said.

"Awe. Ok," he said. "Bye Aunt Ken." He threw his arms around my waist. I hugged him back. "See you in the morning. Normal day," he said with smile.

"What does that mean?"

"I let the kids sleep in this morning."

"Oh," Addison said. "And how did that go waking them up?"

"I didn't," I said. "They got up by themselves and got themselves dressed and ready before they came downstairs for breakfast."

After they left, I went into my office to do work. The phone rang. "Hello," I said on the second ring.

"Hi. The lights are in if you want to come and see it and see if we need to change anything."

"I'll be there in a half hour."

I grabbed my car keys, put my wallet in my pants pocket, and left the house. I drove to the site. The place was lit up like a Christmas tree. My newest project, which I still wasn't sure if I wanted to continue with it after this site was done, was designing apartment buildings. I parked my car among the other five that were there. By the cars, I knew that Alan, Jenna,

Margot, Dillon, and Patrick were here. They are my team. I walked up to the front walk and called Patrick. "Hey, I'm here," I said.

"Ok, I'll be right there."

I looked up at the shell of the building. It still needed walls, doors, windows, and furniture and appliances. Though there were going to be single bedroom apartments, the majority of them would be three to four-bedroom apartments. And each apartment would be its own cubical space. And the building itself would like a pyramid. The top two apartments would be the only two shaped like a triangle. Then from the top, which would be the sixth floor, it would drop down and have four apartments on the fifth floor, eight apartments on fourth floor, twelve apartments on the third floor, eight on the second floor, and four on the first. There would only be thirty-eight units in the whole building.

The five of them came to meet me. "I thought there would be more done than this," I said.

"Nice to see you too," Patrick said.

"It's nice to see you all, but seriously I thought this project would be further along."

"Well, we couldn't get the electricians in before today," Alan said.

"It would help more if you were on the site," Margot said.

"What's there for me to do now, Margot? I designed the structure, helped hire the construction crew, and put it your hands to oversee the production of this project. It's great the lighting is in, but what is here for me to see; other than it is looking like an erect Christmas tree. The design of the structure is there and it's great. And the power is working really well here. I'll be in touch with the construction crew in the morning to find out why there aren't walls, windows and doors yet. This place is supposed to be ready for occupancy by the end of June."

I walked around the rest of site. The pools were marked out where they would be, but they weren't dug yet. Patrick came over to meet me.

"Want to go for drinks tonight?"

"I can't," I said.

"Why?"

I laughed. "Because I can't."

"Fine. Maybe next time."

"Maybe," I said. "I have to run. I'll be in touch with you all soon."

I went home to find cars in the driveway. "What the fuck now is going on in my house?" I said out loud. I got out of my car, which I had to park on the street and walked up the driveway. I went into the house, which was loud with voices.

"Hey," Lennox said.

"Hi."

"Hope you don't mind that we are having a little get together here with our friends to celebrate our engagement."

"Where is Jamie?"

"She's in the kitchen."

I walked in the kitchen to find my countertops lined with wine bottles and liquor bottles. Solo red cups lined the other counter. Jamie was sitting laughing with her friends at the table.

"Oh, this is my sister. Kennedy, these are my friends."

"And this is my house," I said.

"What? Are you mad?"

"A heads up that you are doing this in my house would have been nice."

"This is our house," Jamie said.

"No, James, it's not. It's my house. I bought it from mom and dad."

"But you are turning it into a bed and breakfast."

"Right. Magic words. Turning not turned. It is still my house until I open it."

"Mom said that you wouldn't mind."

"I don't mind you staying here. You didn't let me know that Lennox was coming and staying here when I have Park's kids here. I don't know Lennox. I don't know what kind of guy he is. And yet you let him come into my house and stay here over night without even asking me."

"We will leave."

"No! You've all been drinking, so they can stay, but have the decency to at least ask me next time." I walked out of the room. I went into my office and locked it up and locked up the conference room where I held school.

"I guess she told you," one of her guy friends said.

"Yeah," Jamie said. "I guess she did. Well, fuck it. Fuck her. We are here. Let's party."

I went up to my room and called mom. "Hi," she said answering. "How is everything going?"

"I came home to find a party going on in my house. James said that you told her it was ok."

"Kennedy, it wasn't like that. She asked if it was my house would it be ok to have her engagement party there. I said if it was my house, it would be fine with me."

"She didn't even tell me she was doing this."

"I'm sorry honey. She said that you have been really busy."

"Well, I'm always really busy, but it's still my house."

"I know honey," mom said. "How is home schooling going."

"It's going well. Carter is a sponge. He soaks everything in. I got to take him on his field trip to the Space Center."

"How was that?"

"Oh my god was that fun."

"So does he work all day long?"

"No. We work for about four and half hours and when he is done, we go out and have fun."

"Are the others getting jealous?"

"I don't think so."

"Have you seen them too?"

"Yeah. I had Michael and Kate over yesterday and today, so they too had the experience of home schooling. They enjoyed it."

I stayed on the phone with mom a little while longer and then hung up with her. I needed to be in my office doing work. I went back downstairs. The engagement party had trickled outside by the pool area.

"I'm sorry," Lennox said to me.

"She didn't even tell me," I said. "Oh, sorry. It's ok. Have fun and congratulations again."

I saw a couple walking towards the barn. I ran over there. "Now that's where I draw the line. Get your shit and get off my property," I said. "PARTY IS OVER! Everyone leave or I'm calling the police."

"What is wrong with you?"

"No one is allowed in the barn, James! And yet your horny ass friends were heading there."

"Hey!" they said to me.

"This is why you will never meet someone and be in a relation."

"In the morning, I want you out of here," I said.

Jamie came over to me and smacked me as hard as she could across the face. "JAMIE!" Lennox said. "Ken, are you ok?" I didn't answer him. Hot tears welled in my eyes. I didn't hit her back. I held my stinging cheek and walked to the house. Her guests left. Some of them making rude comments to me on the way out. I didn't care though. I had to stand up for myself. I never did when we were kids. I always went along with everything.

I was in college when I went out with friends and brought a guy, I just met home with me. We had been drinking. My head was swimming. Mom and dad were out of town visiting our grandparents, so they weren't around. Park was already married to Addison, so he wasn't around, and Jamie was on her first music tour, so she wasn't around. We had picked up where we left off with the drinking, we had gone swimming and things started to heat up. The next thing I knew, he had pinned me to the wall of the pool and he was having sex with me. It went from the pool to the shower and to my bedroom. I wasn't a virgin when it happened. No, that first time had been when I was fourteen at Kelly Bishop's fifteenth birthday sleep over party with her cousin Sebastian. It was something that just happened then. This is what I told others when asked when I lost my virginity. After her party, we dated for about a year or so and then his whole family moved away, so it was over. But the guy who came home with me, till this day I don't know his name. It had started off as a great night, and it ended in misery and till this day, I've never told anyone. Jamie had thought what everyone else thought that I had lost my virginity to Sebastian, but the truth is I had lost my virginity to Patrick. He was my first and would always be. And I will always love that.

CHAPTER
FIVE

The next morning, when Addison came, she saw the red mark on my face. "Carter, go get started on your work ok." He nodded and went into the conference room. "Is everything ok?" she asked me. I didn't answer her. She came in front of me and looked at me. "Is everything ok," she asked again. I threw my arms around her neck and cried into her shoulder. In the fifteen years that she's been married to Parker, she'd never seen me cry. "Oh my god, Kenny, what's wrong?" I couldn't talk. I just cried. I sobbed in her arms. Addison saw the barn crew walking that way. She knocked on the window and got their attention. The two guys looked up and signaling for them to come to the house and they did. "Can you please take Carter to the barn with you?"

"Yes, ma'am," one said.

"I'm so sorry. I'm bad with names."

"I'm Juan and this is Miguel."

"Thank you," she said to them. They got Carter and took him to the barn. They always had fun with the kids. They let him swing on the tire rope swing that they had redone to make it secure again. They made piles and piles of hay and tossed Carter in them. He was having the time of his life out there with them.

"Who slapped you?" Addison asked me.

"J-j-j-james," I said.

Addison knew that I hadn't stuttered in years. "Ok, can you fill me in on what happened?"

"I-I-I…"

The cleaning lady was there today. She came in the kitchen and saw me still crying on Addison's shoulder. "Could you please make a cup of tea for us?"

"Yes, ma'am," she said. Usually, Addison would correct her about calling her ma'am, but today at this moment she let it go. Maria made the tea for us and then left the room.

"Here, sip the tea," Addison said. I did. Addison got the tissue box off the counter. "Do you think you can talk now?" I nodded. "Tell me what happened?"

"La-la-la," I gripped the countertop. "Last night," I said.

"Ok. It's ok. Take it slow," she said.

"After you left with the kids," I took a deep breath. "I went to the site to see about the project and to see how along its coming. When I got back, there were cars in the driveway. Jamie was having an engagement party."

"A what?" Addison asked. "She's engaged?" I nodded my head. "Let me see if I can get my mom to take Carter and pick the kids up from daycare and school today." She called her mother, who came immediately. "Don't worry about homework or school with them ok, mom."

"Can I take them to the movies?"

"Yes, of course. Thank you again."

When her mom left with Carter, Addison told me to get in her car. Without question, I did. She called Parker and told him that she would be late tonight and that her mother was getting the kids. She didn't indulge in what was going on at the moment. Then she got in the car, and she drove the hour and half to the beach. When we got there, I was sleeping in the car. She slowly tapped me. I jarred out of my sleep. She couldn't resist asking. "Why do you do that?" I looked at her. "When you are touched, you nearly jump out of your skin. Why?" I lowered my head. "Let's not discuss it now. Come with me," she said. I followed her down the beach, which was nearly empty. We sat close to the water, which rumbled loudly against the shoreline. "Now that we are alone and in a private place, let's talk," she said. "What happened last night?"

"I came home to find Jamie and Lennox having their engagement party. My kitchen was lined with wine bottles and solo cups. I closed off my office and the conference room where Carter and I work. I went upstairs to give them space. Then I came downstairs and they had moved it outside. I lost it when I saw two of her friends heading toward the barn. I told her that I wanted her to leave this morning and she smacked me hard across the face."

"How did you respond to that?"

"I went in the house."

"Ken, you are thirty-nine years old. You need to stick up for yourself."

I lowered my head. "I don't," I said.

"I know you don't, but you have to honey."

"I was raped when I was in college."

She took me in her arms and hugged me. "Do you want to talk about it?"

"I don't know his name. I never knew his name. I went out with friends after our finals and he was there. We were all drinking. I brought him back to the house and we continued to drink. Then we were in the pool swimming and laughing and he pinned me against the wall and…"

"No, no. Don't stop. Say it, Kenny."

"Please don't tell mom or Park."

"I won't," she said. "I feel honored that you are confiding in me. Tell me what happened. I won't judge."

"He had me pinned against the side of the pool and he raped me. I started to sober up and I got away from him, but he wouldn't leave. I went into the bathroom in my room and took a shower and he came in the shower. He again pinned me against the wall and raped me. Then he tied me to my bed and he raped me two more times before he untied me and finally left."

"Why didn't you go to the police?"

"Because I didn't even know his name."

I moved closer to her and sat between her legs with my head resting on her chest. "Why didn't you tell your mom?"

"Because mom was already disappointed in me."

"Oh, Kennedy," Addison said. "Why would she be disappointed in you?"

"Because I was careless. I put myself out there."

"No one asks to be raped, Ken. Did you say no?"

"Yes," I said in a quiet tone. "I tried to push him off, but I couldn't."

"How long ago was that?"

I turned in her arms and buried my face in her shoulder. "Fifteen years ago."

She embraced me like I'd never been hugged before. "Let it out," she said. "It's ok to cry."

"Crying is for babies," I replied.

"No, honey, it's not. It doesn't make you any weaker of a person if you cry. That was a tragic thing that happened to you and you kept quiet about it for such a long time."

"James won't come back."

"Yes, of course she will."

"We've never fought before."

"Sisters fight. It's ok. She needs to respect you and your house. The B & B isn't open for business just yet, so she needs to respect that as does your brother. It maybe their childhood house, but it's your home."

We stayed on the beach for hours. On the way back home, we stopped for dinner. Then we went back to the house. When we got there, Jamie's car was parked out front. Addison walked in the house with me.

"Hi," Jamie said. "I'm sorry about last night and not asking you first about having my friends here."

"Congratulations," Addison said to her. "Maybe in a few weeks we can celebrate your engagement as a family. And if you're pregnant, you want to stop drinking."

"KEN! I only told you that."

"I'm not an idiot, James," Addison said. "I have five kids. You think I don't see the signs? Also, you lay another hand on Ken and you and I will have words."

"What are you? Her mother?"

"No, but I don't like that. You smacked her in front of house full of people."

"You told her that too?" Jamie whined.

"No, she didn't. Some of your friends are friends with Parker and I, so we heard about last night after it happened."

"Ken is a cry baby. Always a tattle tale. You're thirty-nine years old. Grow the fuck up," Jamie said.

"You smack her again like you did, and we are going to have words," Park said coming into the room.

"She told you too?"

"No. She didn't have to," he said. "Martin, Joe, Seth, and Bruce called me last night and told me what happened."

"She threw my friends out of my house."

"This isn't your house anymore," Park said to her. "This is Ken's house. We need to respect Ken's wishes in her house. And as I hear, congratulations are in order," he said. "It would have been nice to be in the loop of your friends last night, so that we could have been in on the celebration."

"It just happened," Jamie said. "I called Megan and told her and before I knew it the house was full of my friends."

"Ken's not one of your friends?" Parker asked. "I can see me not being one of your friends, but Ken? I can't see that."

"But I had already told her," Jamie whined. "Besides she isn't friends with my friends."

"Jamie, you are thirty-nine years old. Grow the fuck up," Parker said to her.

"I just wanted you to know that I am sorry," Jamie said. "Do you forgive me?"

I didn't answer her. "Oh my god, Kennedy, come on," she whined. "For fucks sake. I said I was sorry."

"That's your idea of an apology?" Lennox chimed in. "It needs work, James," he said.

"Jamie's never apologized for anything our entire lives," I said.

"What?" She asked. "Oh, now it speaks."

"It? Really, Jamie?" I said.

"Do you forgive me or not?"

"Yeah, I forgive you."

"So why don't you have anyone in your life?" she asked me.

"I have people in my life."

"No, I mean a guy. Why don't you have a guy in your life?"

"My personal life is mine," I said.

"Would you mind if Lennox and I stayed until the end of the week?"

"No, I don't mind."

The next day with Carter, he wasn't himself. It was obvious after the first half hour. I looked at him. "What's going on this morning?"

"I'll work faster to get the extra work done," he said.

"What extra work?"

"The work we missed yesterday. I'll get it all done."

"Yes, we will get it all done, but can you relax a little please. You are fine."

"Did we miss yesterday because of something I did wrong?"

"Carter, what could you possibly do wrong?"

"I don't know. I'm bad."

"What? Why are you bad?" Then I remembered his teacher Mrs. Evert. "Ok. Get up," I said to him in a soothing way. He got up from his table and came with me. We went out to the barn. I had Miguel saddle up the horses. Juan lifted Carter onto the horse. I mounted up on my horse. When we were both set, I led both horses to the field. "Carter, did you ever tell mommy and daddy what Mrs. Evert was doing to you?" He lowered his head. "No, don't do that," I said. "You hold your head up high always. You didn't do anything wrong. I am so very proud of you. You come here in the mornings and you are ready to work.

"Yesterday, I needed to deal with a few things that came up. That is on me. Not on you. And the way you work, we will have those lessons done in no time. School is work, but school also needs to be fun. You need to enjoy it. Tonight, I'm going to give you a homework assignment."

He smiled so big. "What is it going to be?"

"I want you to read chapter two of Wind and the Willows."

"And do a report about it?"

"No. I just want you to read chapter two tonight for homework."

We rode for an hour. When we brought the horses in, the weather started to change. A Florida rainstorm was on its way. We got to the house in just the nick of time. It was a complete down pour. We went into the house, Addison had snacks set out on the table for us. We ate our snacks and then we went back into the conference room. We worked on spelling and vocabulary. After that he did math. By the time lunch was ready, he had finished up work from both yesterday and today.

"Can I read after lunch?"

"Sure you can," I said.

"Are we going to do anything this afternoon?"

"We can watch a movie," I said.

"Ok."

Addison made lunch. It was to die for. Both Carter and I scarfed down lunch. After lunch, we went into the recreation room.

"What's this room?"

"It's the recreation room. Would you like to help me fix it up?"

"Yes. I'll help you."

"Well, thank you," I said to him.

"So this is a giant playroom?"

"Yes."

"Awesome."

When we had walked into the room, everything had been pushed into the center of the room, so it was a horrific mess. When we were finished in there, the room looked tidy and nice. "Can I play in here?" he asked.

"Yes. If you need me, I'll be in the kitchen or in my office."

I left him in the room. I went into my office and looked over the plans for the B& B again. I needed for the construction of gym to get started. I called Patrick.

"I'm going to send you over plans. Can you let me know if it will work on the space that I have?"

"Yes," he said. "What is the space?"

Carter came in room. "Will you come play with me?"

"Patrick, I'll have to call you back."

I went into the playroom with Cater, and we had a blast in there. It became even more exciting when Jamie and Lennox came in. Lennox was a fun guy. At times, he had Carter on his shoulders as Carter shot darts. When it was my turn to shoot the darts, Lennox held me around the waist and started to dance with me as I threw a dart.

"Could you image doing this with knives?" Jamie said.

Lennox and I laughed. "No," we said together.

I looked for Carter when I was done shooting my darts. He was sleeping on the pool table. I went and scooped him up in my arms. He didn't wake up. I carried him into the living room and put him down on the couch. I covered him with a blanket and went back into the recreation room. The three of us played for an hour. We had fun together.

"So I'm planning my next tour," Jamie said.

"What?"

"Yeah, I need to do about thirty more shows before the baby comes," she said.

"Where would you do them?"

"Canada, the United States, and I'm hoping to get the venue in Japan."

"How long would you be gone?"

"I don't know yet. I need to sit down and work it out with the crew."

"When would you start?"

"I'd want to say in the beginning of May," she said.

In a way, my heart was breaking. This time I wouldn't be able to go to as many shows as I usually went to. Lennox noticed the disappointment on my face before I turned my back. "I have to get some work done. Thanks for the fun today." I walked out of the room and went into my office. I sent Patrick the plans. He called me a half hour later. "What is this to?"

"Something I'm working on," I said.

"Are you going to tell me?"

"Are you alone?"

"Not at the moment."

"Please don't share those plans with anyone else."

"Sure. Are you home?"

"Yes, I have Carter till after six tonight."

"You make the seven-year-old child do schoolwork till after six?"

I laughed. "No, actually my seven-year-old little buddy conked out on me. He's sleeping on my couch."

"Do you have the little guy?"

"No. He likes day care a lot right now," I said.

"Can I come over when I finish here?"

"Sure," I said. "I'll be here."

Dean came over the house to check for standing water. I didn't know he was coming over. Suddenly there he was in my office doorway. "Hey!" he said. I jumped up knocking the chair over. "I didn't mean to scare you."

"It's ok," I said. "Why are you here?"

"Oh, I told Parker that I'd be back to check for standing water. Have you noticed any puddles?"

"It rained today, so I don't know."

"I'll be out checking the yard," he said.

"Thanks."

Addison had seen the encounter. When Dean was outside, she came into the room. "Are you ok?"

"Um. Yeah," I said.

"Um yeah is not an answer."

"It totally is."

"How often does he do that?"

"Not too often. But enough," I said.

"Want me to talk to him?"

"And tell him what? To call before he comes over."

"Yes," she said.

"I have told him that, but he doesn't listen."

"No. This bullshit stops here," she said and before I could stop her, she was walking away fast. She went outside and found Dean. "Can I ask you a question?"

"Yeah, sure," he said.

"What gives you the right to just come here unannounced and sneak up on Ken like that? I saw you watching her. You waited until she was focused on what she was doing before you spoke."

"No, it's not like that."

"Save it," Addison said. "For now on even if Parker gave you permission to come here and to check for whatever it is that you are doing, you need to call first, so that Ken knows that you are coming to the house. My son is sleeping on the couch. Did you think that maybe you would scare him?"

"No, I didn't think about that. I'll go."

"Finish what you are doing, but next time call Ken first and let her know that you are coming."

She did not wait for him to respond. She came back in the house and made sure I was all right. I was quietly standing in the kitchen when she returned. I hadn't noticed that she had returned. Addison calmly put her hand on my shoulder, and I jerked with a startle. "I'm sorry," she said. "I thought you heard me."

"I'm...I'm...I'm..."

"Shh. It's ok," she said. "Take a breath."

I could feel emotions boiling up inside me: Rage. Anger. Fear. Sadness. Terror. I went outside in the backyard and went to the track. I ran the track for an hour. Dean had seen me running and he left walking through the house to get to his car. He bumped into Addison. "She's running," he said.

"She is."

"Is she ok?"

"She is," Addison said again.

"Did I have anything to do with this?"

"Just leave, Dean. And next time please do what I've asked you to."

"I will," he said.

I kept running. Addison watched from the window. I ran even though it had started to rain. I ran until I didn't know if I was wet from sweat or the pouring rain. I walked over and jumped in the pool fully dressed. I swam twenty hard laps. Then I got out of the pool and came towards the house. I striped out of my wet clothing down to my bra and underwear. Then I opened the backdoor to come into the house. Addison looked up at me when I came in. She didn't say anything. I walked over to her and wrapped my arms around her. "Thank you for being here," I said. "Oh, I'm sorry I'm wet."

"It's ok," she said. "You should go take a shower, so you don't get sick." I nodded on her shoulder. I stepped back away from her and turned to leave the kitchen. "Do you want anything?"

"Will you make me a cup of tea?"

"Yes, it will be ready when you come back downstairs."

I went up and showered and dressed in a pair of worn out jeans and a long sleeve shirt. I brushed my hair, but let it air dry, so I went back downstairs.

"Your phone was ringing?" Addison said.

"Thank you." I looked at my phone. It was Patrick. I called him back. He would be at the house in an hour.

"Can I bring my son?" he asked.

"Yeah, that's fine."

"Oh, you are truly a life saver. Thanks."

"How old is he?"

"Five."

I set coloring books, crayons, colored pencils, building blocks, and cars up on the coffee table in the family room. Then I went back into the kitchen. Carter was awake now.

"I would have ran with you," he said.

"Run," I corrected.

"What?"

"Run with you. Not ran with you. It's the verb tenses." He smiled big. "We can maybe start that tomorrow." I was referring to running together.

"Can you explain that?"

"Sure. Today I run, yesterday I ran, tomorrow I will run. It's the tense. You said, 'I would have ran with you.' That's out of context. Would have are adverbs because they describe the verb ran, but you need to put the verb in proper context, so therefore, it would be I would have run with you."

"Ok," he said.

"We will work on that tomorrow too."

Patrick came with his son TJ. A beautiful well sized child for five years old. His hair is the same burnt sandy blond brown hair that Patrick has. TJ has freckles across his nose and cheeks. Though I had never met him, he came over to me and sprang up in my arms hugging me. "Hi," he said. "I'm Turner James."

"Hi," I said to him.

"You give nice hugs."

"So do you. Do you like to color?"

"I like to build things."

"Well, I have building blocks that you can play with." I put him down by the couch. I walked over to Patrick. "He's adorable."

"Thanks."

"In all the years that we have worked together, I don't recall you ever talking about your son. Are you married?"

"No. I'm divorced five years now. TJ lives with me. He is in kindergarten and is usually in daycare until my sister picks him up for me. But today she couldn't do it."

"No worries."

Carter went over by TJ and they played together.

"So this is where you work from?"

"At times," I said. "Patrick this is my sister-in-law and good friend Addison. Addison this is one of my partners at the firm."

"Nice to meet you," they said almost together.

We sat at the kitchen table and looked over the plans for the gym. "Where is the space?"

"Out here," I said getting up and going to the backdoor. I opened the backdoor and showed him by pointing in the direction where I roughly wanted it.

"So it's raining now, so we can't go out there and map it out," he said. "But you have quite enough property to cover it. Do you have anyone here to check for standing water?"

"Yeah," I said.

"A reparable person?"

"Someone we all went to school with and who is still a friend with my brother."

"Trust him or not, he's not doing a great job."

I knew that, but there are only so many arguments that one can get into with my brother.

"Why don't we do this, we will see how the weather is tomorrow and if it doesn't rain, I'll come here on Thursday morning and check it out for you."

"Ok. That will be good."

"Can I come too?" TJ asked from the other room.

"No, you have school on Thursday."

"No, I don't. It's a teacher's workday."

"We will talk about it," Patrick said. I laughed because I was watching as TJ jumped up and came running into the kitchen. He climbed up to sit at the table with us. Carter came into the kitchen as well.

"Can we talk about it now?"

Patrick smiled and took TJ in his arms. "I'm working here right now. So can you please go back in the other room and play?"

"When are you going to feed me?"

"Are you hungry?" Addison asked.

"I'm starving," he said.

"Well, come sit over here and I'll get you something." TJ beamed. "Is he allergic to anything?"

"No. The little devil isn't." The beaming smile never left TJ's face.

Carter came over to me and nudged me. "What do you want?" I asked.

"If he doesn't have school, can he come here and spend the day with us? I'll be with you all day because mommy has to go into the restaurant."

"It's up to his dad, Carter."

"You hear that Patrick," TJ said. "It's up to you."

"You call your dad Patrick?"

"Yeah."

"Yes, he does," Patrick said.

Addison put a bowl of macaroni and cheese in front of TJ. She put a bowl down for Carter too. "Thank you, mommy," Carter said.

"Thank you," TJ said.

After they ate, both boys came and sat at the table with us. TJ climbed on the chair next to me and before I knew it, he was sitting on my lap. Then he turned on my lap, so he was facing me. I looked at him. He spread his arms out wide. I hugged him then he wrapped his arms around me. He put his head on my shoulder and within just a minute he was sleeping in my arms.

"Sorry about that," Patrick said. "Do you want me to take him?"

"No, its fine," I said.

"He's never done that to anyone. Not even his grandmother or my sister."

The comment made me feel good. I held onto him. When Patrick was ready to leave, I carried TJ out to his truck. "He still sits in the car seat."

"I've got it. My niece and two of my nephews are still in car seats."

"So why doesn't the boy go to school?"

"Carter is in the second grade. He was in an advanced class and his teacher didn't want him in the class anymore. I'm the one with the flexible schedule, so I said I'd home school him."

"How is that going?"

"Well, the school year has about twelve weeks left, but Carter and I will be done with his school year in about a month and half."

"Is he an only child?"

"No. Carter is the middle child of five. Michael is ten almost eleven, Kate is nine almost ten, Carter is seven, Tyson is four and Beth is two."

"And these are your brother's children?"

"They are."

"So where are the two younger children?"

"Tyson and Beth are in daycare. They come here every once in a while, since I started home schooling Carter. In the fall Michael is going to go a special school for middle school. He is really smart and he wants to start junior ROTC. My brother Parker found a school that does it just outside of Orlando."

"So are they going to move?"

"No. Michael will board there Monday through Thursday and then I will have him here on Fridays. There might be another school offering the same program closer, but they won't know until the end of the school year.

"Kate will be going into fifth grade in the fall. She is really into music and it hasn't gone to her head how smart she is."

"How are the other two?"

"Beth is a baby still and Tyson." I laughed. "Tyson is his own character. He is into everything and nothing all at once. He is all over the place. He's been here and we've lost him so many times."

"What about you?"

"What about me?"

"Have you been married?"

"No."

"Do you have kids?"

"No."

"Do you want kid?"

"I love kids."

"I could see that. TJ's never taken to anyone like he took to you. It was nice to see."

"Does he see his mother?"

"No. She lives in California with her family. TJ's got me, my sister Ivy and my mom."

"And now me," I said with a smile.

"No, it's the other way around with you. He has you." Patrick brushed his hands through hair. "There is something I've always wanted to do," he said.

"What's that?"

"Can I kiss you?"

"Um."

He planted a kiss on me. I had not been kissed in years. It took my breath away, but only for a second and soon I was kissing him back. We stopped at the same time and pulled away from each other. "I've wanted to do that since the moment I came here."

I looked at him. "What? I never thought you thought of me that way. This way." I said.

"Yeah, well, I have sweetheart."

"I'll see you on Thursday."

"Do you mind if I bring TJ with me?"

"Not at all." He kissed me again and then got in the truck and left. I stayed outside for few minutes. I ran my hands through my hair. "I was just kissed!" I said aloud. I walked to the house hoping that Addison hadn't seen it. She was in the kitchen where I seemed to have left her.

"Everything ok?" she asked genuinely.

"Um. Yeah," I said.

"You're drawing my attention," she said. "Did something happen?"

"Um. Nope," I said with a smile.

"You've never been a good liar." She looked me over. "You were kissed!" she said.

"Shut up."

"That's mature. How was it?"

"Great!" I said sitting down at the table.

"Is there a problem?"

"Not at all."

"Does he work for you?"

"No, with me. We run the studio together."

She smiled. "Well, little man and I have to get going. We will see you tomorrow."

"Ok. Love you."

"I love you too, Kennedy Rose."

"You're the only one who calls me that."

"I know," she said. "Carter, we have to go now."

"Ok, mommy," he called from the game room.

CHAPTER SIX

When Thursday came, I not only had Carter for the day, but I had Tyson and Beth as well. Beth, who had sniffles and was constantly wiping her nose on the bottom of her shirt. The semi nice thing was that Jamie and Lennox were still in town, so I wasn't alone with the kids. Tyson wanted to go outside every five minutes.

"He's a like a puppy," Lennox said. I laughed. "How are you?"

"I'm good. How are you?"

"I pulled an all-nighter. I have teenage children."

"Does James know?"

Now he laughed. "Yes," he said with a smile. "She loves my kids."

"Boys or girls?"

"Two of each. Two sets of twins. Dana and Sebastian are fifteen and Fox and Brianna are thirteen."

"Wait? You have a Dana and Fox?" I said trying to hold back the smirk.

"Yes," he said.

"You named your kids after the X-files' characters?"

"No. Dana was named after my mother and Fox is my ex's last name."

"Bullshit!"

"Jamie!" Lennox called. She came in the room. "Your sister isn't being nice."

"That's hard to believe," Jamie said.

"James, did you know that his kids are named for the X-files characters."

She laughed. "Ken, you're too much. His ex's last name is Fox. And Dana was named after the sweetest woman in the world. His mother."

"Ok," I said with a smile.

"Aunt Ken!"

"I'm coming. Excuse me. Second grade spelling is calling for me."

"How is that going?"

"Absolutely wonderful," I said.

"Can I go outside?" Tyson asked.

"Why don't we watch a movie and have popcorn and candy?" Lennox said.

"Yay! Aunt Ken, are you coming too?"

"No. Carter has to get work done. We will see you in a little while."

We all watched as the four-year-old went to the conference room door, leaned in and said, "Loser!"

"Tyson, four minutes in the time out corner right now."

"Awe!" he said.

"Right now," I said.

He went and sat in the chair. "Ha ha!" we all heard Beth say. "Beth, join your brother in time out right now." Though she cried, she did it. I set two timers. Four minutes for Tyson and two minutes for Beth. Then I went into the conference room and worked with Carter for a few hours. When we were done, I told him how proud of him I was and then let him go join the other two.

Patrick called just as we finished. He was coming over in an hour.

"Aunt Ken, what are we doing for lunch?" Tyson asked.

"Lunch? What? I have to feed you?" He started to cry. "Tyson, I was just playing with you. My friend from work is coming over with his son and he is bringing lunch."

"I don't like you," Tyson said.

"TYSON!" Carter yelled at him. "I'm going to call mom and tell her how bad you have been all day today."

Tyson threw himself on the floor crying. Lennox came over and scooped him up. He took Tyson outside. When they came back in, Tyson was back to himself.

Patrick came with TJ. Tyson started his shenanigans again. He started with TJ. TJ stood his ground and knocked Tyson down. Tyson cried. "Get over it," Lennox said. "Tyson, if you keep up this behavior, you can spend the rest of the day by yourself, and when mommy comes to get you, we are going to tell her how you were today."

"So!" he said. Lennox lifted him and again took him from the room. But when he came back, Tyson wasn't with him.

"I brought pizza, chicken wings, chicken tenders, and brownies," Patrick said.

"Thank you," Carter said.

"I'm going to take a slice of pizza to Tyson," Lennox said. Lennox took two plates of pizza into the conference room on the other side of the living room. He sat with Tyson, who ate the pizza and fell asleep. Lennox came back carrying Tyson. "Where can I put him?"

"Either on the couch next to Beth or in the first bedroom at the top of the stairs," I said. Lennox brought him upstairs and then came back for Beth. When he was done, Lennox returned.

The rest of us ate pizza and chicken and then we all settled in the family room to watch a movie. Carter sat sandwiched between Patrick and me. TJ sat on my lap. We watched an animated movie. The two boys were good together. Jamie snapped a picture of TJ stretched out across me. When the movie was over, the boys asked to watch another movie. Jamie picked one from the library of DVDs on the shelves by the television. She put it on and came and sat next to Lennox. Carter brought pillows down on the floor and was laying on them.

Halfway through the movie, Parker came to get the three kids. He went upstairs first and got Tyson and brought him to the car. Lennox ran up and got Beth. Jamie took Carter outside.

"Who is the guy and the kid inside with Kenny?' Parker asked.

"She works with the guy. His name is Patrick and the little boy is his five-year-old son."

"Oh."

"Why?"

"I was just asking. They make a cute couple."

"I hadn't noticed," Jamie said.

"James, you don't lie very well."

"Hey, I wanted to ask you if over this summer if I could take Katie Bell with me on tour?"

"I think she would love that. I'll discuss it with Addison and let you know in a few days."

"Thanks. I love you."

"I love you too."

"Every once in a while, say that to Ken ok."

He hugged her and then left with the kids. When Jamie and Lennox came back in the house, Patrick was nowhere in sight. I had fallen asleep on the couch in the living room with TJ on top of me. We were chest to chest. His head was resting peacefully on my shoulder.

"I'm going to go see where the dude is," Lennox said.

Patrick was out in the yard in the back properly taking care of the standing water problems. Lennox went outside with him. "What are you doing, mate?" he asked.

"Finding all the places that have standing water."

"Ken has someone covering that issue."

"I know, but he's not doing a great job, so Ken asked me to look into it."

"Cool," Lennox said.

"How long have you known Jamie?"

"Ah. What is it now? Six months," he said.

"Where did you meet her?"

"She was on tour in Las Vegas, and I saw her there and then she went to Washington and I was there for work, so I saw her again. We just kept bumping into each other, so one night after her show, I asked her to go out with me and she said yes. We have been together ever since.

"What about you and Kenny?"

"Ken and I have worked together for the last ten years. We have just been work friends."

"Would you want it to go further?"

"I don't have anything tying me down."

"What about your son?"

"TJ is a bonus and Ken seems to love him and he loves her."

"Yeah, I understand that. I have four teenagers. Two sets of twins."

"Boys or girl?"

"Two of each," Lennox said. "Dana and Sebastian are fifteen and Fox and Brianna are thirteen."

"You have a Dana and a Fox?" Patrick asked. "That is wickedly cool."

"I do. My ex-wife's name is Fox, so she had said that if we had another boy, she wanted to name him Fox. When I told Ken this, she cracked up laughing."

"I love to hear her laugh. Before we started working together, I would see her at the university. She would always be outside working and looking up at buildings and eating and when she laughed, oh did I melt. But then I met Renee. We dated and stayed together for more than five years. Weeks before our sixth anniversary, she learned she was pregnant. Three months after Turner was born, she filed for a divorce, and she went to the judge and told him that not under any circumstances did she want TJ. The judge signed away her parental rights and divorced us all in the same day. By the time, I brought TJ home that evening, all of her stuff had been moved out of the house. I dated, but it never went anywhere. Until the other day, Ken didn't even know that I had a son."

"If I didn't know her and I saw her out somewhere with Carter, I'd have thought that she was his mother. She will be great with your son."

"She already is," Patrick said.

When they came back in, TJ was sleeping right on top of me. I opened my eyes when I heard them come in. Patrick came rushing over. "Wait. I'll move him."

"No, he's ok," I said. "Thanks for coming today and helping with the kids and the standing water problems."

"I marked them out where they are and if its ok with you, I'll come by this weekend and do the work that needs to be done."

"Yeah, that's fine with me. Thank you."

"Also, I'll look to see what kind of materials we will need to build the next building."

"I'd like it to be cement. A good sturdy building."

"It will be the best for the best," he said. We both smiled at each other.

I sat up, caressing TJ, and moving him slightly. "He's little for five, isn't he?"

"Yeah," Patrick said. "He weights twenty-eight pounds though he eats like he's filling an empty dump truck. When I bring him to the doctor, she says he is doing good. But then seeing him next to Tyson today really made me see how small he is. He weighs the size of a three-year-old."

"Would you want me to take him?"

"Would you mind?"

"No."

"I'll call and make him an appointment for early next week."

"That's fine," I said. I stood up with TJ still sleeping in my arms. I went into the kitchen with Patrick following me. I got a bottle of water and drank some.

"So, I know that you haven't been married, you don't have any children, but do you date?"

"I do."

"Are you currently?"

"No," I said. "I thought we had this conversation."

"Tell me more about yourself," he said leaning against the counter.

"Well, I grew up in the house. Went to the local schools. I was popular, but not overly popular. I have always been into building things as you know. I dated this amazing guy when I was in my early twenties. We dated for two years and we were engaged. A month before the wedding, he decided to go into the service, which was fine with me. We postponed the wedding date. When he came home from boot camp, he broke it off with me.

"I graduated college with the bachelor's degree in fine arts and then went to grad school for architecture. I dated while I was doing that but none of them got too serious."

"Do you want to get married?"

"Every woman wants to get married."

"I didn't ask what every woman wants. I asked what you want. Do you want to get married?"

"Yes, I do."

"Do you want kids?"

"If a child or children came with the guy, I'm perfectly fine with that."

"How were you when your fiancé broke it off with you?"

"I knew that we had grown apart and that we were done."

"What did you do with your wedding dress?"

"I donated it."

"So how often do you babysit your brother's kids?"

"I've had them here since the start. Ever since Michael was born. Then Addy started working here; well, Addy always had brought Beth and Tyson with her since she started coming here over a year ago to see how well she could work in the kitchen. When she first started coming, Beth was still crawling and not yet walking. Tyson was three at the time and he took to following me everywhere I went. So, I've had them here for a little over a year now.

"And then Carter's teacher didn't want him in her class anymore. With there being only three months of school left, I said that I would home school him and work with him. When that started, Addy put Beth and Tyson in daycare, so that I could devote all my time to Carter. Within the next month and a half, he'll be done with advanced second grade."

"Will you home school him in the fall?"

"As of right now, no."

"But if they came to you and said that they would like Carter be home schooled, would you do it?"

"Possibly."

"If I asked you to home school TJ would you consider it?"

"Are you serious?"

"He gets teased a lot in school and knocked around quite a bit. I wanted to put him in karate, but they said he is under weight to be in the class."

"He's in kindergarten, right?"

"Yes."

"Does he go to the local school here?"

"No. He goes to Gator Crossing Elementary in the next town over."

Who in the hell would tease and pick on this cute little boy? I'll put a stop to that.

"Does he have school tomorrow?"

"Yeah," Patrick said.

"Want me to take him to school in the morning?"

"No, I don't want to trouble you."

"Tomorrow is Friday. Carter and I have already finished this week's work. So I can do it if you want."

We ate left over pizza, and had a few beers, and talked about life and other stuff until almost midnight. It was so late that it was decided that Patrick and TJ would stay the night. They both stayed in my room with me.

"Wow! This is your bedroom?"

"Yeah."

"This was your bedroom when you were a kid?"

"It was," I said laughing. "How long does he sleep?"

"Turner can sleep the entire night through."

"Wow!"

"What?"

"That's something I've never done. I always stayed up the latest and yet I was always the first one up in the morning. I'd be off doing my chores before my sister and brother were even out of bed."

"What chores did you have as a kid?"

"From the time I was six, I'd take care of the horses. I would run over the whole property to see that everything was secure. Fences, posts, gates, and that kind of stuff. I'd sweep the tennis courts and make sure that the nets weren't dry rotted."

"And what about your brother and sister?"

"Jamie had the inside of the house when we were kids. She would have to check the bedrooms to make sure that everything was tidy. She'd have to straighten the recreation room daily, straighten the library, dust everything top to bottom

"Parker, had to help with the horses, yet by the time he got out there they were all taken care of. He had to sweep the basketball courts, sweep the pool, and climb up to make sure the diving boards weren't yucky. Then he'd have to wash mom and dad's cars every two weeks and mow the lawns."

"Crap."

"It's a ten bedroom house with sixteen bathrooms. And that doesn't include the four bedroom three and a half bathroom apartment in the front of the house. It is a big house that when it was first built, it was an inn or bed and breakfast. Then it closed and sat abandoned for about twenty years and then my parents bought it and brought it back to its glory, yet it was just our house. And then I bought my parents out two years ago, and now I want to turn it back into a B & B."

"I want to kiss you again," he said.

"That would be nice," I said to him.

"Where can I sleep?"

"In my bed with me," I mumbled.

"What was that?"

"In my bed with me," I said louder. He smiled and came towards me and kissed me.

That night was the first time that I had had a man in my bed for years. By the time we went to sleep, it was nearing two in the morning.

I woke up at six and went and took care of the morning work. By the time Patrick and TJ woke up, I had worked hard outside in the rain, showered, and was now in the process of making breakfast. TJ came running into the kitchen.

"Yay!" he said.

I turned from the stove and scooped him up in my arms. I sat him on the countertop. "Did you sleep well?"

"Yep," he said excitedly.

"Why are you so excited?"

"I get something other than cereal for breakfast," he said with a bright big smile on his face.

The phone rang. "Hello."

"Hi, it's Addison. I just wanted to call and let you know that I'll have the kids today. However, Carter is really upset about missing a school day with you."

"Oh, please tell him not to worry. He is doing wonderful. Are you coming this weekend?"

"No," she said. "We are taking the kids to… well, I can't say right now because all five of them are right in front of me. Do you need me to come by and cook for you?"

"No. I can manage through the weekend," I said with a smile.

"Well, if you need me, I'm a phone call away. Love you."

"Love you too, Addison." I hung up with her and finished the pancakes. Patrick came in the kitchen. He kissed me on the cheek.

"Yay!" TJ said.

"Hey," Patrick said to him. "Kenny is going to take you to school this morning."

"No, she's not."

"TJ, yes she is. I have a meeting this morning on the other side of town. Therefore, Ken is going to take you to school this morning."

"No, she's not."

"Why isn't she?"

"Because there is no school today, daddy," he said.

"What?"

"No. There is no school today."

"Are you sure?"

"Yes."

"I'm going to call and find out," Patrick said. He called the school's number to hear the automated message that there was no school today. "I don't know what I'm going to do with him today then."

"I'll keep him," I said.

"Yay!" I said with TJ this time. A smiled widened across his face.

"Are you sure?"

"Absolutely," I said.

"Turner, please behave yourself today. My meeting starts at nine and I don't know how long it will last."

"Just call my cell," I said.

"Bye, daddy."

"Bye, TJ. I love you."

"I love you, daddy."

"Bye, Kenny."

"Bye," I said.

TJ and I had breakfast together. It was Friday. And now I have a precious five-year-old cutie with me for the day. I was going to make this day a day that TJ wouldn't forget. I called Patrick. "I know you just left, but I wanted to ask you is there any place that I cannot take TJ?"

"No. You can take him wherever you would like."

"Ok. I'll text you where I'm taking him."

"Thanks," he said.

TJ was busy building something in the living room. I took my camera and snapped a few pictures and then joined in on the fun. He stopped for a minute and looked at me. "Is this ok?" I asked him.

"Yeah," he said.

"Is something wrong?"

"No. It's just that no one besides daddy has ever played with me."

"Well, let's change that," I said to him. With a block in each hand, he came to me and threw his arms around my neck. I hugged him back. "Come on, let's build something," I said.

We spent an hour in the living room playing and creating different things.

"What are we doing today?"

"What would you like to do today?"

"I'd like to go the museum," he said. "And see a movie on the big screen."

CHAPTER SEVEN

That day, after spending a wonderful hour in the morning after breakfast with a magnificent child, we gathered up things that we would need, which was a few of his toys that he had brought with him yesterday. Then we left for the day. I put him in the car seat and then got into the car. I drove to the museum. We went to the planetarium side of the museum first. We watched a movie about outer space. TJ gripped my hand tight. "I don't like this," he said.

"Ok. Come. Let's go."

"Are you mad?"

"No. Not at all. Come let's go see what the museum has for us to do."

His smile was there, but it wasn't as bright as I had seen earlier. I scooped him up and held him out like he was an airplane about to take flight. The squeal was out of this world to hear. It made me smile.

We went into the museum which was packed with kids. TJ snuggled closer to me even though he was in my arms. We started on the top floor.

"I want to see the movie on the big screen."

"I know you do. Do you want to eat first?"

"Yeah," he said.

"Are you hungry now?" TJ giggled. "What? You're hungry now," I said and dipped him. Then I pulled him up again. "Are you hungry now?" He giggled again. I dipped him again. "Turner, where did you go?"

"I'm here."

"Where? You disappeared."

"No, I'm here."

I felt him tense up. I brought him up to my shoulder again. "What happened?" He was crying hysterical. "Turner, what's wrong? Did I say something wrong?"

"She left just like that," he cried.

"Who? Who left?"

"My mommy. Please don't leave me."

"I'm not going anywhere."

A security guard came over. "Ma'am, is there a problem?"

"No, sir," I said.

"Are you this child's mother?"

"I'm his guardian."

TJ slithered out of my arms while I was talking to the security guard and he disappeared. I looked down and he wasn't there. "Shit! TJ! TJ!"

I took off running. Looking for him everywhere. My heart was pounding. I ran through the whole museum. I went back to the planetarium. He wasn't there. He wasn't anywhere. I called Patrick. He answered.

"Hi, how's your day going?"

"Ah. It was going well, but I lost TJ. We are at the museum, and I was playing with him and then he started to cry. A security guard came over. I was holding TJ and he wiggled out of my arms. One second, he was standing next to me and then he was gone. He's been gone for an hour," I cried. "Patrick, I'm sorry."

"Did you check where the movies are shown?"

"No."

"Check there. About four rows from the top."

"Ok," I said. "I'll call you back."

I went back into the museum and raced back up to the third floor. I flung the doors to the theater open. I walked in and walked down four rows and sure enough there he was snuggled on the seat sleeping. I scooped him up still crying. I carried him out of the theater and called Patrick. "I've got him. He's sleeping."

"He would never leave there. My sister works there."

A tall woman with dirty strawberry blond hair came running over. "Excuse me. What are you doing with my nephew?"

I handed her my phone. "Here talk to Patrick."

"What?"

"Patrick. Your brother. Here. He's on the phone. I am Kennedy Jackson. I work with him at The Studio."

She took my phone. "Some lady has TJ," she said.

"I know. She's watching him for me today."

"What is her name?"

"Kennedy "Ken" Jackson."

"Do you go by Ken?"

"Yes."

TJ woke up. I went and sat on a bench. "You can't run off like that ok. I was worried."

"I'm sorry."

"It's ok. I know that you wanted to see the movie and I was taking you there."

"Do we have to go home?"

"No. Why would we have to go home?"

"Because I was bad."

"You weren't bad," I said to him. "You just did a bad thing. There is a difference."

Patrick's sister came over and squatted down and started yelling at him. "You wait till your daddy gets you. You are going to get a spanking. I'll take him from here."

"Like hell you will," I said.

"Patrick wants me to take him."

"I'll let Patrick tell me that himself. Can I have my phone back?"

She dropped my phone on the bench and then reached for TJ. "I don't want to go with you," he said to her.

"Please stop," I said. "You are upsetting him."

"Pat wants me to take him and bring him home."

"Again, I'm not releasing him to you unless I hear it from Patrick's mouth."

"Aunt Ivy stop it. I don't want to go with you."

"Well, that's too bad," she said.

Ivy slapped me across the face. I got up with TJ in my arms and walked away from her. I called Patrick back. "Do you want Ivy to take him home?"

"No. I told her that I want you to keep him with you."

"Ok."

"She slapped Ken," TJ said.

"Who slapped you?"

"Aunt Ivy slapped Ken,"

"Are you ok?"

"I'm fine," I said. My cheek was burning but I didn't mention it. "We are fine now. We will see you later." After hanging up with him, we went to get something to eat. From there we explored more of the museum. We stayed there till four. We went back to the house. TJ was hyper. It was so nice out that I took him in the backyard and let him run around.

"What's that?" he asked pointing to the track.

"It's a track."

"Like a bicycle track."

"You can ride a bike on it. But it's for running or walking."

"Can we go get my bike?"

"I don't know where you live."

"Can I call grandma and ask her to bring my bike here?"

"If you want to do that you can."

"What else can we do?"

"Do you want to see the horses?"

"No," he said. He took off running towards the track. "Can I use your phone?"

"Sure," I said. I fished it out of my pocket and handed it to him. He called his grandma.

"Hi, Grandma," he said. "Can you bring my bike to me?"

"Where are you?"

"At The Jackson house."

"I don't know where that is," she said.

"Daddy's friend can tell you. Hold on, Grandma." He gave me my phone.

"Hello," I said. "I'm Kenny Jackson. I work with your son."

"He wants me to bring him his bike. Is that ok with you?"

"Yes," I said to her. "That is fine with me." I gave her my address and the directions. Within a half hour she was at the house. When she arrived at the house, TJ dragged me out to meet her.

"Hi, Grandma!" he said.

"Hi, sweet boy."

"This is daddy's friend Kenny."

"Hi," I said again. "Please come in."

"Honey why is your cheek all red?" she asked me.

"Aunt Ivy slapped her across the face."

"Did you miss school today?"

"No. There was no school," he said with a smile. "We went to the museum."

"I'm sorry that my daughter slapped you."

"It's ok," I said.

"Can I go? Can I go ride my bike?"

"Yes," I said to him. "Go ahead."

"Where is he going to do this?" she asked.

"In the backyard," I said. We went into the kitchen. "Can I get you coffee or tea?"

"Coffee would be nice," she said.

I set the cup of coffee up to make. I looked outside. TJ was riding away on the track.

"How long have you worked with my son?"

"For more than ten years now."

"Are you two an item?"

"No," I said.

"Are you married?"

"No, I'm not."

"Do you have kids?"

"Not of my own. I home school my brother's seven-year-old for them."

"Why is he home schooled?"

"Because he is a brilliant young man, who just happens to be smarter than his advanced second grade teacher. He corrected her on something, and he was right about it, and she couldn't take that a seven year old is slightly more intelligent that she is. So therefore, I'm home schooling until the end of the school year."

"Are there more children?"

"My brother has five children. My twin sister is pregnant with her first."

"Do you like kids?"

"I love kids," I said to her.

"What are your intentions?"

"Excuse me?"

"With my son and grandson?"

"I don't have any intentions," I said. "I've worked with Patrick for over ten years and up until the other day; I never even knew that he had a child."

"Why is that?"

"We work together. We have a very professional relationship."

TJ came running in the house. "Come see what I can do. Come see."

"Well, show me," I said getting up without excusing myself from her presence. I went outside with TJ and watched him run towards the track. I walked closer to it. I watched as he mounted his bike and started riding as fast as he could and then he popped a wheelie. "Oh, that's very good, Turner. A few more minutes and then I want you to come inside ok."

"Ok," he said with a smile. "Is daddy here yet?"

"No."

"Do I have to go with my grandma?"

"No."

Before I was at the backdoor, TJ was beside me with his bike. "I'm going to be six at the middle of the August."

I stopped before opening the door and looked at him. "When is your birthday?"

"August thirtieth," he said. "I'll be six," he said proudly.

"Well, now that's something to celebrate."

"You would come to my birthday party?"

"I'd love to come to your birthday party, but I have to be invited first."

"I'll invite you."

Patrick's mother watched the interaction between me and her young grandson. She watched as I scooped him up in my arms and hugged him before turning him into an airplane and flying him into the house. She was smiling when we came into the kitchen. "What did you show, Kenny?" she asked.

"A trick on my bike," he said with a smile on his face.

"Well, I have to get going," she said.

"I really didn't get to introduce myself to you," I said. "I'm Kennedy Jackson."

"I'm Trinity," she said.

"That's a beautiful name."

"Thank you. Are you in anyway related to Bobbi Jackson?"

"She's my mother."

"Where did she and your father move to?"

"The Keys."

"The next time you speak to her, please tell her that Trinity Summers says hello and sends her love."

"I will do that."

We had moved to the living room and were just coming to the door when someone knocked. Patrick stood on the other side of the door. I opened the door and TJ flew into his father's arms.

"Mom! What are you doing here?"

"Young Turner wanted his bike, so I brought it to him."

"Thank you, but you so didn't have to do that."

He came in the house. His mother didn't leave. She came with us into the kitchen. TJ followed behind. He came and leaned against my thigh. It was like an automatic move; I simply bent down and lifted him up. He put his head on my shoulder. I continued in on the conversation. TJ fell asleep in my arms.

"Here. Let me take him," Patrick said.

"I'm fine with him," I said.

"Well, it's getting late," Trinity said. "I'm going to go." With that she kissed Patrick and me good-bye.

CHAPTER EIGHT

June was now upon us. Michael and Kate were finishing there last week of school. The construction for the gym was going smoothly. I had been watching Tyson and Beth, for the day care that they attended closed for the summer three weeks before the school year ended. Addison had been with the restaurant and the new plans that they were doing, which was renovating just about everything except the kitchen. Three stores next to them had closed and they had bought them out and were expanding. The restaurant was going to be huge. Parker's business job was taking him to New York for the next eight weeks.

Carter had finished his second-grade year a month ago. So that he wouldn't get bored, I had gone to the school and met with the advanced third grade teacher at his school and she had given me the books and assignments for him to do. Within a month, we were done with the first quarter of third grade.

Addison had come over with the kids on their last day of school and we had taken them for ice cream and then to the toy store. Once we were back at the house, Addison asked if she could speak to me privately. "I have a favor to ask you and its ok if you say no."

"What is it?"

"Well, as you know Parker is going away for the next two months or so. The restaurant is demanding my attention. Do you think you could take the kids for the summer? I know it's a lot to ask you, but it would be helping me out immensely. You don't have to give me an answer tonight.

But if you will think about it and give me an answer by Monday morning, I'd appreciate it."

It was not a couple days of them sleeping over. It was the entire summer. Because Addison was sugar coating the kicker. In the beginning of August, she and Parker would be taking a three-week cruise to celebrate his birthday. They would be getting back the weekend before the school year started.

Addison had prepared the kids for if I said yes that I would take them for the entire summer. That they would have to be good and listen to me.

And of course, I would be doing it alone because Jamie and Lennox, who now joined her tour as her new drummer, were off on another tour. What the hell would I do with the kids all summer long? And I had to work too. I wanted the B & B to open in August. Now that would be delayed some time. Parker called me that night thinking that I had already said yes to taking the kids and thanked me.

"What are you thanking me for?"

"Are you kidding? For being a god sent and taking the kids for the summer."

"Addison said that I had till Monday morning to decide."

"What? If you don't take them then we will have to hire a nanny to be with them 24/7."

"Did you and Addy give it any thought of what I was planning to do this summer? You just assumed that I don't do anything, so I am available. Park, I work a full-time job. I'm trying to get this place ready to open by August, which now looks like it won't happen until September."

"Please, Kennedy. I am asking you for your help. The kids love you and respect you."

"Will you give me till Monday morning to decide?"

"Yes. If that is what Addison said, then that is fine."

I was just starting to have a bit of a love life. And now the next twelve weeks will be dealing with, entertaining, trying to keep from getting bored and in trouble five kids that really do not have anything other than they are siblings in common with each other. Michael is an all-around athlete, Kate is so into music that she can get lost in a conversation if she starts thinking about a song or a melody, Carter is into space and horses, Tyson is just starting to find his interests which are cars, dinosaurs, and anything that can be put together and taken apart, and Beth. Well, Beth is into everything including getting into trouble every five minutes. I have heard people say the terrible twos and often wondered what exactly that meant and then I see Beth and I understand it perfectly. She doesn't like to share. She thinks that everything is hers. She bites. She kicks. She screams. She has temper tantrums like I have never seen before. Bedtime with Beth is a real issue.

The boys want their own room. They don't want to have to be in the room with their sisters. Kate, who is nine, definitely doesn't want to be stuck in a room with the two-year-old. They fight with each other the most. At least the boys tolerate each other. The age gap for Michael and his brothers are three and five years. The age gap between Kate and Beth is seven years. They both love and hate each other at the same time. Kate was annoyed when she found out that Addison was having another girl and not another boy. She adores her brothers, but there is that love-hate relationship between her and the baby of the family.

Patrick told me a month ago that he has to travel, which I knew about for a work-related project. Patrick had told me that Trinity and Ivy had left for an Alaskan tour right after Memorial Day, and they would be gone all summer long and not returning until Labor Day. This is code for they are making themselves unavailable. Since the day at the museum, TJ didn't want to be anywhere near Ivy anyway. Therefore, Patrick had already asked me if TJ could stay with me from the end of June till the end of July. I had said yes already to that.

I had planned a trip to the Keys to visit mom and dad. TJ would be going with me for that visit. He and I were getting such an attachable bond. When they came over, TJ would snuggle into me no matter what we were doing. When we were out, I'd hear the snickers and the hushed comments.

I had promised that I would take all of the kids to the Space Center. My mouth is a terror at times because I want to do everything in my power to have the kids like me and want to be with me and now I'm not given the choice.

Patrick came over that evening with TJ. When he climbed up in my arms, I could feel the heat radiating off of him. "Patrick, he has a fever." TJ could not settle. He was restless and cranky. "I'm going to bring him upstairs," I said.

"I'll cook the steaks on the grill."

I carried TJ upstairs. I put him in my bed. I took his clothing off him. The only thing he wore was his power ranger underwear. I covered him. Then I went into the bathroom and wet wash clothes with warm water. When I came back, TJ was sleeping. I put the washcloth on his forehead and I thought I heard his skin sizzle. His fever spiked before it finally broke. But I wouldn't leave him. Patrick brought the dinner upstairs to me. I had climbed into the bed and had taken TJ on top of me. When his fever spiked, sweat pored off my body, yet TJ had the chills and his little body shook from it. I had bundled us up even more. We had given him liquids and soup and children's Tylenol to bring down his fever. It was well after midnight when his fever finally gave way like a dam and broke. Sweat poured off him as if he had just jumped in the pool and was now dripping wet on the side of it while waiting for a towel.

Patrick had fallen asleep watching TV. I changed TJ's clothes and the sheets on my bed. When I put him back in my bed, it was in dry clean sheets. He snuggled into me. I brushed his hair back away from his face and kissed his forehead. "Thank you, Ken," he said. "I love you."

"I love you too, Turner."

A bright smile came across his face. "Good night."

"Good night."

I love my nephews and nieces, but the love that I have to Turner is different. I felt maternal feelings for him. Instincts that I have never had kicked in when I was with TJ. I wanted him to be around all the time. I absolutely loved Patrick too. I had to be honest with myself because I'd always secretly adored being around him and having him around. I loved when we would be at a sight and it was hot; he would just casually take off his shirt. I loved his smell.

In the morning, TJ was back to himself. He was bouncing on the bed and jumping off the furniture. Patrick woke up after TJ had launched himself on top of him. The giggling laughter sounded wonderful.

"Good morning," Patrick and I said together.

"My little man is better now," Patrick said lifting TJ above his chest.

"I'm hungry."

I laughed. "Shocker."

We went downstairs. I made pancakes with TJ's help.

"Why are you so quiet?" Patrick asked me.

"Addison and Park have asked me to take the kids for the summer."

"For what? A couple of weeks or something?"

"No. The whole entire summer. Park is going out of town for eight weeks for work, and Addison needs to put the time into the restaurant. Because Jamie is away on tour, she's not available, which leaves me.

"You have already asked me if I could take our favorite five-year-old for a month and I want nothing more than to do that."

"How long until you have to tell them?"

"Monday morning."

"Then what happens?"

"I'm not sure."

"What do you want to do?"

"I didn't want to be tied down this summer. I have fun with Michael, Kate, Carter and Tyson."

"Who did you leave out?"

"Beth," I said.

"How old is she?"

"She's two and a demon child."

"You can't call her a demon."

"Kate is nine years old. I've only seen her cry a few times. Let Beth come within two feet of her and its hysterics from the nine-year-old."

"Can someone take Beth?"

"Addison doesn't want to separate the kids."

The phone rang. "Hello."

"Hi, Kenny."

"Hi, Addison."

"Can I come over?"

"Sure."

"Ok. I'll bring lunch."

I smiled. "I won't reject to that.

"Ok. I'll see you in about an hour."

I hung up the phone. "Addison is coming over."

"So I heard."

"Kenny?"

"Yes, TJ."

"Do you love my daddy?"

"TJ!" Patrick said.

"No, it's ok. Yes," I said.

Patrick looked at me. "You love me?"

I lowered my head and ran my fingers through my hair. "Yeah," I said.

"Since when?"

"Since like the first time I saw you."

He gasped. "You've never let on."

"You were married," I said.

"I wasn't married back then."

"But she told me that you were spoken for."

"Who told you that?" he asked.

"The woman with the purple hair told me that you were spoken for."

"I wasn't married until eleven years ago. That must have been Storm."

"There wasn't a Storm," I said.

"No, it's ok. I know who it was. Go on with what you were saying."

"I always remember when we were assigned to be partners on a project for school. You had said to Tim Jenkins that you'd be doing all the work because girls were not as smart as guys when it came to architecture. Though I wanted nothing more than to punch you, I worked with you on the project."

"I do remember that," he said. "You worked harder than I did. You went above and beyond what the project called for. We were only required to do a 2-D drawing of the structure and you had done not a 3-D, but a 4-D structure. I was blown away," he said.

"You blew me away with the presentation."

"What?" he asked.

"You had started off by saying that when you were assigned a partner for the project that you had wished it wasn't going to be with a girl. Then you said how we met almost every day for a month and we both pulled our own weight on the project and that you were grateful that you had such a great partner."

"Well, I did. I still do," he said.

TJ had gone into the living room and was stretched out on the couch watching TV.

"I didn't know that you were divorced," I said.

"For five years now," he said. "She gave birth to Turner and then she told me that she needed space and her own life. She had divorce papers sent to me at work. Turner was three months old when the divorce went through. I remember being so upset thinking that I was going to lose him. He was there with us. The judge asked to hold him. The divorce decree was signed. Renee got up and walked out. The judge motioned me closer to him and put Turner in my arms. Renee hasn't seen him since that faithful day."

Addison came over. She brought lunch and it smelled delicious. Turner followed her into the kitchen. "That smells soooooo good."

"Well, thank you."

"What is it?"

"It's macaroni…"

"Could I have some please?"

"Yes. Of course," Addison said with a smile.

Addison looked at me. "Beth is going to go spend the summer with my sister. And Jamie called and asked if she could have Kate for the summer. So, could you please take the boys?"

"Yes," I said.

"Oh, thank you so much." Addison took a deep breath. "Beth is going to go with us on the cruise at the end of the summer."

"What? Why?"

"My sister and her husband are going on the cruise as well. They are bringing their twins with them. They are the same age as Beth."

"How are the other children going to feel about that?" Patrick asked. "It's a cruise ship. A vacation of sorts. And you are going to tell them that their baby sister gets to go this time, but they don't. Carter needs to be rewarded for taking being home schooled like a pro. And Michael is starting middle school in the fall. And your beautiful daughter needs to commended for her music ability, and I'm leaving one out," he said with a smile.

"Tyson," I said.

"And Tyson, who is starting kindergarten in the fall. All of your children are at landmarks in their lives and you and Parker are going to only take Beth. If it is a money issue, please let me pay for it. I haven't been around your children all that much, but when I have been around, they are bright and intelligent young people. They are respectful. They are considerate. They are amazing people," Patrick said.

TJ wandered in the room. Patrick watched him look around the room. Then he came and found me. Without a thought, I scooped him up in my arms. He settled in my arms. He kissed me on the cheek and then put his head down on my shoulder and was down for the count. Addison had watched this happen too. "You have the knack," she said.

"What?"

"He's adorable. He came in the room. He looked at me. He looked at Patrick. Then he spotted you. You picked him up like nothing and he snuggled into your arms. He kissed you good night and went right to sleep," Addison said. "Does he do that with his mother?"

"He's never known his mother."

"Oh, my. I'm so sorry."

"She didn't die. She divorced me when he was three months old and went to California. She's never inquired about him."

"I'm sorry," Addison said.

Parker was at his home helping Kate pack her stuff for the summer. She would be spending the next six and half weeks with Jamie and Lennox. She packed jeans and really nice tops. Tyson came in her room and put his stuffed monkey in her bag. Carter and Michael each brought something in too. Parker would be flying with Kate to Memphis and then from there going to New York.

"If mommy is going to be working at the restaurant, and you are going away for the summer, where are we going to be?" Michael asked.

"Mommy said that she would let us know the details when she gets back," Parker said.

"I want mommy," Tyson said.

"She will be home soon. Why don't we make popcorn and watch a movie together?"

"Daddy?" Carter said.

"Yeah, buddy," he said.

"If Beth is going to Aunt Mandy's and Kate is going with Aunt Jamie, where are we going?"

"Carter, it's going to be to ok."

"But you are leaving in the morning with Kate. Do you know where we are going to go?"

"Carter, let's watch a movie and wait for mommy to get home."

He couldn't settle down. When Addison came in the house, the girls were sleeping on the couch. The three boys were anxiously waiting for her to get home.

"Hi," she said to all of them. Big eyes stared at her. "So it's all taken care of," she said.

"Who is going to watch us this summer?" Michael asked.

She sat down on the couch with them. "If the three of you could spend the summer with anyone in the world, who would it be?"

"Aunt Kenny," the three of them said.

"Well, I guess you are in luck."

Addison and Parker both watched as relief settled over the three boys. The three of them huddled together for a hug.

"Were you guys worrying about this?" Addison asked.

"Hell yeah," Tyson said.

They laughed. "Don't worry. You three aren't going there till Monday evening."

It was Carter, who came and snuggled with Addison.

The next morning, I went to Parker's to pick him and Kate up to drive them to the airport. Kate was super excited to be going on a plane for the first time in her young life. They would be taking two flights together. The first from Orlando to Atlanta with a connecting flight to Memphis. Parker would be staying in Memphis just long enough to meet Jamie and have her take Kate for the summer. Then he would be flying into JFK airport, where he would get a car service to take him to his hotel in the heart of Manhattan.

At the airport, I parked the car and went in with them. "I have to go to the bathroom," Kate announced.

"I'll take her," I said.

"Thanks."

I went with her in the bathroom. "Are you nervous?" I asked her.

"No."

"No!"

"No," she said again. "Daddy will be with me. Have you ever flew?"

"Flown," I corrected her. "Yes. I've been all around the world."

"Really?"

"Yes, sweetheart."

"Aunt Ken?"

"Yes."

"Maybe in the fall you could home school me."

"Why would you want to be home schooled?"

"I don't fit in in my school," she said. "I'm not like the other girls. They don't like me. I am never invited to anyone in my class's birthday parties. I love music," she said taking a breath. "I see music. Does that should weird?"

"Why would it sound weird?"

"Because I see music."

"So does Aunt Jamie. She always did. It is a gift baby girl. But we will talk about school when you get back later this summer. Just please do me one thing."

"What's that?"

"Call me every day so we know where you are and so that you can speak to your brothers."

"Ok, I'll use Aunt James's phone."

"Well, you don't have to do that."

"Why not?"

"Because I bought you a present."

When we came out of the bathroom, I gave her a box. "Is this what I think it is?" she asked. She opened it up. "It's a phone. You bought me a phone."

"I did," I said. "It's fully charged. There's a head set in there too."

Parker walked over. "What is this?"

"Aunt Kenny bought me a phone."

"Ken, you didn't have to do that."

"I know, but I wanted to."

"Are the boys getting presents too?" Parker asked me.

"They are."

"What did you get the boys?"

"Michael is getting a phone too. Carter is getting a tablet and Tyson is getting that kids camera that every time we go to the store and he sees it, though he has never asked for it, I know that he wants it."

They called for their flight. "Thank you for bringing us to the airport and seeing us off."

"Sure," I said. I hugged my brother first. "I love you."

"I love you too."

Then I hugged Kate. "Have a wonderful time with Aunt Jamie. And tell her to call me a few times this summer ok."

"Ok," she said. "I will. I love you."

"I love you too."

I watched them board the plane and then I left. I drove home. I would have the next three days to myself before getting the boys for the summer. This gave time to get things squared away a bit. I went into my office, clicked on my computer, and then went into the kitchen to make lunch although it was only ten thirty in the morning. I made a double stuffed grill cheese sandwich and then went back to my office to work. I planned a few fun activities for the boys and I to do. We would not be in the house every day.

I booked a trip to Gator Land. We would be going on a nature preserve and taking hikes the first week. The second week I would be taking them to Bok Tower Garden. Then I would take them to Pounce de Leon Inlet Lighthouse. Following that I would be taking them to Two Tails Ranch. Most of these trips would be a day trip maybe an overnighter if we needed that. And then I would be taking all four boys to Key West for two weeks. While there would be exploring the Florida Keys, swimming, surfing, fishing, and maybe an excursion or two. On the way back from the Keys, we would drive up the beach until we reached Coco Beach or Titusville, where we would finish the vacationing with a trip to the Space Center. Then we would go home, and three boys would go be going home to get ready for their family cruise. This was the plan. I printed out all the details and then went for a swim in the pool.

For the first time I was bored in my own home. It was the first time in months that I was alone in the house. I couldn't take the quiet, so I decided to get showered and dressed nice and go out for a while. I went out by myself. I went to a dance club, but the scene there was younger than I expected it to be. I did not know what to do with myself, so I went to see a movie.

CHAPTER NINE

On Tuesday morning, I drove to Addison's to pick up the boys. Though their bags were packed, they weren't ready to go. Michael was whining that we weren't going to do anything fun. "I know it," he said. "Kate is off with Aunt Jamie having the time of her life and we are stuck here, and we aren't going to have any fun. We will be cleaning up after the horses and taking care of the stuff in Aunt Ken's backyard," he whined.

"Michael, I have to work."

"Why couldn't I go with daddy to New York?"

"We have been over this. Daddy is working in the city and you are almost eleven. You can't be left on your own."

"But what about my friends?"

"Michael, you are still in the same town. I am sure that Aunt Ken will let your friends come over. Now please stop. You are carrying on in front of your aunt." The three of them whined and complained.

I didn't let it get to me. The boys and I were going to have an adventurous summer. The three of them were finally ready to go an hour and half later not that I was rushing them.

"I'll still be in town all summer if you need me," Addison said. "Thank you so much for taking them for me.

"Boys behave yourselves and have a great summer with your aunt. Like I told Aunt Kenny, if you need me, I will be here. I love you all."

"Love you too," the three of them said.

When we left her house, the boys knew the way to my house, but I did not go that way. Instead I drove to Orlando. We got a hotel for the night. The boys and I went swimming in the pool before I took them out for dinner.

"Are we going to my favorite place?"

"Ah. No. We are going to go to some other place that makes noise and is very loud."

Michael screeched. "We are going to The Rain Forest Café! I love that place. We went there after our field trip. Aunt Ken?"

"Yes."

"Are there field trips in middle school?"

"Yes."

"But my friend Dillion, who is in middle school said that there aren't any field trips."

"The correct way to say that sentence is: Dillion said that there are no field trips," I said.

"Ok," he said nicely. "But are there?"

"Yes, Michael, there are field trips."

"Mommy wants him to join band in middle school," Tyson said.

I looked at Michael. "Why is that?"

"Because he was teasing the shit out of Kate."

"TYSON!"

"What?"

"Language."

"But mommy and daddy don't mind. They think I'm cute."

"Well, every time I hear you say a swear word, I'm putting you in time out."

He giggled not taking me seriously. I am going to fix his little ass. He is four soon to be five in a few weeks and he thinks that he is the king. Well, that's going to change while he is with me.

"I want ice cream for dinner?"

"No, Tyson, you aren't getting ice cream for dinner."

"But that's what I want."

"Well, that's not what you are getting."

"But I want it dammit."

We had just pulled in to where the restaurant is. "Michael and Carter please get out of the vehicle and wait for us on the sidewalk."

"Yes, Aunt Kenny," they said together.

"What about me?"

"You are time out for four minutes," I said.

I kept the two boys in my sights. Tyson unbuckled himself from the seat belt and tried to open the door.

"Open the door." I ignored him. "Open the door." Again, I just ignored him. "I want out of the fucking car." That pushed my button.

"Tyson, do you want to be sent to spend the summer with baby Beth?"

"No."

"Then I want you to listen to me. I want you to stop cursing. If I hear it again, I will take to where baby Beth is staying this summer and I will leave you there."

He cried and carried on that he didn't want to go be with Beth. When the four minutes was up, I unlocked the car and got him and went and met the boys. We went into the restaurant. Tyson was as quiet as a mouse until the first crackle of thunder, where he screamed and then came bouncing into my arms.

"It's only noise," I told him. "It's pretend thunder."

He was sobbing crying. "I sorry. I sorry."

"Stop. It is ok. I just want you to be a good boy so that we can all have fun this summer."

He ate his dinner on my lap. Carter squished closer to me. Michael enjoyed the atmosphere.

"So where are we going tomorrow?"

"We are going to… I'm not telling you, but I know that you will like it."

The three boys smiled.

"Can I have ice cream now?"

"Can you say please?" I said to Tyson.

"Can I please have ice cream now?"

"Yes, you can."

"Thank you."

That night at the hotel, after everyone was showered and bathed, we settled in for the night. As we slept, a stormed had blown in. The room lit up from the lighting. Tyson woke up. With the second stroke of lighting, we were all up.

"It's right on top of us," Carter said.

"We are safe. I promise. Come over here if you want to."

I had not finished saying it and I had Carter pressed against me and Tyson trembling behind my back. The storm was close. The light flickered. I thought it was now a good idea to give the boys their gifts. "Michael, come over here please." He did. "I have something for all three of you. Tyson, this is for you."

"What is it?"

"Open it and let's see," I said. "Michael, this is for you. And Carter, this is for you."

"It's a cell phone. Thank you, Aunt Kenny."

"You're welcome."

Carter squealed. "It's a tablet. Thank you."

"You too are welcome."

Tyson was shocked that he was now holding the one thing that he has wanted for months. He came in my arms and threw his arms around me. "Thank you."

"It's loaded with film, so you can take…"

He was off the bed in seconds. He drew back the blinds and put the camera to his eye with his finger on the button and just as the next flash of lighting came, he snapped the picture and caught it. I got out of the bed and went to him. I got down on my knees next to him. "Let's see how you did," I said. "You tap this button to see the pictures that you took." The camera did not have a delete button, so he wouldn't be able to erase anything. We looked at the photo and I was shocked. It was a beautiful picture. I got him away from the window and back in bed with me. The four of us went back to sleep.

In the morning, we were all set and ready to go by eight. We went downstairs in the hotel and had breakfast. "Are we staying here another night?"

"We could," I said.

"Well, what are our plans after this?" Michael asked.

"Well, today is Wednesday. I have to do something at the house on Friday, so we will have to be home early Friday. We will see how it goes ok."

They agreed.

Our first adventure began. The whole day, Tyson took pictures. "When can we see them?" he asked.

"Later today, we will take the time to look at them."

Michael took pictures with his phone and Carter took pictures with his tablet. And as for me, I took pictures with my Cannon Camera and with my phone. By the time we left Gator Land, it was time for dinner. The kids were exhausted. I still had the hotel room for another night, so we went back to the hotel.

"Can we order room service?" Michael asked.

"Yes, we can do that. Why don't you three take showers and then we will order."

"Ok," they said.

Carter looked at his brothers and they seemed to read what he was thinking. "Can you come with us for a minute please?"

"Yes, of course," I said.

I didn't think about where they were leading me until we right there on the edge of the pool and they were all three leaning into me, and we all went flying into the pool. A photographer with the hotel had been snapping pictures and captured it frame by frame. I came up laughing. I grabbed the three boys in a hug and threw myself backwards, so we went under again.

"No bath!" Tyson said.

"Oh, no. You are taking a bath to wash your stinky little body."

"It's all clean now," he said with a smile.

"And just imagine how cleaner it will be after a bath," I smiled back at him.

"Ok. You win," he said jumping into my arms and bringing us under water again.

"Ok. Ok. Let's go so we can eat."

"Yay! We are going to eat," Carter said.

They all said what they wanted at the same time. Michael wanted pizza. Carter wanted pot stickers and egg rolls. Tyson wanted chicken nuggets and macaroni and cheese.

"What do you want?"

"To look at the menu," I said. We went back into the room.

As we sat down at the table that evening to eat our smorgasbord of food: hot dogs, pizza, macaroni and cheese, pot stickers, egg rolls, and hamburgers, the kids spoke about the day.

"Can we go back there tomorrow?" Michael asked.

"We can if you would like, but then we would have to leave from there to go home."

"That's ok," Michael said.

We wound down for the night. Tyson was sleeping two minutes after he was on the bed. I got him under the covers. Carter climbed into bed and he too was asleep shortly after. Michael was wide awake.

"Do I have to go to bed?"

"No. Not if you don't want to."

"Can we watch a movie?"

"Sure."

I took out my laptop and opened it. I had planned to do a little work while the boys slept and before I turned in for the night. But instead went on the movie app that I had and let Michael pick one.

"They have popcorn in the lobby. Can I go get some?"

"Yes," I said.

He put his shoes on, took a twenty and went running to the lobby. Just as he got back into the room another stormy night was starting. We settled onto the king size bed together with the laptop at the bottom of the bed. Within the first hour of the movie, we were both asleep. Though the storm raged on above us, we all slept through it.

In the morning, we packed and loaded the car and then grabbed a quick breakfast and then set back out for Gator Land one last time. Tyson never put his camera down. In a way, I couldn't wait to get to the house and see what was on the chip. Carter had left the tablet tucked away in the car. Michael took a few pictures here and there that day. After lunch, I told the boys that we could visit their one favorite part of the park and then we needed to be on the road heading home. They agreed. An hour and half later, we visited the gift shop and then we were on our way. With Tyson and Carter secured safely in their car seats, Michael sat in the front seat with me.

"Aunt Ken, when we go to The Keys to see Grandma and Grandpa, TJ will be with us too right?"

"Yes. Why?"

"So, we are going to have three car seats in the car?"

"Yes," I said.

"Do you think they will fight who gets to sit next to the window?"

"No, I don't think they will. Patrick has always put TJ in the middle of the backseat, and Tyson likes being on the left side and Carter likes being on the right side, so it all works out."

"TJ. What does that stand for?"

"Turner James," I said.

"Hmm. That's cool," Michael said.

"So, are you excited to start middle school this fall?"

"Excited?"

We looked at each other and I started to laugh. "Ok. Wrong choice of words," I said.

"I think I'll like it. It will be my school for a whole year until Kate moves up. It's last time I'll be in school with Carter though," he said. "He's such a cool little kid too. I love having him as my little brother."

Both boys were sound asleep in the backseat.

"Thank you for taking us, Aunt Kenny."

"You're welcome."

Within the hour we were home. Michael carried Tyson in first and put him down on the couch. The he came back for Carter, who was slowly waking up. When Michael unbuckled him from the car seat, Carter jumped into his arms. Both boys were laughing.

"Mommy's here," Carter said.

Addison pulled in right behind me. I put the bags in and turned to see her.

"I've been calling you," she said.

"Is something wrong?"

"Well, no. But I haven't heard from the kids since you left."

"We're fine, mommy," Carter said with a huge grin.

"Don't alligator…" Too late. He sunk his teeth into Michael's shoulder. "bite your brother," I finished.

"Where have you been? I thought you were coming back yesterday."

"Michael, can you take your brother inside please?"

"Sure," he said to me with a grin.

When the boys were inside, I looked at Addison. "First, do you want me to continue watching the boys?"

"Yes. I need you to."

"Ok, then please don't come here saying that you were worried. I gave you the itinerary of where we would we be going and staying. I am sorry that we didn't call you to check in. I know that you are busy at the restaurant and I am respecting that. We were going to come back yesterday, but we had stayed at Gator Land all day till the park closed. By the time we got back to the hotel, which I did reserve for another night not planning on using it, we did. The boys showered and we got dinner and then we all went to bed.

"This morning, we got up and went back to Gator Land because the tickets are good for two visits. So instead of wasting it, we used it. I got them lunch and we came home.

"If you called me, I don't know why it didn't work. My phone never rang. I'm sorry."

"I miss my kids."

"I know you do," I said.

"I'm sorry."

"It's cool." I looked at her. "While you are here, do you want to eat with us?"

"I'd love too," she said.

CHAPTER TEN

The boys and I worked together at the house over the weekend. I had received my shipment that I had been waiting for for the past four months.

"What's in the boxes?" Carter asked.

"That's my next design," I said.

"What?"

Michael and Tyson came into the kitchen where we were. I gave them breakfast.

"What was the what for?" Michael asked.

"I asked what is in the box. Aunt Kenny replied that it's her next deign. So, my question was what."

I laughed. "Very accurate and thorough, Carter." He beamed.

"What is it?" Michael asked.

"It's my next design," I said again. "Before an architect goes out into the field and builds amazing structures, they first have to build a smaller scale."

"When are you going to put it together."

"When we are in The Keys," I answered.

"Can we help?"

"Maybe. We will see how it goes."

"Ok," they said together.

"So, when is our next adventure?"

"We are leaving in a little while."

Patrick called. He sounded pissed when I answered the phone. "Hello."

"My fucking mother bailed on me. She and my sister went to Ft. Lauderdale to go gambling."

"What's the problem?"

"A five year old little munchkin, who now I have no one to watch."

"Bring him here. Pack enough clothes for the next two weeks for him and bring him here."

"Are you sure?"

"Absolutely."

"But you aren't supposed to get him for another two weeks."

"Patrick, its fine. I'm taking these three to Bok Tower Garden, so adding another boy the to mix doesn't mean much."

"Where is it that you are going?"

"Lake Wales. It's about an hour or so north west of here."

"Ok," he said. "And when will you return?"

"We will stay up there for tonight, go to the gardens tomorrow and Wednesday, and then come home Thursday morning. When we get back, we will be here Thursday and Friday then we will leave Saturday morning for Daytona. We will be there just under a week. Then we will come home for two days again and leave Friday for Gainesville. We will be there just two days. Then we will return home for three days and then we are off to Key West and The Keys for two weeks. From that point when we are driving back, we will be coming up the east coastline till we get to Titusville and we will be ending our trip in the Space Center."

"And you promise me that you don't mind taking him two weeks earlier than you expected?"

"Yes, Patrick. I promise. Everything is going to be fine and work out."

"Can I bring him by within the hour?"

"Yes, of course."

"See you soon."

I called him back. "Don't forget anything that he really needs or sleeps with."

"He said he'll be a big boy and leave Frosty home."

"Whatever Frosty may be, please pack. These three have things that they still sleep with and one is soon to be eleven."

"Thank you."

"I'll see you when you come."

While we waited for Patrick to bring TJ, I played a board game with the boys. Trouble. I loved this game as a child. I hate this game as an adult. I was losing huge when then doorbell rang. I got up bumping the edge of the board and moving pieces around.

"HEY!" Tyson said.

I looked down at him and the pieces that were now in his lap. "You know what that is called," I said with a smile.

"What?" the three of them asked.

"Aunt Kenny wins." The three of them laughed. "Clean it up ok. And get ready because we are going to go real soon."

I went to the door and opened it and TJ bound up into my arms. "Kenny!"

"TJ!"

He smiled so big. I hugged him. He bear hugged me before I put him down. He went over to the boys and sat with them. Patrick handed me Frosty. I looked at it. It was a light blue baby blanket that someone had sewed into a stuffed dog. "This is Frosty."

"It's adorable."

"Frosty is a boy not an It," Patrick said.

"Ok. He's adorable."

"I made that for him when he was born."

I took a step back and looked at him.

"What's with the look?"

"I didn't realize how creative you are."

"Are you shitting me," he said. "I'm a fucking architect."

"This isn't a building, Patrick. This used to be a sheet of fabric and now look at it. It's a friggin' dog. A little worn and tethered, but it's a dog."

"If he gets dirty, he can go right into the washing machine and the drier."

"Ok. Somehow I think you will have to make three of these when the boys see it."

"Find out what they like, and I'll make each of them one. The girls too."

"Wow. Thank you."

"Have you heard anything how they are doing?"

"Kate is having the time of her life with Jamie and Lennox and Beth…" I smiled and laughed. "Well, Beth is Beth. She will go all day without eating. When she does eat, she's doesn't have an off switch. She has grown a full inch in the last two weeks. She never stops running. She runs everywhere she goes."

Within the next hour, I packed the car. TJ's car seat was installed in my car. I kissed Patrick good-bye and we were off to Lake Wales, Florida for the next couple of days. With the four boys, it was quite entertaining all in itself during the drive up. TJ, Carter, and Michael were all talking about school. Tyson chimed in saying that he was starting school in the fall and then he would turn five. It turned out that Tyson and TJ shared the same birthday. August thirtieth.

"Cool!" they both said.

"How old will you be?" Tyson asked.

"Six."

"Hey, TJ, where is your mom?" Michael asked.

"She's in the Hotel California," he said.

"The what?" Carter asked.

"It means she's never coming back," TJ said. "She left me and daddy when I was just a baby. She moved out west to California."

Michael, who was sitting next to me in the front seat asked, "Is that true?"

I nodded my head.

"Aunt Kenny, can you please pull over?"

"We are on the highway. What's wrong?"

"Please, Aunt Kenny?"

I signaled my right turn signal then merged off onto the shoulder. Michael got out of the car and went into the backseat. He took TJ in his arms hugging him tight. "I'm sorry about your mom," Michael said. "If I upset you, I didn't mean to."

"I'm ok," TJ said.

Michael climbed out of the backseat and came back into the car. He closed the door. I glanced at him. This kid had a heart and the compassion that adults don't even have. I was impressed. TJ was quiet from that point on. When we arrived at the hotel, I checked us in. We went to the room with our bags.

"Can we check out the pool?" Carter asked.

"Yes."

"Can we get chips from the vending machine?"

"Ah. Um. No. We are going to go out for dinner."

"Who's turn it is it to pick?"

"It's TJ's turn," Michael said.

TJ looked up at him. "My turn to do what?"

"Were you listening?"

"Nope," TJ said with a grin that could just melt my heart.

"Silly boy," Michael said. "You get to pick where we go for dinner."

"Oh, I want to go to Denny's," he said still smiling that big toothy smile.

"Now that's a place I haven't been since I was…"

"Was it around when you were a kid?" Michael asked.

"Denny's? Yes, of course."

"When did it open?" Tyson asked.

"The restaurant chain has been around since the nineteen fifties."

"Do you remember when it opened?"

"Tyson, just how old do you think that I am?"

He ducked his head. "Old."

"And do you think that I am older than you daddy?"

"Yeah."

"Let's call him," I said. I took out my phone from my pocket and called Parker. "Hi. Your youngest son thinks that I am older than you and that I remember when Denny's first opened."

Parker laughed. "Hi. You made my day. Let me talk to Mr. Tyson. I love you."

"I love you too."

"Well, I thought she was," Tyson said. He laughed at whatever my brother said to him. "I love you too, daddy. I'm being good."

We went to Denny's for dinner. It worked out well, for the boys ordered all different things and then shared everything.

"What's your mom like?" TJ asked after a while.

"Who's mom?" I asked.

"Your mom. What is she like?"

"Grandma is soooo cooool," Tyson said. "She'll let you do anything."

"But what is she like?"

"She's sweet, kind, caring," Michael said. "She's just like Aunt Kenny just older."

"When are we going there?"

"In two weeks," I said.

"I have to go to the bathroom," Carter said.

Michael got up and wound up taking all three boys to the bathroom. When they came back, they were all laughing about something.

"What's so funny?"

"Um. Nothing," Michael said.

"Are you gentlemen done eating?"

I got three yeses and one "can we order pancakes to go."

"TJ, if you are still hungry, you can order something else."

The waitress came by. "Excuse me," TJ said. "May I please have pancakes? No, wait. Can I please have waffles with sausage?"

"Yes, of course."

"Thank you."

Within fifteen minutes, TJ was eating waffles and the other three were eating the order of pancakes that the waitress didn't cancel. By the time we got out of there I had spent almost a hundred dollars for dinner. As we were getting into the car, the manager came out.

"Ma'am?" I turned around to face him. "There was a mistake with your bill. Are the children under twelve?"

"Yes, all four of them are."

"Could you please come back in with me?"

We went back in the restaurant. The boys sat on the couch while I was reimbursed for dinner. Then the manager gave me three gift cards. I thanked him and we left.

"When we get back to the room, do we have to go bed?" TJ asked.

"Oh, no," Carter said. "When we get back to the hotel, Aunt Kenny will let us go swimming for a little while, and then we all shower, and watch a movie together."

"If there is a game room, can we play in there?" Michael asked.

"Yes, of course."

Back at the hotel, we found the game room first on the way to the room. We went into it and it was virtually empty. "AIR HOCKEY!" TJ said. "I want to play."

"Yes, you can play whatever you want."

I went over to the machine to deposit money for five play cards. Just before I did that, a woman from the hotel came over to me. "How many kids and adults?"

"Four children and me," I said.

"Here you go," she said handing me game cards that I wouldn't have to refill. "You are the first ones to come in here in a while," she said. "Are you enjoying your stay?"

"We just got here today, but so far we are. Thank you."

"The cards are good for as long as you are here."

"Thank you, again." I walked away with the play cards to where the boys were. I handed each one of them a card. Then we started to play. I played each boy in air hockey two times before we moved on. Then we played shooting games, we played a shooting water game, a basketball toss game, and skee ball. We played for hours. When we left there, I told the boys that they could go swimming for a half hour if they wanted to. There were a few other kids in the pool. We went to room, so they could change into their bathing suits, and then we went out to the pool. The four of them jumped in together. They all swam to the shallow end, exited the pool, ran to the deep end, jumped in again, and repeated their swim to the shallow end to do it yet again. When the half hour was up, I called for them to get out of the pool and they all four did.

"Four boys!" a woman said. "They must be a handful and a half."

"No. Not really. They are good kids," I said.

"Are they all four yours?"

"Three of them are my nephews and one is my friend's son."

TJ came racing over to me. "Can we go? Can we go?"

"Go where?" I asked.

"To see the man feed the alligator. Please, mommy," he said.

"Yes. Yes." Though he was soaking wet, he bound right up in my arms. "Have a nice evening," I said to the woman. I didn't make a big deal that TJ had just called me mommy for the first time. The truth was, I liked the sound of it. I went with the four of them to see a true American Indian feed an alligator. "Boys, come on. We need to go now." They were really good and came with me.

"Did you do it?" Tyson asked TJ. "Did you? Or did you chicken out?"

"I'm not telling," he said.

"What are we talking about?"

"Nothing, Aunt Kenny."

"Nice try little buddy," I said to Tyson. "We have already had a discussion of what will happen if you do something bad right."

"Yes, Aunt Kenny," he said. "But I didn't do anything bad. I promise."

"Because you said it in front of me, either you tell me what you did to TJ or I'll call your father and tell…"

"I dared him to call you mommy," Tyson said.

"You're in time out for the next twenty minutes and I don't want to hear a peep out of you. If I do, then I'm calling your mother and telling her that she will have make other arrangements for you. Is that clear?"

He lowered his head. "Yes, Aunt Kenny. I didn't mean for it to be mean," he said.

While the others showered or bathed and changed into clean dry clothes, I left Tyson in timeout. When twenty minutes had gone by, I told him he could get up. He came over to me. "I'm sorry," he said almost in tears.

"It's not me you have to apologize to."

"Please don't send me back," he said.

"I'm giving you one more chance. And I am completely serious about this Tyson. One more bad thing and you are going home."

"Ok."

"Please go shower and get ready for bed."

He nodded. He went into the bathroom and I heard him start to cry. TJ came over to me. "Are you mad at me?"

"Why would I be mad at you?"

"I don't know. Because I called you mommy."

"No, TJ, I'm not mad at you."

"I wish you were my mommy."

I do too, little buddy. I do too. "Listen, you can call me whatever you like ok."

"Ok," he said. "Thank you for bringing me." He jumped into my arms and hugged me tight.

Tyson was still crying in the bathroom. I put TJ down and went into the bathroom. "Are you ok?"

"I'm really sorry," Tyson said. "I'll be good. I promise."

"I know, but you have to start thinking about what you say to people. TJ doesn't have a mom like you and your brothers and sisters do. So that could really have upset him. Are you upset that he is here?"

"No," Tyson said putting his head down.

"Tyson!"

"Well, yeah," he said.

"You know that no matter what or who comes into our lives that I will always love you."

"I know."

"Now please hurry so we can at least start the movie."

"Ok," he said.

In the morning, we all woke about the same time. We all dressed and brushed our teeth. Then I took them for breakfast before we went to the Bok Tower Garden. When we arrived, I had a bad feeling that the boys were going to be bored, but they weren't. They loved it. We did the tower first and went all the way up to the eighth floor, which put us two hundred and five feet above sea level. It was a beautiful sight. We learned that the garden was built first and then the house was built to fit the garden. The house has twenty bedrooms. After that, we went to the garden and then to the play area for kids. All four of them loved that. We stayed there till almost four o'clock.

"Are we going to go home now?" Tyson asked.

"No. We are going to stay up here for a few more days."

"Can we go back in the pool?"

"Yes."

"Can we go to the zoo?" Carter asked.

"Yes, we can do that."

The next morning, we checked out of the hotel and we went to Sanford, Florida to go to Central Zoo. Sanford had four main attractions and we had decided to try to do all of them in one day. The first place we went was Zoom Air. It was not a zoo, but it was an outdoor jungle gym for both kids and adults alike. We did have a blast there. From there we went to Black Bear Wilderness Area. It is a huge location.

"We need bikes to do this park," Michael said.

"We can do that." I said.

"Where are we going to get five bikes now?"

"Well, let's just go see, "I continued.

We found a bike store. I bought three Yamaha 12" BMX bikes for Tyson, TJ, and Carter, who were roughly all about the same size. For Michael, who isn't that much shorter than I am, I bought him a 20" Mountain Bike and I bought myself a 26" Mountain Bike. I bought a bike car mount for six bikes. With the man's help, we mounted the bike mount on the car. Then I loaded the bikes on the car, and we were off to go back to the Black Bear Wilderness Area. We went in with our bikes. I paid for our entrance into park and then we were off. The five of us riding together in this park. By the time we were back at the entrance, we were all sweaty, hot, and hungry. I loaded the bikes with Michael's help and then we got into the car.

"That was sooooo much fun. Thank you, Aunt Kenny."

"You're welcome. That was fun."

"I'm hungry," I got from all four of them.

"I know. Let's see about accommodations for the night and then we will get dinner ok."

"Can we just get something and go back to your house?" Carter asked.

"Is that what you all want to do?"

"Yeah," they said.

"We can do that."

I stopped back at the bike shop. I ran in. "Is everything ok with the bikes?" the man asked.

"Yes, they are great. I thought I bought a chain," I said.

It was still sitting on the counter where I left it. "It's right here, ma'am."

"Thank you." I took the chain and ran back out to the car. I chained the five bikes together and then got back in the car. "Where do you want to eat? Or what do you want to eat?"

"Hamburgers!" they all said.

"Great. Let's do it."

We pulled into a parking lot where there were a few restaurants to choose from. The boys picked John's Giant Hamburgers. We went into the restaurant. We got a table and ordered. When the hamburgers came, we ate. I paid the bill and the tip, and we were off for home.

CHAPTER ELEVEN

We were at the house for a few days. We had fun riding our new bikes together all-around town. We went to Addison's restaurant for lunch one day. She was so surprised to see us and so happy. She had opened an Italian restaurant the year after she and Parker were married. Everything was homemade. She loved to cook, and she was great at it. Addison had trained in Italy for two years to be a chef. Everything was authentic and wonderful.

"How did you get here? I didn't see your car," she said.

"We road our bikes," I said.

"Aunt Ken bought us new bikes," the boys said together.

"Ken!"

"We needed them," I protested. "I took them some place that was way too long to walk around, and they said we could use bikes, so I went to a store and bought the kids and I bikes."

"And we had the bestest time," Tyson said.

"It's just best," I said.

He smiled his big, cute smile. "It was the bestest," he said again.

"So, what are your plans now?"

"A few days at the Pounce de Leon Inlet Lighthouse. We will leave Monday morning for that adventure. We will back on Thursday some time. Stay home for the weekend. Leave Sunday midday to go north to the Two Tales Ranch in Gainesville. We will stay up there for a few days and then leave and come home for the rest of the week and then we are going to The

Keys for two weeks and driving home up the coast and then a surprise for all four boys before we come home."

"Sounds wonderful. Are you three having fun?"

"Yes, we are having a great time," they all said.

The lady from Daytona called to remind me of my reservation that started Friday night. It was Friday. When we got home, I told the boys to pack their bags and we would be leaving soon.

"Can we bring our bikes?"

"Of course," I said.

We were all packed and ready to go within the next two hours. Then we left for Daytona. Our hotel was right on the beach. When we arrived, Tyson and TJ were sleeping. Michael took Tyson, I took TJ and Carter by the hand. We went into the hotel.

"Hi, Kennedy Jackson checking in."

"And that would be a double suite," the man said.

"Yes, sir."

"Do you need help with your bags?"

"Yes, we do."

"Aunt Ken, I'll go out with him to get the bags," Michael said. He handed Tyson to Carter. Tyson wrapped his legs around Carter. It was right then that I noticed that Carter had a growth spirt. He was about four inches taller than he was even a few days ago. I looked at him and he looked at me.

"Do you need a pair of new shoes?" I asked him.

"I'm ok. I took a pair of Michael's," he said with that loving smile.

"We will go tomorrow and get you new shoes."

Michael came back handing me my keys. Then we went up to the room with the bellhop. Once the two sleepers were put down, then Michael and Carter went downstairs with the bellhop for the five bikes. They came back upstairs about fifteen minutes later.

"Hey, guys," I said paying the bellhop. "Thank you, sir. Have a nice evening." Then I turned back to the boys. "I ordered dinner."

"Yeah," I heard from the bed. TJ was waking up. "Are we here yet?"

"We are in the room, silly," Michael said.

I went to the back door of the room and opened it up and stepped out on the balcony. The sound of the ocean was profound. It roared and rumbled. In the far distance there was a storm over the ocean. It was absolutely beautiful to see.

"Oh, TJ, I have something for you," I said.

He became all excited. I went back in the room and riffled through my bag for his present. I handed him a wrapped box. He jumped on the bed and then sat down to open it. "Oh my god," he said. "It's a camera. I wanted a camera so bad. Thank you. Thank you so much."

"It can't erase any pictures you take. We can do that when we get home if we need to. I wanted to give it you when we first got you for the summer, but the store was sold out."

Michael nodded. That is what Addison had handed to me before we left her.

"Can I go take pictures?"

"Yes. Go ahead."

Room service came up bringing hamburgers, corn dogs, hotdogs, fried cheese sticks, pizza bites, and a chocolate cake with candles. It was Carter's eighth birthday. Addison, Parker and the family would be celebrating his birthday, and all of the kids' birthdays on the cruise later this summer.

Michael had taken Tyson and TJ to the one of the stores before we rode our bikes back to the house earlier today and they had bought him presents. Tyson had picked a pair of shorts for Carter. TJ picked a soccer ball. Michael picked a duffle bag that dubbed as a backpack. I bought Carter a case for his tablet and a camera as well. "Please wake Tyson up," I said.

Just as I finished saying it, I watched as TJ went over to the bed and jumped on top of him. Tyson squealed and a round of rough housing began. Tyson stopped suddenly. "Stop. Please stop. If I do something wrong, I will have to spend the rest of the summer with Beth, "he said. Then I watched as he started to cry. "I'm sorry. I will be good. Please don't send me."

"Tyson, its ok."

I picked him up and took him outside on the balcony. I sat down on one of the chairs out there and just held on to him. "I'm not sending you anywhere. I promise. Please look at me." He looked up at me. "I'm sorry. I should not have said that to you. If you do something wrong, we will talk about it and talk through it ok. Please stop crying. I love you and your brothers and TJ like you are my children. I don't like to see you sad. You have been absolutely wonderful, but I know you. I've seen you every single day since the day you were born, and I know that you haven't been acting like yourself. So please, Tyson, go back to be that strong headed little guy, who I adore. You are great."

"So, you're not going to send me away?"

"Tyson, where would I send you? I don't even know where your mom's sister lives. No, I am not going to send you away. I promise. I'm keeping my four boys with me. And that's the way it will be."

He grinned through the tears. I wiped his tears away and went back in the room. We had dinner and then I turned off the lights and we sang happy birthday to Carter. He was so surprised. "I wasn't expecting anything. Mommy said that we are going to celebrate our birthdays together at the end of the summer. Thank you."

He opened his presents smiling at every one of them. He loved the shorts that Tyson picked. He liked the soccer ball, which would come in good use tomorrow. He doubled loved the duffel backpack. And then I gave him my presents for him. "You really didn't have to get me anything," he said. "You've been giving us presents all summer so far," he said.

"I know, but these are things that are essential for the rest of the trips."

He really liked the case for the tablet and then he opened the camera. It was similar to the boys' cameras, but it was the upgraded one. It still had the feature that you couldn't erase, which I loved for the kid's cameras. His camera came with a flash, and a built-in removable tripod. "Thank you so much."

Just then my phone rang. "Hello," I said. It was Parker and Addison on the line together. I handed Carter the phone. We all heard them singing happy birthday to him. Carter smiled really big. "Thank you, mommy and daddy."

"How's everything going?"

"It's been such a great summer." He took my phone out on the balcony and spoke to his parents. He told them about the bikes and the park and the trails that we rode our bikes on. He was so excited to be sharing with his parents. He stayed on the phone for over an hour with them. "I love you too, daddy and mommy," he said at the end of the call. When Carter came back into the room, we had cleaned up from dinner. Everyone had showered and was ready for bed.

"Come here, birthday man," I said. He came over and I hugged him so big. "Happy eighth birthday," I said to him. "Now come on over here and we are going to watch a movie before we all go to bed."

We put on a classic. Not the true classical version of it, but it was still a classic. We put on Lassie. All five of us made it the end of the movie. When it was over, I got off the bed and closed and locked the back doors.

"Now for tomorrow we are not on a time limit. We are going to be here till Thursday, so each of us will get a chance to choose how we spend a day."

"Who gets to choose first?"

"Carter does," Michael said. "He's the birthday dude right now."

"I want to go swimming in the ocean tomorrow and maybe for a bike ride on the beach."

"Sounds like an awesome day. Now it is time for bed. I love you all," I said.

"Love you too," they all said.

The next morning, we went swimming in the ocean before having breakfast. We stayed in the ocean till we were pruney. Then we got out and dried off enough to go have breakfast in the restaurant. After breakfast, we went up to the room. Everyone showered and rinsed the salty sand off of their bodies. The boys all decided to wear blue, so so did I. Then we went for a long bike ride together. When we came back, it was lunch time. Tyson asked if he could take a nap after lunch. The other three wanted to go swimming in the pool at the hotel. However, after we ate all four boys went swimming in the pool. I sat on the deck watching them. When they were done, they all stood under the outdoor shower and rinsed off. They toweled off and we went upstairs. I put their names on Popsicle sticks minus Carter. Then I had Carter draw a stick from the group. He drew Michael's name.

"Michael gets to choose what we do tomorrow."

"Can we go out on a boat tomorrow?" he asked.

"Sure, we can," I said.

"Aunt Ken?" I looked at Michael. "I know you got me a phone and everything and I love it, but do you think I can get a camera too?"

"Yes. Why don't we go do that now? Come on guys, let's go do something fun."

"Everything with you is fun," TJ said.

"Can we have group pictures taken?" Carter asked.

"Let's go see about that."

As we got into the car, TJ looked at Michael. "Do moms ever say no?"

"Yeah, sometimes."

"Does Ken ever say no?"

"Yeah, sometimes," he said again.

"Is everyone in and ready to go?"

"Yep," Tyson said and then he laughed.

We went to the mall up there. I had forgotten that Carter needed shoes until I saw him trip over himself. The first place we went was a shoe store. All four boys had their feet measured and then they started trying on shoes. Everyone including me walked out of the store with a new pair of sneakers. Then we found the electronic store. We all went in. Each of the younger boys took a seat on the floor and were playing quietly as Michael and I looked at cameras. After looking at serval cameras, Michael made a decision. He choose a Nikon. I paid for the camera and then we were off and about doing things and seeing things.

"Let's go to a movie," Tyson said.

We went to a movie.

Michael's day: We went to the marina around eight thirty in the morning to see about chartering a boat for the day. We wound up with a thirty-two-foot-long speed boat. We rented life jackets, which I insisted that the boys put them on the second we had them. And then we were off for the day out on the water with a guy name Kirk. Kirk had fishing poles on the boat, so when we got a mile and half out, he let the boys fish.

"So, are they your children?"

"Yes."

"Where is there father?"

"He's working."

"What do you do for a living?"

"I'm an architect."

"Really?" I nodded. "Do you design houses?"

"I've designed a few. I mainly design and build buildings."

"And school sculptures," Carter said.

"School sculptures? Like what?" Kirk asked.

"It's more like ornate playground equipment for the kids," I said.

The boys had heard that I said that they were my kids. Michael looked at me. "Mom, can we go swimming?"

"Yes, but not here."

"Why not here?"

"Because you guys have been fishing here," I said.

Kirk moved the boat.

"Oh, awesome. Look at the lighthouse," Carter said.

"We are going to go there one day this week."

Kirk took us into the inlet and the boys jumped off the boat. I too jumped off the boat. I swam with the boys. We stayed in the water for more than a half hour and then we got out. Once back on the boat, Kirk gave us a tour of the area. The four boys at one point took out their cameras and starting taking pictures. Kirk had taken TJ's camera for a minute and he captured a picture of the five of us together. During the day and at one time or another he had taken each of the boys' cameras and taken pictures of the five of us together. When he brought the boat in for the day, it was around three.

"There is a great seafood restaurant not too far from here," he said.

"Thank you. And thank you for a nice day. Come on boys." They each thanked Kirk for a nice day. Then we were off to get something to eat.

"When can we do the lighthouse?" Michael asked.

"Well, it's something that we would want to go to early, so that we can explore the whole thing."

"How big is it?"

"It's two hundred and five feet."

"Hey, that's how big the tower was right?" Tyson had said.

"Yes, Tyson, it is. That is very good."

"Aunt Kenny, can we get coloring books and crayons like we have your house?"

"Yes, we can do that."

"Can you color in the lines?" TJ asked him.

"Yes. Aunt Ken taught me. If you don't do it right, she makes you do it again and again and again till you do it right."

"Oh."

Just hearing that made me look at TJ. "Do you need help with that?"

He lowered his head a bit. "Yeah," he said.

"No. No. Pick up your head. TJ if you ever need help with anything, you can always ask me. Is coloring in the lines something you want to work on before you go back to school in the fall?"

"Yeah," he said. And then he opened up. "My teacher hit me a few times for not coloring in the lines."

I watched the faces of my nephews and addressed it immediately. "Did you ever tell your dad that it happened?"

He shook his head. "I told my grandma."

"And did grandma do anything about it?"

"She told me not to make up stories."

I wanted to crush the teacher that layed a hand on this adorable little boy. That is when I knew that I had to be more a part of his and Patrick's life. I loved Patrick, but the love for his son was growing on me more and more every day. "Hey, guys, let's go check out the Sunken Pirate Ship," I said. The Sunken Pirate Ship was a place like Chucky Cheese, but everything was boats. There was a ball tank in there and I went in it with the kids. We had so much fun splashing around in the balls. Then we played video games. We had a dance competition. I was shocked to learn that Tyson sure could dance. He was the youngest child with me and the rhythm that flowed through and out of him was just a bit mind blowing to me.

"Where did you learn to dance?" I asked him.

"He watches Kate," Carter said.

"I watch Kate."

"Does Kate know?"

"Nope," they all three said together.

"I know Kate loves music," Tyson said, "but when she starts to dance and tries new moves, I like to watch it," he said innocently. "Can we call Kate?"

"Yes."

"I miss Kate," he said.

"Me too," Carter and Michael said.

"Do you miss Beth?"

And all three did the same thing. They held up their hand with their index finger and thumb about an inch apart and they all said, "Yeah. A little."

TJ had snapped a picture of it.

Though we had a big lunch, by dinner time not only the boys were hungry, but I was hungry too. "What do you want for dinner?"

"Cake!" Tyson said.

"Um. No," I said to him. He grinned at me.

"Can we go to Denny's?" Michael asked.

We went there and the boys were happy. They all ordered something different. Tyson wanted to try Chicken Pot Pie, which he kept calling cake.

"It's not a cake," I said with a smile. "It's a pie."

"It looks like a cake," he said.

When it came, I told him if he didn't like it, he didn't have to eat it and that he could get something else. Needless to say, he loved it. Carter ordered Sheppard's Pie. Michael ordered a hamburger and TJ ordered waffles. I ordered a chicken pot pie as well. After we had all ate, the boys wanted dessert. I told them we would stop at the grocery store and pick up a few things. They were happy about that.

Back at the hotel, I took the remaining Popsicle sticks out and put them in front of Michael to pick. He had picked me.

"Lighthouse Day tomorrow," the boys said together.

The Lighthouse is painted bright red. We arrived there at nine in the morning and we went on a tour of the lighthouse learning the different parts and learning the history of lighthouses and the way they were so important and their purpose.

"Like in Pete's Dragon," TJ said.

"Yes," the lady conducting the tour said.

"The new one doesn't have a lighthouse in it?" Carter said.

"I didn't see the new one. I saw the old version with them singin' and dancin'," TJ said.

"Aren't you going to correct him?" Michael asked me. "Aunt Ken?"

"Yes, Michael."

"Aren't you going to correct him?"

"Yes, but there is a crowd of people around and I didn't want to embarrass him."

"Oh. Sorry."

"No, that's quite alright," I said to Michael.

The sweat was pouring down my back. I was hot and dying of thirst, which probably meant that the kids were too. When we finally made it to the top, the guide offered us water. We all drank. The view was spectacular, and all four boys pulled out their cameras and shot pictures first of the views and then of each other. Then the guide asked if we wanted a picture together. We grouped together, smiled for the first one, made funny faces for the second, and then took a real serious looking one.

"Whenever you are ready, we will start the descend," she said.

"Thank you."

I stood with the four boys within my arm span just looking out. I wasn't aware of the photographer, who had been following us around since we went to Bok Tower Garden. He was snapping one after another of the five of us together.

TJ had asked if I could pick him up. I lifted him into my arms, kissed him on his cheek and we just stood there for a while. The photographer captured one after another again and again.

"Aunt Ken," Carter said. "What was so special about lighthouses?"

I looked at him. "There weren't streetlights or lamp post on the piers a long long time ago, so when the boats were sailing in, they were aware of jetties and the banks because of the lighthouses. They all served their purpose back then and they still do today."

"How is that?" Tyson asked.

"When immigrants come on boats, if they see the light at night from the lighthouses, they know that land is close. It was the same back when they were built."

"Awesome!" I heard all four of them say.

"Are you ready to move on?"

"Can we stay a while longer? Please?" asked Tyson.

I looked at the guide. "That's fine. Besides, you called and made reservations, so it's yours for about another hour," she said. "You can come down whenever you are ready."

"Thank you."

We stayed the rest of the hour up there. The sights were breath taking.

"I see dolphin!" TJ said.

"Me too!" said Carter and Tyson.

It took about twenty minutes to descend from the top of the lighthouse. Michael carried Tyson and piggy backed Carter. And I carried TJ.

"Michael, are you alright?"

"Yeah," he said a little winded. "I'm good."

"You know what I could go for right now?" Carter said. Then the three boys said together, "Mommy's rice balls."

"What is a rice ball?"

"It's a gooey mess of rice, peas, and meat all rolled into a ball, covered with bread crumbs and fried to perfection," Michael said.

"Your mom makes them?"

"Yep," they all said.

"I wish I had a mom."

Very sincerely Tyson, the youngest in the group said, "You have Aunt Kenny."

Once we were down the stairs, I put TJ down and I took Tyson from Michael squishing him with hugs. "You are such a wonderful young man," I said. "I love you, Tyson."

"I love you too, Aunt Kenny."

We went for lunch. We had a fish basket with fries with iced tea to go with it. We ate lunch under a pavilion. Carter pulled his backpack up on the table opening it quickly. He drew out The Wind and Willow. "Will you read it to us?" he asked me handing me the book.

"I wondered where my book disappeared to," I said with a smile.

"Is it ok?"

"Yes, it's more than ok. Let's finish lunch first."

We finished lunched, cleaned up, and then moved down to the beach. Though it was a warm summer day with the kids out of the school, vacationers here on vacation, the beach was nearly empty. We had picked a spot where we could all sit together. I put a blanket down on the sand watching each boy take their spot. They left me the middle of the blanket.

I sat down. Within seconds of me sitting, the boys moved in closer to me. With Michael leaning on my left shoulder, TJ resting between my legs leaning back against me, Tyson laying on his back with his head resting on my left thigh, and Carter on my right facing away from me but still leaning against my side, I opened the book. I started to read the first chapter. The boys listened as I continued to read. I had read a few chapters when a warm breeze blew over us. It drew my attention from the book. I looked up at ominous clouds in the sky. "We need to hurry," I said. Jumping up, Michael managed to take the hands of the other three boys. I grabbed the blanket, and we ran together where our bikes were parked. I tossed the book in Carter's backpack then threw it over one shoulder, mounted my bike and rode with accuracy and sped to the hotel. We dismounted the bikes under the overhead just as a hard rain started pounding the ground.

We walked the bikes into the hotel to the elevator. Once upstairs, with the bikes resting against the wall, everyone took their turn in the bathroom showering. I had gone to the back door overlooking the beach. I unlatched the lock then opened the back door. The sound of the fast hard pounding rain was satisfying. Michael had gone in Carter's backpack taking the book out. He walked towards me handing it to me. "Will you continue?" The four boys settled on the king size bed together. Within the next couple of hours, I finished reading the book. Tyson sat up. "That's it?" I couldn't help but laugh.

"Thank you," Carter said.

"We can bring books with us when we go to The Keys. We can pick different spots or places to go and I'll read to you guys if you want."

We spent the next two days doing what Tyson and TJ wanted to do. Tyson wanted to spend his day playing video games at the arcade down the street. We had pizza for lunch and hamburgers for dinner. The next day, our final day in Daytona, we spent riding our bikes on the beach, playing kickball together, having a picnic on the beach, and flying kites. It would be our final night in Daytona as well, with the car windows down, I drove my car on the beach up and down quite a few times. The boys loved it. We had someone take our picture in the dying light of the day. That night, in the room, I put my computer on, put a movie in, then the five of us settled together on the over plushy carpet, with popcorn, candy and drinks all the while watching a movie.

CHAPTER TWELVE

As we drove home, music played in the car and it was loud as the boys sang along with the music. Tunes from The Beatles, Simon and Garfunkel, Third Eye Blind, Adele, and others the boys all whaled out their songs. I smiled singing along with them.

"Daddy listens to country music," TJ said.

"We could give it a try." I changed the station finding country music. To my surprise the boys belted out Garth Brooks "I have Friends" loudly.

"Do you know it?" TJ asked.

"I do," I confirmed.

"Mommy has the next verse," he said with a bright smile.

I started with "I guess I was wrong…" and the boys howled from the backseat. We all laughed and sang along.

"Can we go to mom's restaurant for dinner?" Tyson and Michael asked together.

"Sure. Call her and let her know that we are coming."

Michael took his phone calling Addison. "Hi, mommy," he said. "Is the restaurant overly hopping?" he asked. My brother was famous for that expression. I heard Addison laugh. She answered him. He covered the hole at the bottom of the phone, "Mommy wants to know when we will be there?"

"In about thirty or forty minutes," I said. He repeated it to Addison.

"Ask if she has rice balls," Carter piped in. Michael nodded after asking the question.

"With gooey cheesy sauce?" Tyson asked. Michael just nodded without asking the question.

Just as we were pulling into the restaurant parking lot, John Denver's "Country Roads" starting play. "Do you know this one," I asked the boys. They looked at me for a moment. I sang "Almost heaven, West Virginia. Blue Ridge Mountains. Shenandoah River…" by the time I got the chorus of the song, the boys were singing along with me. "Country Roads take me home…" We finished the song. "I'm going to have so much fun with you guys when we are heading down to The Keys."

"When are we going there?"

"In a week."

"Are we only going to stay a few days?" Michael asked.

"No. We are staying there for two weeks."

"Where are we going next?" Carter asked.

"We are going to see the elephants for two days in northern Florida and then we are coming home for a few days before our trip to The Keys."

As we sat down for dinner, my phone rang. It was the hotel in Daytona. "Hello," I answered.

"Ms. Jackson?"

"Yes," I said.

"I'm calling you because you left your bikes in the room."

"Oh, my god. I'm so sorry. I can be back there within the next two and half hours."

"We are experiencing bad weather here, ma'am. If you come tomorrow that will be ok."

"Thank you so much. We will be there tomorrow before noon. Thank you again," I said.

"What was that?" Addison asked walking over with a tray of food that we had not yet ordered.

"We left our bikes."

"What are we going to do about it?" Tyson asked.

"We will go get them tomorrow morning."

"Promise?" TJ asked.

"Oh, for sure," I said.

"Maybe I can go with you tomorrow," Addison said.

"Oh, mommy, that would be so great," Carter said.

"What's a rice ball?' TJ asked.

Addison turned to him with a smile. "This is a rice ball."

"It looks like a giant meatball."

"It's better than a meatball," Tyson said.

TJ poked it with his fork. "It's like a Poke' Ball," he said. He cut into it and cut a piece. He put it in his mouth and chewed it cautiously. I couldn't help but smile and laugh. "This is really good," he said. "Thank you."

We ate dinner and then Michael and Carter went in the kitchen with Addison and they washed dishes for her. TJ was playing a game on my phone while he was sitting on my lap. The photographer that had been following us around for the last couple of weeks was there in the restaurant and he took pictures of us together. I looked up and saw him. He tried to turn away quickly. I waved over the waiter. He came over. "Could you please sit with them for just a minute please?"

"Yes, of course, Ms. Jackson."

"Thank you."

I got up from the table and went like I was going to the bathroom and then I walked right up to him and grabbed his camera. "HEY!" he shouted.

"Tell me who the fuck you are right now?"

He got up to try to take the camera from me.

"Addison, call the police," I said.

"No. Please don't."

"Who are you?"

"Wesley Smith. I'm a photographer."

TJ came over. "Hi, Uncle Wes."

"This is your uncle?"

"Well, he's not a blood relative, but he's daddy's best friend."

"Why are you following us? How long have you been following us?"

"I've been there since you took him to Bok Tower Garden," he said.

"Why?"

"Pat asked me to," he said.

I pushed Wes down on the chair still holding his camera. I called Patrick. He came to the restaurant immediately. I went outside with him.

"You don't trust me with TJ?"

"What?"

"You don't trust me with your son that you have your private investigator follow me and take me pictures of me with TJ and my nephews."

"It wasn't supposed to be like that."

"Then please enlighten me and tell me how it was supposed to be."

"I asked Wesley to follow you because I thought that Renee was trying to get Turner."

"Who is Renee?" In my anger I forgot his ex-wife's name.

"TJ's mom."

"Do you honestly think that I would let her take your son?"

"No, but she has people."

"Why would she want him now after five years?"

"I don't know. It was a feeling."

"Patrick! A feeling? You could have just told me that one of your friends… your best friend was going to be following me and taking random pictures of me with TJ."

"Then you would have been looking for him and looking for the camera. These are natural in the moment shots, Ken. I'm sorry I didn't tell you. Are you still going to keep TJ for me?"

"Yes, of course," I said. "Is he going with us to The Keys?"

"No."

"Will someone else be there?"

He didn't answer me. "Can I kiss you?"

"If you want to," I said.

He stepped closer. I leaned into him and raised my head. He kissed me on the lips and then deepened it. He wrapped his arms around me. He held the back of my head. I wrapped my arms around him. If it was possible, Patrick deepened the kiss even more. I felt electric currents shoot throughout my body. When we stopped, I kept my eyes closed for a minute longer.

"Are you ok?" he asked.

Slowly opening my eyes, I looked up at him and nodded. "Yes, I'm wonderful," I said half breathless.

We walked back inside the restaurant. TJ came running over crying. I squatted down taking him in my arms like a mother would to her young impressionable son. "What happened?"

"I thought you left me."

"No, Turner, I wouldn't leave you." He put his head on my shoulder sobbing. I stood up with him wrapped snug in my arms. "Don't cry. I'm not leaving you. I promise."

"Here. I'll take him," Patrick said.

"No, daddy. Please don't make her leave. Please," he cried.

"No, baby, he's not making me leave. Shh. It's been an extremely long day. It's time to go home. Come. Let's go home."

I looked at Patrick. "Please if you would like, please come to my house."

Addison brought the boys home to grab some of her stuff for tomorrow to go with us to Daytona. Then she came to my house. By the time she got there with the boys, I put TJ to bed.

"Is he ok?"

"He is."

"How old was he when his mom left?"

"He doesn't remember her at all," I said. "He's probably never felt the loss of his mom until he's been with me and the boys."

"Have the boys been nice to him."

"Oh, god yes. You have great kids."

"Did Patrick come?"

"No."

"Do you love him?"

I turned away from Addison. I lowered my head.

"Hey, what's wrong?" she asked. "Come. Sit. Let's talk. I walked over closer to her. She pulled me into a hug. "Kennedy, it's not going to change what happened to you in the past, but honey, its ok to love someone and let them love you.

"You called him tonight, and he dropped everything he was doing to come to you. That speaks volumes, Ken."

"I don't want him to know."

"He doesn't have to know right now. If you feel more comfortable down the road with him and you want him to know then tell him."

"Is it lying if I don't say something?"

"No, sweetheart," she said. "No. Not at all."

In the morning, I woke up early and went to do stuff around the house.

I checked on the horses. I fed and watered them. I brushed them then mucked their stalls. I checked all the things on the property. Everything looked good and in order. Then I went back to the house. Everyone was awake and, in the kitchen, when I came in.

"Are you ready to go?" I asked them.

"Yes." "Yep." "When are we leaving?" They said together.

"We are leaving hopefully within the next half hour or so," I said.

A half hour late, we were getting in the car. TJ was extremely quiet in the backseat. The other three were talking about our next adventure. TJ hadn't spoken a word the whole ride to Daytona. When we got there, he stayed back by the car when we all got out at the hotel. I squatted down next to him. "Are you ok?" I asked him. He nodded. "TJ, nodding isn't an answer."

"I ruined everything," he said.

"How did you do this?"

"That's why my mom left too."

"TJ, I promise you that you had nothing to do with that."

"I'm scared."

"Of what?" I asked.

"Of losing you."

"I assure you that I'm not going anywhere."

I hugged him. He jumped into my arms. I stood up holding him. He was crying. "What's this all about?"

"I don't want you to go."

"Go where, Turner?"

"Go away."

"I'm not going away. We are going to go get our bikes and then we are all going home."

"Why don't you take him for a walk," Addison said. "We are here. We can get the bikes in a little while," she said.

TJ wrapped his legs around me. He kept his head on my shoulder. I started to walk with him. I rubbed his back. I felt his breathing change. He was now sleeping in my arms. I walked back over to Addison and the kids.

"Is he ok?" she asked and looked up from helping Carter with something. "He's conched out," she said. "Why did he think you were leaving?"

"I think he got really scared at the restaurant with the photographer and then I called Patrick, and TJ thought that he did something bad. He thought I was sending him home to his father."

"He's really becoming attached to you."

"I know," I said.

We went into the hotel and got the bikes. Addison helped load the bikes on the car.

Again, I was not aware of a photographer taking pictures. It was a woman with short, cropped hair. Still holding TJ, I dislodged his car seat putting it in the back of the SUV. Addison said that she didn't mind driving. Michael climbed in the front with her. Carter and Tyson climbed into their seats. I gently climbed in with TJ now resting on my lap. He slept the whole way home. I too had fallen asleep in the SUV while Addison drove.

When we got home, I carried TJ in the house. I finally put him down on my bed. Afterwards, I went downstairs. Addison was in the kitchen already whipping something up. I sunk into one the chairs at the table.

"Welcome to motherhood," she said to me. I looked at her. "What's on your mind?"

"What do you do when they are inconsolable?"

"You do just what you did, Kennedy. You handled that situation beautifully."

"I wish you could go with us to The Keys."

"Yeah about that," she said. "Rachel said that she is going to take over when we are on the cruise," she started. "We had been in the kitchen together when I asked if she wanted to start a bit earlier and she said that she is available. Starting Monday, she will take over for me until the end of August."

"So, you will be free?"

"Yeah," she said. "I'll be free."

"Would you want to go with us?"

"I'd love that."

"When is Parker coming home?"

"He's going to fly to Alaska to meet up with Jamie and Kate. He will go to the concert there and then he will bring Kate home. On his way home, he'll stop in Atlanta for Beth."

The house smelled wonderful from Addison's cooking. The smell of freshly baked cookies warffed through the house. The boys came in from playing outside. "It smells good in here," Michael said.

"Aunt Ken's house always smells like a delicious bakery," Carter said.

Addison did not go with us to see the elephants. I took the boys to Gainesville to see them. Two Tale Ranch is open to the public. It is a preserve for elephants. We were able to feed them. The boys went for rides on them. We stayed there only a few hours. We were staying in a hotel, so we went to the hotel. Everyone showered and dressed. Then we went to a museum. Walking around in the air conditioning felt wonderful. The museum offered a painting experience, so we all decided to do it. We were all given a canvas with a pre-drawn picture on it. The woman instructing of the details first said to wet the whole canvas with a paint brush. Then she informed us to follow the steps: to paint the background first. The picture that we painted was a mother elephant with a baby. When we were finished there, we left our paintings to dry and went for lunch.

I took the boys on a nature walk after lunch. We played I spy something. Michael started. "I spy something blue," he said. Everyone stopped and started looking for blue things.

"The sign," Tyson said.

"Good, but no."

"The bird," Carter said.

"Yep. Your turn."

Carter did not go right away. We walked a bit further into the trail. "I spy something orange."

"The sign," Tyson said.

Carter nodded. "Carter, we can't hear a head nod, "I said. "Tyson it's your turn."

"I spy something black," he said.

"Black?" I asked.

"Yeah," he said with a smile.

"What the hell is black?"

All four boys laughed. I started looking all over the place. Not once did I think that he was talking about my shirt. The boys all seemed to get it because they were all laughing watching me look for something black.

"Is it close by us?"

"Ah-huh," he said. I took off my sunglass to wipe away the layer of sweat that covered my face. I then took the collar of my shirt and pulled it away from my skin.

"Is it my shirt?" His grin spoke volumes. "Oh, that's it," I said and started to chase him. He was giggling and screeching as I ran after him. I caught him, lifted him over shoulder and let him hang there for a minute. "You little rascal," I said. His fit of laughter was contagious.

"Are they all four yours," a woman who was watching asked.

"Yes," I said.

"It looks like you all are having a great time."

"We are," Michael said.

"Is it my turn yet," TJ asked.

"Yes," I said.

"Can it be multiple colors?"

"Yes."

"Awesome. I spy something red and blue."

"Tyson's shoes?"

"No, Michael," TJ said.

"My shorts," Carter said.

"Nope."

"That big bird over there," I said.

"No. Keep guessing."

I put Tyson down. He was looking up. He started jumping up and down. "The Spider-Man kite?"

"You got it," TJ said.

"It's Aunt Kenny's turn."

"I spy something brown."

"The trunk of the trees," Carter said.

"No, but great guess"

"The ground," Tyson said.

"That's good too, but no."

"The squirrel," Michael said.

"No."

"The sign," Carter said.

"No. Keep guessing."

"This thing," TJ said.

"Yes. But what is it called?"

"Porcupine," Carter said. "Poke' ball," Tyson said.

"A poke' ball? Really, Ty? And no to both of you."

"It's that thing that we decorated at Christmas time," TJ said.

"Mommy would know what it is," Michael said.

"Come on. Don't give up," I said.

"It's a pine something," Carter said.

"It looks like an ice cream cone," Tyson said.

"A pine cone," they all said together.

"Good. And nice working together. You all did great."

"Aunt Ken?" Tyson said.

"Yes."

"When we go to Keys, can we bring our bikes?"

"Yes, of course."

"I have to go to the bathroom," TJ said.

"Me too," Carter said.

"Well, then let's go."

The boys all smiled. We went back to the museum, used the bathrooms, and then went to collect our paintings. They turned out really well. "Ok. I want each of you to write your name, today's date, and your age on your picture," I said.

They each took a pen. Tyson Jackson Julye 11, 2017 Age: 4

Carter Jackson Age: 8 7/11/17 TJ Alexander Age: 5 July 11, 2017

Michael Jackson Age: 11 7/11/2017 Ken Jackson Age: 39 July 11, 2017

"What are you going to do with them?"

"You'll see," I said to Michael.

We went to put the paintings in the car. "Can we go back to the hotel?" Carter asked.

"Yes. Is that what you all want to do?"

"Yes," they said together.

We went back to the hotel. I left the five paintings in the back of the car. As we walked past the pool, TJ playfully bumped into Michael, who lost his balance and fell in the pool with a big splash. TJ covered his mouth to hide the smile. "I'm sorry," he said. "I was playing around."

Michael reached up from the pool, grabbing Tyson around the waist and pulling him into the pool. Carter jumped right over his brothers' heads into the pool. TJ went to grab me, but I grabbed him instead. And I got a running start and jumped in with him in my arms. We had a splash war in the pool. We spent a half hour just goofing off in the pool and having fun.

The next day, we went home. I had to meet with the contractors about building the gym. "Listen boys, I need for you to be good for the next hour."

"We are always good," TJ said.

"Yes, that's true and I love you all for that. But I need for you to please stay in the house. The contractor is coming over and I don't want any of you getting hurt or anything while he is here."

"Is it daddy?" TJ asked.

"No, baby, it's not daddy. It's someone else."

"How come you didn't go with daddy?"

"TJ, do you know what your daddy does?"

"Yes. He builds buildings."

"Close. Daddy and I design buildings and then other people build them for us."

"Aweeeesome!"

I laughed.

"Is it Dean?" Carter asked.

"Hell no," I said.

Carter had just taken a drink of water and now spit it across the room laughing and choking all at the same time.

"Stop that," I said. He continued to laugh. "Carter, stop that."

"You are too funny."

There was knock on the door. I ran to get it. The contractor was a huge man. He stood six foot seven, he was lean but muscular. He had to crane his neck to get into the house. "Hi," he said to coming in.

"Hi."

"Oh, what are they playing?"

"We are building a castle," Michael said.

"What is your name?" TJ asked.

"I'm Walter."

"Do you want to play with us?" Carter asked.

I stood back and watched this huge man walk over to where the boys were in the living room and sit down on the floor with them.

"Aunt Kenny, you are going to help too right?" Tyson asked.

In that precious moment I had forgotten why Walter was there. I joined the boys and Walter on the floor, and we built a castle. It was Tyson that snapped my brain back into function. "Aunt Kenny, can the gym look like this?"

"What? Oh, the gym. Yes. No."

Tyson looked at me like I had two heads.

"Yes, that's why I'm here," Walter remembered too. "Sorry, ma'am."

"No, its fine. Thank you."

He stood up and then took me by the hand pulling me to my feet. Walter looked at the castle. "It's missing something," he said.

"What?" the boys asked.

"A bridge to get in and out. When I'm done with your aunt I'll come back and help you put it in."

"Can it go in the playroom?" Carter asked.

"I think it might be able to," I said.

"Part of our summer vacation with Aunt Ken," he said with that beautifully bright smile.

Walter and I went out in the backyard. He went over the marked-out the layout. "This is good, but I can make it better," he said.

"Whatever or however you think. I'm not judgy," I said.

"So, which one belongs to Patrick? We have worked together for the better half of eight years and I never even knew that he had a child. Is he married?"

"No."

"Where is the boy's mom?"

"I'm not sure," I said.

"If I had to guess which one his was, I'd say he's the little one with the brown hair and green eyes."

"No, that is my nephew Tyson," I said.

"My next guess would be the one with dirty blond hair and blue eyes."

"No. That's my nephew Carter."

"They aren't related, are they?"

"Yes, they are brothers."

"Adopted right?"

"No. Biological," I said.

"So, Patrick's son is the little guy with brown hair and grey eyes."

"Yes," I said with a smile. "He looks just like Patrick."

"He looks like he could be your little one."

"What? No."

"If I didn't know any better, I'd say he was yours over being Patrick's."

I didn't answer him. We wrapped things up outside. Once we were back in the house, TJ came racing over me to. "I won. I won. I won."

"What did you win?" I asked scooping him up into my arms.

"In the game room. I won," he said. "I love you."

"I love you, TJ."

I put him down. "Hey, guys, Walter is back. We can finish the castle now," TJ said.

"Is Aunt Ken here too?"

"Yeah," he said.

They came running into the room. "We ordered pizza for lunch," Michael said.

"That's fine."

"We didn't think you would mind?"

"I don't. It's fine," I said.

"Mommy is going to bring it," Tyson said.

I knew that. She texted me already. I asked her to please bring an extra pizza and her famous rice balls.

We had gone back in the living room where the castle now stood. TJ came and sat on the arm of the couch watching. "So, you and daddy don't do this part."

"Nope," I said. "I'll be right back." I went into my office and got a set of blueprints. Then I came back. "TJ." He looked at me. "This is what me and daddy do," I said unrolling the blueprints.

"Aweeesome!" he said.

When Walter was done with the castle, it not only had an operating draw bridge, but he gave it a mote too.

Addison came. The three boys went to her and hugged her. Walter stayed for lunch. Addison had made bite size rice balls for the boys. TJ was in heaven. "Thank you, Aunt Addison." Her eyes filled with tears. "Did I do something wrong?"

"No," she said. "I just like the sound of that."

TJ came and curled up on my lap after we ate. I thanked Walter for the day: coming here, building the castle with the boys and I, and of course his main reason for being here – the gym. "Production can start when you get back from vacation," he said. "See you in a couple of weeks."

"Thank you," I said to him.

TJ had fallen asleep on me. I carried him over to the couch and put him down. I covered him with a blanket then returned to the kitchen.

"When are we leaving for The Keys?" Addison asked.

"Whenever you want to go," I said. "We can go earlier if you want."

We had been talking. I told her that we could stop by the house in the morning and get her and her bike. We were laughing about an incident that happened when we were children when TJ started to yell out in his sleep.

"NO! I DON'T WANT TO GO. MOMMY! MOMMY!"

I got up from the table and raced over to him. I scooped him up in my arms. "TJ, its ok. I have you," I said.

"Mommy!"

"I have you. You are safe."

Patrick had come by to see us before we left. He didn't bother to knock when he heard his son yell and call out. He witnessed me rushing to TJ's side and lifting him. Rocking him and letting him know that it was ok. Patrick came rushing over; first I thought he was going to snatch TJ from my arms, but instead he embraced both of us. "I love her, daddy," TJ said.

"I know you do, buddy."

TJ was still crying. "Can she be my mommy?"

"I'd love to be your mommy," I said aloud. Then I looked at Patrick. "I'm sorry. I shouldn't have said that."

"No," he said. "It's ok."

"I love you," we said together. "I'd love to marry you," I said just as he said, "Will you marry me?" "What?" we asked together. "Yes," I said. Patrick kissed me and kissed me.

"Daddy! I'm in the middle here." We both stopped kissing and laughed. Patrick took off his necklace and opened the chain. He took off the ring that was on it. He took my hand and placed the ring on my finger, and it fit like a glove. I looked down at it and smiled.

"I remember this ring," I said. I beamed. "I always wanted it. I thought I'd never see it again."

"I haven't taken it off since that day," he said. "I wish I knew where the other one was."

If it was possible, I smiled even bigger. I had it. It was a project that we had done together in school. There were two rings. I designed one and he designed the other and in our project, they were interlocked at the entrance to our model building. When we finished the project and long after it was graded for our final, we each took our ring back. I had always wanted the one that he had designed and made.

I looked at Addison. "I'm engaged," I said. "Oh my god! I'm engaged." I jumped up and down and hugged Patrick again. I hugged TJ. "When can I adopt him? When can we get married? Can we do it right away? I'm sorry. I'm asking too many questions."

Patrick kissed me. "I had a feeling about you," he said. "From the moment you met TJ, I saw it in your eyes that you adored and loved him like a son. I had the papers drawn up. We can go to the court tomorrow."

It was TJ who answered. "So tomorrow it will be real?" he said. "Tomorrow, she will be my mommy?"

"Yes."

"We can elope tomorrow," I suggested. "And then do a wedding for family and friends later on."

"We need a witness."

"We have Addison," I said. Addison was beaming too. She went racing upstairs and picked out "my wedding outfit". She came downstairs with a few things. She held each of them up and asked the boys what they thought of it.

"I like the blue one," Michael said.

"What blue what?" I asked.

"The dress you should get married in," Addison said.

"What?"

My head was literally spinning. Tomorrow I would be a wife and mother.

"So, Kenny, there are living arrangements that we must talk about," Patrick said.

"We are moving in here, daddy," TJ said.

"Yes, that would be wonderful," I said.

CHAPTER THIRTEEN

Addison was wonderful. She helped me do my hair. She picked my dress. The boys were excited. We went to the courthouse and met with the judge. I slipped the ring that I had made in architect school on Patrick's finger. He looked down at his hand and smiled. Patrick and I were first married and then the adoption came second. I was now a wife and a mother, and I was on cloud nine. Within forty minutes time, my life changed forever.

"So, when are you leaving for The Keys with our son."

I smiled. "That sounds so good. Our son," I repeated. "We are leaving tomorrow morning. We will be gone for two and half weeks."

"I'll move in when you get back."

"Ok."

Addison walked over. "Would you like me to take TJ for the night, so that you two can be together?"

"Would you mind?" Patrick said.

"No."

Patrick took TJ by the hand and led him to the bench. "Turner, today you are going to go spend the day and night with Addison and the boys."

"Ok," he said. "Have fun with mommy." He hugged Patrick and then came running towards me. He bounced up in my arms. "Love you, mommy," he said. "See you tomorrow morning."

"I love you too," I said kissing him.

Addison left with the boys. Patrick and I went and signed the papers that legalized all of this. Then we went back to the house. We went up to my bedroom and we stayed up there most of the day. We made love over and over during the day and into the evening. We shared passionate moments all day long.

"My husband," I said.

"My wife."

"I wanted to be your wife since that first day of class when you bumped into me."

"What?" he said.

"You don't remember?"

"I remember most moments with you," he said kissing me. "Remind me though."

"We had just finished orientation and our first class started about a half hour after that. You had that crimson backpack tucked under your arm. You were looking at the clock tower and walking backwards. I too was looking at the clock tower walking forward and you walked into me. It was at that point that I wished you would ask me to marry you."

"I remember the first time I thought about marrying you," he said.

"When was that?"

"We were all at a party after finishing our first year. You were in blue jeans and that blue jay colored shirt. Your hair was down. You were standing talking to someone and you looked over at me and waved. I can remember thinking "she just waved at me. I want her to wave like that at me forever. Then you left with someone."

I lower my head. "You know thinking back after that night you changed. You were quieter. You didn't want anyone to get to close to you." Then the realization of that night came to him. "Oh my god," he said. "Kennedy, did something happen that night?" I started to cry. "Did he rape you?" I buried my head in his bare chest continuing to cry. "Did you go to the police?" I shook my head. "Why not? Look at me. Kenny, look at me," he said. "Honey, why wouldn't you have gone to the police?"

"What would I have told them? I didn't even know his name. I was drunk. He brought me home and it happened…" I choked on my words.

"GOD! I wish I would have known."

"What would you have done?"

"I would have beaten the shit out of him. I would have been there for you."

"Then we wouldn't have TJ," I said. "I can't bear children of my own.. I didn't think that I could be loved after that. We have been working together for so long and I have stood back at times just to watch you work."

I didn't know that he had done the same for me over the years.

We finally went down to eat something. Addison had come back with the boys. She had brought food. We were coming down the stairs when she came in with the boys. I ran down the stairs and threw myself into her arms. She stumbled back a little but kept us steady. "You can't have a wedding with a wedding cake," she said. Addison held me. "Are you ok?"

"I told him," I whispered.

She looked up at Patrick. He continued his descend down the steps. He smiled at her. "Did you say we have a wedding cake?"

"Yes," she said.

"Thank you so much."

"Are you ok with the news that you learned today," she asked still holding me.

"A thousand percent," he said. "I wish I would have known back then. I would have annihilated him."

"Do you know who he is?" she asked.

By his look, Addison knew that he knew him. "I'll take care of it," he said.

I drew back from Addison. "No. Please. I don't want anything to happen to you. Please, Patrick. It's in the past. Things are different now. Please."

"Ok," he said taking me in his arms and hugging me. "Ok. If that's what you want."

The boys came in the house. We ate together and then we had wedding cake. The woman photographer was there. She had been at the courthouse too. She took pictures of us getting married and of the adoption. Patrick introduced her to me. "Kennedy, this is my best friend, Storm Meadows," he said. "She is also TJ's Godmother."

"I remember you," I said to her. "Hi. How are you doing?"

"I'm good. Congratulations and best wishes."

"Thank you."

"If it's ok, I'd like to accompany you to The Keys and take pictures of you and my Godson."

"Yes, that is fine," I said.

She had given me an engraved card that read:

Congratulations Mr. Patrick and Mrs. Kennedy Alexander

The next morning, I went to Addison's house to pick her and the boys up. The SUV was packed, the six bikes were loaded on the back, and we were off. "Did you tell mom yet?" Addison asked.

"No. You and the boys and Storm are the only ones that know."

"How are you going to break it to mom?"

I looked at her and smiled. "I don't know yet."

Addison and I had split the drive. It took us four hours to get there. TJ had been awake the whole trip until we hit the seven-mile bridge and then he finally fell asleep. Michael and Carter helped Addison unload the car. We put the bikes in the port, and I locked them together. Then I went back to the car. I threw my duffle bag over my shoulder, grabbed TJ's bag, throwing that over my shoulder as well, and then I went and released him from his car seat. By that time, mom and dad knew we were there. They had already greeted Addison and the kids. Mom came over to see if I needed help. I handed her the duffle bags. Then I went back to getting TJ out of the car. He was in a deep sleep. He didn't even stir when I lifted him.

"And who is this?" mom asked.

No time like the present. "This is my adopted son Turner James Alexander," I said.

"Your son?"

"Yes, ma'am," I said.

"And when did you adopt him?"

"Yesterday."

"Do you have any other surprising news?"

"Yes," I said.

"What's next? Are you going to tell me that you're married?"

I stopped what I was doing and looked at her. "I am," I said.

"Well, congratulations," mom said hugging me.

"You aren't mad?"

"No."

"Are you disappointed?"

"No. A little surprised, but I think it's wonderful. I love the ring," she said to me looking at my left hand. "How old is my grandson?"

"He's five almost six," I said. "He's birthday is the same as Tyson's."

We went into the house. Dad looked at me. I looked at him. "Is there something you want to share?" he asked tossing the newspaper on the table.

And there it was, Patrick, TJ, and I in court. "I didn't know about that," I said.

"Is it true?"

"Yes, sir."

"Well, at least I'll be able to give one daughter away," he said.

My heart sunk in my chest.

"Todd!"

"No, Roberta, it would have been nice to be told."

"I wanted to tell you face to face."

"And who is the boy?"

"This is Turner James. TJ. He is my adopted son. Mom. Dad, Patrick Alexander and I eloped, and I adopted his son yesterday, but we are planning to have a wedding and a celebration."

"Why so sudden though," mom asked.

"I have loved Patrick forever," I said.

"That is Trinity's son, right?"

"Yes," I said.

"Does she know?"

"No. Not yet."

Just then the phone rang. I heard Trinity through the phone. "So, it looks like we are finally related," she said. "I was damn furious when I first found out, but then Patrick explained it to me, and I couldn't be happier. My grandson for the first time in his life has a mother, and not some cold hearted bitch either who would just want to be my son's wife and not TJ's mother, but your daughter opened her arms and her heart up the first time she layed eyes on my grandson. I'm not thrilled that they eloped, but I am beyond thrilled that she adopted my TJ," Trinity said. "Now we will have to make arrangements to get together to plan these two one hell of a celebration."

"Yes, we will have to do that. Congratulations," mom said to her. Trinity said it right back. "Who would have thought after all these years that our kids would marry each other," mom said.

When mom hung up the phone, she turned to see where I had gone. Addison had taken the boys down by the water. TJ was still sleeping. I had gone out in their backyard, which overlooked the water, and had taken a seat in one of the Adirondack chairs. TJ was sleeping in my arms still. Mom came outside.

"I'm sorry," I said. "I should have called you and daddy and told you what was going on. It literally just happened."

"You married Patrick on a split decision?"

"Yeah, kind of," I said. "I love this little boy. He has been calling me mommy on and off for the past few weeks. I met him about a month ago. Mom, he came running over to me and jumped up in my arms without even knowing who I was. My heart melted when that happened. He has been travelling with the boys and me.

"When he was sick, I took care of him. His mother walker out and didn't ever look back when he was three-month-old. For some godforsaken reason, she didn't want to be part of this beautiful, funny, loving child's life. From the moment, I held him in my arms, I never want to put him down and now I don't have to. Yesterday, was beyond amazing. Marrying Patrick, who I have loved for the better half of twenty years now maybe longer. And he married me, mom. And he gave me this treasure," I said looking down at TJ.

I took my phone out and called Jamie. Her voice mail picked up the call, "James, when you get this please call straight away. I need to talk to you right now. Please, James, call me."

I hung up and calling Parker. He answered his phone. "Hello."

"Parker, I have something to tell you."

"Are you ok?"

"Yes, I'm great. I wanted to tell you that I got married yesterday. I married Patrick Alexander."

"Well, it's about time. When I get back with Kate, we will have to celebrate. Congratulations, Kenny."

"Thank you." My phone buzzed. "That's Jamie. Let me take this. I love you."

"Love you too," he said.

I clicked over. "Are you ok?"

"Yes, I'm fine," I said to her. "I have something to share with you. I got married yesterday and I adopted the cutest little boy. He was part of the marriage package."

"Oh, wow. That's wonderful. We will have to celebrate when my tour ends."

"Thank you, James. Are you mad?"

"No," she said. "Why would I be?"

"I don't know. I thought you would be mad."

"No. Not at all. I love you. I'll see you soon."

"See you soon."

TJ slowly began to wake up. "What did I miss?" he said.

"Nothing," I said.

"Are we here?"

"Yes, sweet boy, we are here."

"Oh, the ocean. Can we go please? Please, mommy, can we go?"

I smiled and laughed. "Yes, of course we can go, but first I want you to meet someone."

He had been looking at the ocean. Now he turned and looked at me. I saw fear in his face. "W-w-w-hat if t-t-t-hey don't l-l-l-ike me?"

"TJ, I promise you that everything is going to be ok. Come on. I want you to meet my parents."

I picked him up and brought him in the house. "Mom. Dad, this is TJ. TJ, this is my mom, Roberta and my dad Todd."

"C-c-can I c-c-call t-t-them…"

My dad took TJ from me. He is a large man, standing six foot five. He is about two hundred and fifty pounds of muscle. My dad hugged him. "Hello, my grandson," dad said.

"I never h-h-had a grandfather," TJ said.

After he met my mom and dad and they loved him and he loved them, we went swimming just like I promised. After that, when he was in the shower, I called Patrick.

"Hi, my love," I said. "I have something to ask you. Does TJ stutter?"

"Only when he is nervous," Patrick said.

"It's just that I never heard him stutter before."

"He's never been nervous around you," he said. "Even when I told him that he was going to be meeting someone new and when we walked into your house, he just jumped in your arms and that was that," he said. "How is everything going?"

"Good. I guess. My mom took the news well. My dad not so much. Apparently, it wound up in the newspaper." TJ came back in the room. "Hey, let me go. I will call you back in a little while. I love you," I said. He said he loved me too and then we both hung up.

"Why don't we get a blanket and go watch the sunset together," I said. We all went on the north side of the island. Addison and I put down blankets facing west. Mom and dad sat down together. Tyson sat between mom's legs, Michael sat next to dad, and Carter cuddled up next to Addison. I took a picture of them all together. I sat down and within seconds, TJ was sitting on my legs. I put my arms around him. Storm snapped picture after picture. We watched the sunset.

"Where does it go?" TJ asked.

"Where does what go?"

"The sun? Where does it go"

"So, you know that the Earth turns on what is called an axis. The sun stays up in the sky and the Earth turns around it," I said. "So now countries on the other side of the world are getting sun. There day is starting. It's already tomorrow in other countries," I said to him.

"TJ?" dad asked. He looked at him. "How old are you?"

"Almost six," TJ said.

TJ seemed to melt into me and Storm captured it.

"Grandma, mom says that I have to go back to school this fall," Carter said.

"Yes, that's right. Aunt Ken home schooled you for a few months," mom said. "How did that go?"

"I loved it," he said. "We would do my school work in the mornings and then in the afternoons we would go places."

"How did that happen?" dad asked.

"My teacher didn't like me."

"Carter!" dad said.

"No, dad," Addison said. "He's a hundred percent correct. His teacher did not like him. She was going to put him in a younger class, and we said no. She said she wasn't taking him back in her class, so Ken opened up her life and home and helped me out."

"And that was fair to the others?"

"They did try it," I said.

"And what happened?" dad asked.

"Kate and I couldn't get used to it. We tried it for a week. I mean it was at Aunt Kenny's, and we always have fun there without having to do work, so when we had to do our schoolwork there, it was really hard."

In the morning, Addison had taken the boys for a hike. I was left back as was TJ. We went into the kitchen for breakfast and dad told us.

"Addy took the boys hiking," he said.

TJ looked at him with his big grey eyes. Then he looked at me. "They didn't ask me to go."

"I know, baby," I said. "It's ok. We will do something right after breakfast." Dad saw that I was a little hurt by that. I didn't say anything to him about it. "Did mom go too?"

"No, your mother went to the grocery store."

Mom came back with a car full of groceries. She saw that TJ and I were still here at the house. She saw the hurt in both of us. I had taken her kids everywhere this summer. I didn't leave anyone behind. Now on our first full day down here, she takes the boys and leaves TJ and I behind. If she weren't with us, we would have been out on a boat together. It is a trip that I had previously paid for.

"TJ go get your stuff together. We have to go."

"Home!" he asked.

"No, silly. We have plans that I don't want to waste." I looked at my parents. "Mom and dad, would you like to go with us?"

"Yes," they both said.

We went down to the docks and I introduced myself. We met our captain. We got on the boat and he took us out for a long day on the water.

Dad and mom stayed on the boat, while TJ and I went swimming. We saw coral, and school after schools of fish. We stayed in the water for a long time. When we came back on the boat, mom gave TJ a snack.

"What grade are you going into in the fall?"

"First grade," he said.

"Are you excited?"

He shrugged. Mom smiled and laughed.

"I'm excited to finally have a mommy," he said. The words must have sunk in because he looked up at me and started to cry. I scooped him up in my arms.

"It's ok," I said. "I'm here. Mommy is here," I said.

Dad watched this display with tears in his eyes. He had watched Addison with the kids ever since they were born and he had watched Parker with the kids again ever since they were born, and now he was watching me with a pint sized five almost six year old, and he watched with pride and love in his heart.

"When did he start calling you mommy?" dad asked me.

"About a month ago," I said. "We were on a trip and he came up to me and called me mommy."

"How did it make you feel?"

"My heart melted," I said.

"You do know that he is sleeping?" dad said.

"Yes, I know," I said with a smile.

"He's small for his age."

"Yeah, he is, but he's great."

When we got back to the dock, we thanked the captain. Then we went back to the house. TJ was awake now. He was telling mom all about the bell tower I took him to see.

"It was really really tall," he said. "Right, mommy. Wasn't it tall?"

"Yes, sweet boy, it is really really tall."

"How tall?"

"Two hundred and five feet," TJ said. "The same size as the lighthouse we went to."

"Yes, TJ that is right."

"What color was the lighthouse?" dad asked him.

"Fire engine red," TJ said.

"Not quite, but it is red," I said with a smile.

"Mommy. Mommy. Look. It is a fire truck. Can I go see it?"

"Go ahead," mom said. "Take your son to see the fire truck."

I scooped him up and put him on my shoulders. I walked over. "Oh, cool!" TJ said from perched on my shoulders. That is when I saw Patrick. TJ saw him too. "DADDY IS HERE! DADDY!" TJ slithered off my shoulders and ran to Patrick. He jumped up in his arms. I walked over to them. I hugged Patrick. We kissed. "I'm in the middle again," TJ said.

"Hi. I didn't know you were coming."

"That's the purpose of a surprise," Patrick said.

Mom and dad walked over. "Hi," mom said to him. Patrick hugged her.

"It's good to see you, Roberta. Hi, Todd."

"Congratulations!" mom said.

"Thank you."

Patrick kissed me again. He hugged me tight.

We went back to my parents' house. TJ was bouncing between Patrick and me. I didn't mind. I loved every second I was with him. Mom fixed lunch for all of us. We were all laughing and having fun when Addison came in with the boys. They were all smiles.

"Hi," Addison said.

"You left without us," TJ said.

"What?" Addison said.

"You didn't tell us that you were going hiking. You left without us. Mommy never left without the three of them or even you," TJ said.

"Turner!" Patrick said.

"No, he's right," mom said. "You knew that Kenny paid for a day out on the water."

"I didn't know that was today," Addison said.

"Mom, it's ok. TJ, come over here," I said grabbing him and squishing him with hugs.

"What are the plans for tomorrow?" Addison asked.

"We are going to see Hemingway's House," I said.

"He has cats with six toes," Carter said.

"I'm sorry. I haven't seen or spent much time with my boys all summer. I didn't think you'd mind me taking them."

"It's ok. I don't mind. After all, they are your kids. I will give you the agenda for the next few days and if you don't want to do it or the boys don't want to do it that'll be ok. But at least I'd know in advance."

Patrick couldn't stay. He had to get back for a work conference. "TJ, please behave yourself," he said.

"I will, daddy. Mommy is here."

"I know she is, buddy," he said. Patrick turned to me. "Now Ken, please try to behave yourself," he said with a smile. I bit his shoulder. "Have a great time, and I'll see you both in a few weeks. I love you."

"I love you too," I said.

"I love you most," TJ said.

"Thank you for coming."

"When you get back, we are will start planning our wedding."

"I know," I said to him with a smile. "I can't wait."

The next day, it was rainy and stormy. I sat on the living room floor starting my model. "Can we help?" Carter asked.

"Not just yet," I said.

"What can we do? It's raining," he whined.

"Why don't the four of you play a game?"

"What game?"

"Grandma has tons of games. Go ask her to show you."

He went and found mom. She brought him to the hall closet and showed him all the games. He took Trouble. The four of them sat at the kitchen table and played. Addison had run to the store and now came in wet. She came in with groceries. She went into the kitchen unloading the groceries then she was putting things away.

"What is it going to be?" dad asked.

"It's a replica of what the added building of the house is going to look like. Apparently, the contractor cannot picture it although blueprints have been drawn up."

"Added building?" dad said.

"Yeah, we are going to build a gym."

"When do you plan on opening the Bed and Breakfast?"

"I originally planned to open it at the middle of August, but then that got pushed back because of taking the boys for the summer. Not that I would have traded that for the world."

"So, you moved really quick with the wedding," dad said.

"Yes, sir, I did. But I have loved him for an exceptionally long time. Him having TJ was the icing on top," I said to dad. "Dad, I fell madly in love with that little boy the second Patrick brought him to my house, and he bounced right up in my arms like he'd known me his whole entire life.

"I took care of him when he was sick and that just deepened the bond between us. When we were traveling, one night he had a nightmare and called out saying mommy. Dad, for the life of me, I couldn't help but rush over to him and take him in my arms and rock him and let him know that he was safe."

"Where is his mother? Will she come back for him?"

"No. She won't come back for him. She is in California with her new family. She walked out on them when he was three months old. Patrick said that he's never taken to a woman like he did to me."

The boys started to argue at the table. I got up from the floor to go over and see what was going on. Addison was right there in the kitchen. She stopped what she was doing to see what was going on as well.

"What is this about?" she asked.

"TJ is cheating."

"How am I cheating?"

"Mom, he's cheating," Carter said.

"I am not," TJ said. TJ started to cry.

"Oh, go cry to your mommy!"

TJ got up and took off running. "Nice one, Carter!" I said. I went running after TJ. He was fast like lightning. For his small stature, he could move quick. "TJ! Turner, stop." He kept running. "Turner! Turner, stop!" I was running faster to get him. After five full minutes, I caught him. He was crying. He thought he was in trouble. He was trying to pull away from me, but I had a good strong grip on him. "What is this about? Stop. Honey, please stop. It's ok."

I sat down on the curb with him in my arms. My legs were burning from running like that. "I wasn't cheating."

"It's ok."

"I wasn't cheating," he said. "Tyson wasn't being nice. He kept moving my game piece around and I put it back to where it was."

"It's ok, but you can't take off like this. You made me worry."

He drew back in my arms. "Worry? I made you worry?"

"Yes, TJ, you made me worry."

"Mrs. Hopper said that only mommies worry about their kids."

"Well, daddies do too, but yes mommies worry about their kids."

"And now I have a mommy."

"Listen, kiddo, I am not going anywhere. I am not going to just take off and leave you. I won't do that. I promise."

"What if you grow tired of me?"

"What?"

"No seriously. What if you grow tired of me?"

"TJ, I don't think you realize that I fell in love with you the second I saw you? I love you. Are there going to be times in the future when you piss me off? Probably. Does that mean that I don't still love you? No. I am here for you."

We walked the mile back to the house. When we got there Tyson and Carter were in time out.

"Just because she adopted you, doesn't mean you are family," Tyson said.

Dad went over and picked Tyson up and took him out of the room. He took him into their bedroom and scolded him. "He is family. He is your aunt's son. And don't you ever ever say that to him again. You need to be kind. You were moving his game piece around the board. STOP IT!" he yelled at him. "He is now your cousin. You will be nice to him. Do you hear me?"

"Yes, grandpa," Tyson said.

"Now you go sit on the couch and don't say a word till I tell you you can get up."

"Yes, grandpa."

Dad came out of the room and took Carter in the room. "You will be nice to that little boy. His whole life just changed, and it is all new for him. He is your cousin now and you will be nice to him. Do you hear me?"

"Yes, grandpa," Carter said.

TJ just noticed the piano. "Owe! Can I play it?"

"Yes," mom said. She walked over and opened it up. TJ climbed up on the bench and started playing the piano.

"Looks like I will have to get one," I said.

"Daddy can bring ours," he said.

"Yes, he can." I watched in amazement as this almost six year old little boy was playing the piano without music.

"I want to take violin lessons," he said.

"We can look into that for the fall."

He played for a few more minutes and then turned and jumped away from the piano. Later that night, when I was putting him to bed, I asked him, "Where did you learn how to play the piano?"

"Daddy plays," he said. "He started to teach me when I was three," he said. "Do you play?"

"No."

"Are you mad at me?"

"Turner, why would I be mad at you?" He shrugged. "No, kiddo, I'm not mad at you. I love you."

"Will you read to me?"

"Yes. Let me go get the book." I left him alone for two minutes. When I came back in the room, he was sleeping. I kissed him on the cheek then turned the light out before leaving the room.

Tyson and Carter were waiting for me. "Hi, guys," I said to them.

"Hi. Can we talk to you please?" Carter said.

"Yes."

I went to the kitchen table with them. "We are sorry," Carter said.

"Want to tell me why you both are acting this way?"

"We have always been your boys," Tyson said.

"What?"

"We have always been your boys," Tyson said again. "Now we're not. Now you have your own boy."

"So, you guys think that just because TJ is now in my life that I'm going to stop wanting to be with you?"

"Yeah," Carter said running his hand through his hair.

"I know that things are different now, and that it all happened really quick, but that doesn't mean that I am going to stop wanting you guys around. I love you so much."

With that finally settled I went back and sat down on the floor with my project. My cell phone buzzed. I looked at it. It was Storm. *Can we meet?* She wrote.

Yes. You can come to my parents' house.

Be there in about ten minutes.

Ok. C U then. 😊

She came to the house. "I saw that Pat was here. Is everything ok?"

"Yes. As far as I know," I said. "Would you like a cup of coffee and a piece of key lime pie?"

"Yes. Thank you."

"How do you take your coffee?"

"Black, "she said. "Pat has spoken about you over the years," she started. I looked at her. "No, it's true. He says that you have awesome talent with the stuff that you do. When he would get frustrated with things, he would say that he'd wish he could discuss things with you."

"Why are you telling me this?"

"Listen, I have been in Pat's life since we were elementary school. Wesley and I were best men at his wedding to the piece of shit Renee. I threw that bitch a baby shower. When she had TJ, she obviously had post-partum depression. She had it right away. She didn't want to hold him. She didn't want to see him. She refused that. Patrick on the other hand melted when he saw him. And when he held TJ for the first time, well, it was the most beautiful thing that I had ever seen. Within three months, she had packed up all of her things, she served Pat with divorce papers, and she had relinquished all of her rights of TJ. She never held him. She never touched him.

"Patrick never struggled with being a father. He stepped up to the plate and then some."

"Would she ever come back?"

"Renee?"

"Yeah," I said.

"No," Storm said and sipped her coffee. "Thanks for the coffee. I'd really like to be your friend."

"Is Storm your real name?"

"It is. My parents were earthy people," she said with a smile. "My siblings are my sister Rain, and my brothers River and Wolf. I am the youngest of us all. When I first met Patrick, he was this adorable brown hair little boy with grey eyes. The teacher said "we have new student. Her name is Storm Meadows." The whole fucking class laughed except for Patrick. He pulled the empty chair out from the desk next to his and gestured for me to come and sit next to him. We have best friends since that day.

"I remember him talking about you when he went to architectural school. I was a photography student there, and we would be roomed together in college."

"Did you ever hook up with him?"

"No," she said. "Don't get me wrong. I love Patrick with all my heart, but I prefer women over men. Renee always had a problem with that. Will you?"

"Why would I?" I said.

"I don't know. It freaks some women out."

"Storm, as long as you love my husband and my son and we can get along that's all that matters. If you want to come hang out at my house and go horseback riding with your nephew and godson, then come over. I'm the new person in the mix here. You've been a part of their lives, so why would I want to change that?

"You made my wedding announcement. I cherish that. Diversity is good for kids. TJ has lived a remarkably diverse life: not having a mother, being the son to a single father, having you and Wes in his life, and..."

"And now you. I've seen Pat date over the years and when he introduced TJ to them, TJ would hide behind Patrick. He never engaged in conversations with them, and then when he saw you. My god, I saw that little boy open up in a way that he never has before.

"When we would get together for Sunday night dinners, you were all that he would talk about. I'd hear, "Ken does this, and Ken does that, and Ken has horses, and Ken has a park as her back yard, and Ken took him for ice cream before dinner."

I smiled. "Yes. Yes, I did do that."

While she was there, TJ had a nightmare. I heard him talking in his sleep. "No. No. I don't want to go with you. No. No. I don't want to go.

MOMMY!" I went running into the room. Sweat poured off his body. I picked him up taking him on my lap. Mom came to the door.

"Is he ok?"

"Yes. He's ok."

I was rocking him. He was crying. I spoke to him in a low voice. Reassuring him that he was safe. "What were you dreaming?"

"There was a man in a van," he took a deep breath. I took his shirt off him. Sweat beads sat on his skin. "He had a doggy. I was playing with the doggy and then the guy picked me up and put me in the van. I didn't want to go with him, mommy."

"It was just a dream," I said. "You didn't go with him."

Then TJ told me about the man by the school that was there every day. He had a puppy that kids played with and he would try to get some of the kids to go over to his van.

"What color is the van?"

"Yellow. Bright yellow."

"Is there writing on the van?"

"Yes. It says Happy Puppy on it in red letters with blue around it."

"Did you ever go by the van?"

"No. I was too scared to."

"And that is ok, TJ."

"He's going to be there again when school starts."

"Did you tell daddy?"

"Yes."

"Tell me what does the man look like?"

"He's tall like you and daddy. He has a round head with black hair." TJ continued with a full description of this person. I finally calmed him down enough to go back to sleep. I went back into the kitchen with Storm and told her about his dream and then everything he had just told me.

"I'll tell my detective friend tomorrow about it."

"He's had this dream before, but this is the first time that he has told me about it."

A storm had moved in with wicked lightning, so Storm stayed the night. Her hotel was on the northern side of the island.

In the morning, I woke up to TJ sitting on me. "Aunt Storm is here," he said. "Is she here to take me home?"

"What? No," I said. "What time is?"

He shrugged. "I can't tell time yet."

"We will work on that before school starts up again," I said. "Get dressed please. We have a busy day."

"Ok, mommy. Can Aunt Storm come with us?"

"Yes," I said sitting up with him in my arms. I layed him back between my legs and tickled him. His laughter was like music. It was a beautiful sound.

"Is daddy coming back?"

"No. We will see daddy in two weeks."

I tickled him a little more and then we got up. I showered and dressed in jean shorts and a short sleeve shirt. TJ came back into the room after I was dressed. "Aunt Storm is different," he stated. I turned and looked at him.

"What?"

"She's different."

"How is that?"

"Well, how you love daddy, she loves women."

"TJ!"

"But she does, mommy."

"Does it matter?"

"No. I love her. She plays catch with me; she takes me to the movies. She takes me places and we have fun. But why is that?"

"People are different, TJ. Everyone is different."

He jumped off the bed and turned back. "Mommy?"

"Yes."

"When school starts, are you going to be there?"

"Come here," I said picking him and sitting with him on my lap. "Now I know that this…that having me in your life is new, and if you have to ask every day if I will be here, I want you to know that every time you ask this question I am going to give you the same answer. Yes, TJ I will be there. I am going to be here."

I knew he was insecure, and it was coming out more and more. This was the farthest away he had ever been from Patrick. That day, while exploring the Hemingway House, he never left my side. Afterwards, we went out on a lunch boat for lunch and a boat tour. He sat on my lap the whole time.

An older woman had taken notice. "Is he your son?"

"Yes, he is."

"He's adorable. How old is he? Three or four?"

"No, he's almost six. He's just little."

The boat hit a wake. TJ got scared. I looked over at Addison just in time to see Carter react the same way. We smiled at each other. Tyson had taken to Storm. He was sitting on her lap and he had fallen asleep.

"Want me to take him?" Addison asked.

"No, it's ok. I'm ok with him."

"We share a birthday," TJ said. "I'll turn six and he'll turn five."

Michael was sitting with dad. "Can we go fishing?" he asked.

"Sure. When we get back to the house, I'll take you fishing."

"Can we watch the sunset again tonight, mommy?" Carter asked.

"I think we can do that," she answered him.

We had lunch on the boat. The four boys had chicken fingers and fish sticks with French fries. The five of us adults had shrimp cocktails and a Waldorf salad with Brie and hummus with crackers.

When the boat docked back in, dad took Michael fishing while the rest of us went with mom to the tennis courts. Tyson and TJ were given their first lessons in tennis. Carter played a game with mom. Addison and I played each other. When we were done, I played Storm. She was happy to be a part of the group.

CHAPTER FOURTEEN

We stayed with my parents for ten days. Then we left for our start home driving up the coast. We had stopped in each Key on the way back up north doing the tourist thing in each one. We got a hotel in Marathon. We took a boat out there watching sunset on the boat.

The next day we went Islamorada. It was more of the same things that we had been doing for the last week and half. Going to the beach, swimming, riding jet skis, boating, and more swimming. When I planned this, I thought this would be fun. Now it was just plain old…

"This is boring," TJ whined. "Can we do something else?"

"What would you like to do?"

"Can we go bowling or do something indoors?"

"Sure," I said to him.

The other three were excited to do something indoors too. We took them bowling. Because there were six of us, we split into teams. I had TJ and Carter on my team, and Addison had Michael and Tyson. "The best of three games," Addison said.

"Are you sure?" I asked her.

"Oh, yeah, girlie, I'm sure."

I laughed so hard. "You haven't called me girlie since I was thirteen."

"Well, bring your A game," she said.

"Consider it brought."

"What are they doing?" TJ asked.

"It's called trash talking," Michael said. "Good luck."

TJ smiled.

There was a little difference though. The bowling balls weren't bowling balls. They were skee balls. "What the fuck is this?" Addison asked. I burst out laughing. "No. No. Wait a minute. You knew about this."

"No, of course not."

"How hard can it be, mommy?" Michael asked. He took a skee ball and brought it back like a bowling ball and threw it hard down the lane and he got a strike. He turned to face us with a broad smile plastered on.

"Cute, Michael," Addison said. "Move over. It's my turn." She took her ball and brought it back like Michael did and threw it down the lane and gutted it. I laughed. "Shut up, Kenny," she said. Tyson went next. He hit four pins. Then we were up. Carter went first and hit a strike. Then I went and hit a strike and TJ knocked down four pins.

Round two: Michael again scored with a strike. Addison knocked down one pin. Tyson gutted it. "It's ok, baby," Addison said to him. Tyson still smiled as if he had rolled a strike. Carter got a strike, I got strike and TJ knocked down six this time.

"Let's go do batting practice," Michael said.

"Yeah!" all three younger boys chimed in.

"Oh, this will be good," Addison said.

For Tyson and TJ, we got t-ball tees for them to swing off of. Carter wanted to try it without the tee. Michael got up, took the bat to the plate and cracked the very first ball. "Wow! I'm signing you up for baseball in the fall," Addison said. He cracked another and another. It was damn impressive. Then Carter went. He struck out for the first one, but hit the second and third one. "Your turn, sister," Addison said to me. I looked up from the squatted position that I was in. I stood up, put on the helmet that she handed to me, took the bat, and went into the cage.

"Oh, shit," Michael said. "She means business." Addison went in the one next to me. "Guys, come watch our moms," he said to the others. They all stopped what they were doing and came running over to watch. TJ stood in front of Michael. Michael had his hands on TJ's shoulders. Tyson stood in front TJ with TJ's hands on his shoulders and Carter stood next to the three of them, with his hand on TJ's shoulder leaning in on them. I put the bat down, turned to them and took a picture of the four of them. Then I picked up the bat.

"Let's do this," I said. Our balls came at the same time. I hit mine. Addison missed.

"I wasn't ready."

"Ok, baby, we can restart it."

"Shut up, Kenny," she said between her teeth.

The next ball came and again I hit it. She hit hers. Another ball came, I hit it. Addison missed. The third ball came, I hit mine, as did Addison. We had six balls in the machine. I hit the fourth as did she. I hit the fifth, and she missed. I got cocky and threw my head back laughing. When I looked up, I took a line drive right to my left eye. Addison hit her ball. She came running into the cage. "Are you ok?" I didn't answer her right away. "Kenny, are you ok?" I slowly nodded my head.

The guy that ran the place came over. "Hey, are you ok?" he asked. He looked at me. "Well, you sure are going to have a shiner."

"Mommy!" TJ said.

"I'm ok," I said.

"Let me get you some ice."

"Thank you," I said.

"Can we tell daddy that mommy hit you?" Carter asked.

"What?" Addison asked. "No."

Carter laughed.

The guy came back over with ice. He handed it to me. I put it on my eye. "If your kids want to play in the arcade, it's free," he said.

"Thank you," I said to him.

"Are you ok?"

"Yeah, I'm ok."

The kids played in the arcade. Because we were staying overnight there, I drank a beer. Addison had a margarita. "Are you sure you are ok?"

"It's a black eye, Addy. I'm fine. God knows it not my first one."

She looked at me. "When the hell did you have a black eye?"

"I've had my fair share of them," I said to her.

"When?"

"When we were kids, Jamie punched me in face once...twice. I was in that fight at school with Melody Barker or Baker."

"I remember her. Baker," she said. "Wasn't she a grade ahead of you?"

"She was."

"Why did she hit you?"

"She thought I was Jamie," I said with a smile.

"What?"

"You've never heard this story?"

"Obviously not," she said.

"Yeah, that bitch Melody was dating oh god what the hell was his name? Max Stewart," I said. "Jamie liked Max and he liked Jamie, so they kissed in the hallway outside of Mr. Campers room…"

"Oh, Mr. Camper. He was such a sweet man," Addison said.

"So, I was at my locker, and Melody came over. She tapped me on the shoulder and when I turned to look at her, she cold cocked me right in the face."

"Did you hit her back?"

"Oh, yeah," I said with a smile.

"Did she get into trouble?"

"Who knows. I was suspended for five days for fighting."

"Why? She hit you first."

"Because after I got my bearings, I hit her repeatedly. Nice man Mr. Camper had to separate us. He dragged me all the way to the office. When the principal asked why I kept hitting her, I told him it was because she wanted to hurt Jamie. My last one was when the… well, it was a long time ago," I said.

TJ came running over. "You have to play. Please, mommy, come play."

"Ok, sweet boy," I said getting up. Addison stayed at the table. She watched as I went and played with our kids. I looked over at her. Then I looked at Carter and Tyson. "Go ask her to come play and don't say that I said it."

Carter ran over. "Aren't you going to come play too, mommy?" Addison got up and Carter took her hand pulling her over to play with us.

"Did your Aunt tell you to come over?"

"No. We thought you would have come with her," he said.

"Mommy! They have the trampolines," Michael said.

We went to where they were. Again. We teamed up. This time we switched, so now I had Tyson and Michael and Addison had TJ and Carter. So, it was dodge ball on a trampoline. This was going to be fun.

"I don't know how to play," TJ said.

"It's easy, baby," I said to him. "You take the red ball and you throw it at either me, Michael or Tyson, and if you hit one of us then we are out. If we catch it, then you are out."

"Sounds coooool!" he said.

"TJ, how do you spell that?" Addison asked.

"Spell what?"

"The last word you just said to your mom."

"C-o-o-o-o-o-l." he spelled.

"Yep, that's how it sounded," she said picking him and kissing him on the cheek.

So, we started to play. I thought this would have been one, two, three; and we are done, but it didn't happen like that. We literally played trampoline dodge ball for an hour. It was so much fun. In the end, Addison, Carter, and TJ won by a point.

"I'm starving," Michael and TJ said at the same time. They high fived each other.

"When are you and daddy and Beth leaving on the cruise?" Michael asked.

"Let's not discuss it now," Addison said to him.

"But it's coming up right?"

"Yes, it is coming up. But again, Michael, let's not discuss it." Addison's phone rang. "Hello," she said. "Hi, honey, how was it being with Aunt Jamie?"

"Oh my god, mommy, it was great."

"Are you and daddy home yet?"

"No. We stayed three extra days with Aunt Jamie and Uncle Lennox. He is so much fun, mommy. We are on our way to get Beth."

"Oh, good," Addison said.

"Where are you at?"

"I'm in The Keys with Aunt Kenny and the boys."

"So, I hear I have a cousin now."

"You do."

"Is he little?"

"He's five. Almost six."

"I can't believe Aunt Kenny got married and I wasn't there."

"Sweetheart, it wasn't a wedding like you are thinking. They went to the courthouse and it is called eloped. They are going to have another wedding with all of the family and their friends soon, but it had to happen so that she could adopt TJ."

"So, she adopted him?"

"Yes."

"So, he is now her little boy?"

"Yes."

"Does that mean that she's not going to take us places or do things with us anymore?"

"Absolutely not," Addison said. "Aunt Kenny is not like that. It just means that she will have her own child there along with you guys. The fun you have with your Aunt isn't going to change."

"Will she still take me for Girl's Day Out day?"

"Yes, of course. We were talking about that earlier. She said that she has to set up that appointment with you and that she cannot wait to see you and hug you and talk to you. She misses you. God. I miss you and Beth."

"Thank you for letting me go this summer, mommy. Thank you so much. I love you."

"I love you too."

Addison came back over to join us. "Your sister sends her love," she said to the boys.

TJ looked at them. "You have a sister?"

"Two sisters," they all three said together.

"Kate and Beth," Michael said.

"Where are they?"

"Kate was touring with Aunt Jamie and Beth spent the summer with mommy's sister Aunt Mandy in Georgia."

"Oh," he said.

I looked at him. "What's wrong?" I asked him.

"If you and daddy have children, you'll forget about me."

"What?" literally came from both Addison's and my mouth at the same time.

We both rushed to him. I scooped him up and yet he was in both of our arms. "That would never happen," I said.

"But that's what Renee did," he said. It was the first time he said her name and had not called her his mom.

"You are in our family now," Addison said, "and everyone is going to love you for forever."

"TJ, I love you so much. You are now my son. Nothing can change that now."

"What if you and daddy get a divorce?"

"You will still be my son."

"He needs counseling," Addison said. "He's really struggling with you leaving him."

"I know," I said.

"Kennedy, if you ever go away for a business trip, you are going to have to take him with you. He understands that Patrick isn't going anywhere and he can be away from him, but he can't be away from you. A least not right now."

"Well, I'm not going anywhere."

"I remember when I thought I wanted to be psychiatrist and I did all my schooling and my internships; I saw a young girl who was like him. She couldn't cope with being alone. He's almost there," Addison said. "If you step out of sight even for a minute, you can see him searching for you. He is terrified that you are going to leave him.

"Maybe it wasn't a big deal when it was just him and Patrick. I don't know, but since you came into his life, you altered him. Now he's so afraid that he will be bad, and you will leave, or he will love you and you will leave."

"I know," I said. "I've loved Patrick for a long time. We went to school together. We worked on projects together both when we were in school and now that we are at the same firm. I knew that he married and I heard talk that they divorced, but I never knew about TJ. Then the first time I met him, he just bounced himself right into my arms and I fell in love with him that second.

"I don't know how to reassure him that I will be here no matter what."

"When we get back, you might want to take him to a doctor and just see what they say."

The next day we left The Keys. We drove into Miami. The boys were excited. We stopped at Viscaya. We toured the house first before going into the gardens.

"The other one was better." Carter said.

"Definitely," Michael chimed in.

"Without a doubt," TJ answered.

"What was better?" Addison asked.

"The Bok Tower Garden," Michael said

"It was spectacular," TJ said.

"I love the vocabulary," I said to him with a smile.

"Mom!"

"What, sweet boy? It's a complement."

Tyson just listened. He was quiet today. I went over to him. "What's up, buddy, you've been quiet today."

"Yeah," he said and walked away.

"Ty, what is it?" I said going after him.

He looked to see that Addison couldn't hear him. "It's just not fair, Aunt Kenny."

"What's not fair?"

"That mommy and daddy are going to take Beth with them because she's the youngest. My birthday is going to happen when they are on the cruise."

"Please don't think about that now. Try to enjoy our time together."

"Oh, I am," he said. "It's just that..." Tears ran down his face. I scooped him up in my arms.

"I promise you that everything is going to be ok. Do you trust me?"

"Yeah," he said.

"Do you believe me?"

"Yeah."

"Have I ever lied to you?"

"No," he said.

"Well, then I guess everything is going to be ok."

"Ok, Aunt Kenny."

"Come. Let's go. We are going to go get lunch."

"Oh, good. I'm starving."

Our next stop for the day was the Miami Seaquarium. We first ate lunch before going to see the shows. The kids loved it. I hadn't been there in a long time. Mom and dad took us when we were kids. I vaguely remembered it. Addison had never been. We watched the dolphin show, the whale show, the seals, the dolphin show again. We saw the sharks.

"Mommy!" I looked at TJ. "Were there sharks in the water in The Keys?"

"Yeah, sure there were," I said.

"But we didn't see them."

"Just because you don't see them doesn't mean that they aren't there."

"Were we safe?"

"Yes, TJ, we were and are safe."

"Cooool," he said.

"Mommy?" Tyson said. "Aunt Kenny just said that we swam with sharks."

"No, that's not what she said, baby," Addison said. "There were sharks in the water, but we didn't see them. We were safe," she assured him. "We are safe right now."

Carter and Michael were ahead of us. They were looking in the giant tank in front of us. Carter was standing in front of Michael and Michael had his arms around Carter's shoulders. I stepped to the side and took a picture of it. I wondered where Storm had been. I hadn't seen her since that night at my parents' house.

"Where are we staying tonight?" Carter asked.

"We are staying a little further up north in Broward County. In Fort Lauderdale. Tomorrow we will be having a fun full day up there."

"Aunt Ken," Michael said. I looked at him. "Thank you for this awesome summer."

"You're welcome."

"This has been the best summer of my life," TJ said.

"Mine too," Carter and Tyson said.

"Thank you for keeping me with you and not sending me to be with Beth."

I hugged Tyson.

That night we checked into the hotel right on Fort Lauderdale beach.

Addison opened the backdoors and we could hear the ocean. Bedtime hadn't been discussed, but they were all in bed and sleeping by nine thirty.

"You've taught my children manners," Addison said.

"No, they've always had them. Well, always around me."

"That's what I mean. I have been busy ever since I first got pregnant with Michael and it never stopped. Not even when I was pregnant with Beth. I have five beautiful children that I don't know a lot about them."

"It's not too late, Addy."

"They are all afraid of losing you."

I looked at her. "What?"

"They are. Even before this summer started, I over heard Carter and Michael talking. Carter said that he had the best time with you this year. He was so excited that you home schooled him and that he spent every day with you. Michael is afraid that once he starts middle school that he will change, and things will change."

"It won't change my relationship with them. Not with any of them. I miss Kate. I am thrilled that she got to spend the summer the way that she wanted, but god, I miss my girl. And Beth. She is almost three now. I can't wait to hug and kiss her.

"Just because I adopted TJ doesn't change my love for your kids. I still consider all of them my kids."

"Are you going to move in with Patrick?"

"No!" She looked at me. "They are moving into my house. I'm not moving away from my place. I own that place live, stock, and barrel and I mean every word of that. I'm going to open the bed and breakfast. Maybe later than I wanted to do so, but it will happen," I said.

"Did you move rooms when you bought the house?"

"No. I'm still in my childhood bedroom for right now. Patrick and I will choose a room to live in and TJ will have his own room."

"I can't believe you kept the trip going."

"Why?"

"Well, you are married now," she said with smile.

"He's working," I protested. "He's away on business right now. He's not even in the state, so what was I to do; cancel the plans that I had with the boys and my son to stay home to talk to him on the phone every night. I can do that from anywhere that we are."

"You speak to him?"

"Every single night. Even before we were married."

"When?"

"When the kids are safely tucked into bed and when the moment is right. I have spoken with Park every night too and James. Hell, I'd like to speak to this Addison bitch person that I speak to every night as well."

"Why don't you?" she asked with laughter in her voice.

"Because that bitch won't answer her phone. When I get back from this trip, I'm going to talk to her about this." We both laughed. "Addy, thanks for being here. I'm glad that we have this time together."

"Me too," she said.

In the morning, I woke Addison up first. "Hey, wake up."

"Is everything ok?"

"Yes. Let's take the boys for an early morning bike ride on the beach."

"Ok," she said. She got up. Together we woke the boys. They were excited to get up early. We took the bikes outside and rode them to the Bahia Mar hotel on Seabreeze Boulevard up to Commercial Boulevard where the Fort Lauderdale pier is. We made it just in time to go out on the pier to watch the sunrise together. All four boys had their cameras and took gorgeous pictures of the sunrise. On the ride back, we stopped at a restaurant off Oakland Park Boulevard named First Watch. We had a great filling breakfast.

"I need to stop in the drug store," Michael said.

"For what? What do you need?" Addison asked.

"Film for my camera."

I looked at him. "Good one. I love it," I said.

We all laughed. We got back on our bikes and rode back to the hotel. Everyone; including Addison and I jumped into the pool. Then we finished the walk to our room with the bikes. We all took turns showering and getting dressed.

"Look they have a Discovery Center here," Tyson said.

"I know they do," I said to him.

"I wish we could go there."

"Your wish is my command."

He got all excited and jumped up and down.

"Kennedy, did you sleep at all last night?"

"Yeah, why?" I asked Addison.

"When did you finish this? I went to bed well after midnight."

"I finished it after that," I said with a smile.

"You didn't sleep."

"Yes, I assure you I did."

"What? like an hour?"

"Um no. A little more than that. I'm fine," I said to her. "Come on. Let's go have fun."

We spent the next six hours playing and having a wonderful time in the Discovery Center. We took an indoor airboat ride through the Florida Everglades. We experienced what it would be like to be in a tornado. Of course, we did the space thing for a long time before moving on to see a movie. Before leaving there, we all went in the gift shop. The boys each picked something that they wanted. I bought a little something for all of them as did Addison.

"Mommy, can I have money?" TJ asked me.

"Here, TJ, let me help you," Addison said. "What do you want to buy?"

He looked at her with tears in his eyes. "I want to buy something for mommy."

"Ok. I'll help you with that," she said. "Come on."

"Aunt Kenny, I have to pee," Carter said.

"Me too."

"Me three," Tyson said.

"Go ahead. I have him," Addison said to me. "Thank you for taking them."

"Sure."

I walked back into the main building with the boys and sat on the bench to wait for them to come out of the bathroom. They all three came out together. "Could you give us money and not ask what it is for?" Michael asked.

"Yes, I could do that."

"Like a hundred dollars?" Carter asked.

"But what about for mommy," Tyson asked.

"Hold on. We will be right back. Will you stay here and wait for us?"

"Of course."

This woman walked over and took a seat next to me on the bench although all of the other benches were vacant. "Are those your children?"

"Yes," I said. "Well, they are my nephews."

"Do you have children?"

"Yes. I have a son."

The boys came back. "We need a hundred and fifty dollars."

"Excuse us please," I said to the lady. We walked out of the museum and outside into the fresh air. "Ok. Here," I said handing them two hundred dollars. "I would like change please. I'll wait for you right here."

"Thank you," they all said hugging me tight. They ran into the store. I sat with their bags of goodies from the store. Toys, Astronaut ice cream, along with Rock Candy and other candy bars. Addison came out with TJ, who was beaming from ear to ear. He ran up to me, jumped in my arms hugging and kissing me.

"Where are my three?"

"Are you kidding?" I asked. "They are in the store."

"Should I go back in?"

"No. They will be fine," I said to her.

"I can't believe the money you have spent on my children."

"It's material things," I said. "I have money and up until just recently I didn't have a little one to spend it on, so I spend it on our children. I'm very wealthy," I whispered. "It's good. It's not going to break me by spending money on our children. Hopefully before you all leave on the cruise, I can have my Girls Day with Kate and maybe start one with Bethy too."

"Is it wrong not to tell your four older children that they too are going with us on the cruise?"

"No, it's a surprise for them."

The boys finally came out of the store with two bags. "This is for..."

"No," TJ said. "We are going to do it back at the hotel."

"Oh, ok," Michael said.

"Are you guys ready?"

"I have to pee," TJ said.

"Come on. Let's go," I said picking him and carrying him back into the museum. We both used the bathroom and then we left. We went back to the hotel. Everyone put their bags by their own stuff. "Our day isn't over yet. Come on. Let's go," I said.

"I want to change," Michael said.

All four of them changed. They each put on jean shorts and changed their shirts to collared shirts. They all four looked handsome and cute as ever.

"Where are going now?"

"We are going to… oh nice try, Ace," I said to Michael.

"Damn! I almost got her."

I laughed. We left the room. We got in the car and I drove a few blocks to Los Olas Boulevard, where we boarded the dinner cruise boat taking it up and down the Intracoastal Waters.

"Is this the same water that is by us?"

"Yes, TJ," I said.

"How far up does it go?"

"All the way to Maine."

"Really?"

"Yeah," Addison said.

"So, we can take a boat from here all the way up there?"

"Yes. But no, we are not doing that, Carter."

"Well, maybe that can be our trip next summer."

"We will give it some thought," Addison said.

CHAPTER FIFTEEN

Due to cutting a few days out of The Keys and heading back up north a little sooner, we decided to spend a few days in south Florida. The boys were loving the beach and doing other things as well. For the three days that we were there, we got up early every morning and took long bike rides together. Then we stopped for breakfast at the same place First Watch every morning before returning to the hotel, jumping in the pool, swimming together for fifteen minutes on the first day, a half hour on the second day, and this morning, we went from being in the pool to taking the bikes to the room, grabbing an armful full of towels and racing to the beach to swim in the ocean. The day was perfect. We ate lunch on the beach with our toes buried in the sand.

Then the storm blew in. We gathered our things running to the hotel. We made it just in time before the pounding rain started. For the rest of the day, we stayed up in the room watching the boats traveling in this wicked weather up and down the Intracoastal. I went to my duffle bag and found a book. I sat down on the floor at the bottom of one of the beds and started to read from The Borrowers. Addison joined me on the floor. The four boys got on the bed behind us. I read the whole book out loud to them.

"Will you read another one please?" Tyson asked.

"It's mommy's turn to read," I said.

Addison went to the duffle bag and unzipped it. She pulled out a few looking each of them over and then picked one. She picked A Wrinkle in Time. The boys came and sat with us on the floor. TJ sat between my legs leaning against me, Carter sat between her legs leaning against her and Michael had Tyson between his legs leaning against him. We all listened as she began. She did not read the whole book. She stopped reading when she looked up to see that both Tyson and Michael were sleeping. TJ could stay up for days if I allowed him. He was afraid of missing out and Carter seemed the same way.

"Thank you, mommy," Carter said.

"Oh, you're welcome."

I stood up and then squatted down lifted Tyson off of Michael and I put him in bed. Then I went back for Michael. I lifted him up and put him in bed as well. Just as I covered him, he opened his eyes. "I'm awake."

"No, it's ok. Close your eyes, sweetheart. It's ok." I kissed him on the forehead. He was toasty warm from being out in the sun. He turned on his side and went back to sleep.

Carter and TJ sat quietly with the building blocks that I had brought. I took the model out and my paints.

"You paint them too?" Addison asked.

"Yeah. Sometimes."

"What is our plan for tomorrow?"

"We are going to start heading back up north. We will stop in Palm Beach for the night or maybe even go a little further."

"When are we due back in Daytona?"

"Not for another three days."

"Would you want to take the boys to Sea World?"

"Sure."

"We can drive straight up there tomorrow and get a hotel close by the park and take them there and then go on to Daytona."

"Yeah, that sounds great. Hey, thanks for reading with us."

"How often do you do that?"

"What? Read to them?"

"Yeah."

"Every day."

"Again. When do you find the time?"

"I don't know. I find the time," I said. "With Tyson not yet reading, and TJ just recently finishing kindergarten and Carter loves when I read to him, so does Michael. So, I find the time."

"Yes, but they are my children and I can't seem to find the time."

"You just have to find even five minutes to do it. It would be a start."

"Yeah," Addison said.

"Tyson reads," Carter said.

"What?"

"He does. Ask him later or tomorrow. He reads pretty good. And you are not missing out, mommy. You are here for us," he said and hugged her.

The storm raged on. With the thunder crackling loud over us, I knew that TJ wasn't going to sleep any time soon. I took out the coloring books and crayons. I just put them down on the table without saying a word. TJ went to the table and took a book. He colored for a while.

"I'm hungry."

"I'm going to go to the lobby and see what places are around that we can order from."

"Can I go with you?" TJ asked.

"No, I'll be right back."

The second I walked out of the door, he threw himself down on the floor kicking and screaming crying. Addison tried to console him, but it wasn't working. Carter came flying out of the door. "AUNT KENNY, STOP. IT'S TJ!"

I raced back to the room. "What happened?"

"You left."

"No. I am going to the lobby. I'm not leaving the hotel." He wouldn't stop crying. He was inconsolable. I took him in my arms and rocked him. "I wasn't leaving you. Shh. Shh. Calm down. Calm down."

He cried himself to sleep. I rocked him still. Tears sat on the brim of his eye lashes. I wiped them away.

"Jesus, Kenny, I've seen my kids throw temper tantrums, but I've never seen that. That's not good."

"I know."

"What are you going to do about it?"

"I'll call Patrick and…"

"No, Ken, you have to deal with this."

"I just don't know how."

"We will figure something out," she said.

I put him down on the bed and then went to the lobby to find out where we could order from. I went back upstairs with our options of pizza or Chinese food. We decided on Chinese food. They had a surprisingly good selection for the kids.

The next day, we packed the car and got back on the road. We took the boys to Orlando. We checked in to the hotel, which was a block away from Sea World. Our food choices were plentiful being right on International Drive. We took the boys out for dinner, but before dinner we had seen a guy flying, so the boys wanted to check it out. I pulled the car over. Then we walked over to where the event was happening. All six of us wound up doing it. It was fun. After being shot like a rubber band in the sky and then coming back, leaving the surface again and coming back three times, the ride was over; we went out for dinner.

"Can we go swimming when we get back to the hotel?" Carter asked.

"We will have to see what time it is," Addison said.

"Excuse me a minute," I said. "I have to use the bathroom."

TJ stopped what he was doing and looked at me. "Mommy!" he said in lowered voice.

"I'll be right back."

I got up from the table proceeding to the bathroom. I heard Addison talking to him, but when I returned, he was crying. "TJ, I had to go to the bathroom," I said. He started to calm down as he moved to my lap. I kissed him on the head.

When we got back to the hotel, it was still early. Addison said that they could go swimming. "I have to do a little work, so I'm going to the room."

"Ok. I'll watch the kids," she said. "What do you have to do?"

"I have to take pictures of the model and get them sent off for approval."

I walked back to the room. I called Patrick to tell him how much I loved him. "How is our boy?" he asked.

"He's experiencing extreme separation anxiety with me. The second I walk away he starts to cry and carry on."

"Oh, do you need me to come?"

"No. I just wanted to let you know that it is occurring. Other than that, he is great."

"Where are you all now?"

"We are in Orlando. We are taking the boys to Sea World tomorrow."

"Oh, that's great. Teej has been bugging me to take him there. What are you doing now?"

"Taking pictures of the model to send out."

"It can wait," he said. "Go have fun with our boy."

"Yeah. I will," I said. "I love you."

"I love you too."

The next morning, we had an early start. We all woke up pretty early, so we decided to go for a bike ride. Who would ever have thought that all of us could ride five miles? It was surprising to both Addison and me. When we got back to the hotel, everyone showered and prepared for the day. We went to the restaurant in the hotel for breakfast and then we were off for a day of fun at Sea World.

Upon entering the park, we took a map. We sat with the kids to see where they wanted to start. The four of them picked the sea lion show, so we were off to that side of the park. We watched that show moving to the walrus show. By noon, the park was full of people. Everything had been going really nice. At three o'clock we went to the whale show. We watched it enjoying every minute of it. We were seated in the splash zone, so we were drenched by the end of the show. When it was over, TJ was standing right next to me. We were exiting the exhibit and then he was gone. It literally took me less than a minute to realize that he was gone. My heart started to pound.

"TURNER! TJ!"

Addison too was distracted with her kids. "What happened?" she asked turning and looking at me.

"He's gone."

"What?"

"He was right here next to me and now he's gone."

"Ok. Don't panic," she said.

"TJ!" I started moving all around looking for him. "I'm going to go find someone to report it to," I said. I took off running screaming his name everywhere I went. A park official rushed over.

"Is there a problem?"

"I lost my son."

"Ok, where was the last place you were with him?"

"We had just finished watching the whale show. We were in a crowd of people. He was right next to me one second and gone the next. Please help me."

"What does he look like?"

"He's a five-year-old little boy. He's about…maybe just under four feet. He has brown hair and grey eyes. He's wearing blue jean shorts and green t-shirt."

In the meantime, while we were looking for TJ, he had followed a crowd and was in the shark exhibit. It was then that he turned to see where we were. Not seeing us, he stayed where he was. I left out the detail that he had a jacket. He put his jacket on and went and stood close to the tank watching the sharks. He had his I-pod with him, he put his headphones on and put music on.

In twenty minutes after his disappearance, the park was locked down. No one was allowed in or out. Places were being thoroughly searched, but precious time was slipping by.

"Patrick will kill me," I said. "Where can he be? He freaks out if I'm out of sight."

An hour had gone by and still no TJ. Two hours had escaped us and still now TJ.

"Maybe he is inside somewhere," Addison said.

In the third hour, the weather changed bringing in an evening thunderstorm. My heart was in my throat. The park lifted the lock down even though TJ still wasn't found.

He had sat down with his back against the tank. He pulled his baseball hat out of his bag and put it on. He had his knees pressed to his chest. He pulled a snack out of his bag and ate it. He ate a Smucker's peanut butter and jelly sandwich that I had put in his bag that morning. He was still calm. He hadn't realized how much time had gone by. People ignored him. He was content. He closed his eyes for a second and now was sound asleep in the shark exhibit. It was cold, dim, dry, and safe inside the exhibit.

Addison took the boys with her, so they wouldn't miss out on a day of fun. I stayed with the park officials. "I should be looking for him. He must be so scared right now. He is only five. Everything scares him."

It was nearing closing time when a woman park official asked me to come with her. I was a complete nervous wreck. For the first time all day the shark exit was empty and now a camera showed a small child resting against the shark tank. "That's him!" I said. I took off running as fast as I could. Park officials ran with me. I ran past Addison and the boys.

"Did you find him?"

I didn't answer. I just kept running. We got to the shark exhibit. A man grabbed a hold of me. I was still in motion and came to abrupt stop. I looked at him. "What?"

"You need to calm down, ma'am."

"Ken. My name is Ken."

"Ken, calm down. He appears to be fine."

"Please let me go. Please let me go in there."

He slowly let me go. I started to run again, and again the man stopped me. "Ken, you have to go in there slowly. Can you do that?"

"I don't know," I said. "I just want to go get my son. I want to hold him in my arms."

The overhead speaker came on: "THE PARK WILL BE CLOSING IN TEN MINUTES. THE PARK WILL BE CLOSING IN TEN MINUTES."

TJ woke up. "Mommy!" He jumped up. "Mommy! MOMMY!" He started to cry. "MOMMY!" He picked up his bag. He was whaling now. "MOMMY!"

The man let me go for the second time and I rushed into the entrance of the shark exhibit just as TJ was rushing to come out of it. He ran right into me. I stumbled backwards. The man caught me getting me steady on my feet. TJ jumped into my arms. "MOMMY!"

"It's ok now. I have you."

Trinity had seen it on the TV. She called Patrick. "Have you heard from your wife?"

"Yes, mother," he said. "She took the kids to Sea World."

"She's on the news. As is my grandson."

"What?"

"There has been a child missing in the park since three o'clock today. Obviously, it was your son."

"Mom, why do you look into things?"

"I'm telling you. They are on the news right now."

Patrick turned the TV on and sure enough, we were right there on his screen. Both of us with our heads buried in each other's shoulders. "See I told you," Trinity said. "And this is the person that you picked to be his mother."

"I'll call you back," he said. He hung up with her and called my cell phone. I didn't answer it. He called me again and again and again. I still didn't answer. He called Addison. She answered. "What the fuck is going on?" he asked.

"I can't talk right now," she said.

"Where are you staying?"

"The Hilton on International Drive."

We weren't allowed to leave the park. It closed for the night, yet we were still there. We were all taken into a room. TJ was taken by a lady in a room separate from me. I was told to take a seat. A woman and man came into the room.

"Can you tell us your name?"

"Kennedy Alexander."

"Mrs. Alexander," the woman said.

"Ken. I go by Ken."

"Ken, when you lost sight of the little boy, did you report it right away?"

"Yes, of course."

"About how long after he went missing did you report him missing?"

"A minute or two."

"Are you related to the boy?"

"Yes. TJ is my adopted son."

"Where is his father?"

"He's home working."

"Has your son eaten today?"

I lowered my head. "I don't know," I said. "Yes. We had breakfast at the hotel this morning before we left to come here, and we had lunch at one I think."

My phone rang again. "Can I answer this? It's my husband."

"No," the man said. "We aren't done questioning you. Why when you gave the description of your…" he did air quotes "son" "didn't you say that he was wearing a jacket and a hat?"

"Because he wasn't wearing them when we were together."

"Did he steal the jacket?"

"No. It's his jacket."

"Did he steal the hat?"

"No. I bought it for him before the whale show."

"So then why didn't you say he was wearing a Sea World hat?"

"Because he wasn't wearing it when we were watching the whale show."

"How long were you separated from your child today?" the man asked.

"From three thirty or so until nine fifty this evening."

"So, in the almost six hours that he was away from you, did you enjoy the park?" the man asked.

"What? No. Of course not. I was with park officials from the time I reported him missing until the woman from the park told me to come with her."

"Did your husband know that you were taking his son here," the woman asked.

"He's my son too. I adopted him. And yes. I told him we were coming here. Can I please go be with my son?"

"No," the woman said. "Did you have other children with you today?"

"Yes. My three nephews."

"And when you realized that your son was missing, you just abandoned them."

"No. They were with their mother."

"But you said that they were with you," the woman said.

"Yes. My sister-in-law and I brought the four boys here today. When TJ went missing, I left her with her boys."

"How old is your son?"

"He's five for another month."

"Do you know a Trinity Alexander?"

"Yes, of course. She is my mother-in-law. What does she have to do with this?"

"Ken, please stand up and put your hands behind your back."

"Excuse me? Are you arresting me?"

"I'm not going to tell you again to stand up and put your hands behind your back," the man said.

"Why I am being arrested?"

"For child neglect. Mrs. Trinity Alexander is pressing charges."

"What?"

The man came and yanked me out of the chair. Then he wrestled me to the ground. I couldn't believe what was happening to me. He had my hands behind my back and his knee pressing down into my back. He put handcuffs on me. The door opened behind us.

"Kennedy!" Patrick said.

I turned my face away from him.

"What are you doing with my wife?"

"Sir, Mrs. Trinity Alexander called us to inform us of child neglect."

"My wife is not neglecting our son. Please get her up and take the handcuffs off of her."

"Mrs. Alexander claims that Ken was traveling alone with four boys. If she was off looking for one all day long, then she neglected the safety and well-being of the other three children."

"My sister-in-law is with me," I said. I started to hyperventilate. "I...I...I can't breathe!" Hot tears dripped down my cheeks. "We were all brought here together. I don't know where she is now. I was brought in here."

"Please get her up and take the cuffs off of her," Patrick said again. The man did get me up, but he left the cuffs on me.

Meanwhile, Addison had left the park with Tyson, Carter, and Michael. She took them out for dinner thinking that I was taking TJ back to the hotel to have time with him. She had no idea that we were still in the park and that I was being interrogated and possibly arrested.

"Is Aunt Ken going to meet us?" Carter asked.

"I don't know. Let me call her and see where she is. She might have taken TJ back to the hotel."

"Is he going to be in trouble?" Tyson asked.

"No, honey. This was something that just happened today, but that is why you all have to know your surrounds and when you don't see us with you, you go to an adult from the park or get a police officer and tell them that you are lost."

"Do you think TJ knew to do that?" Michael asked.

"No, honey, he didn't. If he did, this would have been over a long time ago today."

She called my cell phone. I didn't answer it. I couldn't answer it.

"Where did you get the black eye from?" the woman asked me in alarm.

"I got hit by a baseball in the face when we were in The Keys," I said.

Patrick was taken out of the room. He was brought to where TJ was. TJ saw him and started to cry. "Where's mommy?"

"She's a little busy right now," Patrick said.

"Are you here to take me home?"

"No."

"Why are you here?"

"Because of what happened today. Want to tell me what happened?"

"We went for a five-mile bike ride this morning," he started. "We had breakfast at the hotel and then mommy and Aunt Addison brought us here. We saw the sea lions, the walrus, the penguins, and then we had lunch. Mommy bought me a hat. See," he said showing it to him. "Where is mommy?"

"Finish telling me about your day," Patrick aid.

"We went to the whale show. There were a lot of people," he said yawning. "Mommy told me to hold her hand and I was, but then I let it go and I got pushed into the shark place. There were still a lot of people. I thought mommy and everyone was with me, so I was watching the sharks. When I turned around, she wasn't there. I wasn't scared because I liked where I was. I was cold so I put on my jacket and my hat and put on my music. I thought I was only away from them for a few minutes, daddy. How long was I away from mommy and everyone, daddy?"

"Almost six hours, buddy," Patrick said.

"So is mommy in trouble?"

"I don't know yet, bud."

TJ started to cry. "Mommy is in trouble because I am a bad boy."

"No, TJ, you aren't a bad boy."

I am going to kill my mother. Patrick thought. *How dare she start this shit with Kenny.*

I was taken to the police station where I was put into a holding cell. In my whole life, I have never once been arrested. Tonight, for the first time ever, I was arrested.

Patrick called Trinity. "What the fuck did you do?"

"What?" she asked all innocent like. "Pat, it's late."

"I don't fucking give a shit that it is late. My wife was arrested because you called the Orlando police department and said that she neglected and endangered four children's lives. What is wrong with you?"

"I wanted to see my grandson," she said. "She's been gone a long time now with him."

"Drop the charges right now or you will never see him or me ever again."

Ivy had just arrived home. "Mom, it's late. Who are you on the phone with?"

"With Patrick," she said.

"Why? Is something wrong? Is he ok? Is Kenny and the kids ok?"

"Ken has been traveling alone with the boys and today she lost TJ. When she did that, she left the other three boys to fend for themselves."

"No. That's not true. Addison is with her and the boys. What did you do?"

"I called the Orlando police and reported her."

"My god, mom. She will be arrested," Ivy said.

"She's been arrested!" Patrick yelled.

"Mom call the police back and tell them you want to drop the charges," Ivy said.

"I want to see my grandson."

"MOM!" Patrick and Ivy said together.

"Patrick, I'll get Bruce and we will come there. See you soon."

Ivy went to Bruce's house. "Hi, we have to go to Orlando right now. My fucking mother had my sister-in-law arrested for child neglect. Will you please help her?"

"Yes, of course. Wait! When was there a wedding?"

"They got eloped, but they are going to have a wedding with family and friends. She legally adopted TJ."

Ivy and Bruce came to Orlando. Bruce dropped Ivy off at the hotel, where Addison was in a panic. It was well after midnight. Ivy found Addison and Patrick by the pool side.

"Bruce will get her out."

"Did mom drop the charges?"

"Yes."

"How long ago?"

"About a half hour ago."

I was still in a holding cell. I sat on the floor in the far corner because I was afraid that someone was going to come in and grab me again and put me in handcuffs. At the police station, I had been searched and treated like a criminal. I was cold because I was in shorts and a t-shirt.

"Ken!" I heard my name, but I couldn't focus. I was exhausted from the long day and so hungry. "Ken!" the man said again. "My name is Bruce. I am a friend of Patrick and Ivy." The cell door was opened. He came in. I cowered from him. "No, honey, I'm not going to hurt you. Come on." I couldn't move any further away from him right now. "I'm going to lift you up. Can I lift you up?" He squatted down in front of me. "I promise you; I'm not going to hurt you." I was shivering. He turned to the guard behind him. "Can I have a blanket to put around her?"

"Yes, sir."

"Why is she sitting on this ice-cold floor?"

"Sir, I had to do my job," the woman officer said.

He turned back to look at the woman officer. "So, what did you do to her?"

"She had to be searched."

"For what? What could she possibly have on her person?"

I was still cowering from him. He put his hand on my shoulder and I started to scream. "No. No. I swear I'm not going to hurt you. Kenny, I'm a friend of Patrick and Ivy. I'm going to bring you to Patrick and TJ." The guard came back with the blanket. Bruce opened the blanket draping it over my shoulders. I pulled it around me and when I did, Bruce lifted me into his arms. I put my head on his shoulder and everything went black.

When I woke up, Patrick, Addison, Ivy and Bruce were standing around the bed. For a second, I didn't know where I was. "It's ok," I heard Patrick say. "Are you ok?"

"Where is TJ?"

"He's sleeping in the next room."

I got up from the bed. I went into the adjoining room going over to where TJ was sleeping. I climbed in bed with him taking him in my arms and fell back to sleep.

In the morning, I was quiet. There was a knock on the door. Addison opened the door to find someone from Sea World standing out there. Addison let the man in. Patrick, Ivy, and Bruce took the kids for breakfast.

"I'm here to present Mrs. Kennedy Alexander with free passes to Sea World. And I also wanted to let you know how deeply sorry I am for the way you were treated last night," he said to me. "We honestly didn't know anything like that was going to happen. I do hope that you weren't hurt last night. And I also do hope that you and your family will come back to our establishment"

He left the room.

"How are you?" Addison asked.

"I'm fucking pissed," I said. "My mother-in-law had me arrested last night. I was fucking strip searched. I was pulled out of a fucking chair and wrestled to the ground with a guy holding me down with his knee in my back. I was handcuffed and treated like a fucking criminal.

"I shouldn't have married Patrick," I said.

They came back from breakfast. TJ was lethargic when they came back in the room.

"What happened?" I asked.

"We were talking," Patrick said. "I told him that I was thinking of taking him home."

"But our trip isn't over yet," I said. I got up from the chair I was sitting in. "Can I talk to you outside please?" Patrick and I walked out of the room. With tears in my eyes, I said to him, "Please don't take him home. Yesterday was just something that happened. And I know that I probably don't have a say in this, but I don't want him around your mother right now. If you take him home, he's going to blame himself. Patrick, please don't punish him or me by doing that. It was a mistake. I love you and him so much."

"Fine," he said. "I love you too. Are you going to be ok?"

"Yes. We are going to be fine."

"That's not what I asked. I asked if you are going to be ok."

"It's a lot to take in that my mother-in-law doesn't like me, and she doesn't think that I'm good enough for you or to be TJ's mother."

"What?"

"I heard her say it last night when she called to drop the neglect charges. She was on speaker. She told the captain that she called in with concerns because she doesn't like me and I'm not good enough to be your wife or your son's mother."

"I didn't know about that."

"I know you didn't," I said to him. "I will recover from this, but if you take TJ home now, he may not recover from this. And that would crush me."

"That would crush me too," he said.

Bruce and Ivy came out of the room. "Sorry to interrupt, but we have to get going," Ivy said.

"Thank you for everything," I said. I hugged Ivy. "When we get back, you and I will have to go for coffee or lunch or something."

"I'd like that," she said.

"Thank you, Bruce, for getting me out of there. It was nice meeting you."

"Nice meeting you as well. Sorry it had to be under these circumstances."

"Yeah," I said. "All is well now."

"I'm going to go home, and bitch slap my mother," Ivy said.

I smiled and laughed. "See you soon."

We went back in the room. My three nephews were playing on their I-pads for the first time in weeks. TJ was sitting by himself almost in the corner. I walked up to him. "Hey, buddy," I said. His shoulders shook from him crying. "TJ, please look at me," I said.

"I'M SO SORRY, MOMMY!" he cried. "Please don't be mad at me."

"Mad at you! TJ, I'm not mad at you. I was so scared yesterday when I couldn't find you. But honey that was a misunderstanding and misunderstandings happen sometimes. I'm so proud of you."

"You are?" he cried. "For what?"

"Because you didn't freak out yesterday. You stayed right where you were. It just took a long time to spot you with all those people around. But you didn't do anything wrong."

There was knock on the door. A woman in a business suit came into the room. "I need to talk to Kennedy Alexander."

"Yes, that's me," I said.

"Mrs. Alexander, could you please come with me to the lobby?"

"Yes, ma'am," I said. I kissed TJ on the head. "I'll be right back. I promise."

I got up and went with the woman to the lobby, where I was taken into a conference room. Another woman in a business suit and a man in a suit were in the room. The man started. "Will you please sit down," he said. I sat without speaking. "We were made aware of what occurred yesterday with you and your son and with the fiasco that occurred as well. On behalf of the Hilton, we'd like to pay for your stay here now and also give you a full paid trip to any Hilton of your choice for you and your family."

"Thank you so much."

"Are you ok?"

"Yes, sir, I am."

"Is your son ok?"

"He's working on it, "I said honestly.

"We heard that you will be going to Cape Canaveral when you leave here."

"Yes, sir," I said.

"Consider your accommodations completely paid for."

"Sir, I don't know what to say. That is so kind of you. Thank you again."

My cell phone buzzed as I walked back to the room. I looked at it. It was mom and dad. "Hello."

"Oh my god is everything ok?"

"Yeah," I said.

"I can't believe she had you arrested," mom said. "That bitch! And she is supposed to be my friend. Why did she do it?"

"I lost TJ for almost six hours yesterday. She thought I was alone with all of the boys and that I was neglectful to all of them."

"Are you ok?" dad asked.

"I'm getting there," I said to him.

"Is TJ ok?"

"He too is getting there."

"We will be at the house when you get there."

"We won't be home till the beginning of next week."

"That's ok. Whenever you get there, we will be there."

"Thank you, mom and dad."

I made it back to the room and hung up with mom and dad just before walking in.

"Oh, good you are back," Patrick said. "I have to go back for work. Are you sure that you are ok?"

"Yes, honey, I'm fine."

"TJ, you take care of mommy for me ok."

"I will daddy," he said with that bright smile.

"I'm going to go strangle my mother," Patrick said. Patrick kissed me goodbye. I kissed him too.

"Ewe!" Tyson and TJ said together. I turned and kissed Tyson first because he was closest. "Oh, mommy, make her stop," he said.

"Nope. You brought this upon yourself. TJ, let's go walk daddy to his truck."

"Ok, mommy," he said.

We walked Patrick to his truck. While we were in the lobby, I saw the newspaper. There were pictures of me laying cuffed on the floor with the guy's knee in my back, there were pictures of police putting me in the patrol car. MOTHER CHARGED OF NEGLECT AFTER LOSING HER SON IN SEA WORLD

"That explains a lot," I said.

"What's that?" Patrick asked. He looked at me holding the paper. "No, put that down."

"My parents saw this. They will be at the house sometime this week."

"That's ok. I love your parents."

"Too bad it's not precipitated by your mother."

"I'm so sorry about that."

"It's ok," I said. "We will deal with things next week when I get back with the kids. I love you."

"Love you, daddy."

"I love you too, buddy. And I love you, wife," he said to me. "My Kenny," he said kissing me again.

He stepped up into the truck. We waved him goodbye. Then we walked back in the hotel. I scooped TJ up. "Today, when we go out, I'm getting a harness for you."

"Aunt Addy beat you to it. She got one for me and one for Tyson and she told us both that we would have to wear them today. He wandered off too, but he wasn't gone as long as me."

"We need to talk about something."

I sat him down at a table by the pool. "If there is ever a time again that we get separated, you are to go to an adult that works in the park or find a policeman or police woman and tell them that you lost your mommy or that you are lost, so that what happened yesterday won't ever happen again.

"But like I said before, I am very proud of you for yesterday. You handled yourself pretty damn well. Now promise me that you will go and tell someone that you are lost if something like that ever happens again."

"I promise you, mommy."

We went back to the room. "Boys, you have five more minutes on those I-pads and then we are going to go have another fun filled day."

They put their I-pads away immediately. "What's the plan?" Michael asked.

"Well, I was presented with free passes for Sea World, so we are going back there. Get ready. And today the color is red. We will all be in a red shirt. I want everyone ready to go within the next fifteen minutes."

They went and got ready. I walked over to Addison. "So, what's this I hear that you lost Tyson yesterday."

"Oh, my god. Yeah. I did. He was only gone for five minutes, but I was in such a fucking panic. After we found him, I went into one of the gift shops and I bought him and TJ a harness. Tyson wore his for the rest of day yesterday.

"I am so sorry that all of that happened yesterday and last night. Why were you strip searched?"

"Because the bitch of a mother-in-law that I have told the police that I had paraphernalia on my person."

"She's a cold-hearted snake."

"That she is."

We took the kids back to Sea World. We were able to go into Aquatica as well. We went on everything. We did all the rides. We saw all the attractions. We had a wonderful time. TJ rarely let go of my hand all day long. If he did, he was reaching for my pocket. As the day wore on, we let the kids pick their favorite things to do for the rest of the evening. Thought it wasn't the Fourth of July, we knew we were going to be in the park watching fireworks. The fireworks had gone off last night just as I was hugging TJ last night when he was found. Tyson and TJ were both getting tired. Michael picked Tyson up. Seeing Tyson wrapped around Michael like that made Addison and I see that Michael had a growth spurt. I put TJ on my shoulders as we walked around.

Two park officials came over to me. "Mrs. Alexander, could you please come with us?" the taller one said.

I was slightly nervous.

"Mrs. Jackson, could you please come with us as well?"

Addison and I exchanged glances and then we went with the two officials. They brought us into one of their gift shops. "The four children can pick whatever they want and it's on us," one of them said. "That also goes for the two of you as well. Whatever you like, is yours. We are terribly sorry for the occurrence yesterday."

"Are you folks staying for the fireworks?"

"Yes," Addison and I said together.

"When you are done here, we will escort you to the best spot to watch the fireworks in the park."

"Thank you," I said.

TJ came over with a stuffed orca, a blanket, and a backpack. "Mommy, can I have these?"

The one official bent down next to him. "Why don't we go fill that awesome looking backpack," he said to him. He took TJ by the hand and they filled the backpack with notebooks, pencils, crayons, folders, and toys. The man measured TJ for a t-shirt and a sweatshirt.

Three other store employees met with the boys and did the same with them.

"Do you see anything that you like?" a woman asked me.

"I like the birthstone necklace," I said. "I like the one with the animal charms."

"How many is your family?"

"There are three of us. My birthday is September. My husband's is in May, and our son's birthday is in August."

Addison was looking at the necklaces as well. She too got one. She also got a bracelet for each of the girls.

When we were done, we were taken to a platform area to see the fireworks. We were the only ones there with the park officials. When the fireworks started TJ jumped and screamed. I picked him up in my arms and just held on to him while we watched them.

"I'm sorry about yesterday," he whispered in my ear. I looked at him. "What?"

"I'm sorry about yesterday, mommy."

I hugged him tight to me. "Please let it go, Turner."

"You are mad at me."

"NO! No, TJ, I'm not mad at you. I wasn't mad at you yesterday when it happened and I'm not mad at you today. I was scared yesterday, but I wasn't mad at you."

"I love you, mommy."

"I love you too."

CHAPTER SIXTEEN

The next day, we left for Daytona. When we arrived at the hotel, we were met by the manager, who told us that our stay was free. He then picked up TJ and hugged him. "Glad to see you are safe, my boy."

"Thank you," TJ said.

"We upgraded your room," he said. "Your room isn't quite ready yet, so we would love for you to enjoy a meal on us."

"No, this is way too much," I protested.

"Not at all, ma'am," the manager said. "Please accept this gift."

"Thank you so much," I said.

We went to the restaurant. We were given menus, but I don't understand why, for drinks and appetizers kept flowing. Then the chef's special was brought out to us. When we were done eating, desserts were brought out to us. The manager appeared. "Your room is ready," he said. "Please come with me." He picked Tyson up carrying him to the elevator. We went up to the penthouse. The manager opened the door for us. Just standing out in the hallway, I was blown away with this room. There were flowers galore around the entire room. The manager walked into the room where he put Tyson down.

"Wow!" the four boys said.

"This is our room?"

"Yes, Michael," the manager answered him. "This is your room for your whole stay."

"Wow!" he said again.

"Please enjoy your stay. If you need anything don't hesitate to ask. Your things have been brought up for you already. The bikes are downstairs waiting for you."

"Thank you so much, Jeffrey," I said trying to hand him a tip.

"No. No. Your money isn't good here," he said. "Enjoy."

After he left, I looked at Addison. "Did I miss something?"

"Yeah, girly, you sure did."

"What? What did I miss?"

"You are loved everywhere you go, Ken. People have taken notice of you with these kids. And then in one instant things changed, but that doesn't change the way people view you."

I sat down on the oversized fluffy chair.

"Your love for TJ bursts out of you," Addison said. "You're like a mother holding her newborn baby for the first time, but with you, he's a five almost six-year-old boy. But you beam when you are around him."

"Well, I love him," I said.

"That is above abundantly clear, Kennedy."

"Mommy!" Tyson said. Addison looked at him. "Can we go swimming?"

"Sure," she said.

"Yay!" he said.

We went downstairs with the boys. TJ didn't go in the pool right away. He looked like he wanted something. I went to him. "Hey, what are you doing?"

"Could we go to the drug store?"

"Why do you want to go there?"

"I just want to see something. Can we go?"

"Yeah," I said. I told Addison I was taking him to the CVS, which was on the next block. We walked there. When we went in, he went to the cards. I followed him to keep him in sight. I watched him pick up one and read it and then put it back. He did this repeatedly for five or six cards. "TJ, what are you looking for?"

"A thank you card."

"For who, baby?"

"For you."

"TJ, you don't have to give me a card."

He started to cry. I scooped him up in my arms. He was sobbing crying. I walked out of the store and back to the hotel with him in my arms. I took him up to the room.

"Grandma wants to take me away from you and daddy."

"What?"

"She does."

"How do you know that?"

"I read it on your phone."

"What? Where?"

He took my phone and found the message, which was now marked as read. I read the message. She wrote: *Kennedy when you return home, you and my son will lose Turner James forever. I will be taking full custody of him when you return and neither you nor my son will ever see him again. Enjoy your time with him, for it will be your last.* I closed the message and called Patrick. "Hi, sweetheart," he said. "How is everything?"

"It was going well until TJ saw a message on my phone from your mother."

"What? What does it say?"

"For me to enjoy my time with him because when we get back, she is getting custody of TJ and you and I will never see him again."

"Are you fucking kidding me?"

"No. No, I'm not. I'm forwarding you the message right now."

I heard the clap of thunder before I saw the lightning strike. Within ten minutes, Addison came in the room with the three boys. "DID YOU SEE THAT LIGHTNING?" Carter asked.

"No, but we heard the thunder."

"The lightning was so thick, Aunt Kenny."

"I believe you."

"Did something happen?" Addison asked.

"My mother-in-law sent me this message," I said handing her my phone.

"What? Did TJ see it?"

"He did," I said pointing to him crouched in the corner.

"Did you call, Patrick?"

"Yes."

"What is he doing about this?"

"I don't know yet."

"Is he taking this serious?"

"Yes, of course."

Michael went over to TJ and put his arm around him. "What are you doing in the corner?"

"It's safe here."

"Safe from what?"

"My grandma."

"She's not here, TJ," Michael said.

"She's going to take me away from mommy and daddy."

"What? Are you kidding me?"

"No. She sent mommy a text message."

"TJ, do you think that your mommy is ever going to let that happen?"

"No, but grandma can be mean."

"You do know that your mommy is a superhero, right?"

"What? She is?"

"Sure, she is," he said. "She's the best kind of superhero too."

"Really? How?"

"Because wherever she is everyone is safe. But she doesn't let people know that she has secret powers, but she does. See every time she takes you in her arms and hugs you, she is adding another layer of protection on you.

"Although we got separated the other day in Sea World, you were safe and protected from harm because she hugged you just before you were separated from us."

TJ listened to every word that Michael told him. The five-year-old believed every word he said too. "Ask Carter and Tyson. They will tell you. Ty! Come here. Carter, come here," Michael said to them. They came over. "Tell TJ that his mommy is a superhero."

"Oh, she is," Tyson said. Not even hearing the story that Michael had just made up to TJ, Tyson said, "When she hugs you, she puts a bubble around you, so you are safe."

"See. What did I tell you?"

"It's true," Carter chimed in. "She came to the school and hugged me, and I was protected from my mean teacher. She's a true superhero."

TJ looked over at me.

"You will be extra strong because of all the hugs that she has given you," Michael said. "But TJ, you can't tell anyone about this. You have to keep it a secret."

"I will," he said. He stood up and came over to me. I took him in my arms. He snuggled into me. "Why don't we watch a movie on this rainy night," I said.

TJ sat cupped in my arms while we watched the movie. I played with his brown hair. Occasionally, I kissed him on the forehead.

"Extra protection," Carter said.

"What, Carter?" Addison said.

"Oh, nothing mommy," he said.

The next day, we went for a long bike ride. TJ though he stayed with the group, he stayed off a little ways from us all. When we went on the beach to swim later that day, he did the same thing.

"Is he withdrawing from me?" I asked Addison.

"No, I don't think so."

"Can we go back to the lighthouse and show mommy the top?" Tyson asked.

"Sure," I said.

"Can we go today?"

"Well, it's getting late today, but we can go in the morning," I said. "It's nicer in the morning when there aren't a lot of people there."

"Ok," Tyson said.

"When are we going to the Space Center?"

"In two days," I said to Addison.

When we were done swimming and sunbathing for the day, we went into the hotel and into the arcade. We all played video games, did the basketball toss, played skee ball, and air hockey.

"Can we do the miniature golf game?" Carter asked.

"Yes," Addison said.

We all went and did that. Addison and I had a good laugh watching the kids when they first tried to hit the ball with the clubs. Addison showed Michael and Carter how to do it. The other two just kept on doing what they were doing. Surprisingly, Tyson was the first one to hit a hole in one. After that Michael hit one and then Carter did too. TJ was still having fun hitting his ball off everything. And then the last hole, he did it. He hit a hole in one. He came running to me bouncing up in my arms. I squished him in hugs. He giggled. I placed him on my shoulders.

"What's next?" he asked from his perch.

"A bath and bed," I said.

"But mommy the sun is still out."

"Oh, so what are you saying?"

"It's way too early for bed time, mommy."

"Oh, ok."

I reached up and pulled him around me. Cradling him like a baby, I kissed him a few times.

"Can I have a hug or two?"

"Sure, pumpkin."

"Oh, my god, we are going to have the best Halloween this year, mommy," he said.

"Oh, are we?"

"Yes, mommy. Can we make a haunted house?"

"It's something to think about. What do you and daddy usually do?"

"We go to the monster's house."

"Who is the monster?" Addison asked.

"My scary grandma."

I couldn't control myself, I laughed. I shouldn't have, but I did. "Why is she scary and a monster?"

"Because she wants to take me away from you and daddy."

"Ok, let's not worry about that. And your grandmother isn't a monster."

"But she is, mommy."

"Why is she?"

"Because she has the witch's wort on her face."

I laughed again. "What on earth are you talking about?"

"Mommy, you haven't noticed it. It's a big scary wort right under her left eye. That's the witch's eye."

I laughed yet again. Maybe I shouldn't encourage this kind of talk, but it was priceless listening to him talk about Trinity.

"And what the hell kind of name is Trinity?"

"Turner!"

"No, really."

"It's her name."

"What are you going to call her?"

Fucking bitch.

"Um. I don't know you yet."

"What is she to you?"

"Well, because she is your dad's mother that makes me her daughter-in-law."

He left it at that. We moved back to the Halloween conversation and haunted houses, and what he may want to be.

"We have to decide pretty quick," he said.

"Why?"

"Because we have to get it first before it's no longer around."

"TJ, its July. We have plenty of time before Halloween."

"Oh, what about Christmas? Do you believe in Santa Claus?"

"Yes, of course I do," I said. "Do you?"

"Yeah," he said.

"Tell me. How do you and daddy celebrate Christmas?"

"We get a gigantic tree. We load it up with lights and ornaments. Then Santa brings tons and tons of presents."

I laughed and smiled at his description. "What about the Easter Bunny?"

"Oh, he's stupid!"

"What?" I asked laughing. Addison started to laugh too.

"Who is stupid?"

"The Easter Bunny," TJ said.

"Yes, agreed," said Carter.

"What? Since when? You love the Easter Bunny."

"Mommy," Tyson said. "The damn thing bit me."

"What?" We were both smiling and laughing as we listened to this bizarre story.

"Mommy, I was afraid of getting the bunny sickness."

"Disease," Michael said.

"Don't encourage this," Addison said to him.

"Mommy, I'm eleven and that thing was scary."

"Where did your father take you?"

"To the mall," Carter chimed in. "He had fangs, mommy."

"Guys, bunnies have big teeth."

"Fangs, mommy."

"Like a vampire," Michael said. "Ask Katie. She ran away screaming."

"Oh, I have to ask Kate right now," Addison said.

Michael pulled out his phone and called his sister. "Hey, where are you now?"

"Home. We got home yesterday."

"Welcome home," he said.

"Where are you all at?"

"In Daytona for a few more days. Hey, do you remember the Easter Bunny?"

"MICHAEL! I'll have nightmares."

"Wait tell mommy. Hold on. Love you."

"I love you too."

Michael handed Addison his phone. "Hi, sweetheart."

"Hi, mommy."

"So, your brothers were telling me about the Easter Bunny at the mall that your father took you to see."

"It bit Tyson. The thing had fangs, mommy."

Michael overhearing his sister said, "See. Told you, mommy."

"Go. So, I can talk to your sister."

Addison spoke to Kate briefly because for the first time all summer, Tyson and Carter started fighting. It started off innocent with just pushing each other and then slaps followed and then they went big time punching each other.

"What the hell is going on?" Addison said seconds after hanging up the phone. Carter was sitting on Tyson. "Get off your brother."

"He bit me like the Easter Bunny."

"Stop it. This is ridiculous," Addison said. "Carter get off of your brother."

Tyson is four and small, but he's strong. He flipped Carter off of him. Then he pounced on top of him and sunk his teeth into Carter's shoulder.

"TYSON!" Addison yelled. I came back in the room. "Where the hell were you?"

"What?" I asked. "We needed ice." I looked at boys. "Hey! Are you fighting? Do you want to go home before this trip is over?"

The boys separated.

"Timeouts begin now," I said. "Pick your spots and stay there for the eight minutes, in which you should know better than to pick on a four-year-old."

"He bit me twice."

"He wouldn't stop teasing me about the damn Easter Bunny."

"Listen, both of you. All four of you. The Easter Bunny in the mall…"

"Daddy took you guys to see the wrong bunny," Addison interrupted. "He feels really bad about that. It won't happen again. The Easter Bunny isn't a vampire. Now timeouts for both of you."

"Yes, mommy," they both said.

"You almost told our kids that there is no Easter Bunny."

"I know. Thank you for catching me."

"Sure. Don't mention it."

"Where on earth did Parker take the kids?"

"He took them to the strip mall, where there were freaky bunnies. I could stab him," she laughed. We both laughed.

"And five. Four. Three. Two. One."

"I'm hungry."

Addison looked at me. "How did you know that was coming?" I looked at the clock as did Addison. "Oh, I see," she said.

"Hey, guys, you have five minutes to get ready for dinner," I said. "And doing it nicely."

The boys got ready. I changed as well. Upon seeing what I was wearing, Addison changed too.

"It's over five minutes," Carter said. "Mommy's on timeout."

"After dinner," I said.

"Really, Kenny?"

"Oh, yeah. And why does it stand?"

"Because you didn't follow Aunt Kenny's directions," Tyson said.

"But I'm older."

"We know," the three boys said.

TJ laughed at them.

"Come let's go, children," I said. "Addy that goes for you too."

"You just wait, girly."

"Owe, I'm shaking."

The four boys laughed.

"Do we have to call daddy?" Michael asked.

And Addison and I burst out laughing.

We continued the fun and laughter in the elevator. As the doors opened on the first floor, we all gained our composure before stepping out of the elevator. We went into the restaurant at the hotel and then changed our minds and decided to go out for dinner. We went to a nice restaurant right on the beach. We choose a table outside. There was a pleasant summer breeze. TJ went and stuck his toes in the sand. He turned back to face us with a wide grin.

"I love him so much," I said.

"Mommy, can I go in the ocean?"

"No. Not now. We are going to have dinner soon."

"Can I just put my toes in the water?"

"Not right now."

He came back over and sat on my lap. He leaned against me. Within a minute's time, he was sound asleep. Tyson had climbed in the chair with Michael and he too was sleeping.

"Two down," I said.

Michael took Tyson on his lap. He let Tyson snuggle into him. "Mommy, I can't believe he is starting school this fall."

"I know."

"I think you and daddy should have another baby."

"Well, that my boy isn't happening."

"Why not?"

"We will discuss it another time."

"Sure, mom," Michael said.

"Can I eat Ty's chicken nuggets?" Carter asked.

"Yes."

"Can I eat his grilled cheese sandwich?" Michael asked.

"Yes."

We ate dinner and then went back to the hotel. I put TJ to bed. Michael kept Tyson with him. "What's on your mind?" Addison asked.

"I'm starting middle school. Who's going to be there to walk him to class?"

"Kate and Carter will be there, baby."

"But I won't be there, mommy."

"Michael, its ok. The middle school is right next door to the elementary school. Middle school starts a half hour later than the elementary school. You can walk your brothers and sister to class if you want."

"I really miss Kate."

Just then there was a knock on the door. I opened it to find Parker and the two girls. I hugged my brother first, then Kate and finally Beth. They came into the room. Carter ran to Kate and hugged her. She hugged him back. Then she moved to where Michael was.

"Hi," she said.

"Hi." They hugged each other. "I missed you."

"I know. I've missed you too," she said. Kate kissed Tyson on the cheek.

"Wow! We are all finally back together," Carter said. "Hi, daddy."

"Hi, bud," Parker said picking him up to give him a hug. "Where's your little guy?"

"Sleeping," I said pointing to the bed.

"Has he been out long?"

"For about two hours now."

"Will he sleep all night?"

"No."

"How is that going with him?"

"It's wonderful," I said.

"Where's Patrick?"

"He's finishing a project in Georgia this week."

"You know mom and dad are at the house?"

"I do know that."

"Is everything ok?"

"It's getting there."

"What's going on?"

"His grandma threatened to take him away," Carter said.

"What?" Parker said. "Carter!"

"No, it's true," Addison and I said together.

"Why?"

"Let's move this conversation away from small ears," Addison said to

Parker. "Michael, you are in charge. We are going to be downstairs. If you need us, call my cell phone."

"Ok, mommy."

"Why don't you put on a movie," Parker said. He got them situated with a movie and then we adults went downstairs. "So, what's going on?" Parker asked.

"I lost him in Sea World," I said. "One second he's there holding my hand and the next he was gone. It took six hours to find him. Trinity called Patrick and told him it was on the news, which it was. Then she called the local police here and reported that I neglected four boys. I was arrested. She has sent threatening text messages saying that when we return, Patrick and I will never see him again."

"Do you believe her?"

"No," I said. "She will have to fight us damn hard to get him. Patrick is a great father."

"And what about you?"

"I'm new to the parent thing," I said.

"Yes, but you do it so well."

CHAPTER SEVENTEEN

Just as the three of us adults were getting ready for bed, TJ woke up and he was starving. I went into the bathroom and changed my clothes. Afterwards, I took him in his pajamas downstairs to see about getting something to eat. It was then that I wished I would have ordered him another grilled cheese sandwich. The hotel bar and restaurant were still up and running. I took a menu and then sat with TJ to see what he wanted. I looked at him. He was taller now by at least an inch. His grey eyes sparkled in the dim light.

"I want a philly cheese steak sandwich."

A man walking by, who worked in the restaurant and bar heard him say that.

"Would you like French fries with that as well?"

"Yes, please."

"And ma'am, can I get you anything?"

"I'll have a cup of your French onion soup please."

"Would you like it to go?"

"Yes, thank you," I said.

"Those are cool pajamas," he said to TJ.

"They come in adult sizes too. My daddy has a matching pair."

"Well, then I'll have to look into those," he said with a smile. "Your food will be right up."

We waited in the lobby. "What are we doing tomorrow, mommy?"

"We are going to have a fun filled day."

"Around here?"

"No, we are going somewhere special."

"To the lighthouse?"

"No. Even more special."

"Back to the garden tower?"

"No."

"I liked it there."

"I know you did."

"Maybe we can take daddy there."

"Yes, I think we can arrange to take daddy there."

"Are we going to the planetarium?"

"Nope."

"Are we going to the beach?"

"No. Stop guessing because I'm not going to tell you."

"I miss daddy."

"We will see him in two days."

"Am I going to have to go live with grandma?"

"No."

"Are you in trouble?"

"Turner stop worrying please. I'm not in trouble. I didn't do anything wrong."

"Grandma smokes."

"I know she does."

"No not cigarettes."

"How do you know that word?"

"I've been around," he said. I couldn't help but laugh. "She smokes chocolate things."

"TJ, stop. We will have this discussion upstairs."

"Can I go watch the cartoons?"

"Sure," I said. I moved with him. He sat on my lap watching Bugs Bunny as we waited for our food.

Ten minutes later, our food was brought to us. I paid for it and then we went upstairs. So, we wouldn't wake anyone, we sat outside on the balcony. We could hear the roar of the waves and thunder in the distance. He ate more than half of his sandwich plus he ate all of his fries. Of course, the five year old that he is had to play with every single one of them before he ate them. I ate my soup and then finished his sandwich. After we were done, we went back in the room. I went into the bathroom and changed into my pajamas. When I came out, I scooped TJ up in my arms and carried him to our bed. I put him down on the bed and then pulled the blankets down. He climbed to the top of the bed. Dove headfirst onto three pillows and to my surprise was back to sleep before I even turned the lights off. I fixed him putting him in a more comfortable position and then I got into bed. I covered the two of us, rolled on my side facing TJ and fell asleep.

In the morning, we woke up at seven. TJ and I had only slept about five hours. Well, I had only slept about five hours. We all got ready for the day. "Are we checking out?" Addison asked.

"No. We have the room until tomorrow."

"Oh, great," she said.

We went from being a party of six to now being a party of nine. I wondered how we were going to do driving arrangements and then it dawned on me that Addison and kids would ride with Parker and TJ and I would be on our own. When we went downstairs, we had breakfast first and then we went to the cars.

"I want to ride with daddy!" the three boys said together.

"Me too," said the girls.

"Ok, I'll ride with Aunt Kenny and TJ."

"But mommy we want you to ride with us too," Carter said.

"Go ahead," I said to her. "It's alright."

"Are you sure?"

"Yes, of course. It's fine."

I put TJ in the car before climbing in. He and I sang in the car. The almost hour drive south on I-95, I made fun and entertaining for him. Just as we were pulling into the Space Center, TJ said, "So I guess we are getting left out today."

"Oh, honey, don't say that."

"They dumped us like hot potatoes to go with Uncle Parker."

"I know it looks that way, but it won't be that way when we go inside."

My heart had sunk by his expression. He wasn't yet six, yet he's extremely intelligent.

"Listen. I promise you that no matter what happens today, we are going to have a specular time. Do you believe me?"

"YES!"

"Good. Now come on. Let's go join the group."

We went to the ticket window to add on three more extra tickets. TJ was standing in front of me leaning against me. I looked over to see Storm snapping pictures. When she was done, I waved to her. She came rushing over, lifted TJ for a giant hug and kiss and then she hugged me.

"How are you?"

"Fine. How are you? Where have you been?"

"I've been around," she said. "In the shadows," she smiled. "I'd like you to meet my friend, Claudia. Claudia, this is my best friend Patrick's wife, Kennedy, but she goes by Ken."

"I've heard a lot about you. It's nice to meet you."

"Nice meeting you too."

"Hi, Aunt Claudia."

"Hi, Turner James," she said picking him up to hug him.

"This is my mommy."

"I know," she said to him. "My god, it's so good to see this child smile like that. I didn't know you had so many teeth in your mouth. Let me see those choppers." TJ smiled at her. "Any loose ones yet?"

"Nope."

"Well, your mom or dad will have to bring you to see me when that changes."

"Aunt Claudia is a dentist."

"I kinda figured that."

"Hey, wait. You know Parker and Addison," Claudia said to me.

I laughed. Parker turned around. "Claudia! How are you? This is my sister Kenny and her son, TJ."

"I know TJ," she said. "I didn't know you had a sister."

"I have two sisters. Kenny and Jamie. They are twins."

"Wow, it's a small world."

"Mommy, are there dinosaurs here?"

I laughed again. "No, baby, we are at the Space Center."

The words just crossed his mind and he became scared. "Like a black hole? Like that kind of space?" He started to cry. I bent down and took him in my arms.

"TJ, I promise you that you that we are going to have the best day."

"But grandma said," he kept saying over and over.

"What, honey? What did grandma say?"

"That that's where my mom is."

I wanted to slap Trinity. She may not have liked Renee, and I know that she doesn't like me, but to scare her grandson by saying such cruel things to him at this young and impressionable age.

"TJ, you know that Renee is in California. That's not a black hole. It's just across the country, baby. And I'm not in a black hole; I'm not going in a black hole now or ever. Grandma just says words, baby. That's all. It's ok."

He stopped crying. Carter came over and squeezed him in a hug. "You're going to love this place. Aunt Kenny brought me here for a field trip. It's so much fun."

We finally went inside. TJ gripped my hand. His palm was sweaty and sticky. I put my other hand around his shoulders.

Beth was nervous. She clung to Addison's leg. Tyson had big eyes as he tried to take everything in all at once. Carter looked like he just stepped into his house and was welcomed with open arms. Kate and Michael got a map to see what we should do first.

"The Space launch," they said together.

"Yeah, because that takes the longest," Carter said.

Michael sunk his arm around Carter's shoulders. He took Tyson by the hand. We all walked together to the bus to take us out to the launch pad. It was a warm sunny day with not a cloud in the sky, which made it even that much more hotter. The tour was the same as it was on the field trip, but now having almost everyone in my family together, it was quite the experience. Everyone was happy with smiling faces. I didn't have to worry about losing sight of TJ, for he was glued tight to me.

"Why are your hands sticky?" I asked him.

He laughed. Just as Addison asked Tyson and Carter the same thing. The boys were laughing.

"We had licorice."

"Where did you get that?"

"From daddy," Tyson and Carter said.

We made it out to the launch pad, and we were given the full tour. Carter was in his glory. His young eight-year-old self could barely contain himself. He was happy and grateful to be back here. Beth had fallen asleep in Parker's arms. Kate wasn't the slightest bit interested. Michael was enjoying himself, but nothing like Carter. Tyson liked it, but lost interest in it as well. And TJ couldn't wait to try the flight simulator.

"Mommy, I could do this when I'm older," he said.

"Yes, you could."

Carter was filled with excitement just as he was when I brought him for his field trip. He had remembered just about everything from that first tour. They were picking kids to sit in the seats. Carter had wanted to do it so bad when we were here for his field trip, but he wasn't picked. Now he was just about jumping up and down.

"I remember you," a woman in a flight suit said. "Come this way," she said to him. "And you," she said to TJ. TJ and Carter went up together. They were put into the seats and the rocket started to shake as if it were ready for takeoff.

"Thank you so much," Carter said as they were brought out of it.

TJ's face was precious. "Thank you, ma'am," he said. "That was totally awesome." He came racing to me and bounced up in my arms. "What's next?"

"All the inside stuff. You'll see," I said.

We went back on the bus to the main building, where there were tons of things to do.

"Is there music in space?" Kate asked.

Carter chimed in, "When the Apollo 10 Mission went up there were two spaceships that went up that mission and the astronauts said that they heard music and whistling on the far side of the moon."

An employee at the Space Center looked at him. "Where did you hear that?"

"I read it," Carter said. "The rocket was called Snoopy and the pilot's nick name was Charlie Brown."

I looked at Carter with a smile. "That's my third-grade genius."

"But it wasn't music. It was feedback between the two radios."

Beth woke up. She's adorable. She looked around. "Oh, we are still here," she said and put her head back down on Parker's shoulder and closed her eyes again.

We spent the whole day there. When we were leaving to go back, Carter and Michael came with TJ and I. Parker and Addison took Kate, Tyson and Beth. Beth, who was now wide awake, for she slept most of the day. The boys never stopped talking the whole ride back to Daytona. Just before we were pulling off the exit, Michael asked, "Are we going home tomorrow?"

"Yes," I answered him.

"Are we still going to stay with you?"

"No, sweetheart. Your dad is back now, so he will be with all of you."

"So that's it."

"What's it?"

"So, we aren't going to see you for the rest of the summer?"

"Michael, I'll still see you every day. We just won't be together at night."

"But how are we going to see you every day?"

"Because you and your brothers made a deal with me before this trip started remember?"

"I remember," Carter said.

"Go ahead and remind your brother."

"Aunt Kenny said that she would take us on an adventure if we promised when we got back from the trip that we would read every day and brush up on schoolwork, and we all promised. And Aunt Kenny said that she would help us.

"Ty has to color in the lines every day and start working on his alphabet and numbers, and you and I have to read aloud every day and we have to read chapter books without pictures."

"I remember the deal," Michael said. "And if we do all that every day, you'll take us for ice cream and to play games during the week."

"Yes. So, you see, I'll still see you every day."

"But things are different now."

"Why? Because I'm married and I have a child."

"Well, yeah," he said.

"Michael, things won't change that much ok."

For our last night at the hotel, we had a bond fire on the beach. We all sat around with hotdogs on skewers and cooked them in the fire. We listened to the crackling of the fire and the roar of the ocean. As the night wore on, Tyson had fallen asleep in Michael's arms, Beth had fallen asleep in Addison's arms, and TJ was fading to sleep in my arms. Carter, Kate and Michael were still wide awake.

"Are we leaving early in the morning?" Michael asked.

"I have to head back first thing," Parker said.

"I'm going back with daddy," Kate said.

"I'll take Beth with me too."

"Kate, you can come with us," Michael said to her.

"There's not enough room for me," she said.

"That's not true," Addison answered. "There is plenty of room for you."

"I want you to see the lighthouse," Michael said to her. "I want you to go back with us. I've missed you." Kate looked at her eleven-year-old brother as if seeing him for the first time. "So, you mean the whole time you were with Aunt Jamie, you never thought of us?"

"I did," Kate said. "I mean I was having fun and everything, but yes, I thought of you all."

"Kate, you don't have patronize me," he said. "Go home with daddy if you want to so you can go hang out with your friends."

"Kate!" Addison said.

"Mom, I did miss him. I missed everyone, but I was having a lot of fun too. Making music with Aunt Jamie and getting to play the piano on stage and the violin. Mom, it was the most amazing thing ever. Thank you for giving me that opportunity."

Carter took a picture of her. Then he turned and took a picture of Michael with Tyson in his arms with the fire behind them.

"Mike, please don't be mad at me."

"My name is Michael. Not Mike. I hate being called Mike."

"I'm sorry," she said. "Can we go up to the room?"

"Sure," Addison said. "I can put your sister and brother to bed. Michael, are you ready to head to up?"

"No, that's ok," Parker said. "Here, Michael, I'll take him. Come on, Carter, you need to go upstairs too."

"But, daddy, it's our last night. Can't I stay down here with Aunt Kenny and Michael?"

"Ken?"

"I'll bring them up in a little while," I said.

Parker took Tyson from Michael. Then he, Addison and Kate walked up to the hotel. I sat with the boys on the beach still.

"I can't believe her," Michael said. "And today at the Space Center "Is there music in space?" he mocked her saying it. Then he turned to Carter. "Where the hell did you hear that about Apollo 10?"

"I read about it," Carter said. "I want to know all there is to know about the space program. When I'm old enough, I'm going to take flying lessons. I want to be a pilot and an astronaut."

"Wow," Michael said.

"What? Are you making fun of me?"

"No, Carter. You are eight years old and you know what you want to be when you grow up."

"Well, don't you know yet?"

"No. I guess I never really thought about it. I mean I love sports and playing sports, but I don't know if I want to be an athlete when I get older. You amaze me."

Carter took a picture of me with TJ.

"Can we go for a bike ride in the morning?"

"I think we can do that, Carter," I said.

"Aunt Kenny, thank you for such an awesome summer."

I smiled at Carter. "You're welcome."

We stayed on the beach for a half hour longer and then we gathered our things and headed back for the hotel. Just as we entered the hotel, it started to pour unbelievably. Hard pounding rain. We went up to the room. I unlocked the door with the card, and we went into the room. Everyone else was asleep when we came in. The boys put on their pajamas. I undressed TJ down to his shorts before putting him into the bed. The boys climbed into bed together. I went into the bathroom and showered and then dressed for bed before climbing into the bed with TJ. Everyone was sound asleep, most of them snoring, and now I couldn't sleep. I got out of bed because what was the point in staying in bed, if I couldn't sleep. I took out my laptop and started working on my newest project, which when we get home needs to be done by Tuesday. The project was to do a layout of a new apartment complex. The design needed to be fresh and new. I had no clue what I was going to do until I looked around the room seeing everyone sleeping. Michael was sleeping with Carter sleeping on top of him and Tyson was on top of him. So, I did a rough sketch of a three tier with largest being on the bottom, then medium and smallest and then reversed it so I would have a six story building. I grabbed my camera and took a shot of the boys sleeping.

```
[____[]____][____[]____][___[]____][__[]____][____[]____][____[]____]
   [___[]_____][___[]____][___[]___][___[]___][____[]___]
      [__[]___][__[]____][__[]___][____[]___]
      [__[]___][__[]____][__[]___][____[]___]
   [____[]____][___[]____][___[]___][__[]___][____[]___]
[___[]____][__[]____][___[]___][__[]___][__[]___][___[]____]
```

THE MCT APARTEMENT BUILDING

Just as I was climbing back into bed and making my second attempt to go to sleep, Beth woke up.

"Aunt Kenny?"

"Yes, sweet girl."

"I'm really hungry," she said almost starting to cry.

I got out of bed pulling on my jeans and a jacket. I scooped her up in my arms so she wouldn't wake anyone else up. Then I slipped out of the room with her. We took the elevator downstairs. It was four thirty in the morning. The kitchen in the restaurant was starting their morning prep services. I went to the girl behind the front counter, who had her head down and was obviously working on her school studies. "Excuse me," I said softly so as not to scare her. She looked up.

"Oh, hi. Can I help you, ma'am?"

"Is there anything open where we can get something to eat?"

"The kitchen is starting their morning prep service. Let me call them and see what can be done for you."

"Thank you," I said.

She called to the kitchen and told them it was for a VIP guest. She came over to where Beth and I were waiting. "They said to let them know what you would like, and they will gladly make it for, ma'am."

I looked at Beth already knowing what she was about to say. "Oatmeal and sausage on the side," she said.

"Can you make that a double order please and I'll have French toast please."

She told the kitchen what we wanted and in twenty minutes we had our order. I took Beth to a table in the lobby, where we ate our breakfast. "So, missy you haven't told me how your summer was with Aunt Mandy."

"It was ok," she said.

"Well, what did you do?"

"We played a lot outside. We made sandcastles in the sand box."

"Did she take you anywhere?"

"We went to the park."

"Anywhere else?"

She shook her head. She had spent eight weeks there with Mandy. I knew that Addison was mad at Mandy, but I didn't hear why yet.

"She has a new boyfriend," Beth spilled. "He spanked me."

"What? Why?"

She put her little head down on the table and started to cry. I picked her up immediately. "Shh," I said to her.

"I didn't mean to break it."

"To break what?"

"Porsha's doll."

Porsha is a year older than Beth. She has already turned four and Beth will be three next month.

"How did the doll break?"

"Porsha had been banging her head around all day and then I picked it up. She was yelling and screaming that I was touching her things. Aunt Mandy's boyfriend came over and grabbed the doll from me and her head came off. He then threw the doll on the floor and spanked me."

Now I became pissed off. "Don't cry. It's not your fault. And I'm sorry that he spanked you. Did he hurt you?"

She nodded her head.

"Ok, well that will never happen again ok."

Shit. Now I felt horrible because I just wanted the boys for eight weeks and not Beth. I already knew that I wasn't going to have Kate. I just thought it would be difficult with her because she is two and still naps and now, I find out that Addy's sister's boyfriend layed a hand on my precious niece. Oh, I'm pissed off now. I should go to Georgia and kick his ass for spanking a child that isn't his. That son of a bitch. I better never meet him, or he will get a swift kick in the balls before I even say hello to him.

After calming Beth down and she finished her breakfast, we went upstairs. She slipped right back into bed with Addison and Parker. I made my third attempt to hopefully and finally get some sleep, but it didn't happen. Tyson from a dead sleep smelling remnants of breakfast food woke up. He looked around the room and saw that I was awake. "Aunt Kenny."

"Yes, Tyson," I whispered.

"I'm hungry."

Parker heard him. He stretched big. "What time is it?"

"It's five forty-five," I said.

"Are you hungry?" he asked me.

"No."

"She took Beth for breakfast without inviting anyone else," Tyson said.

"Lower your voice please," I said to him.

"I want breakfast too," he said.

"Ok. Ok." I got out of bed pulling back on my jeans and jacket.

"Do you mind taking him?" Parker asked.

"No."

"When you come back, please make sure I'm awake."

"I will do," I said.

I took Tyson downstairs and ordered him breakfast. Cream of wheat with bacon on the side and two pancakes. He didn't just eat his breakfast; he scarfed it down as if he hadn't eaten in days. "Slow down. You are going to choke. It's not a race," I said to him. I was now on my second cup of extremely strong coffee. When he was done, we went up to the room. He climbed right back into bed with his brothers and fell back to sleep in what seemed to be a split second. And now I was definitely wide awake. I woke Parker, who went into the bathroom and showered. Then he gathered his and the girl's things. I went downstairs with him as he packed up the truck before going back upstairs to get the girls up. Addison was awake when we came back.

"Kate is going back with us," she said to Parker.

"Oh, ok."

He woke up Beth and they left to go back home.

After eight o'clock, slowly the children began to wake up. I dressed for the day and as the boys woke up, I made them pack their bags to go home.

"Why don't you do it for us?" Tyson asked.

"The same reason I haven't done it for you all summer. And why is that?"

"So that we know that we have everything we brought," he said.

"Good boy."

They finished gathering their things. My stuff was already packed up and ready to go. Addison gathered her stuff.

"Mommy, daddy took my clothes," Kate said. "I don't have anything to wear."

"It's ok," Carter said. "You fit in my shorts. He took out a pair of clean brand-new blue jean shorts and handed them to her."

Carter took his things out of his bag and found a green and blue striped t-shirt and handed it to her.

"Thank you, Carter," she said. "But I don't have shoes."

She wore the same size shoe as Michael. He went in his second bag, which was just for his shoes and took out two pairs of sneakers for her choose from. She picked his colorful New Balance shoes, in which she had almost the exact same pair. He tossed her a pair of socks.

"Thanks, Michael." She hugged her brothers and then went into the bathroom and got changed. She called Addison to come into the bathroom. Addison went in.

"What seems to be the problem?" she asked her daughter.

"I sat on the edge of the tub to put on my shorts and my panties got wet. I don't have any other panties."

"Let's see what we can do."

"I'm wearing all boys' clothes."

"And you're going to be ok with that for today."

Addison came out of the bathroom. She measured the boys' boxer shorts and they would all be too big for Kate. I was tucking a pair of TJ's in his bag. "Can I see those for a second?"

"Sure," I said.

She held them up to Carter's and Michael's and they were definitely a smaller pair. Tyson's would have been too small on her. Tyson's all were cartoon printed. TJ's, well the pair that she was holding was plain printed. She went back in the bathroom and gave them to Kate, who was tall and extremely thin. TJ's boxers fit her perfectly.

"Thank you, mommy," she said.

"Get dressed and I'll braid your hair."

"Ok. Thank you."

Kate got dressed and came out of the bathroom. Although her whole outfit belonged to the boys, she looked adorable.

The boys went into the bathroom together dressed and brushed their teeth. When they came out, we went downstairs for breakfast. Tyson, who had eaten at six, now ate another full breakfast. Once we were done, we took our last trip upstairs to the room to retrieve our bags. Then we went downstairs once again.

"Mommy," TJ said. I looked at him. "Don't forget the bikes this time."

"Oh, that's it," I said with a smile. "Now you're going to get it."

When the elevator doors opened, he jumped out of the elevator. He tried to run, but he was carrying his own stuff, which consisted of a duffle bag, a backpack, and his bag from yesterday that held his stuffed teddy bear. We couldn't leave it in the car overnight. I reached and grabbed TJ, who started squealing and laughing. He loved the affection, the interaction, and the game of it.

The valet brought around my SUV. We loaded the back with the bags. I pulled the protective shield over everything before closing the back.

"Can you please repark my vehicle?"

"Yes, ma'am," the valet said.

"Thank you."

We went to the front desk and soon after our bikes were brought around.

"How am I going to come with everyone?"

"You can ride with me," Michael said.

"How though?"

"You can sit on the handlebars," he said to her. He mounted his bike and then like a pro helped her on the front of the bike. He stood up to balance them out and waited for everyone to mount their bikes. Then he walked the bike a ways until it got rolling and he could start pedaling.

Storm was there in the shadows to snap a beautiful picture of the two of them.

We rode to the lighthouse. Michael's wish. I paid the donation, in which the woman running the lighthouse though she was extremely grateful came off that she was annoyed that I was giving them yet another donation. She did not expect it. We went all the way up. Upon stepping out, Kate became a little anxious. Michael sunk a reassuring arm around her shoulders. He whispered to her, "Take a deep breath. It's ok." With his arm safely around her, she stepped out onto the balcony. I once again lifted TJ up. Addison did the same to Tyson, and Carter stood sandwiched between all of us. And once again Storm was there…somewhere unseen… taking elegantly beautiful pictures of all of us together. We stayed out there for an hour and then began our descend down for the last time on this trip. Once again, we climbed on our bikes, Michael helped Kate and then we rode back to the hotel.

The valet brought my SUV around. Addison and I mounted the bikes on the bracket. With the SUV in the valet's supervision, we all went into the hotel to use the bathroom before starting for home. Then everyone climbed in.

"Addison, would you mind driving?"

"No. I don't mind. Are you tired?"

"Yeah. I was up all night."

"Oh my god, Ken, why didn't you say anything before? We could have just packed up the car and headed home earlier."

"No. It's ok," I said. "I'm just starting to feel it now."

Addison climbed into the driver's seat; I got in next to her in the passenger seat. Carter's car seat along with TJ's car seat was now tucked in safely in the back. They were sitting in seats like two little big people. Both of them were beaming. Michael put a movie on for all of them. About ten minutes into the drive home, I dozed off and woke up as Addison parked the vehicle.

"Hey, it looks like we have company," she said to me.

I opened my eyes stretching. I looked around and sure enough my driveway was full of vehicles. Parker's truck, so we knew he was there, Patrick's two trucks, mom and dad's car, Addison's SUV and there was another one that I didn't know.

"Monster ma is here," TJ said. "Mommy!" he said in a shaky voice.

I turned to look at him. "TJ, I promise you that you are not leaving this house tonight."

"Why is she here?" he cried.

"Hey, if Aunt Kenny says something it's true," Kate said. Then she put her arm around him. "It's so nice finally having a boy cousin in the family," she said kissing him on the cheek.

"Mommy, she's kissing me again."

"And she will do that for the rest of your life," I said with a smile.

"I've been girl kissed," he said.

We all got out of the vehicle and went inside. TJ seeing Patrick went running to him and jumped up in his arms. "Hey, there's my buddy," Patrick said. "And you've grown since I last saw you."

"A whole inch," he said with excitement.

"I see that," Patrick said with a smile.

"Why is grandma here?"

"It's ok," Patrick reassured him. "Everything is ok."

I hugged and kissed Patrick. "It's good to be home," I said.

CHAPTER EIGHTEEN

Trinity came out of the kitchen with a glass of wine in her hand. "Aren't you going to say hello to your grandmother?" she asked TJ.

"Hi," he said and then he ran upstairs to my room.

"What's wrong with him?"

"Are you serious?" I asked.

"What?" Trinity asked all sweet and innocent like.

"Mom, stop it."

"Well, let's get our cards out on the table. I don't like who you picked to be my grandson's stepmother."

"I am not his stepmother. I adopted him. He is my son."

"Sweet thing, he will never be your son."

"Mother! If you ever want to see your grandson again, then you will stop this right now. I love, Ken."

"Ken is a man's name," Trinity said.

My mother had come into the room upon hearing this turmoil. "Trinity, you have been my oldest and dearest friend. I hate the fact that you had my daughter arrested. I hate to think of what could have happened to my four grandsons because of that. If she had been alone with all four children, my grandsons would be a ward of the state right now. Hell. So, would yours.

"My daughter can be called anything she wants to be called and no one including you is going to make her feel less about herself."

"Who elopes?"

"Mom, I have already explained this to you. I talked to my lawyer a few months ago and told him that I wanted Kennedy to adopt Turner. He said that adoption could go through, but it would be awkward if we weren't married. And I have loved Ken since the day I met her. She is my soulmate."

"I just don't think that she is a good influence on my grandson."

"Now you wait a minute," Parker began.

And Addison picked up, "She has been in our five children's lives since the day they were born. Last school year; when I was called to come back into work and I didn't have a place for my four and two year old to go, Ken stepped up and had them here in her house, which she is trying to turn into a Bed and Breakfast. Then when Carter's teacher had an issue with him, Ken said she would home school him, and she did. She worked two full time jobs this past spring and didn't say a word. She worked with Tyson, who will be five in a few weeks and he can write and spell his own name. And this fall, when four of my children will be in school, Ken will help out with Beth.

"She took my three boys, and TJ and they had an adventure. She didn't just take the kids to Chuckie Cheese and call it a day. She took them to wonderful places, and they explored magnificent things. She read them stories every day and listened to them and talked to them."

"Well, maybe I miss judged her, but now with you living here, I'll never get to see him."

"Of course, you will get to see him," I said. "I didn't marry Patrick and adopt TJ to keep you out of their lives."

"Why did you marry my son?"

"Because I have loved him since the moment I laid eyes on him," I said. "And as for TJ, I don't know who wouldn't love that little boy. When he first met me, he came running at me."

"He was always looking for that woman; who was meant to be his mother; who would catch him, hold him, cuddle with him, and struggle when she has to put him down."

"Kennedy fits that description to a tee, grandma," TJ said from his perch on the fourth step up.

The fact that he was crying, made me run to him and scoop him up in my arms and hide him for protection. Trinity watched our interaction.

He had his arms wrapped strong around my neck and his legs wrapped around my waist. His face was buried deep into my shoulder as he sobbed. I held him tight and whispered in his ear. "I'm not going to let anything happen to you. I promise you that. I love you."

Trinity watched in disbelief. Mom and dad watched as well. I started to rock him still trying to get him to stop sobbing. After ten minutes, he started to settle down a bit. I heard Trinity say that it usually takes about an hour to calm him down.

"She has the knack, mother," Patrick said.

"Why don't you go find the others and you can watch a movie in the den." He shook his head and clung a slight bit tighter to me. "It's ok. I have you."

"Maybe I should leave," Trinity said.

"Not before you do what you came here to do," Patrick said.

"I am truly sorry, Kennedy. Turner, I am sorry. I would never take you away from your father."

"But you would take me away from mommy," he said. "Do you know what happened when mommy was arrested in Orlando?"

"No," she said.

"I saw them."

"You saw who?"

This was the first time I was hearing this. God! I want to punch her.

"The police. I saw them coming for mommy. I saw him jerk mommy up out of the chair and then wrestled her to the ground." Big extra wet tears dripped from his eyes. "The police officer held her down on the ground with his knee in her back. Then he jerked her arms behind her back and put the bracelets on her. When he pulled her up on her feet, he did it by her hair.

I hadn't told anyone that. "TJ, that's enough now," I said to him.

He looked me right in the eyes, "Maybe she'd like to watch it."

"What?"

"I recorded it on my camera."

"No, honey, that's ok."

"No, mommy, make her watch it. Make her see."

"Go get your camera." I put him down. He looked back at me. "I'll be right here when you come back."

Patrick stepped closer. "Did that happen with your hair?"

I nodded as I put my head on his shoulder. TJ came back. "Here, mommy."

I took his camera, turned it on, and went to his videos. It was the fourth video in his camera. "I was brought in here," TJ said. "They told me that mommy will be here soon." There is a large clicking sound. TJ points the camera to the hallway door that was closed and is now wide open. The police come down the hall. They come into the room where I am. TJ stands on a chair in the room where he was in to make himself taller. You can clearly see me sitting in a chair behind a table. The bigger of the two officers, takes the table by the edge and flips it away. Then he jerks me out of the chair and wrestles me to the ground. "Don't be mean to my mommy. MOMMY! MOMMY!" I must have heard him calling because I looked over to where his voice was coming from. The officer's knee is pressed hard into my back. He jerked my arms back just like TJ had said and cuffed me. Then he grabbed the collar of my shirt, but mostly my hair and pulled me up.

"Oh, my god," Trinity said. "They told me that he wouldn't see anything."

"Well, I did," TJ said.

"No. No. Don't be fresh to grandma," I said.

"But that wasn't right."

"I know, honey, but neither is you being fresh to her." I thought for a minute. "Well, that would explain his nightmares," I said to Addison.

"I'm sorry. I wasn't allowed to be with him," she said to me.

"Mommy!" Carter said. Addison looked at him. "I have some of that taped too."

"What?"

"I didn't want to upset Aunt Kenny," Carter said. "I was afraid if I showed it to you or her that we would have come home sooner."

"Mommy," Michael said. "I thought the same thing. I too have it on film."

Carter's video was of the police officer taking me down the hallway and putting me in the car. He had pushed me into the door jam in the hallway and he shoved me up against the car, where he pressed himself against me. Then he opened the car door and jerked me into the car.

Michael's recording had the whole thing. From the time I was brought into the room and shoved down into the chair. The man pushing me down in the chair pushed me in extremely close to the table. Then the police coming into the building. The woman officer telling him she would be the good cop and he would be the bad cop. Then them coming into the room and everything else was the same as that the other two had recorded.

"Why were they so mean to you?" Trinity asked.

"Because they heard that I abandoned my son and my three nephews. Neglect charges is a criminal act," I said. "They were treating me like a criminal. Also, they were informed that I was in possession of contraband."

Patrick looked at his mother.

"They were rough, but it became nasty when I was brought into the station." I stopped talking and kissed TJ on the head. "Please go play with you cousins." Finally, TJ left the room. "They emptied my pockets so rough that I was knocked off my feet. Then my clothes were stripped off of my body. I had to stand with my legs spread apart while a woman officer with gloves on put her hands and fingers in places I'd rather not mention and felt around for drugs, which I don't do. Once that was over, I given my clothes back to wear, my hands were cuffed again and I was walked to a cell, where I was shoved into."

"I am so truly sorry," she said again. "I'm going to go now. Kennedy, I am deeply sorry."

After Trinity left, in which we couldn't get TJ to come back into the room to say goodbye to her, we had dinner. Mom noticed that I was extra quiet at dinner. She let it go until we were in the kitchen cleaning up.

"Are you ok?" I didn't answer her. I was trapped in a trance. The fear of losing TJ had a grip on me that was unshakable. Mom touched my arm. I nearly jumped a foot. I looked at her. "Are you ok?" she asked again.

"Um. Yeah."

"You're not," she said. "What's wrong?"

"He chose me, mom, to be his wife and the mother of his precious son. The fear of losing TJ is intolerable. Trinity has sent me threatening texts for the last almost two weeks. I'm scared to be home."

"Nothing will happen to any of you at this house or on the grounds of this house. And I think she changed her mind tonight."

"How is that, mom?"

"Because you didn't see what the rest of us saw tonight."

"What?"

"When that little boy was on the steps crying, you didn't stop to think, you didn't hesitate, you didn't even miss a beat, Kenny, you ran to that child. You scooped him in your arms, and you comforted him. When he was in your arms, nothing else mattered to him. Nothing else mattered to you. The room was full of people, and yet it was empty seeing you with him wrapped up in your arms. Kenny, that's what moms do. They protect their young. My god, honey, if you were an outsider looking in, you would never know that you have only been in this little boy's life since the start of the summer break.

"Kenny, TJ calls you mommy. Now you know that when you were young, my friends the Ericson's adopted Tony when he was about TJ's age, to this day he has never called Martha mommy let alone even called her mom.

"Although, your father and I were not present when you met him, it's abundantly clear that he took to you immediately. He accepted you and you accepted him without anyone telling you what to do. It is beautiful to see you two together. And you and Patrick. Well, you all just fit together."

"Thanks, mom," I said. We finished in the kitchen. Upon entering the den, and TJ spotting me from his perch on the arm of the couch, he stood up and launched himself at me. Patrick spun around saying his name, just as I caught him in midair pulling him close to me and smothering him with kisses. Laughter and squeals filled the room.

"Turner! You have to let someone know that you are doing that."

"Ok, daddy. But mommy will always catch me. Right mommy?"

"Yes, Turner."

"I don't like my name," he said out of the blue.

"What?" Patrick said.

"I don't like my name. Turner. What am I a book? A page turner? A spatula? I don't like my name," he said again.

"What do you want your name to be?" I asked him as I walked closer to Patrick.

"Well, if you had a son, what would you name him?" TJ asked me.

"I have a son," I said to him.

"Mommy! If you had your own boy what you name him?"

"How about if we changed Turner to something else with a T?" Patrick said.

"Well, before we make a split decision, why don't we think about this for a few days," I said.

"Did Renee name me Turner James?"

"No," Patrick said. "I named you. You turned my life around. When you were born and Renee didn't want to hold you, the doctor handed you to me. And you turned your head and looked up at me with those big grey eyes. You never turned your head away to look at Renee. When you turned and looked up at me like what else, you melted my heart."

"Ok, daddy, I'll keep my name. I'm sorry."

"Can I ask a question?" dad said.

"Sure, dad."

"Did TJ always refer to Renee by that?"

It was TJ that answered. "No. I used to say my mom, but she's not my mom. She has never been my mom. A mom sticks around and is someone you can count on," he said.

He spoke beyond the five-year-old child that he was. He was more mature than other almost six-year olds. But he was an only child in an adult house. They all spoke to him like an adult. So, at times when he knew he needed to speak up, he did, and he told it as it was.

That night as we settled down and got ready for bed, TJ was in the room with us. He had already been sleeping for hours. I knew that he would get up in another hour. Patrick and I started to kiss. "We can't be too intimate with him in the room," Patrick said.

"No. I know," I responded still kissing him.

"He needs his own room. How will that work here."

"He can have his own room. Of course, that can be done."

"How are we going to live here when you open the B&B?"

"We will take the deluxe apartment, which is where my parents are right now. It is their room. But it is essentially an apartment. All three of us can live in there. It is a four three and half split. It was built that way when this was originally built, for it was a B&B. Then it closed and the owners sold it as a house. My parents bought it back in the early eighties.

My parents having three children with completely different personalities couldn't all be jammed up in an apartment and my parents knew that, so we all had our own rooms and bathrooms. This place was the place to be at the holidays. My parents threw massive parties here when we were kids.

"However, we grew up with responsibilities. We had to clean our own rooms and bathrooms. We had to take care of the horses, and the property. We had check for standing water and go to the furthest points of the property to check the fences and gates. We had to maintain the pools.

"Park could have gone all the way on a football scholarship, but he didn't. He went to school for accounting. He played sports in college, but not on a full ride scholarship. James has always been into music. I used to tease her saying that she came out of the womb singing and dancing. I played sports but went to college on a full ride scholarship for chess."

"Do you still play?"

"No. I was in my senior year at Florida State, and we had travelled to Washington DC for a tournament. I was the elite. The captain of the chess team. It was the first time in a long time that it was a girl that held this position. We had won taking the whole tournament by surprise. We had been in Washington for almost a week. There was a party that we went to…"

I stopped. This was the first time ever that I was talking about this. Patrick and I were lying in bed side by side. He saw the look on my face. There was fear in my eyes. "Did something happen?" he asked. I went to get up, but he held my hand. "Have you ever mentioned this to anyone?" I shook my head. "Tell me."

"The party was getting too wild and out of the control. I left to go back to the hotel. It should have been an eight-minute walk, but halfway there, a van pulled up and the guy I had beat earlier that day got out of the van.

"My hair was so long then. He grabbed me by my hair. He came at me and punched me hard in the stomach. He told me that he was going to do to me what his father had done to him, and he kicked my ass. Every time I tried to get away, he grabbed me by the hair. Pull me back towards him and then he would hit me harder and harder. He had gotten me on the ground. Then he shoved a knight in my mouth and held me down. He was trying to shove it down my throat. Some of the party goers were coming back and seeing what was happening started to scream. He punched me once more in the face before getting off of me and running off to his van.

"I spit the knight out. I was carried back to the hotel. The next day on the flight home, I could barely move everything hurt. I went to my classes ignoring the fact that I looked like a monster with bruises over most of my body. I was in my architecture class, which was dark, when the professor turned the lights on, I heard her gasp. She managed to finish class and dismiss everyone. Then she came rushing over to me. I heard her talking but she seemed so far away. She called in another professor, who just so happened to be my chess coach. I had avoided him when we left DC, on the flight home, and for the past couple days since I'd been back. And now when he came in the room, I heard him gasp as well. Things were blurry. I remember closing my eyes and then being lifted out of my seat. I was taken to the hospital. When I was released, I told him that I would never play chess again and I have not touched a board since.

"After that I picked up on my architecture classes and the rest you know."

"I'm sorry that happened," he said.

He kissed my cheek. He pushed my hair back and saw a hidden scar right above my ear. He rubbed his finger over it. I moved closer to him turning my body so now my back was against his chest. He held me in his arms. He ran his top hand up and down my skin and he felt little nicks of old scars. He again took hold of me and just held me tight.

"Did anything else happen to you in your youth?"

I closed my eyes as tears brewed and then dripped down my face. I whispered, "I was raped."

"Look at me," he said. I turned in his arms and looked at him and then buried my face in his chest and shook from emotions that were pouring out of me.

"Thank you for marrying me and loving me."

"Kennedy."

"You're the first person I've been this honest with all my life. Thank you for making me safe. I love you."

"I love you too," he said. "Wait. You never told your parents?"

"Patrick, there are so many things that Todd and Roberta don't know about me. It would rock their world if they even got a glimpse of what has gone on in my life since middle school. As long as our chores were getting done on time, and we had good grades, Todd and Roberta didn't know their kids business."

"Didn't you have a curfew?"

"No."

"Did you have family dinners together?"

"On Sundays. Monday through Saturday, my parents worked."

"What did they do?"

"Dad was a pilot and constantly traveling. And mom worked in a bank. She left the house at seven in the morning and didn't get home till after seven at night most nights. That started when James and I were in middle school. When she didn't have to be here to drive us and pick us up from school. Plus, dad ran camps here at the house. Basketball camps, tennis lessons, horseback riding lessons, the middle school and high school ran track here at the house."

"Were you into sports?"

"Yeah, I was. James not so much."

"Do you have a volleyball court here?"

"Yep. Both sand courts and hard courts."

"So then how would you get away with things?"

"I said he ran camps here. I didn't say that he was always here."

"What's the worst thing you've ever done?"

I propped myself up on his shoulder and looked at him. "The worst thing I've done. Hmm. That's hard to say."

"Kennedy!" he said in a loud tone.

"Shh. You don't want to wake the boy," I said.

He smiled at me. "I'm waiting."

"I stole my parents' car and went to Daytona to go to the beach."

"How old were you?"

"Twelve."

"Did you get into trouble?"

"Not the first time."

"How many times did you do this?"

"Five times safely and the sixth time I got busted."

"Who caught you?"

"My dad."

"What did he do?"

"He spanked me."

"Had he done that before?"

"Yeah."

"Would you ever spank your child?"

"Our child?" I asked. "No. There are better ways to deal with reprimanding a child."

"Did you ever get hit for something that Jamie did?" I looked at him and he knew the answer. "For what?" he asked.

"When we were five, we had been playing outside and mom had said that we needed to be in the house before it got dark. Jamie had been practicing her music. She had begged my parents for a clarinet, and she got one from Santa that year. So, we had been outside playing. I saw that it was getting dark, so I cleaned up all the tennis balls that I had knocked around the courts and I went into the house.

"It had been dark for over an hour when Jamie came in. My mom asked if we were in before dark. Jamie turned to my mom and said, "I was in before it got dark, but Kenny just came in the house, mommy and she left tennis balls all over the courts." My mom looks out on the courts and there were tennis balls scattered everywhere. My mom sat her in a chair at the kitchen table, she called me over, in which I was showered and dressed for bed with wet hair, and my mom calls me to her. Then she picked me up and put me over the dinner table and spanked me. Jamie sat there watching it with her mouth hanging open."

"Was that the only time?"

"God no," I said.

"Did she ever get hit for you?"

"I don't think so."

I got up to use the bathroom. When I came back, Patrick had fallen asleep. Just as I was getting into bed, TJ woke up. "Mommy?" I got out of bed and went to him. "I'm so cold, mommy," he said. I put my hand on his forehead and he was burning up. I sat with him on the bed and then I climbed into bed with him. I put my arms around him. His body was so hot, but he was so cold. He shivered from the fever. After a few minutes, I got out of the bed and picked him up and brought him downstairs. I sat with him and gave him juice.

Mom was up. She came downstairs. "Is everything ok?"

"He's burning up with fever."

"He needs liquids."

"I'm giving it to him."

I brought him in the den and sat with him on the couch. I put a blanket on him. I sat with him for the rest of night and into the morning hours. When Patrick woke up, not finding either of us in the room, he came racing downstairs. I had just closed my eyes for the first time all night when Patrick asked if everything was ok. I opened my eyes and looked at him. "He's been burning up most of the night or morning," I said.

"Yeah, he has battled fevers most of his life."

"Maybe we should find out why."

"I've taken him to doctors, but they can't seem to explain it. Why don't you get some rest? I'll sit with him."

"I'm going to take him upstairs," I said, "And put him in our bed and see what happens."

By nine in the morning, his temperature had spiked higher. I got up, showered, and then carried him downstairs. I put him the car and took him to the doctor. Blood work was taken, and he was given a shot with antibiotics. I brought him home. The doctor called later that day and informed me that TJ had a hidden respiratory infection. It was the cross between a viral infection and bacterial infection that settled in his chest. She said that I needed to bring him back so they could start treating him immediately.

Two hours later, we were back on our way home with a nebulizer machine for breathing treatments, and an inhaler, and antibiotics. The rule was we had to keep him inside in a cool place with not a lot of light. This kid loved being outside, so this was going to be torturous for him for the next week. She had given him something to sleep, so he slept now. When we got to the house, mom came out to meet me. She took everything in the house for me. I picked him up and carried him.

"What's the problem?"

"He has a hidden respiratory infection."

"Oh, you had those when you were young," mom said.

"What the hell causes it?"

"Change of atmosphere, going from hot to cold constantly, breathing in too much damp air."

"Oh, great. So, he got it from being with me," I said.

"No," mom said. "He's an active little boy."

I held him in my arms while he slept. Patrick came home from work. I filled him in.

"Crap!" he said. "I was hoping that he had outgrown it."

"What?"

"When he was born, his lungs weren't fully developed, so I've dealt with this with him all of his life."

"So, this isn't my fault?"

"What? No. How would this be your fault?"

"From taking him with me and going to so many places."

"No that's probably the best things for his lungs," Patrick said.

The next day, mom and dad were going to Atlanta to see Jamie in concert. Apparently, so were Addison, Park, and the kids. Patrick had meetings in Jacksonville, so he would be gone for the next three days. And TJ was still with a high fever. I needed to get work done as well, but as of this moment that wasn't happening. And now I too spiked a fever. I called Ivy, but she was out of town with Bruce.

"Shit!" I said. I then called Trinity. "Look I know you don't like me all that well, but TJ is sick with a fever and so am I and everyone else is out of town. Can you please come…" My phone died.

Trinity was at the house twenty minutes later. "Kenny? Ken? Kennedy?"

I was upstairs burning up with a fever like I had never had before. I shook with the chills. Trinity came upstairs. "Kenny?"

"I'm… I'm in….in the… the bath…bathroom," I said through chattering teeth.

She came in. "No. No. Don't take a shower."

"I…I have…have to…to warm…warm up."

"I know," she said. "Come on." She took hold of my hand.

"Please…please don't…don't take…take TJ away."

"No, I won't. Now please come with me," she said. She led me to my bed. "Climb in."

I climbed into bed and she covered me to my chin.

"I'm so cold."

"I know you are," she said. "It's ok. You are going to be ok."

"Mommy!" TJ whined from across the room.

My instinct was to get out of bed and go to him. "No, you need to stay in bed," Trinity said.

"Please don't take him."

"I'm not going to take him. I promise you," she said.

"Mommy!" TJ whined again.

"I'm…I'm here," I said to him.

He got up from his bed and came to my bed. He started to cry when he saw Trinity. "She's…she's here…here to take me."

"No, honey," Trinity said to him. "I promise you; you aren't going anywhere. Now please get back in bed. You both are burning up with fever."

TJ got into bed with me. His body was so hot. Trinity took both of our temperatures. TJ's was one hundred and two and mine was one hundred and four. She stepped out of the room and called her friend, who was a doctor. "They are both so sick," she told her friend. "My daughter-in-law's temperature is one hundred and four and my grandson's is one hundred and two. Can you come and help me please?"

He was at the house in ten minutes. He gave TJ a shot with antibiotics first. When he went to give me a shot, I freaked out a bit. Trinity rushed to the bedside and sat on the bed with me. "No…no needles," I stammered out.

"It's ok," she said. She took me in her arms. "My god, her body is so hot."

"I know," he said. "After I give her the medicine, I'm going to put her into a cold bath. Hold her still," he said. He managed to give me the shot. I gritted my teeth and groaned. Every touch hurt. Then he lifted me into his arms and brought me in the bathroom. "Trinity, this is going to shock her body. We may have to hold her down in the water."

A man came in with bags and bags of ice and put it into the tub. Cold water was added and then he put me down into the water. I let out a scream. Trinity was right there by my side. "It's not for long. We must lower your body temperature. Look at me," she said. "Look at me. Look at my face."

I made eye contact with her briefly and then passed out in the tub. They didn't keep me in there long. The doctor and his friend lifted me out of the tub and carried me back to the bed. Trinity pulled my freezing wet clothes off me and they put me into bed. She covered me and then sat on the bed with me rubbing her hands up and down over the blanket. "I need to call my son," she said.

"Grandma," TJ said.

"Hi, honey," she said. "How are you doing?"

"I'm really hungry."

She put her hand on his head and for the first time in three days he no longer had a fever. "My friend John will take you downstairs and get you something to eat."

"Is mommy sick?"

"Yes, honey."

TJ ran downstairs and called Patrick. Patrick answered immediately. "Kenny? Is everything ok?"

"Daddy, mommy is sick."

"What? Is anyone there with you and her?"

"Grandma," TJ said. "Your mom is here."

"I'm coming home," he said. "I 'm a few hours away, but I am coming home."

Patrick hung up with TJ. He told his business partners that he had to go. "My wife and son are sick."

"Why don't you fly home then?"

Patrick went to the airport and flew into Orlando. He rented a car and came rushing home.

When he got home, they were giving me my second ice bath. I screamed out again. TJ was crying. Patrick came rushing through the front door. He scooped TJ up in his arms and came racing up the stairs and down the hallway to our room. He came running into the room. He put TJ down and came into the bathroom just as I passed out for the second time.

"What are you doing?"

"We need to draw her temperature down," the doctor said.

"Please tell me that she is going to be ok?"

"Can you pick her up?"

"Yes, of course." Patrick lifted me into his arms. He carried me to the bed and put me in bed and pilled the covers up on top of me.

Trinity sat with me. "Patrick, we need to give her an IV, but every time that we have tried, she has freaked out. She needs fluids." As Trinity spoke to Patrick, the doctor drew my arm out from under the covers and he was just about to put the IV in my arm when I woke up seeing the needle and started to kick trying to free myself from the covers. I kicked and squirmed and just about bucked to get out from under the covers.

"No! No…no I… I don't… don't want… want that."

"Kenny," Patrick said. "I'm here, my love. It's ok."

"No. Pl…please."

"Kenny, you are very sick. They need to give you medicine."

I managed to get free from the covers. I was in my bra and underwear, which were both wet. I stood up on the bed, saw the open door, and jumped off of the bed. I took off running. Patrick and Trinity ran after me. "Christ she is fast," Trinity said.

"She runs five to ten miles every day, mom," Patrick said. He caught up to me. He reached around me. I screamed and kicked as he lifted me off my feet.

Trinity watched. From my reactions that she had seen since she had been at the house, she knew that something awful must have happened to me when I was younger. Trinity, who had overlooked seeing the scars on my body; her eyes were now drawn to the claw marks down my back. Claw like marks that were three wide going down from each shoulder blade to the top of my buttock. Patrick held me in his arms. I was still fighting trying to get free. He brought me down on the floor. He was seated with his legs out. He had me between his legs. He held my arms in front of me across my chest. I was kicking still. He brought his legs over mine and finally pinned them down.

"NO!" I screamed.

"It's ok."

"NO!"

"Honey, I've got you now. You are safe."

"I can give her more antibiotics," John said.

"NO!"

"Do what you need to do please," Patrick said.

"NO!"

"Please stop screaming," Trinity said.

He gave me another shot. I tried so hard to get free. I was fighting under Patrick's strength. I started to convulse and shake violently in Patrick's grip. "What the fuck do I do?"

"Just hold her until it passes," the doctor said.

It lasted three minutes before I went rigid in his arms. My head flopped down and my body went completely limp under him. "Mom," Patrick said with his voice quivering.

"Let's get her back upstairs."

Patrick stood with me in his arms. My head flopped back against his shoulder. My arms hung. Trinity got a blanket off the couch and covered me before they brought me back upstairs. Patrick undressed me completely and put me into bed. I was unresponsive. John put the IV in my arm and started fluids going into my body.

"What should I do?" Patrick asked.

"You need to go to the store and buy her juices," Trinity said. "She needs a lot of liquids."

"TJ, get dressed," Patrick said.

"Is mommy going to be ok?"

"Yes," Trinity said.

"TJ, please get dressed," Patrick said again.

"You can leave him here?"

"No. If she has another screaming fit like that, I don't want him to see that and I'm sorry to say mother, but I don't trust you enough to leave my son with you right now."

TJ got dressed and Patrick took him to the store. He called Storm. "Hey, where are you?"

"In the studio."

"Are you busy?"

"Not really. Why?"

"Can you please go to Ken's house? She is burning up with fever. My mom is there with her doctor, but I'd like to have a friend there with her."

"Sure. I'm on my way."

In Patrick's absence, I convulsed two more times. Each time, Trinity sat holding me. I was convulsing even more violently now when Storm came into the room. She rushed to the bed. She got me on my side and held me.

"Kenny, can you hear me? It's going to pass, honey," Storm said. "Can you hear me? Honey, try opening your hand."

I slowly opened my right hand.

"Good. That is good. I know this hurts, honey," Storm said. "I know it hurts, but it will pass."

Trinity took hold of my open hand.

"Hey, it's good to be back home again," Storm started to sing John Denver's song. She sang the first couple verses and finally started to feel my body starting to relax. "See honey, it's starting to pass." She continued to sing, and it was soothing. Finally, I was limp against her. She climbed in the bed with me. She sat with her back against the headboard. Then she gently pulled me so that I was against her. "Can you find a shirt to put her in?"

Trinity went into the closet and came back with a t-shirt. She came back to be bed. Storm leaned me away from her and put the shirt on me. Then she pulled me back against her.

"What's wrong with her?"

"Both she and TJ have hidden respiratory infections."

I started to shake with the chills again. Patrick got back and came upstairs. "How is she doing?"

"If I hold her can you make her drink a little?" Storm asked.

"Daddy!" TJ said with tears in his eyes.

"I can do it," Trinity said. "Patrick, you should take TJ away from here."

"Mom, please tell me that she's going to be ok?"

It was Storm, who spoke. "She will be better," she said. "Now please go with TJ, so he doesn't get this again."

Patrick went to TJ, who was crying and upset.

Trinity sat on the bed after pouring some of the juice in a glass. Storm eased my head back a bit and Trinity got a little bit of juice into my mouth.

John's wife had heard about this. She came with soup and warm tea. She came into the room. She disconnected the IV and took it out of my arm. "This isn't going to work with this," she said. The three women worked together to get liquids into me. My fever spiked again and again I had convulsions. However, this time there was no ice bath. Instead, they held me through it. Storm telling me that it would pass soon. Trinity holding my hand and allowing me to squeeze the life almost out of her hand. And then Julie did something that no one had done, she put an oxygen mask on me. "Just breathe. Let it in, baby girl," she said. "Do you remember me? I'm an old friend of your mom."

I opened my eyes for the first time in hours and looked around.

"Welcome back," Storm said. "I know this hurts, but it won't last forever. Just breathe."

"Hold me," I said.

"We have you."

"Trinity. Thank you."

"Shh. There's time for that later."

I leaned back against Storm as another wave of convulsions went through my body. I cried out. "I know," she said. "I know it hurts. Close your eyes. It's better that way. Just close your eyes. I have you. We have you. You are safe. You are in your bed at the house. Patrick and TJ are downstairs."

I did close my eyes and soon after it was over. My fever started to break. Sweat poured from my entire body.

"She's soaking wet," Storm said.

"Honey, we have to get you into dry clothes," Trinity said.

I turned my back to them and took off my shirt. Trinity and Storm saw the scars on my shoulders and back. Nicks on my right side. Scars that weren't properly treated because I was ashamed to show them to anyone. Trinity got another t-shirt. I put it on. I managed to get out of the bed and go into the bathroom. I came out in a pair of shorts. I just barely made it back to the bed before sleep over came me. Storm grabbed me as my body fell forward on the bed. Trinity helped to get back under the covers.

My sleep was restless. I turned a lot. Pretty soon I was soaked in sweat for the second time. Storm went downstairs and got Patrick. "She's soaked through as if she were out in the pouring rain or as if she jumped in the pool fully clothed."

He came into the room. The three women left the room. He lifted me though I was sleeping and brought me into the shower. When the water hit me, I cried out. Trinity sat on the steps with tears in her eyes. I woke up startled and fighting.

"Honey, you are safe. Honey, it's me."

I pulled away from him and sunk to the floor of the shower. "I don't want you to see," I said.

"See what, Ken?"

"The scars."

"Kenny, do you think I'm going to love you less because of it?"

"How long does this last?"

"Storm said that your fever is breaking, so not too much longer. You didn't answer me."

"I've kept away from men for an awfully long time, Patrick. The scars are…"

"They are there, honey. It doesn't make you less of a person. I love you no matter what."

I got myself up. I managed to shower and get into pajamas. I got in bed by myself and slept for the rest of the night without being bothered.

CHAPTER NINETEEN

It took a few days for the fever to completely go away. Trinity stayed with me the whole time. She was there for the few more spikes that it took and then she was there when the fever finally broke. It had drained me. I took a shower and got dressed in a pair of blue jeans that a week ago fit me perfectly and now they sagged and hung and I had to wear a belt. I managed the stairs by myself too for the first time.

"Mommy is down," TJ said. He came running towards me and hugged me. I hugged him back.

"How are you?" Patrick asked.

"I'm hungry," I said.

"I got it," Trinity said.

"Daddy signed me up for Tee ball."

"Oh, that's great."

"I have a game over the weekend."

"I can't wait."

"I'm sorry. I have to take him."

"No, it's ok," I said.

Trinity and I were alone. "May I ask you a question," she asked.

"Yes, of course."

"The other day, I saw the nicks and the scars on your left side. How did you get them?" I didn't answer her. "Do you parents know?"

I shook my head.

"When did it happen?"

"When I was a teenager," I said.

"Were you in a violent relationship?"

I shook my head again. "It wasn't a relationship. It was barely a one-night stand. I was at a party. Everyone was drinking. I had just graduated high school. I was still just seventeen. There was this guy there. He said he would drive me home. When I got into his truck, I didn't think anything different. He said he would drive me home. Instead he drove to a wooded area off the Turnpike. He drove the truck into the woods. He pulled out a knife. He held pressed into my left side. Every time he told me do something that I didn't do, he's used the knife to flick away bits of skin."

I hadn't heard the door. My mother stood behind me.

"He striped my clothes off of me and he pressed the knife into my ribs as he raped me."

I heard my mother gasp. I spun around.

"Kennedy!" mom said in a low voice.

I lowered my head. "I'm sorry," I said.

"Why are you sorry? I'm sorry that I never knew."

"I still have nightmares from it," I said.

"Why didn't you tell us?" dad asked.

"I thought you'd be disappointed."

"Why don't you play chess anymore?" dad asked.

"I…I got bored of it."

"I don't believe that," he said. "Something changed when you were away at college."

"I grew up," I said.

"You came home broken," he said. "And I want to know why."

"Why now?"

"Why not now? What in the hell are you so afraid of at almost forty years old, Kenny? I want to know," he said.

"We had gone to Washington DC for the chess tournament. I don't know how I did, but I did it. I won the whole tournament. We had gone to a bar not far from the hotel to celebrate before flying home the next day."

Addison came in the kitchen with Parker, Lennox, and Jamie. Patrick was back with TJ. "It's raining," TJ said. "No, practice."

"TJ, can you go watch TV in the game room?"

"Sure, daddy."

TJ hugged me again and then ran out of the room.

"Why are you so thin?" Jamie asked me.

"I've been sick for a few days."

"What happened?" mom asked.

"I got sick from TJ."

"Why didn't you call us?"

"Because you were in Georgia seeing James's concert."

"Who took care of you?" mom asked.

"Trinity and Patrick and his friend Storm."

"And some other people," Trinity said.

I looked at her.

"They are professional people, Kenny," she said.

"Did they see me naked?"

"No, they didn't. Storm and I did," Trinity said. "And Patrick did."

I lowered my head again.

"Who raped you?" Jamie asked.

"I don't know. I don't know his name."

"Describe him?"

"He was tall. Like over six feet. He had long wavy hair. He has green eyes."

"That fucking bastard," Jamie said.

"You know who he is?"

"Yes."

"Who is he?" I asked. She didn't answer me. "Jamie, please. Because of this guy, I haven't been in any relationships. So, I deserve to know his fucking name."

"Joe Sullivan," she said.

I turned and threw up in the kitchen sink. "I have to go," I said.

"Where?" Mom, Trinity, and Addison asked.

"I don't know, but I have to go." I looked at Trinity and mom. "Will you go with me?"

"Yes," they said together.

"I have to go get something."

I tried to run, but I was out of breath. I walked as fast as I could to the garage. I unlocked a cabinet and took out my clothes from all those years back that I had put into a plastic Ziplock bag. I had a few things from that night. I came back in the house.

"TJ!" I called. He came running. "Hi, sweet boy, do you want pizza for dinner?"

"Yeah!" he said so adorable.

"Ok." Though I was weak, I lifted him up and hugged him. "I love you."

"I love you too," he said.

I went back into the kitchen. Mom and Trinity came with me. As they were getting in the car, though I didn't want to leave Jamie out, I went back into the house and asked Addison to go too.

"Are you going to be here?" I asked Jamie.

"Yes," she said. "I'm going to give Katie Bug a music lesson. Are you ok?"

"I'm better now," I said to her. I went to her and wrapped my arms around her as she wrapped her arms around me. She felt my bones under her touch. "Thank you so much. I love you."

"I love you too, Kenny."

The four of us went to the police station. When we walked in a sense of bravery swept through me. I went over to the front desk. "Hi, I'd like to speak to a woman detective if I can."

"What is the issue?"

A woman heard me ask. "It doesn't matter what the issue is. She asked to speak to a woman. I can help you," she said. "Please come this way."

"Can my mom and…"

"Yes, they can come too."

We all followed her to a room. Once inside the room I handed her the bags of my ripped up clothes. "I was raped," I said.

"When?" she asked.

"Twenty-one years ago."

"Why did you wait so long to come in?"

"Because I didn't know who raped me, but I do now. His name is Joe Sullivan."

"Did he cut you?" she asked.

I lowered my head. "Yes, ma'am," I said.

"Can you show me?"

"I…"

"It's ok," Trinity said.

She closed the blinds to the room. I lifted my shirt to reveal my left side. I heard mom draw in a breath. The woman detective, whose name is Brenda Strongman came over. She touched my skin. I jumped. "Is this ok?"

With my eyes closed tight, I nodded my head.

"I'm going to bring in someone to take pictures of this."

"I don't want a lot of people to see this," I said.

"I know you don't," she said. "But this needs to be documented."

They had given my clothes to the medical examiner. The shirt that I was wearing that night matched the nicks that he had made with the knife. He had taken the blade and dug into my skin and then flicked the knife blade out making these rosebud like nicks up and down my whole torso. The scars started from the back of my head, down my back; on the front of me, from my nipples down my torso to my mid thighs. The nicks were also on the tops of my shoulders and scattered here and there down my forearms to my elbows. There are scars in my arm pits as well.

Brenda touched some of the nicks. Some were small and others were bigger. Then she touched the scar that ran from my left side to my belly button. I drew back a little.

"Does it go lower?"

"Yes," Trinity said. "The nicks cover most of her body."

"Will you take your pants down?" Brenda asked.

The photographer came into the room. It was Storm. I went to her and wrapped my arms around her and cried into her shoulder. She put her arms around me and hugged me back. She felt the nicks.

"Ken, get dressed. We are going to go somewhere else and take the photos," she said. I pulled my shirt back on. "Detective, are you coming with us?"

"Yes."

Storm stepped closer to her so we couldn't hear her. "I have photos of these from years ago. I didn't know her then. But when we were called to the scene of the crime, she was laying bleeding on the grass. I had taken pictures and it is still an open case. When she was put into the ambulance, although she was weak and out of sorts, she put a good long fight until she passed out. She went out screaming and fighting hard.

"She's married to my best friend."

"Can you do this professionally?"

"Yes, ma'am," she said.

"Then take us where you are going to take us to."

I was quiet as we got into Storm's truck. We drove a few miles and then went into a building. I realized that we were at her apartment. "I want you to lay on the table. I want you to take off your clothes and just relax. I promise you, I'm not going to hurt you," Storm said to me.

"Do I have to get naked?"

"It will be better that way. I promise you it won't be for long."

I looked around and saw a picture of a younger Storm with long brown wavy hair.

"You were there," I said.

"I was."

"You covered me so the men at the scene wouldn't see."

"I did," she said.

I lowered my head.

"No. Don't do that," she said. "This wasn't your fault."

"Can I use your bathroom?"

"Sure," she said.

I walked into the bathroom and puke again. Storm had known how sick I'd been in the last couple of days. When I came out, she gave me some warm tea. I turned away from everyone in the room and undressed. Then I sat on the table still facing away from everyone.

"You are ok," Storm said. "If you want to sit, I can get pictures of it that way first. Lift your left arm."

"Do we need to measure them?" Addison asked.

"Yes."

"I can do that for you," she said. "I can hold the ruler or whatever you use. Kenny, is that ok with you?"

I nodded my head.

Trinity took mom and they went and sat on the couch. "How is it that you saw this, but I never have?" mom asked.

"She had a fever," Trinity started. "John came over and put her in an ice bath to try to draw the fever down. When he was putting her back in bed, I took her shirt off of her and put her into another shirt. She was laying on her right side. She said she was cold, so I was trying to warm her up and I felt them."

"It's been twenty-one years and I never knew."

"Our kids will hide the bad things away from us," Trinity said. "You have to think. When was the last time you saw her naked?"

"With Kenny, she was probably nine or ten."

"Kids grow up. Their bodies become their own. They don't want to show them to their parents."

Storm took pictures with Brenda holding up my arm and Addison measuring each one. When they got to the scar on my side to my belly button, Brenda touched it again. I dropped my arm to try to cover it up. "Did you get stitches for this?" she asked.

I shook my head.

"At some point, you are going to need to verbalize your answers."

"No," I said. "When I got…" she touched the scar again. "When I got home that night, I super glued the skin back together." I remember things in fragments. I didn't remember going to the hospital.

"Kenny, I need for you lay on your side now," Storm said.

"It was deep," I said. "I stood in the bathroom at my house and put glue and then worked the skin back together."

"I'm all done," she said. I pulled my clothes on.

Storm went into her office and game back with a file that she handed to Brenda. "Don't open this now," she said.

"Is that me?" I asked. "From that night?"

"Yes," Storm said.

"Can I see them?"

"Why don't we go back the precinct," Brenda said.

We went back. We went into her office again. I sat down. "Tell me about that night," she said. "Start with how old you were?"

"I was seventeen. It was graduation night. Jackie Breaks was having a party. The whole senior class was there. There was liquor flowing. Everyone was dancing and partying really hard. I wanted to go. This guy said that he would drive me home. But he didn't drive me home. Instead, he drove and got off the Turnpike in a wooded area. He asked me if I was a virgin."

"Weren't you?" mom asked.

"No."

"When did it happen?"

"The end of middle school," I said. "I had been sexually active in high school with a few chosen guys.

"He took the knife out and opened the blade. Then he pressed the knife first into my hip. He pressed it in and I remember crying out and then he scrapped it forward. He told me to take off my clothes. When I didn't, he pressed the knife under my arm and did it again. Then he kept doing it over and over again."

"When did he slice you?"

"While he was raping me," I said.

"Did he rape you just once?"

I shook my head. "No."

"Do you remember how many times?"

"He did this inch by inch by inch. Every time he raped me, he would drag the knife another inch."

Addison had measured it. "Seven," she said out loud. Then she sat next to me and put her arms around me and hugged me.

"When he was done having his fun, he dumped me out of his truck. I don't know how long I was there before people came," I said.

"Were you alert when they came?"

"Yes," Storm and I said together.

I reached onto Brenda's desk and took the file. I looked at the pictures and I could see it. I didn't cry when I looked at the pictures.

"When he left you, were you dressed?"

"No," I said.

"So why didn't you report it when it happened?"

"I thought people would say it was my fault."

It was just Brenda and I in the room now. "What did you do afterwards?"

"I acted like nothing had happened and I packed my shit and went away to college."

"Where did you go?"

"FSU."

"Did you date anyone?"

"I went on a few first dates, but never let it go any further."

"When did the nightmares start?"

"Right away."

"Have they stopped?"

I shook my head. "No."

"When was the first time you ever mentioned this?"

"About the rape?"

"Yes."

"Earlier this summer. When I started getting really interested in Patrick. I told Addison only about the rape. Not about the torture."

"Have you told Patrick?"

"Yes. He knows I was raped, but he doesn't know how I got the scars."

"Are you going to tell him?"

"I'll have to tell him," I said.

"Are you just dating Patrick?"

"No. We are married. I adopted his five-year-old son two months ago. The day that Patrick and I eloped, I adopted TJ. He calls me mommy."

We finished up and I went to find mom, Trinity and Addison and we went home. When we got there, music filled the house. I went and found Patrick. "Can I talk to you alone please?"

"Sure," he said. When we were alone, I looked at him. "What's wrong, sweetheart?" he asked.

"Are you mad at me?"

"What? Why in the hell would I be mad at you?"

"I don't know," I said. "Patrick, when I was seventeen, the night I graduated high school, I went to a party and got drunk. A guy said that he would drive me home, but he didn't. He took me to a wooded area off the Turnpike and he not only raped me seven times, but he did this to me," I said showing him the nicks and the scar. "I know you've seen these, but I wanted to tell you where they came from. Joe Sullivan was extremely violent. He had a knife with him that night and every time I didn't do something, he told me to do, he would press the knife into my skin and then flick away a chunk of skin. When he started to rape me, he put the blade into my skin and dragged it along an inch.

"Marrying you this summer and adopting TJ has been such a wonderfully great experience for me. If I didn't get sick and your mother didn't see the scars, then I probably wouldn't have talked about it. We haven't slept too much together yet, but I have to let you know that I still have nightmares. Sometimes I will wake up in a complete sweat."

"I'm ok with that," he said. "I love you."

"I love you too."

Due to the fact that I had preserved the clothes from that night, they were able to draw Joe's DNA and his sperm from the fabrics. A few days later, Brenda came to the house. I was playing outside with TJ. We were hunting catepillars. Brenda pulled up in the driveway behind the SUV.

"Hi," she said getting out of the car.

"Hi."

"Can you come to the station?"

"Yes, but I'll have to bring him with me."

"That's fine," she said.

I got TJ and we went to the police station.

"We need you to view a line up."

"How does that work?"

"There will be men lined up and you see if can identify Joe Sullivan," she said.

TJ was kept out of the room with another officer. I went into the room with Brenda. "Do you remember what he looks like?"

"Yes."

"If you were to meet with a sketch artist, do you think you could give a composite identification of him?"

"Yes."

A sketch artist was brought in. I described Joe Sullivan to him. "He has green eyes, he has black hair, he has a deep widow's peak, and he had long hair back then. He has a scar on his right cheek. I described other things too. He had a tattoo of a parrot on his lower stomach, he had a pirate with a patch covering its right eye tattoo on his left front side of his shoulder. I described a few other things too. How his pointer finger on his right hand pushed to the left.

"And I bit him back then."

"Where?" Brenda asked.

"I bit into his top of right shoulder. I sunk my teeth deep into his shoulder. It was after that that he pushed me out of the truck."

The picture of the description I had given was drawn up. Then there were five men standing on the other side of a class window. "Can he see me?"

"No. Is he there?"

"Yes. Number four."

I had positively identified Joe Sullivan. They had enough evidence to book him.

"The knife was never found," Brenda told me.

"I have it," I said.

She went back to the house with me. I took her out to the barn. I climbed up in the loft of the barn with her and then handed her a box. Inside the box was the bag containing the knife.

"You've done really well," Brenda said. "How did you get the knife?"

"He left it sticking in me when he dumped me out of the truck."

His name was not Joe Sullivan like Jamie had said. I had identified the right person, but with the wrong name. Because of that detail they could not hold him or even book him. The man, who raped me, had cut claw marks down my back. He had nicked my skin from the back of my head, across the tops of my shoulders, down my whole front and back and now for the first time, it was known.

CHAPTER TWENTY

The end of July was upon us. The first week of August, Parker, Addison, and the kids would be going on a two-week cruise. Patrick and I had talked about going on a cruise. I told him that I would go with him and TJ, but I'd want the whole family to be there and then we would have our wedding ceremony with the whole family. I didn't know that Patrick booked us on the same cruise with Parker and Addison and that Jamie and Lennox were going too and mom and dad, and Trinity, and Ivy and Bruce, and Dillion, Margot, Jenna, and Alan from work, and Dean, and Connie and her daughter Pepper, and Storm, and Wesley.

Patrick, TJ, and I went shopping. We drove to Orlando for this. "For our reception are you going to wear a dress?"

"No," I said with a laugh.

"Do you have any dresses?" TJ asked.

"Um. No," I laughed a little harder.

"Are you going to wear white?"

"Yes."

We went to a bridal shop, where Patrick picked a pair of white sparkly pants for me that had a matching top with sheer long sleeves. Then we went to get a suit for him and for TJ. We got TJ a shiny black suit with a cobalt blue shirt to go with it.

"Do I have to get dress shoes?" TJ asked.

"No. We are going to get you a new pair of sneakers," I said. I picked him up.

"Are we going somewhere special?" TJ asked.

"Maybe we are, buddy," Patrick said.

Then we went and bought clothes for the three of us before going home. When we arrived home, Addison was there with the kids. Carter was sitting on the steps. "Hey, bud," I said to him when we walked up the sidewalk.

"Can you take me somewhere?"

"Yes, of course," I said.

"Hi, Aunt Kenny."

"Where do you want to go?"

"I want to get something forTyson for his birthday."

"My birthday is the same as Tyson's."

"I know," Carter said to him.

"Daddy, am I going to get birthday presents?"

"Of course you are," Patrick and I said together.

"I'll be back in a bit," I said.

I took Carter to the store.

Patrick went into the house with TJ. "Hey, can you watch the kids for a bit?" Addison asked him.

"Yeah, sure," Patrick said.

"What size does TJ wear?"

"He's a six."

"Daddy, can I have drumsticks for my birthday?" TJ asked.

"Well, now I know what to get him," Addison said with a bright smile. She kissed Patrick on the cheek. "See you in a bit, Brother-in-Law."

"Hey, when is Kenny's birthday?"

"September twentieth."

Music filled the house. "James, can you turn that down please," Patrick called out.

Jamie came into the kitchen.

"If that's not you then…"

"That's Kate."

"Where is she?"

"She's in the game room," Jamie said.

Patrick went in the room with Jamie. He stood there listening to her sing and play the keyboard. Lennox filmed it. Michael came into the room. He tapped Patrick. They left the room together. "Can I play basketball?"

"Yes."

"I've looked all over the place for Carter. Do you know where he is?"

"Your aunt took him to the store. Where is Tyson?"

"He's not here," Michael said. "He stayed home with dad."

Jamie was with Kate, so Patrick went out in the back and played basketball with Michael.

"Can I ask you something?"

"Sure."

"Who is that lady with the short hair that always comes over?"

"You didn't meet Storm?"

"Yeah, well we did, but who is she?"

"She's my best friend."

"My friend's dad is a cop. He said that Storm was taking pictures of Aunt Kenny."

"Yes, that's true. She was."

"So is Storm a cop?"

"No. She's a photographer."

"So, does she take pictures of crime scenes?"

"Sometimes."

"Can I tell you something?"

"Yes, Michael, of course."

"When we were away with Aunt Kenny, I saw that she has scars on her body. I want to ask her about it, but I don't want to upset her."

I had just gotten back with Carter and seeing Patrick out back with Michael, I came outside to hear the tail end of that Michael's statement. "Don't want to upset her who?" I asked.

Michael looked up at me. "You," he said.

"Why would you upset me?"

"Can I ask you something?"

"Yes, of course."

"Why do you have scars on your body and a long scar from your ribs to your belly button? And then those marks that look like claw marks down your back?"

"I was in accident when I was young," I said.

"Do you cry out in your sleep because it still hurts?"

"What?" I asked him.

"You do," he said. "You cry out in your sleep."

"I'm sorry if I scared you," I said to him.

"But you didn't scare me or the others. We were just concerned for you. Whenever you were sleeping on your left side, you would cry out. Then you would move and stop. It wasn't every night. It happened after you were arrested though."

I hugged Michael. "I love you," we said together.

"Can Uncle Patrick take me to the store?"

"Why are you asking me? Ask him."

Michael looked at Patrick. "Can you please take me to the store?"

"Yes," Patrick said.

"Just the two of us?"

"Yes."

"Thank you."

My phone buzzed. It was Addison FaceTiming me. I accepted it. "Are you alone?"

"No, but I will be."

"Oh, wait. Is that Michael?"

"Yes."

"Ask him if he likes this backpack."

"No!" Michael said. "Uncle Patrick is taking me to the store."

"Oh. Ok."

She had walked past a purple backpack with musical notes floating all over it. "Mom, you should get that for Kate."

"It's the only one they have, and it has a hole in it."

"We will look for Katie," Patrick said. "Come, Michael."

I went back into the house and into my office and closed the door. "I'm alone."

"Is this good for TJ?" She showed me the cutest outfits.

"Yes, those are great. What size are they?"

"Patrick said he wears a six."

"He wears a boys' medium," I said.

"Well, that changes things. I can have fun with that. He's the same size as Tyson."

"Where is Tyson?"

"He's home with Parker. He's determined to be able to read before starting school."

"Your children are egg heads," I teased.

Music resonated into my office.

"So, who is in the house with you?"

"TJ, Carter, and Kate. I'm going to go play with the kids," I said.

I hung up and went to find the boys. They were playing with Lennox.

"Mommy, I want drumsticks for my birthday," TJ said.

"Well, that's a good gift," I said.

Parker called. He was going to come over with Tyson. When he came, I sat with Tyson and read to him. And then he whispered a secret. "I know there are letters on the page," he said. "But they are fuzzy."

"Parker!"

He came into the living room. "What's up?"

"We have a situation here."

"What is it?"

"You tell him," Tyson said.

"He said that the words on the page are fuzzy."

Parker called the pediatrician and then he took Tyson to the office, where they had an eye doctor on staff. Tyson was checked out and fitted for his first pair of glasses. He picked blue frames with Spider-Man on them.

That night, after tucking TJ into bed, I came back downstairs to get work done and to wrap his and Tyson's birthday presents.

Patrick came into the kitchen. He started to kiss my neck. He lifted me putting me on the granite countertop. We continued to kiss.

"I need you to pack for a trip," he said after a few minutes.

"Where are we going?"

"I wasn't going to tell you."

"No, is it a surprise?"

"Yes."

"Then I'll just pack. Don't tell me."

We went upstairs and I packed. Patrick had taken the outfit I picked at the wedding shop and had given it to Ivy to bring. He had also given her the suits for him and TJ. He had called everyone and told them about the reception that we were going to have on the cruise. My mom and Trinity had gone shopping together and had bought dresses. Addison bought a dress for her, Kate and Beth, and she bought suits for the boys.

That night, we went to bed. I cuddled into Patrick. For the first time in my adult life, I loved the contact. I snuggled closer to him and fell asleep. About two hours into sleep, a nightmare started. I cried out. It woke Patrick. I cried out a second time. Patrick sat up and took me in his arms. I started to struggle. "Kenny, wake up, honey," he said soft and gentle. "Kennedy," he said again. He loosened his hold on me. I startled and bolted from the bed. "Ken."

I turned and looked at him. "I'm sorry," I said.

"No, it's ok."

I went to my dresser and took out a pair of dry clothes. I striped out of my sweaty clothes and put on the dry pajamas.

"Do you want to talk about it?"

I shook my head. I didn't look at him. He took me in his arms and kissed me. He put his hand on my left side. "No. Don't," I said.

"Does it hurt you?"

"No."

He lifted my shirt up leaving my breasts covered. Then he rubbed his flat open hand on my left side. I closed my eyes. He felt me tense up. "Kennedy, relax," he said. When he got to the long scar my breath caught in my chest. For most of it, it was just a thick line on the surface of my skin. The closer it got to my belly button, the more it had puffed out and a raised scar about a quarter of inch thick ran three inches to my belly button. When Patrick put his mouth on it, I ducked my head and cried. He kissed every inch of the elongated scar. I tensed up. "Kenny!" I didn't realize I was trembling. I laid there and tears ran down my cheeks.

"I'm sorry," I said. I curled up in a ball. Patrick didn't leave me though. Instead he took me in his arms and held me.

"Have you been with anyone since then?"

"I've been with you."

"Have you been with anyone before me and after him?"

I nodded my head. "Yeah, but it never went farther than one night."

"Why not?"

"Because I didn't know how I would explain the scars. I trust you. I feel safe with you."

"Can I touch it again?"

"Yeah," I said.

CHAPTER TWENTY-ONE

The cruise ship was leaving out of Fort Lauderdale on Friday afternoon. As a family, we drove down on Monday to Fort Lauderdale. We had rented a house for the week. We went to the beach, took the kids to the museums, we went to the movies and saw a double feature. Thursday night, Patrick, TJ, and I went out for dinner. We went to Commercial Boulevard and found a parking space. Then we decided on Greek food for dinner. We went into the restaurant not knowing that our parents had planned ahead, and we were having a rehearsal dinner. Both my parents and Patrick's mom were hosting the dinner for us.

"But we are already married," I whispered to my mom.

"Please just have fun tonight and give this to your father and I to do. Can you do that?"

"Yes, ma'am," I said.

We all sat at a very large table and when the wine was brought to the table, my dad stood and said he wanted to toast Patrick and I.

"To my eldest daughter of my twin daughters, I wish you all the happiness in the world. May god bless you now and always throughout your life. I have always been, and I am so proud of you. Congratulations."

I turned and looked at my mother. "Dad does know that I am the youngest of the three of us kids, right?"

"No, dear. He's never known that."

"Great."

"Daddy," Jamie said. "I'm older than Kenny by eight minutes. Ken is the youngest of the three of us."

"What?" he asked. "No. It goes Parker, Kennedy, and Jamie."

"No," the three of us said together. "It's Park, Jamie and then "Ken," Park said. "Kenny," Jamie remarked. "me," we all said at the same time.

"Well, whatever it is, I am so proud of you. Congratulations."

"Thank you, daddy."

Trinity spoke next. She too stood up and held up her glass. "To Patrick, my only son, and to Kennedy, congratulations."

And last to go was mom. She stood up. "Kennedy, you never cease to amaze me. You came into the world a screaming little tiny thing, and you have grown into the beautiful woman you are today. You have always been one to make quick decision; however, they have never been wrong decisions. As we all know that you eloped back in June, we are hosting this dinner for you both because you so deserve it. I have never seen love like the love that you share between you two. You both are bursting with love that is felt all around. Congratulations.

"I'd also like to toast the newest member of this family, Turner James. You have a glowing light that burns bright inside of you and I hope that it never dies.

"Congratulations to the three of you, who have made this family more complete."

We all toasted. I went up to my mother and kissed her on the cheek. "Thank you."

After dinner, with it still being light outside, we all went on the beach and played soccer. TJ kept creeping closer and closer to the water's edge. "TJ, don't do it," Patrick warned. And he would stop and then he would inch a little closer. "TJ, I'm warning you," Patrick said. But Patrick nor TJ expected what I was going to do. I came charging at TJ, lifted him up in my arms and dove right into the water. He clung to me, but he was having the time of his life. We came out of the water both dripping. I smiled at Patrick.

"I warned our son. I never thought I'd have to warn my wife as well."

"Yeah, well," I said with a smile.

And then the linebacker that my brother once was, charged at Patrick lifted him on his shoulder and drove him straight into the water.

"Yay! Daddy went for a swim."

I couldn't help but laugh. I kissed TJ on the forehead.

Lennox picked Jamie up and carried her sweetly into the water. "Aww. That's romantic," I said.

Dad hugged mom. "Todd, don't you dare," mom said, but dad kept moving mom backwards. He then danced with her and tangoed her right into the water. We all laughed. Patrick looked at Trinity, who looked left out. He went up to her and lifted her in his arms and brought her into the water. Addison jumped on Parker's back and he ran into the water with her. Ivy took Bruce's hand and they ran in together. TJ took me by the hand. He's pretty damn strong for a five almost six-year-old. He pulled me to the water's edge. I lifted him up and ran into the water with him again. He squealed with laughter. Tyson picked up Beth and ran to their parents. Carter looked at Michael. Together they lifted Kate and brought her into the water.

"Good now everyone is soaking wet," Addison said. "Now what?"

"Now we go back to the house and go swimming," Michael said.

"We need to get some sleep. We have to be up early to go to the port," Trinity said.

We went back to the house and we all went swimming in the pool together for about a half hour. Then we went to our rooms and showered and got ready to settle in for the night.

"What's it going to be like on the ship?" TJ asked Patrick.

"It's going to be big. Remember when we went to New York City?"

"Yes, I do," TJ said.

I came out of the bathroom and laid on the bed with them. "What are we talking about?' I asked through a yawn.

"What's it going to be like on the ship?"

"It's going to be a lot of fun. There is going to be swimming pools, a surfing station, and basketball courts, there is a museum, there's a park, there will be shows on the ship."

In Parker and Addison's room, Tyson was asking the same types of questions. Parker told them that the ship is like a huge floating city.

"Are you going, and we are going to stay here?" Michael asked.

"No, we are all going."

"But you said that you were only taking Beth."

"Michael, at first; when this summer started, it was only going to be your father and I going. Aunt Kenny was going to have all five of you, but then Aunt Mandy asked if Beth could come to her this summer and Aunt James asked if she could have Kate for the summer…"

"Aunt Jamie is Jamie not James. She's not like Aunt Kenny."

"What do you mean?"

"Well, she's not. Aunt Kenny knows us and I mean really knows us, but Aunt Jamie has come and visited and then she leaves and takes off for a long time and we don't see her and she doesn't call us to see how we are doing. With Aunt Kenny, not even a day goes by that we don't hear from her or she doesn't hear from us.

"So, we are all going on the ship tomorrow?"

"Yes, baby, we are all going on the ship."

"Is Aunt Kenny going?"

"Yes."

"I was afraid when she got married and adopted TJ," Carter said.

"What?" Addison asked.

He came over and plopped down next to Michael. He looked at his mother. "It's true. I was afraid that she wasn't going to want us around anymore. I mean now she has a husband and kid of her own, so I was afraid that she was going to say to you that she couldn't take care of us this summer."

"Aunt Kenny isn't like that," Michael said.

"No. I know, but I was nervous."

"You were what?" Parker asked coming over and join Addison and the two boys.

"I was afraid when Aunt Kenny married Uncle Patrick and adopted TJ," Carter said.

"Are you still afraid?" Parker asked.

"No." Carter climbed on Parker's lap. "Daddy, you should have seen Aunt Kenny when TJ disappeared. I've never seen anyone look so scared ever. And I know if mommy weren't there, it would have been harder on her because she would have been alone with the four of us boys. But she didn't leave us right away after he went missing. She made sure that mommy and all of us were safe and then she took off running.

"After he was found and they brought them into the building and they put TJ in one room and Aunt Kenny in another room; when the police came, they wrestled her to the ground."

"It's true. That one big guy slammed her so hard into the ground."

Parker looked at Addison who just nodded that it was true what they were saying.

"After Uncle Patrick showed up, we all thought it was going to be ok and that we would all leave together, but that didn't happen. They told us that we could leave, and that Uncle Patrick could take TJ, but Aunt Kenny was detained." Carter said. "But we saw the police wrestle her to the ground and then cuff her. We saw him drag her across the room and then he yanked her up by the handcuffs and her hair"

"Why are we talking about this now?" Addison asked.

"Because we saw him."

"Saw who?"

"The police officer that was rough with Aunt Kenny."

"Let's not worry about it," Addison said.

Friday morning, I went for a long walk along the beach before anyone got up. We would be leaving to go to the port at eleven. On the way back, I stopped to watch Patrick and TJ playing. TJ looked up and saw me. He waved big over his head and he started to run towards me. I sped up a bit and caught him in midair.

"MOMMY!"

I noticed a man watching us. I walked up to Patrick carrying TJ and I kissed Patrick. The man continued to watch us. We went back to the house and showered and got dressed for the day.

"I'm hungry," TJ said.

"Ok. Let's go get breakfast," Patrick said.

"Is mommy coming?"

"Yes, I'm coming. I'm starving."

I picked TJ up and we left the house. We went to the restaurant near the house and there once again the man was there. I turned so he couldn't see me. "Patrick, do we know that man over there," I asked.

Patrick facing the way that I was talking about looked over.

"Which man, honey?"

"The guy with the bald head."

Patrick saw him. "No. Why?"

"He's been watching us."

TJ looked and then clung tighter to me. "TJ," I said.

"He's a police officer."

"What?" Patrick and I asked together.

"He's a police officer from Orlando. He's the one that slammed you into the ground."

"What?" Patrick asked. I looked down. "No. Don't lower your eyes. You have nothing to be…"

He walked over to us. "Excuse me, are you Mrs. Alexander?"

"Yes, sir, I am."

"May I talk to you for a minute please?"

"No!" Patrick and TJ said.

"Please, ma'am, I just need a minute of your time."

I put TJ down. "Mommy!" he said between his teeth.

"It's ok. Daddy is here and he won't hurt me."

I walked away from them. "Please tell me what I just told my son is true."

"Yes, ma'am," he said. "It's true. I'm not going to hurt you. I thought that you would like to have this back," he said and held out my necklace.

"I thought I lost this forever," I said. "Where did you find it?"

"It was in the backseat of the patrol car."

"Thank you so much."

"I'm sorry about that night in Sea World."

I looked down. "Yeah," I said.

"Ma'am, we were getting information that you were hurting the boy and that's the reason he ran away from you."

"That's not what happened," I said.

"I know that now, but at the time we were told to get you away from the child. We were also informed that you had contraband on you."

I nodded my head still looking down. "Yeah, I know."

"Are you ok?"

"Yes, sir, I'm fine."

"Whatever came out of it?"

"Nothing besides the fact that I was given a night I'll never forget in my life and that goes for my son and nephews too."

"I didn't know that he was your son."

"I adopted him earlier this summer after I married my husband."

"The woman who called in was frantic that you had kidnapped the boy and that you were using drugs and had drugs on your possession."

I nodded again.

"Well, I won't keep you any longer. I just thought that you'd like to have that back. And I'd also like to apologize for the way you were treated and the way I treated you."

"I know that you were just doing your job."

"That may be true, ma'am, but I didn't know that you had already been held for most of the day."

"It's... It's fine," I said. "Thank you for returning my necklace."

A girl about Tyson's age came running over to where we were. "Daddy!"

He bent and scooped up the child.

"Who's this?"

"I'm Kenny," I said.

The little girl smiled. "I'm Dale," she said. "You know my daddy?"

"Yeah, I guess."

"We are going on a ship today," she said.

"Well, I hope you have fun." Then I walked away. I walked back over to Patrick and TJ.

"Is everything ok?"

"Yeah," I said.

"What did he want?"

"He returned my necklace to me."

"Why is he here?"

"He and his daughter are going on the cruise."

"What?" TJ asked. "But he's not nice."

"No, baby, it's ok. He was doing his job that night in Orlando. He was going off the information that he was given, and he reacted to that. It's ok."

A beautiful blond woman joined him and the girl. I looked at her. "I know her."

"What?" Patrick asked.

"I do. I know her."

I took Patrick's hand and we walked over. "Samantha Jones?"

She turned around and we were face to face. "Oh my god if it's not Kenny Jackson. How the hell are you?"

"I'm great."

"What did you become?"

"I'm an architect."

"Somehow I thought you'd be that."

"You know her?" the cop asked.

"Yes. Kenny was one of my best friends when we were kids. She constructed that art piece at the school that I work at."

"I go to that school," TJ said.

"I'm sorry," I said. "Samantha this is my husband Patrick Alexander and our son TJ."

"This is my husband Adam Heyward and our daughter Cynthia."

"Hi, Cynthia," TJ said.

"Mom, my name is Dale. Hi, TJ."

"Well, it seems that our kids know each other."

Adam shook hands with Patrick. "How are you doing?"

"Great," Patrick said.

"So Sam, you are back in town?"

"We officially moved back a month ago. Where are you living?"

"Still in the same place. I bought it from my parents. How is Jessie?"

"She's great. She is a doctor. She's around here somewhere. What brings you here?"

"We are celebrating our marriage on the cruise," I said. "Patrick and I eloped earlier this summer."

"Congratulations."

"It's going to be a big celebration," Patrick said. "Why don't you join us."

"Yes, we'd love that," Samantha said.

A woman my height walked over and gave me a little nudge. "Hey, how have you been?" she asked me.

"I've been great, Jess. How are you?"

"Wonderful."

A woman walked over to her with two small children.

"This is my wife Nicole and our children Reese and Ryle."

"It's nice to meet you," I said to her.

"How do you know her?" Nicole asked.

"We went to school with Kenny and her sister Jamie."

Jamie came in the restaurant. "Oh, no," she said with a smile.

"Is everything ok?" Lennox asked.

"Yes, it's fine. Come with me," she said taking his hand. She strolled over to us. "If it isn't the Jones's twins. What the hell are you doing here?"

"Family vacation," Jess said.

"It's nice to see you."

"And you. Wow, you're engaged."

"I am," Jamie said with a smile. "Are you going on the cruise?"

"Yes."

"Great. Us too," Jamie said.

Parker came in with the kids. He was carrying Beth.

"It's Mrs. Heyward," Carter said. "Can I go say hi?"

"Yes," Parker said.

Carter came running over. "Hi, Mrs. Heyward."

"Hi, Carter."

Carter saw Adam and stepped backwards. Patrick stopped him. Patrick bent down. "It's ok." Patrick picked Carter up.

"Hi," he said to Adam.

"Hi," Adam returned to him. "So, is this your son too?"

"No. This is my nephew Carter," I said.

Michael walked over with Tyson. "Why are you here?" Tyson asked.

"Tyson!"

He looked up with his big blue eyes. "He hurt you, Aunt Kenny."

"Let it go," I said. "And please be nice."

Addison came into the restaurant. She rushed over. "Why are you here?" she asked Adam.

"My family and I are going on the cruise today."

"Honey, am I missing something?" Samantha asked.

"Please just let it go," I said.

"The little boy said you hurt her," she continued.

"Remember the missing child in Sea World," he began. "Well, it was her son, but that's not the report that we received. We were told that a woman matching Kennedy's description had kidnapped a little boy and that she had drugs in her possession.

"I didn't know that she and the staff of the park had searched for hours on end looking for the little boy. They had just found him when we were called in. When we got there, she was holding the child described to be that of the kidnapped child. My partner took TJ away from her and I brought her into a room."

"I'm asking again to please stop. What's done is done. I'm fine. My son is fine. And we are here to have fun as I am sure that you and your family are. Samantha it is great seeing you. Please Patrick can we go?"

I walked away. My appetite was destroyed. I went back to the house and gathered all of our things. There was a knock on the door. I went to it and opened it. Samantha and Adam were standing outside. "May we come in?" Samantha asked.

"Yeah," I said.

"He had told me about that call the morning after it happened," Samantha said.

"What happened after you were taken to the station?" Adam asked.

"I wasn't treated nice," I said.

"Do you know who made that phone call to us?" he asked.

I nodded. "My mother-in-law. She thought that I was neglecting the boys. Before this trip, it had been just me traveling with the four boys. We traveled to different places in the state. It was while I was home that Patrick asked me to marry him and to adopt TJ. We were married in the courthouse and the adoption went through in the same day and then I continued to travel with the boys. His mother did not approve of the marriage or it could have been the fact that we eloped and now her precious grandson, who has never had a mother all of sudden had me in his life. She didn't want to share his love and attention, so when we were in Sea World and TJ got separated from us, she saw it on the news and used it to her advantage."

"Oh my god, Kennedy," Samantha said.

"She called the Orlando police station after telling Patrick what happened and after he left home to come to Orlando. I had been terrified all day long because he's so little and we had spent six long hours looking for him. It wasn't until the park had closed and everyone had cleared out from the shark exhibit and tank area that he was finally spotted on camera. When they told me, he was found and where he was, they couldn't contain me any longer. I raced to get him, and they had stopped me before letting me get to him. I carried him all the way back to the entrance. I thought that that was going to be it. That we were going to be able to leave the park, but I was being led back to the offices. And then TJ was taken from me again. I was brought into a room by a male officer, who told me to take a seat in the chair and then he left the room. Moments later, he returned and…" I lowered my head. "and grabbed me out of the chair. He was yelling at me and then I was slammed to the ground and he wrestled me. I was handcuffed and laid on the floor with a man's knee pressed hard on my back, yet I hadn't been fighting.

"My son saw that. My nephews saw that. The four of them watched from separate rooms as I was yanked to my feet and brutally dragged out of the room and down the hall and to the patrol car, where they watched me being thrown into the back of the car.

"At the station, after mug shots were taken, I was brought into a room and told to undress." A tear ran down my face. "My mother-in-law said that drugs were inside my body, so I was stripe searched. When they found nothing, the woman cop slammed me into the wall told me to get dressed. I did and again cuffs were put on me and I was brought to a holding cell.

"By that time, my mother-in-law had called the station back and said that she had made a mistake, but what was done was done. I spent the night in a holding cell. When a man came to tell me that I could leave, I couldn't even move. I remember him coming in the cell and coming towards me and I had nowhere to go because I was already against the wall, and he bent down and lifted me off the floor."

"I am truly sorry for all of that," Adam said.

"My mother-in-law had enjoyed hearing that I was arrested and taken in. She did not think it would go as far as it did. She wanted to scare me away. She wanted me to stop loving not only her son, but TJ too. She thought she called in before the searches took place, but she didn't."

"Were you hurt?" Adam asked.

"What people don't know is that I had been interrogated all day long by the security team at the park and every time that they asked me if I knew where he was and I said no, one of them would knock me hard in the ribs. This went on for almost six hours. One second we were watching the whale show and when it ended, I had TJ's hand and at some point he let go of my hand, but there were so many people that we were pushed ahead and he was in a crowd too and he went with the crowd thinking that we were there with him.

"When you came and told me I could sit in the chair that was first time all day that I had sat down. I know that you had told me to get up and to put my hands behind my back, but I was too exhausted to move."

"Why didn't you tell me that?"

"Because you had not stopped yelling from the time you came back into the room. And then you hauled me to me feet. I thought you were just to going to cuff me and walk me out of the room, I didn't know it was going to be like that. Before that day, I had never been arrested."

"I'm sorry," he said again.

"I know that you were just doing your job."

The door opened and TJ came running in the room. I looked at him and knew he was going to jump in my arms. I braced myself and caught him. "Daddy said to tell you that everything is ready, and we are waiting for you."

"Ok," I said. "Come. Let's go."

CHAPTER TWENTY-TWO

When we got to the port, we had to go through the security checks. Our passports were checked; our luggage was checked and then checked in. We were given our room keys and a map to follow once we were on the ship. After that, when we were all cleared, we went through a series of mazes; following directions of where to go and then finally we were brought to the cruise ship. We walked on the ramp to get on the ship. TJ was excited and nervous all at once. TJ was walking between Patrick and me holding tight to our hands. I let go of his hand for a second and he stopped stopping Patrick along with him. I turned to him and lifted him up. Then I took Patrick's hand and we continued to board the ship.

We were staying on that level along with the rest of the family. We went to our room to see how it was. For just the three of us, the room was huge. Patrick had purchased the outside estate room for us. We had an ocean view and though the view wasn't pretty right now, it would be.

"Mommy? When school starts in a few weeks, are you going to take me?"

"YES!" I said with excitement.

"Why are you thinking about school?" Patrick asked TJ.

"Because I'm going into the first grade and I'm excited."

"What are you most excited about?"

"I'll have you and mommy there for open house," he said.

My heart melted. This is the sweetest kid ever.

"Are you looking forward to seeing your friends?" I asked.

"I didn't make any. And I don't have any and this is a new school."

"What? Why not?"

"Because I didn't want to be invited to parties and have them ask about my mom."

Patrick sat on the bed. "I'm sorry buddy."

"It's ok, daddy."

"Things will be different this school year."

"I know," TJ said.

We left the room and went to go see about the dining halls. Patrick had already paid for our food services. I lifted TJ up so he could see everything.

"Can I have a cookie?"

"Which ever one you want," the lady serving the food said.

"Thank you."

"Is this the only dining…"

"No. Not at all," she said to Patrick. "Here is a map," she said handing him one. "This has all the dining facilities on the ship. There are hamburger places, there is a fish fry place, and there is the buffet. There is a pretzel stand and a hotdog stand. There are international food stations. There are places to eat everywhere on the ship."

"Thank you."

"What do you want to eat?"

"A pretzel dog," TJ said.

"Well, let's go find that," I said to him.

"Don't overindulge in him," Patrick said.

"Why not overindulge in him? He's all we have."

TJ smiled so bright.

We went walking around the deck that we were staying on, which offered a lot. We found the hotdog stand and TJ got his pretzel dog. Then we continued to walk around.

"So, when do we leave the port?"

Just then the motors kicked in. TJ got scared and turned into me. I reached down and picked him up. "It's ok. We are going be ok and this is going to be the best trip ever."

"This summer has been the best summer ever," TJ said.

"How's that?" Patrick asked.

"I got to go to New York with you at the beginning of the summer and I didn't have to stay with grandma. Then I got to go with to Mommy's house, where I met mommy. She took me to the most awesomest places and then you got married and I got a mommy. It's been a busy fun summer and I'm not even six yet," he said with that beautiful bright smile of his. "The only bad thing is that I got lost and grandma…"

"That's over with now," I said to him. "We have to let that go."

"But why, mommy?"

"Because sometimes you just have to make a choice to move on from things, Turner. This is one of them."

"Ok, mommy."

I loved hearing him call me mommy. I still hold the memory close of when I first heard him say it. Yes, it was said from a dare, but still he called me mommy. I have never felt a love like this. Where it doesn't matter what is going on in my life or how chaotic my life is or maybe, when TJ calls me mommy, it's like finding the pot of gold at the end of a beautiful rainbow.

The cruise liner finally pulled out of port at four o'clock that afternoon. We stood on the deck and waved good-bye to land. We would be on this cruise for seven days, six nights. We would be going to the Bahamas, Saint Marks, and into the Caribbean.

TJ and Tyson's birthday was the next day. We had not seen any of my family members or Patrick's for that matter since we boarded.

"Are we having dinner together?" Patrick asked.

"I don't know," I said.

"Are they staying on our floor?"

"Patrick, darling, you are the one who booked this vacation. I have absolutely no clue where they are staying."

"Well, should we go back to the room and get changed for dinner?"

"Yes," I said.

"When can I go swimming in the pool?"

"Maybe after dinner," Patrick said to him.

We went back to the room and changed for dinner. There was a knock on the door. Patrick opened it. It was Addison and Jamie. "Hey, come on in."

"Sweet room," Jamie said.

"Thanks. How is your room?"

"Oh, it's great," Jamie said.

"Ours is wonderful," Addison said.

I came out of the bathroom. "Hey," I said and hugged my sister first and then Addison. "Where are you guys staying?"

"On this floor," Addison said. "We are staying right off the elevator. We have the first room on the left of the elevator, Jamie and Lennox are right next to us, then your sister and Bruce, mom and dad are next to them, and your mom is next to them."

There was a knock on the door. I opened it this time. Storm came into the room. "You made it," Patrick said to her.

"Yes, of course," she replied.

The kids found us. "Wow, cool room, Aunt Kenny," Kate said.

"I'm hungry," Tyson said.

"Me too," Michael, Beth, TJ, and Kate said.

Carter was quiet. I looked at him and noticed he had his headset on. I tapped him on the shoulder. He looked at me and smiled. "Hi, Aunt Kenny."

"Hi, Carter."

"Mom, dad said to tell you that he's hungry," Carter said to Addison.

"I swear it's like having a sixth child," Addison said. "Go get your father and we will go."

"Who has to go get him?" Carter asked.

"I'll go," Michael said.

"Thank you," Addison said to him.

"Where do you want to eat?" Patrick asked.

"The main diner," Carter said. "They have a buffet and it looks great."

Addison looked at him. "How do you know that?"

"Mom, I've checked out most of the eateries today," he said.

Addison smiled at him.

We went for dinner. The whole entire family. We didn't separate the kids form the adults. We all sat together. The main diner had a touch of everything: Italian, Japanese, Chinese, Indian, Latin, and much much more. All cultures were represented. After dinner, we let the kids go swimming. Because it was dusk, the slides were closed.

"Can we watch the show?" Michael asked.

"Yes, we can watch a little bit of it," Parker answered. "Remember the deal."

"Yes, I do," Michael said.

"What's the deal?" Jamie asked.

"The kids have to read for thirty minutes every day."

Kate had brought her book out with her, so when she was done swimming, she curled up on a lounge chair, wrapped in a towel and she was reading.

"Do I have to read too for thirty minutes every day?" TJ asked.

Patrick and I both said yes.

"But I didn't bring a book."

"That's ok. We will find you one tomorrow," Patrick said.

"Aunt Kenny has books with her," Kate said. "She always has entertainment for us no matter where we are."

"I want to read," TJ said.

That did it. That got us moving from the pool area back to the room. Except this time when we went in the room, we were not alone. We had all the kids in the room with us. They all put on dry clothes then they found places to go and each one of them except for Beth sat down with a book. I gave Beth a coloring book with stickers and she was content.

In the morning, I woke up first and wanted to go for a run. I got up and got dressed. TJ woke up shortly after I did. "Where are you going?"

"I was going to go for a run."

"Can I come?"

"Yes. Put your sneakers on."

He went into the bathroom and when he came out, Patrick was awake now too. Patrick went to him and lifted him up. He carried him to the king size bed and tossed him on it. I jumped on the bed, so the three of us were together. Patrick and I sang "Happy Birthday" very softly to him. TJ was so excited.

"Do you want your presents now or later?" Patrick asked.

"I have presents?"

"Of course, you have presents," Patrick answered.

"But I… this is so cool,"

I took a duffle bag out of the closest and brought it over to the bed. TJ unzipped the bag to find it was loaded with wrapped gifts. He took them out and put them on the bed. Patrick had bought him the new shoes that he was raving about after seeing a commercial for them while watching cartoons. They had lights along the bottom of them. Then he opened clothes. "Cool," he said. "I got a new bathing suit. Look, it has sharkies on them." Next, he opened a box of toys and games. After that, he found the box of books that we had seen at the bookstore not too long ago. His last gift for the moment was a jacket with superheroes on it. He hugged it first and then put it on. Then he hugged each of us. "Thank you, mommy and daddy."

"Are you ready to go have breakfast?"

"YEAH!" TJ said all excitedly. "Can I have a brownie for breakfast?"

"You can have whatever you like for breakfast," Patrick and I said together.

"Can I wear my sharky shorts?"

I smiled at him. "Yes, of course."

"This is the best birthday ever."

We went to breakfast just the three of us. We were meeting the family for lunch today and then we would be dining alone tonight maybe.

"Are you going to go for that run, mommy?"

"Definitely going to put that in the schedule for today," I said.

"Can I go with you?"

"I'll think about it," I said lifting him up and putting him on my shoulders. We walked into the buffet, where there were tons of different foods to choose from. "What's wrong, baby?" I asked TJ.

"I don't see a brownie."

"Don't worry. We haven't made it over to the dessert station yet."

I purposely skipped it because Patrick was getting him a brownie with birthday candles. We made up three plates of food and found a table. TJ was wearing his shark bathing suit and his superhero jacket.

A woman came over just as I lowered TJ to the chair. "Can I ask you a question?" she asked.

"Yes," I said.

"How did you ever manage having a child on your shoulders and carrying three plates?"

"She's multied talented," TJ said.

I smiled and laughed a little.

"Where did you find the crepes?" she asked.

"They are on the second station by the door," I said.

"Thank you. Enjoy your day."

"Thank you. You too."

"Do you have kids?"

"My husband's children are with us," she said.

"Are they around my age? I'm six?"

"No, sorry sweetie. They are teenagers."

A girl with lime green hair came over to the table. "Hi," she said to everyone. "Hey, cool jacket."

"Thank you," TJ said.

"I'm Lizzy."

"Hi, Lizzy," TJ and I said together.

"Steff, dad said I had to ask you if I could go swimming."

"Yes, but I want you back in the room by ten ok?"

"Yeah. Thanks," she said.

"Teenagers," Steff said.

Patrick walked over with a teenage boy following him. He had the plate with a brownie and the candles on it. TJ jumped up on his seat. "Is that for me?" he asked.

"Yes," Patrick said.

"Hi, Steff," the boy said. "Dad said to ask you if I could go play basketball?"

"Yes," she responded. "But be back in the room by ten please."

"Yep. Thanks." He leaned in and kissed her on the cheek.

"Want to sit with us and have some breakfast?" Patrick asked. "I'm Patrick; this is my wife Ken, and our son TJ."

"Hi, nice meeting you all"

She sat with us at the table. Six candles were on the brownie.

"Are you in kindergarten?"

"Nope. I'm going into the first grade," TJ said with a smile.

"Where are you from?" Patrick asked her.

"We are from New Jersey, but we just moved to the Orlando area. Max took a job as a construction site manager."

"Max Benning?" I asked.

"Yeah," she said surprised. "You know him?"

"Yes," I said. "Patrick and I are architects. Your husband is great to work with. Have you two been married long?"

"For three years now. How long have you two been married?"

"A month and half now?" Patrick questioned.

"Yeah, I think that's right," I said.

"But you've been together long enough to have a six-year-old," she said.

"He was all mine originally," Patrick said.

"Mommy adopted me the same day they got married," TJ said.

"Well, then aren't you the lucky one," Steff said to TJ with a smile.

"Yeah, I really am," he said.

"What do you do?"

"I'm a schoolteacher," she said me.

"What grade do you teach?"

"Fifth," she said.

"My cousin is in fifth grade," TJ said.

We shared our breakfast with a stranger. TJ ate his brownie, which he was very happy and thrilled to have it for breakfast. Patrick made him eat a slice of ham, bacon and some fruit before we left there. As we were leaving, Parker and Addison were coming in with the kids.

"Happy birthday, Tyson," I said and bent and kissed him on the head.

"Thank you," he said with a smile.

"What did you have for breakfast today on your birthday?" Parker asked TJ.

"A brownie," TJ said.

"Oh, wow," Tyson said to him. "Happy birthday."

"Happy birthday."

We left them to have their breakfast. We were meeting at two for lunch, so we still had all morning to do whatever we wanted to do. We let TJ decide how he wanted to spend the morning. He wanted to try surfing, so we went there first. He had fun and Patrick and I each took turns doing it with him. Then we went and played basketball. For a six-year-old, he knows how to move on the court. From there we went swimming until we were told that we had to get out of the pool due to a storm out on the ocean, so we went back to the room and showered and dressed. We played with a couple of his games that he got. We played JR Monopoly first.

"I don't know how to count money," TJ said.

"Oh, well let's show you," I said. I went to my wallet and took out money. Patrick took out change from his pocket. We put it all on the table. "If I give you five dollars and tell you to go buy a drink that costs a dollar, how much would you be given back?"

I watched as he used his fingers. He held his hand up and then put his thumb down. "Four," he said.

"Ok, that was an easy one where you could use your fingers, but you can't always use your fingers to count money," Patrick said.

"So, what do I do?" he asked.

We spent the next forty minutes going over money with him. He loved every minute of it and when we were done with the lesson, he had really got it.

By two o'clock, the storm had moved on. Everyone once again met in our room. Tyson did not look happy. "What's going on with him?" Patrick asked Parker.

Tyson looked up with tears brimming. "I'm not getting any presents," he whaled.

I couldn't control myself. I turned and lifted him in my arms. He put his head on my shoulder and cried a hard cry. Sometimes I thought my brother could be mean.

"Where are Michael and Kate?"

"They are with Lennox getting a table for us for lunch," Addison said. Just then her cell phone buzzed. "The table is ready," she announced to the room. I carried Tyson, who was slowly starting to calm down.

"Everything is going to be ok, sweetheart," I said to him.

"He's being a baby," Beth announced.

"And that's ok, Bethy," I said. "It will get better."

By the time we got to the restaurant they picked, Tyson was sleeping on my shoulder. They choose the sit down and order restaurant for lunch and because of the previous weather conditions, the place was packed. I sat with Tyson on my lap and TJ next to me. I gently woke Tyson, who woke up just as the waiter came over. We placed our orders. Patrick and Parker both got up from the table and told the rest of us that they would be right back. After we ate lunch, the waiters and waitresses came over with two cakes singing happy birthday. Both boys were smiling so big. After the candles were blown out and the cakes were cut, we went back to the cabins. Once again, everyone came in our cabin. A man followed us into the room carrying bags and presents. I tipped him and he left. Neither birthday boy realized what had just happened. Tyson was checking out TJ presents from this morning.

"What's Twister?" Tyson asked.

"A fun game that we can all play," Parker said.

Addison and I set up the gifts for the boys. Mom and Trinity blocked the view of the boys so they wouldn't see.

Over the loudspeaker an announcement was made about the weather conditions. We were supposed to dock into port, but due to the weather we couldn't, so we would be waiting out the storm for the time being. Passengers were free to move about the ship.

After the announcement was made, Addison got the boys attention. "Tyson and TJ, how about you both come over here," she said to them. Both boys turned to see the two mountains of presents. They both came racing over. They sat in the chairs at the table and waited.

They both got new backpacks for school and school supplies, and coloring books, and toy cars, and Lego sets. Our room was now cluttered with toys, but everyone was having a great time.

"Mommy is taking me to my first day of first grade," TJ announced.

Mom got teary eyed as did Trinity.

The whole trip went so well. We got off the boat as a family and did excursions together. We went zip lining, we went white water rafting, we hiked and climbed a mountain, and then on the second to last night on the ship, with our family all dressed up to the nines, we had our wedding reception, which fell on August tenth, which is the day our paths crossed over fifteen years ago at orientation for school.

We walked into the banquet hall, where the cruise ship had given us the room for the night. We walked in holding hands and the announcer announced us, "Now entering the room is bride and groom: Mr. and Mrs. Patrick and Kennedy Alexander and their adorable six-year-old son, Turner James Alexander. I was carrying him. Patrick whispered for me to put him down, but I didn't. The three of us walked out on the dance floor and we danced together. TJ started to cry. We finished the dance and then attended to him.

"What's wrong, sweetheart?" I asked.

"I'm just happy," he cried.

"I know you are."

"Let's toast to the happy couple," the announcer said.

We thanked him.

"Who wants to give the first speech?"

"I will," I said. I walked to the center of the room. "It was fifteen years ago today that I saw this gorgeous looking guy standing in the middle of the lawn on campus just looking around. I remember thinking, I hope he looks my way and then he did. I smiled at him. Fast forward, years later, we have worked together in the same space for more than ten years now; however, we didn't really know what happened to the other when the lights were turned off at the office or on whatever site we were working on. I did not know that Patrick had an adorable son, who would come to be our son this summer. I am so glad that all of those years ago, I smiled at him and waved hello."

Patrick came and stood next to me. "Fifteen years ago, today, I knew I saw the woman I was going to marry. Although life and circumstances kept us apart, it also kept us together. I am so glad that Kenny said yes to marrying me and my...our son. She is my soulmate, my best friend and now she is my wife."

"I love you," we said together.

We danced most of the night. Waiters and waitresses came in with the dinner plates and we stopped dancing to eat dinner together with everyone. I did not think about the wedding cake, but mom and Trinity did. A waiter pushed in a cart with a beautifully decorated cake. Perched on the top of the cake, was a figurine of a man, woman, and child. The kids took a ton of pictures.

"Will the loving and happy couple please come cut their cake."

Both Patrick and I stopped dancing and turned to see a three tiered cake. "Oh, wow," I said. "Did you do this?" I asked him.

"No. I thought you did."

"No, it wasn't me."

I looked at Addison. She shook her head.

"If she didn't do this, then who?" Patrick asked.

"I don't know," I said.

Our mothers were standing close to the cart with the cake on it. As we walked closer, I noticed a wedding knife in my mother's hands. I looked at her and smiled with tears in my eyes. She had gotten us an engraved wedding knife. Trinity was holding two bronze plates that had our wedding date engraved on it. Wednesday: June 28, 2017 at 12:00 P.M.

Patrick and I both smiled at each other. "At least someone has our wedding date written down," he said.

There was a third and smaller bronze plate that said: Kennedy Rose Jackson-Alexander becomes Tuner James Alexander's mother on Wednesday: June 28, 2017 at 12:30 P.M. *To the start of a wonderful family: Patrick, Kennedy and Turner Alexander Congratulations*

We finally made it the rest of the way to the cake, where my mom handed me the knife. Patrick and I took it together and cut the first slice. I took the figurine off the cake and held it up. TJ came running to us. I scooped him up in my arms as the cake was cut. We went to our table. Mom came over. "You don't have to hold on to the figurine," she said. "It's yours."

"I know," I said with a smile. "But I don't want to put it down."

"You look stunning in that."

"Thank you, mom."

We had such a wonderful time that evening. Everyone enjoyed themselves. By the time we returned to our rooms, everyone was exhausted. TJ like Beth, Tyson, Carter and Kate had fallen asleep at the reception. I carried TJ, Patrick carried Kate, Addison carried Beth, Parker carried Tyson and Michael carried Carter. Addison and Parker agreed to take TJ for the night, so that Patrick and I could be alone. We all went into their room. We put the kids down. I took TJ's dress pants off and his shoes and shirt.

"Thank you for keeping him," Patrick said.

"Sure. It's no problem."

I reminded her that he has nightmares and if she needed to call our room not to hesitate. She assured us that everything would be fine and with that we went to our room. Patrick and I showered together starting off the sexual connection between us. We had intercourse in the shower that was riveting. Patrick carried me to the bed, where we went again. We had intimate passionate sex. It wasn't rough or aggressive. When we done, we laid as close as possible. I remember glancing at the clock and seeing that it was a quarter till four in the morning before I closed my eye.

Not even an hour later, with Patrick sleeping soundly, my cell phone buzzed. I got up out of bed, going to my phone. I looked at the text.

Please come ASAP. TJ is screaming and we can't get him to stop. Parker wrote.

On my way. I responded back. I pulled on a pair of shorts and t-shirt and my sneakers and left the room. I went to my brother's room. I knocked on the door and Michael opened it.

"Is everyone awake?" I asked.

"The younger kids went to sleep in Grandma's room with them."

"I'm so sorry that this happened."

I went rushing over to TJ. He was screaming. I sat with him on the bed. "TJ, it's ok. I'm here now," I said.

"I think he's still sleeping," Michael said.

I touched his arm and he jolted backwards. I grabbed a hold of him. He quieted down. I took him in my lap. I caressed him. "MOMMY!" he yelled out. "MOMMY!"

"I'm here, TJ. Open your eyes and see."

Slowly he opened his eyes. Sweat poured off his body.

"I want to go to our room," he said.

"I know. Come on," I said standing up and taking him with me. "Thank you for all your help and thank you for tonight," I said to Addison.

I carried TJ down the hall to our room. I unlocked the door and then once in the room, I changed his clothes and put him to bed. I climbed back in bed with Patrick and snuggled close to him.

"Did you get up?" he asked.

"Yeah. I brought TJ back in our room."

"Why?"

"He had a nightmare and wouldn't stop screaming."

"Is he ok?"

"Yeah, he seems to be. He's in his bed now."

We went back to sleep and slept till eight in the morning. It was our last day on the cruise ship before it docked into port tomorrow morning, so we were going to have a fun filled day.

Patrick and I spent an hour packing our things and getting everything together. Then we showered and dressed for the day. TJ was still sleeping. We let him sleep while we tidied up the room. We put his new things in his backpack. We cleaned up Tyson's things as well and put all of his things in his backpack as well.

"I'm going to go for a run if you don't mind," I said to him.

"No, I don't mind," he said.

"I have my phone. Text me when you are ready to go for breakfast."

I put on my sneakers, took my phone and ear buds, and put money in my pocket and then left the room. I went to the track on the ship and ran five miles. Just as I was finishing my last lap, my cell phone buzzed. I waited till I finished the lap to look at it. They were ready for breakfast. I picked up my jacket, put it on and then went to meet them.

"Good morning," I said to TJ. He looked up at me and smiled.

"Good morning, mommy."

We had breakfast. Then we went together to have fun. We did the surfing again, we played all the games that were available, and when the weather changed to dark and stormy, we went back to the room and watched a movie together. We went for dinner that night and just enjoyed the entire atmosphere.

That night when we put TJ to bed, both Patrick and I climbed on the bed with him. We snuggled with him. I closed my eyes for a minute, and I wound up sleeping the whole night. Patrick had done the same. The three of us slept in the smaller bed together all night long.

CHAPTER TWENTY - THREE

When we departed the cruise ship, we were all going back up north including mom and dad. We all got into the RV that Patrick had rented, and we started our journey home. I was driving the first leg, but we really didn't need to stop other than if we needed gas, but Patrick had fueled this thing before we left it a week ago.

I drove to the rest stop north of Fort Pierce, Fort Drum. We weren't empty, but we were low on fuel. I pulled into the gas station at the rest stop.

"I have to go to the bathroom," Tyson, TJ, Carter, and Michael said.

"Well, let's go," Parker said.

I went with them as did Kate, mom, Trinity, and Storm. We went in and used the bathroom and when we came out, Kate started the kids off with "I'm hungry."

I ran out to the others and told them that the kids were hungry and did they want anything. Addison came back with me. We ordered chicken sandwiches, French fries, and onion rings and then we went back out to the RV. We all ate. Taking that first bite into the sandwich, I hadn't realized how hungry I was. Parker took over driving.

"Do you have plans for when we get back?" mom asked.

"Well, I have to go into the building and see how the projects are coming along. Why?"

"Your father and I are leaving on Wednesday to go home, so we want to spend time with each of you."

"We will definitely spend time together."

Parker pulled into his neighborhood. He unpacked their bags, we all exchanged hugs and then I got back in the driver's seat and drove to the house. The Jackson Estate looked beautiful as we pulled into it. I heard mom sigh. I parked the RV on the street. We all got out and took bags into the house. I went back for more of our stuff. Michael and Carter rode up on their bikes.

"Hey, guys."

"Mom wants to know if you want her to come over to cook for everyone."

"Why didn't she just call me?"

"Because she took your phone by mistake," Carter said. "Here, Aunt Kenny."

"Thank you."

"So, do you want her come over and cook for everyone?" Michael asked.

"Please say yes," Carter chimed in.

"You all know that you are always invited," I said.

I took another bag from the RV and Michael called Addison. "Aunt Kenny said yes, mommy. She said get here right now and cook us all a damn meal," Michael laughed.

I found it to be really amazing that in just a few weeks, Michael would be going to middle school and he still calls his mom mommy. Carter got off his bike and went in the RV and took a few things. Patrick came back out to get stuff.

"Oh, hey, guys."

"Hi," they said together. "Mommy is coming over to cook."

"Oh, ok."

The boys parked their bikes in the garage and helped carry in more things. I went back in the house to check on TJ and found him sound asleep on mom's lap. I stopped and took a picture of it. "Addy is coming over to cook dinner."

"Why don't they just move closer to you?"

"I don't know. I've mentioned that too a few times over the years."

"The house next door is on the market," dad said.

Parker came to the house with the rest of the kids. "Addison made a stop, but she will be here soon."

"You know, Parker," dad started. "The Miller's house is on the market."

Parker nodded his head. "Yes, sir, I noticed that."

"Why don't you and I go over there?"

"Right now?"

"Yeah," dad said.

"Oh. Ok."

He and dad went over there. It wasn't right next door although it was next door. It was about two hundred yards away. They spoke with the Millers and dad wound up purchasing the house right there on the spot.

"Will mom be mad?"

"I don't know," he said.

"I can't believe that you did that."

"Why not?"

"So, do you want to move back up here?"

"No. I love living in Key West," he said.

"Then why did you buy it?"

"Because I always wanted it."

"So will Ken own it?"

"No."

"Are you going to give it to Jamie and Lennox?"

"No."

"Then what are you going to do with it?"

"Parker, stop asking questions."

They came back into the house.

"Dad, Frank Miller called for you," I said.

"What on earth would he want?" mom asked.

"I just bought his house."

"You did what?" Mom, Jamie, and I asked.

"I did. I just bought their house."

"Why?" mom asked.

"Roberta, you know that I have always wanted to own that house."

"Yes, I know that, but are we going to sell our house?"

"No."

"Then what are you going to do with?"

Addison walked in the house. "Hi," she said. "Mr. Miller is dancing around in his driveway," she said.

"Dad just bought their house."

"For who?" she asked.

"For you, Parker and the kids," dad said.

There was hard knock on the door. Patrick opened it. Mr. and Mrs. Bankers were standing there. "Please come in."

They came in. "Frank and Trish just said that Todd bought their house."

"I did," dad said.

"We too want to put the house on the market," Jane Bankers said.

"How much are you asking for it?" Lennox asked.

"I don't know," she said. "How much did Frank sell for?"

"Six hundred thousand," dad said.

"Our house isn't as big as their house," Jane said.

"How big is it?" Lennox asked.

"Four bed rooms, three and half baths and three car garage."

"Can I see the house?" he asked.

"Yes, of course," Jane said.

Within the next fifteen minutes, my brother and sister were now my neighbors. The Millers would be moved out of the house at the end of month and the Bankers said that could be out by the first few weeks in September.

Just as we sat down for dinner, there was a hard knock on the front door. I went and got it. A woman with green hair stood outside. "Can I help you?"

"Do you know Lennox?"

"I do."

"Do you know where he is?"

"Yes, I do."

"Can you get him?"

"Please come in. Who are you?"

"Meg," she said.

"And how do you know Lennox?"

"I'm his sister."

I went into the kitchen. "Lennox, there is someone here to see you."

"What? Who?"

"A woman with green hair named Meg."

He got up and rushed out of the room. Jamie sat looking at me.

Lennox went into the living room. "What are you doing here?"

"Listen. I know I'm the last person that you want to see right now."

"You could say that again. Why are you here?"

"I needed to tell you that I'm sorry."

"Do you even know what you are sorry about?"

She looked at him. "Yeah, I think," she said.

"Meg, I don't need this shit from you anymore. I am in a relationship with an extraordinary woman, who is going to have my child. I am done playing your games. Go back to mom and dad's and don't contact me again."

"It's not that easy."

"Why not?"

"They threw me out."

"Little girl, you are not staying here. Wherever you are trouble follows. I don't want you here."

"Please, Lennox?"

"No. Get out."

Jamie came into the room. "Hi," she said.

"Hi," Meg said.

"Who are you?"

"I'm Meg."

"Who are you?"

"I'm Lennox's sister."

"Are you the one who stole from me?"

Meg shrugged. "I don't know. I guess."

"You stole something that is really important to me and I want it back."

"What is it?"

"A gold tipped guitar pic," Jamie said. "It means so much to me and I want it back right now."

Meg dropped her purse on the couch and fished through it. She pulled out several guitar pics.

"Oh, my god," Jamie said. "You little bitch."

Kate came into the room. "Aunt Jamie?"

"Not now, Katie bug."

"But Aunt Jamie."

Jamie looked at her. "She's the one who stole the pin that you gave me." Kate, who hardly ever cried started crying.

Meg looked at Kate who was just about sobbing. She fished through her purse again and pulled out the elusive pin. She held it up.

"Lennox, with your permission I'd like to call the police," Jamie said.

"You don't need my permission," he said to her.

Jamie took her phone out of her pocket and she called the police. Four officers showed up a few minutes later.

"Never a dull moment," Trinity said when the police arrived.

"No. Not at all," mom answered. "My kids don't play around. And for that I am extremely proud of all three of them."

The police were explained the situation and how everything was with Meg. That she was a druggy and she stole money from Lennox, she stole from Jamie and she stole from Kate.

"Do you want to press charges?" one officer asked.

"Yes." Lennox said.

"But you're my brother?"

"And you are thief."

The police took pictures of the couch with merchandize on it. Then they put her in handcuffs; when this happened, I looked away. She led her out of the house. They took everything that was on couch in for evidence.

"You will have to come to the station to claim your possessions," one officer said.

"Thank you," Lennox said.

When they left, Jamie apologized to him. "Why are you apologizing?"

"Because your sister was arrested."

"Look if it's going to get her the help, she needs then so be it." He went to Kate and hugged her. "You are such a brave young lady," he said. "I'm very proud of you."

"What did I do?"

"You stood up and told the truth. I don't know too many kids that would do something like that. I know that some would clam up and not say anything, but you have done something right from the start. You never backed down even when Jamie yelled at you."

"You yelled at my daughter?" Addison said coming into the room.

"I did," Jamie said. "I thought she was being irresponsible and that she lost the pin that I gave her. I had it special made for her. One day she was wearing it and the next it was gone."

"It's ok, Aunt Jamie," Kate said giving her a hug.

"No, sweetheart, I'm sorry."

"Are you ok?" Addison asked Kate.

"Yes, mommy," she said.

Jamie and Lennox went to the police station. Meg was booked and held at the station. Lennox and Jamie were able to reclaim their things.

"When will she be arraigned?"

"Tomorrow, sir," the woman behind the counter said.

"Thank you."

Everything at the house finally started to settle down after ten that evening. TJ was still wound up. Parker took Beth and Tyson home. Carter, Kate, and Michael were playing in the game room. Addison sat with mom on the couch. Addison closed her eyes for a second and was soon asleep.

"Are we spending the night?" Michael asked.

"It looks that way," I said to him. "I want you all to go upstairs and get ready for bed please."

"Ok. Sure, Aunt Kenny."

Michael went and gathered TJ, Kate and Carter and they went upstairs. Mom and dad went to their room. I got a blanket to cover Addison with. When I put it over her, she opened her eyes. "Are the kids ready?"

"It's pouring rain right now. Why don't you stay the night? Besides the kids are upstairs and in bed."

"You're sure you don't mind?"

"No. Of course not."

My cell phone rang. I looked at it. It was Parker. "Hello."

"Is Tyson there with you?"

"No. Didn't you take him home with Beth?"

"I did, but I just went to check on them and he isn't here. Where is Addy?"

"She's sleeping on the couch. I will go and see if I find him."

I didn't hang up with Parker. I ran to the front door and went to leave and there standing in front of me was Tyson drenched. "Parker, he's here."

"Is he ok?"

"He's soaking wet. I'm going to give him a bath and then put him to bed."

"Tomorrow he's getting it," Parker said. "Good night."

"Good night. I love you."

"I love you too," Parker said.

I picked up Tyson. "How did you get here?"

"I road my bike," he said.

"What? Tyson that is over ten miles."

"I know, but I wanted to be here. I wanted to be with you and everyone else. Where are they?"

"They are upstairs sleeping. Come. Let's get you dry and warm."

I took him upstairs and put him in the shower. Then I put him in pajamas. Mom heard us and came to see what was going on. "How in the hell did he get here?"

"I rode my bike, grandma," Tyson said.

"You did what?"

"I rode my bike here."

"In the rain?"

"Well, it wasn't raining when I left the house," he said.

"How did you come?"

"Mom, that doesn't matter now. I'm going to put him to bed, and he can tell us in the morning."

"Yes, that's fine," mom said.

I took Tyson to the room just off mine and where I knew his brothers and sister would be sleeping. I opened the door and saw the light go off. "Who is awake?" I asked.

Kate uncovered herself. "Is it ok?"

"You really need to get some sleep."

"What is he doing here? How in the hell did you get here?"

"I rode my bike."

"TYSON!" Kate scolded. Tyson looked at her. He put his hands on his hips as if making a statement.

Michael opened his eyes. "Where's Tyson?"

"He's right here."

Michael shot out of bed. "What the hell? How did you get here?"

"I rode my bike."

"Does daddy know that you are gone?"

"Yeah."

Michael picked him up and brought him on the bed with him. He made him lay down. "You need to go to sleep."

"You all need to go to sleep. Good night," I said to them.

I went in my room. Patrick had gone to bed hours ago. TJ was snuggled in bed with him. I turned the TV on and the lights off and got into bed. TJ opened his eyes and came closer to me. I took him in my arms. I pushed his hair back away from his face and kissed him on the forehead and then I drifted off to sleep.

In the morning, Parker was at the house before anyone got up. He came upstairs and got Tyson. He brought him downstairs and scolded him severely.

"But I told you that I wanted to stay with mommy and the others."

"And I told you no. If you do it again, I will tan your hide. Do you hear me?"

"Yes, daddy."

"You lost your bike for two weeks."

"But we are going bike riding with Aunt Kenny today."

"And you aren't going with them."

"But daddy, I want to go."

"No, Tyson, you aren't going. You don't listen. You don't get to go."

"I'm sorry."

"Tell me what you are sorry for?"

"I'm sorry that I didn't tell you I was going to ride my bike to Aunt Kenny's."

"Nope. That's not it. You still aren't going with them today. Now go outside in the back yard and run around the track till I tell you to stop."

"Ok, daddy."

I came downstairs in my workout clothes. I looked out of the window seeing Tyson running hard around the track. I walked outside to see how he was doing. "Hey, what are you doing?"

"Running."

"For how long?"

"Till daddy comes out and tells me I can stop."

"How long have you been running?"

"It was still a little dark," he said.

I looked at my watch. It was nearing eight. "You can stop," I said to him.

"I can't. Daddy is mad at me because I came here last night. He said I have to wait for him to tell me to stop."

"I'll be right back ok, buddy."

"Sure, Aunt Kenny."

I ran to the house to find Parker. I found him working in the side garage. "How long are you going to leave a five-year-old boy running?"

He did not hear me. He had his earphones on and music playing loudly in his ears. I walked over and slammed my hand on the table he was working on. "What the fuck?" he said. He pushed his earphones off. "What the fuck," he repeated.

"How long are you going to leave Tyson running around the track?"

"What? He's in the house now."

"No, he's not. He's running around the track because you told him to do it until you came out and told him to stop."

"What?"

"I'm not repeating it because I know that you fucking heard me."

Parker put down what he was working on and went out in the back yard to find Tyson still running around the track. He ran over to him. "You can stop now. Go in the house," he said to him.

"Yes, sir," Tyson said.

He walked with his head down into the house. Addison was in the kitchen cooking when Tyson came in. "Good morning," she said to him.

"Is it? I don't know," he said.

"What? What happened?"

"Nothing, mommy."

Beth was in the kitchen with Addison. She was sitting at the table. "Daddy had him running around the track," she reported. Addison turned and looked at Tyson. His shirt was stained with sweat at the neckline and the arm pits.

"Is this true?"

"Yes, ma'am," Tyson said.

"Why?"

"Because I rode my bike over here last night. He said I can't go with Aunt Kenny on the bike ride. He said I'm grounded from my bike for two weeks."

"But why did you have to run around the track?"

Tyson shrugged.

"Go take a shower and then you can have breakfast."

"Ok, mommy," he said.

He came upstairs and went into the bathroom and showered. He got dressed and came back downstairs.

"You're in trouble," Beth said.

"What?" Tyson asked.

"You're going to get it," Beth taunted.

Tyson got scared that he was going to get it because Parker threatened to tan his hide earlier. He ran out of the room and went and hid in the cabinet in my office. Addison came back in the kitchen seeing Beth giggling. "What's going on, Missy?"

"Tyson is funny," Beth said.

"Where is he?"

"I don't know," she said with a smile.

Addison went looking for Tyson with no luck. Carter came in the kitchen with Michael and TJ. Addison came back in the kitchen. "Have you seen Tyson?"

"No," the boys said together.

"Could you help me look for him?"

"Sure, mom," Michael said.

The three boys left the room and ran throughout the house looking for him. TJ went in my office and looked for him, but never thought to go into the cabinets. They looked for him again, but still didn't find him.

"Mom, I don't know where he is."

"Can you get your dad?"

"Sure, mom," Michael said. He ran to the garage. "Dad, we can't find Tyson."

Parker dropped what he was working on and ran into the house with Michael. "When did you last see him?"

"He came in and told me that you had him run around the track and that you punished from his bike for the next two weeks. Then he went upstairs to take a shower and that's the last time I saw him."

"TYSON!"

I came back from the grocery store. "Is Tyson with you?"

"No. Why?"

"We can't find him," Addison said.

Beth was giggling again at the table. Addison turned and looked at her. "Where is your brother?"

"I don't know," she said.

"What did you do?"

"I told him that he's in trouble," she said with a smile.

"BETH!" Parker and Addison yelled at her together.

Lennox came into the kitchen. "What's going on?"

"Have you seen Tyson?"

"No."

I grabbed my car keys and went looking for him. I drove by the park, the school, and their house. I went into their house and looked for him but didn't find him. I locked their house and doubled back searching for him. When I got back to the house, the police were there. Parker was sitting on the couch in tears. "I was so mad at him this morning. I came here and woke him up and I scolded him for riding his bike here alone last night. I told him that he is grounded for the next two weeks from his bike. I told him that I would tan his hide if he ever did anything like that again."

"Do you have surveillance cameras?"

"Yes. For outside the house," I said. We watched the video from about the time that he went missing, but he never came out of the house.

Kate was sitting on the couch crying. "We searched the whole house and he's nowhere to be found," she said.

My phone rang in my office. I got up and ran in there. "Hello," I said. It was a work call, so I sat in my chair and turned and looked up and I saw that one of cabinets wasn't closed all the way. I stood up and opened it. Tyson was curled up sleeping. "I have to call you back," I said. "Tyson," I said softly. "Ty." I reached in and gently pulled him out. He woke up in a panic.

"No. No. Daddy is going to spank me."

"No, he's not," I said. "We have been looking for you for hours." I carried him out of my office. "I found him," I said.

Parker stood up and ran over to me. Tyson started to cry really hard. "Please don't spank me."

"Spank you!" Parker said. "No, buddy. Come here." Parker took him from me and just hugged him.

The police left the house. Parker still held tight to Tyson. "Why do you think that I was going to spank you?"

"Because you said it," Tyson cried.

"I'm not going to spank you."

"Beth said I was in trouble and I was going to get it."

"She's three," Parker said.

Tyson put his head on Parker's shoulder and continued to cry. "I'm sorry, daddy," he said.

Addison had come over and sat with them. The other kids slowly left the room leaving Addison and Parker to deal with Tyson. Lennox picked up Beth and brought her out of the room. Tyson went to Addison climbing up in her arms and snuggling close to her. "It's ok," Addison said. "Everything is ok."

Lennox brought Beth in the room where he and Jamie were staying. "So, what did you do?" he asked Beth.

She shrugged.

"Oh no, munchkin, what did you do?"

"I told him he was going to get it. It was funny. He runned out of the room."

"And you think that this is funny?"

"Yep," she said.

"Beth, that's bad," Lennox said. "You can't do that."

She smiled and laughed. "Ok," she said.

With everything worked out now and all the kids accounted for, I went back into my office to return the phone call. "Mr. Bruno please," I said to the woman's voice on the other end of the line. He came on the line. "Mr. Bruno, I'm sorry about before. What can I help you with at this time?"

"I want to change the windows," he said. "I want them to be ceiling to floor windows."

"In which rooms?"

"In all of the rooms," he said.

"Well, let me pull the blueprints and see what we have to work with."

"I want to be able to look out from anywhere I am in the house. From the first and the second floor."

"Yes, I understand that, sir. Let me take a look and I'll get back to you within the next hour."

I hung up with him and went to find Patrick. "Hey, Mr. Bruno called."

"What the hell does he want now?"

"He wants ceiling to floor windows throughout the whole house."

I laid the blueprints out and we looked over them. "So literally he doesn't want walls," Patrick said.

"That's what I'm understanding."

I called him back and told him that we could put in storm windows throughout the house."

"And when do you think construction will be complete?"

"Ground was just broken, so it will be at least two months."

"And I want a glass bottom pool."

"We've already discussed that, Mr. Bruno," I said.

"Yes, I know, but I'm going to keep on trying."

After hanging up with him for the third time, I thought of tempered glass. We could make his house out of that and his pool as well. It would be an above ground pool, but it could be done.

"Hey, babe," Patrick said to me. "We need to run a background check on this guy."

I laughed. "It's being done."

"He wants a house with no walls, and he wants a glass pool."

"Yeah," I said.

"I mean I know this man has money to spend, but something is off here."

"I'm going to go out to the site and see how things are coming."

"Ok. Can you take TJ with you?"

"Yes," I said.

"I have to get ready to go to Daytona."

"I know," I said.

I rolled the blueprints back up and went and found TJ. He was playing basketball with Carter. Addison was wrapping things up in the kitchen. "Hey, we are going to head out for the rest of the day and take the kids to the movies. There is dinner in the fridge. You just have to warm it up."

"Thank you," I said.

"So, when is this place going to open up as B&B?"

"We have to wait for that building in the back to be complete. It will be at least another two weeks and then we will get in the gym equipment and from there Patrick, TJ and I will move into mom and dad's apartment in the front of the house and then we will open."

"How many maximum occupants can there be?"

"Well there are ten bedrooms not including mom and dad's apartment, so couples with kids can be two adults and six kids in three different rooms, or it can be up to eight adults in those rooms, and then there are smaller rooms, but each room can comfortably fit six adults or families and still have room."

"I just need to know how many people I would be cooking for."

"Let's say a hundred and fifty," I said. "That would be guests and employees."

"Are we going to open up the banquet hall for meals?"

"No. We have a full formal dining room."

"What? Where the hell is that?"

I started to laugh. Then I went to a door to the left of the kitchen and opened the door to reveal a large dining room.

"Has this been here long?"

"Ever since the place was built," I said.

"Wow. Every day this place has new surprises." She looked at her watch. "Oh, we have to get going. Michael, Carter, Kate, and Tyson we have to go."

"TJ, come on in."

The kids came into the house. Addison and Parker left with the kids. Patrick came downstairs with a duffle bag packed. TJ looked at him. "Where are you going?"

"I have to go to Daytona for a few days."

"Oh. Ok."

He kissed TJ on the forehead and then he kissed me. "Be good for mommy."

"Always," he said.

"I love you. I'll see you at the end of the week." With that Patrick left.

Mom and dad came into the kitchen for the first time today. "Hi," dad said.

"Hi. I didn't know you were here," I said to them. "Can I get you something to eat?"

"No. Addison told us there is plenty to choose from in the fridge."

TJ started to giggle. I looked at him. "What's up, buddy?"

"Grandpa's shirt is missed buttoned," he said.

I looked at dad's shirt and sure enough it was. Dad looked down and then looked at mom and they smiled at each other.

"With that, TJ and I need to run out for about an hour."

"Where are you going?" mom asked.

"I am going to go check the site of a house that I am designing. The homeowner wants to change things on his house, so I have to see what we will be dealing with before I can sign off on the possibilities of his plans for his house."

"When you get back, let's have lunch," mom said.

"Yes, that will be nice."

I took TJ to the construction site with me. There was a chain link fence up, and big trucks on the property. And of course, you couldn't miss the giant mountain of rocks and dirt that were piled up at least twenty feet high.

"Can I climb that?"

"No."

"How come there is a fence around this?"

"Because of what you just asked before the fence question."

"So, you want to keep people out?"

"Yes. Precisely."

My phone rang. "Hello, Mr. Bruno."

"Can we start with the landscape?"

"No, Mr. Bruno."

"But I want a lot of trees. I want a forest behind my house."

"Mr. Bruno, your house isn't the only house in this development. We have already been over this."

"Well, how many houses are there going to be?"

"There will forty houses in this development."

"And where will my house be in the development?"

"Just where we discussed. Your house will be in the front of the development."

"Can I come get a look?"

"No, sir. Like I discussed earlier with you today, they just broke ground, so there is nothing really to see."

"And what about the pool? Am I going to get a glass pool?"

"Like I have already told you, I need to speak with a different pool facility to see about this."

"And I want the pool to be twelve feet deep."

"Yes, sir, I know this."

"Mommy, I have to pee."

"Do you have a child on the site? How come a child gets to see it and I don't?"

"Because he's going into the first grade when school starts in the fall and he has no say of what or what doesn't go into this site."

"But I want to see the layout again."

"Then why don't you meet me at the office in an hour and I will happily show you the layout of the land once again."

"In an hour?"

"Yes, sir, in an hour."

"So that will be at four o'clock?"

I looked at my wrist. "Yes, sir."

"Ok. I will see at four. At the site?"

"No, sir. At my office."

"Yes, of course," he said.

I hung up the phone. "Mommy. I have to pee."

"Why don't you go right over there," I said to him.

"Where?"

"Right," I took him by the hand and brought him over to a spot. "here," I said. "This is a good spot."

"What will be here?"

"Mr. Bruno's pool," I said with a smile and laughed. He smiled and peed. "Let's go. And this stays between us."

"Ok."

CHAPTER TWENTY - FOUR

I took TJ to the office. "Wow!" TJ said jumping up and down.

"You're acting like this is the first time you've ever been here?"

"It is," he said.

"What?"

"Mommy, did you even know that I existed before daddy brought me to your house?"

I gave it thought and then lied to him. "Yes, I knew you existed."

"Can I go climb on that?"

"On what?"

"On the thingy that looks like a squirrel."

"It is a squirrel and I'm very proud of you for seeing it like it is."

"Can I climb on it?"

"Yes."

"Who builted it?"

"Built not builted. And daddy and I did that."

"Cool! So, I can climb on it?"

"Yes. Look. My office is right over there. Stay where I can see you."

"IS THAT A POOL!"

"No. It's a fountain."

"It's so deep. Can I go swimming in it?"

I thought for a minute. "Just don't pee in it," I said.

He took off his shoes and socks, his t-shirt and shorts and was standing in a pair of Batman boxer shorts.

"Have fun."

"Thanks, mommy."

TJ jumped into the fountain. He swam to the far side of it and swam back repeatedly. I left him and went into my office. I pulled up the layout and then set the light to the drafting table then I shot the layout on the light table.

Mr. Bruno came into the building. He was a large man at over six eight. He saw TJ swimming in the fountain and walked over and sat down on the edge of it. "How's the water?"

"Warm."

"Are you the little boy that was at the site today?"

"Yes, sir," he said.

"What does it look like?"

"Like nothing," TJ said. "There's a huge fence, a couple large trucks, and huge piles of dirt and rocks."

"Thanks, little kid."

"TJ."

"Hi, TJ, I'm David Bruno."

"Mr. Bruno," I said coming out of my office.

"Is that your mom?"

"Yep. I mean yes, sir."

"Yep is fine, TJ," he said. "Have fun swimming in this beautiful fountain."

TJ smiled at him and swam to the far side again.

"How old is he?"

"He just turned six."

"He's cute. Oh, should he be climbing on that?"

"Yes, he's ok."

We went over the layout. "I decided that I don't want a glass pool anymore. I want a pool like that fountain."

"That can be done."

Mr. Bruno looked over to see where TJ was. He was back in the fountain. "Can we go out there by him?"

"Yes, sir."

When we came out of the office, Lynn and Kara came into the building. "There is a child swimming in our fountain," Kara said. "Hey, what are you doing?"

"He's fine, Kara," I said.

"Who in the hell does this kid belong to?"

"He's Patrick's and my son," I said.

"Oh, shit, I'm sorry."

"Welcome back from Tokyo. How was the trip?"

"It was great," Lynn said. "We learned a lot. How was your summer?"

"It was wonderful."

"Wait. Did you say that Patrick and you have a son together?"

"We do."

"Where in the hell have you been hiding him for what, four or five years?"

"I'm six."

"I adopted him at the beginning of the summer when I married Patrick."

"What? We missed the wedding?" Lynn said.

"No. We eloped and the adoption went through the same day."

"Congratulations," they said together.

"Hi, Mr. Bruno. What brings you in here?" Kara asked.

"I'm having a house built."

"That's wonderful to hear. How are your wife and daughter?"

"They are fine thanks."

"Well, we will leave you to do whatever," Kara said.

"Welcome back ladies," I said.

They walked away. We walked closer to the fountain and sat in the chairs that were in the lobby. TJ was splashing in the middle of the fountain.

"So, you didn't tell them that you were married?"

"No, sir."

"Why not?"

"Honestly, I didn't think that they were coming back from Tokyo."

"Why would they stay there?"

"To work on our international projects."

"What are you doing internationally?"

"Constructing hotels."

"When were they due back?"

"Mid to late September."

"Would you have to go over there?"

"No. It's one of my projects, but I trust the team that is over there now working on it. It's more than seventy-five percent done."

"When will it open?"

"Just before Christmas."

"What is it called?"

"The Double Slayer."

TJ climbed out of the fountain. I tossed him one of Patrick's workout towels. He dried off and then went into the bathroom and changed his clothes. Then he came and sat on my lap. I pushed my fingers through his wet hair.

"Well, thank you for the time for showing me the layout again. I'll be in touch."

"Thank you, sir," I said.

TJ fell asleep in my arms. I stood up and shook hands with Mr. Bruno. He left and I went to find Lynn and Kara.

"We need to talk right now," I said. I put TJ in my office and closed the door. "If you ever come in here again with the attitude that you had, you can find yourselves other employment. How dare you come into my building and start that bullshit in front of not only a client, but my child."

"Can we explain?" Kara asked.

"I don't want to hear it."

"The child was swimming in the fountain."

"He can swim wherever he wants to swim and wherever Patrick and I permit him to."

"But it's a fountain. Not a pool."

"Kara, I'm aware it's a fountain, I designed it and had it constructed. It's not shallow. It's a deep fountain, but to a six-year-old boy, it's a swimming pool."

"So, did you know that Patrick had a son?" Lynn asked.

"No."

"Where is his mother?"

"I'm his mother," I said. "And that is that."

My cell phone rang. I looked at it. It was Mr. Bruno. "Hello," I said and walked away from Kara and Lynn.

"I'd like to invite you and your adorable little boy to dinner at my condo tonight at seven. Please come. You can meet my wife and daughter."

"What can I bring?"

"Nothing more than yourself and your son."

I went into my office and picked TJ up. I carried him to the car. Kara had called Patrick and told him that I scolded both her and Lynn. I had just put TJ in the car when my cell phone rang. "Hi, honey," I said.

"Hello. So, Kara called me and told me that you yelled at her and Lynn."

"Did they mention why?"

"No. I told them if you yelled at them then they deserved it. Kara hung up on me. I think it's time to bid her fair well."

"Let me investigate how they did on the Tokyo job first and then we will go from there."

"It's a plan," he said. "What are you doing?"

"I'm leaving the office with TJ and we are heading home to change before joining Mr. Bruno and his family for dinner."

"How is that going? Is he still carrying on about the glass pool?"

"No. He now wants a pool built that resembles the fountain."

"What in the hell changed his mind?"

"Turner was swimming in the fountain when Mr. Bruno came to the building."

"He was what?"

"He was swimming in the fountain."

"It's deep enough?"

"Yeah. He was standing in it and the water came to shoulders."

"You made it that deep?"

"Apparently so," I said smiling.

"Was he naked?"

"No," I laughed. "He swam in his boxer shorts."

"You're wonderful," he said.

"So, I never realized that you never brought him to the building."

"I didn't?"

"No. When we walked in, he was blown away by everything. He climbed on our squirrel a few times. He had fun."

"Did you show him the plane?"

"No. He fell asleep before I could give him the full tour of our building."

We got to the house. Dad told me that they were going out for dinner with Jamie and Lennox. I woke TJ up. "Go shower and change please."

He went running upstairs and showered and put on a pair of jeans and a grey t-shirt. It matched his eyes. Then he came downstairs. "Where are we going?"

"We are going to have dinner with Mr. Bruno and his family."

"Cool," he said.

My cell phone rang. "Hello, Mr. Bruno."

"If you would like, bring your bathing suits."

"Oh, thank you," I said.

I showered and put on a pair of blue jeans and a black t-shirt. We left the house and I stopped at Publix and bought cookies and a bottle of wine. Then we went to his condo. When we got there, Mr. Bruno was waiting for us in the parking lot. I parked where he pointed to and we got out of the truck.

"Kenny, you don't have to keep calling me Mr. Bruno. You can call me Dave or David. Come. My wife and daughter are waiting for us."

We went up to the penthouse. TJ's expression: a wide-open mouth said it all. "You live here?" he asked.

"Yes."

"And now you want a house?"

"Yes," David said.

"Why?"

"TJ!"

"No, he's ok," David said. "More room."

His wife and daughter stood by the door and waited for us to come in. When we did, I handed her the bottle of wine and the box of cookies. "Thank you," she said. "I'm Gwen and this is our daughter Hayley."

"Nice to meet you both."

"Nice to meet you too," they said together.

"I'm Kennedy, but everyone calls me Ken and this my son TJ."

"He's adorable," Hayley said. "How old is he?"

"I'm six," TJ said.

"Hayley will be starting college in the next few weeks," David said.

"Where are you going?"

"To the University of Central Florida."

"Oh, so will you commute?"

"Yeah," she said.

"Congratulations."

"Thank you."

"Please come and sit down," Gwen said.

We went into the living room and sat down. TJ was wandering around. "TJ, stay in here please."

"He's fine," David said.

"So, Dave tells me that you are the one responsible for building our house."

"I am the architect."

"I'm sorry if he is driving you crazy."

"He's fine," I said.

"He told me today that he no longer wants a glass pool. He mentioned that he now wants a fountain pool. I don't know what that is."

I took out my phone and showed her pictures of the fountain at the office. "Oh my god, that is stunning."

"Thank you," I said.

TJ wandered back into the room. He looked at me. Then came and squished himself on my lap.

"Would you like to play a game with me?" Hayley said. "Do you like games?"

"Yes," TJ said excitedly.

"Dinner will be ready soon," David said.

Hayley took TJ into another room, where they set up Jenga blocks. Before they could start to play, David announced that it was dinner time. He made hamburgers and ribs.

"Do you have hotdogs?" TJ asked.

"TJ!"

"I was just asking," he said to me.

"We do have hotdogs. How many would you like?"

"Two please."

"Two dogs coming right up," David said.

They had side dishes of potato salads, two different kinds of macaroni salads, a cucumber salad, fruit salad, black beans and rice, corn on the cob, grilled zucchini and yellow squash, an Asian pasta salad, seaweed salad, and rolls of sushi, and a spicy chicken salad.

"Please help yourselves,"

I made a plate for TJ with a little bit of everything on it. Then I made my own plate again with a little of everything on it.

"How long have you been an architect?"

"Almost twelve years," I said to Gwen.

"Do you have a famous piece of work?"

"I do. It's a statute outside the elementary school. Actually, it's their play ground that I designed and built."

"Is that the school that I'm going to?" TJ asked.

"Yes," I said to him.

David had cut up the two hotdogs and put them on TJ's plate.

"Thank you," TJ said.

"So, TJ do you fish?"

"Yes, sir with my daddy."

"What have you caught?"

"Together we caught a Sword fish."

"Did you get to keep it?"

"Yes, sir," TJ said and stuck a piece of hotdog in his mouth.

"Would you like to go swimming?" Gwen asked TJ.

He looked at me. I nodded my head.

"Yes, please."

Hayley took him inside the apartment to change. Then he came running back outside and jumped cannon ball style into the pool.

"He's such a sweet kid. You should be proud of yourself."

"That would be my husband's doing," I said to Gwen.

"Don't sell yourself short."

"No, ma'am, I don't, but it is true. Until the beginning of this summer, I didn't even know that Patrick, who is my work partner and now my husband, had a son. The day I met him this summer, he jumped right into my arms. Two weeks later, while on a trip with my three nephews and TJ, the boys dared him to call me mommy. He ran up to me and said mommy and then started to cry. I scooped him up in my arms and it's like I've never put him down. He melted my heart.

"About two weeks after that I married Patrick and adopted TJ."

"You married your husband on a whim?" David asked.

I lowered my head and ran my hands through my hair. "I've loved him since the day I saw him when we started architectural school. We would work together on projects and I would feel the chemistry between us, but he dated other women and I dated other men and then we built our firm together, but we had our own lives. I knew that he got married, but I didn't know that he had a child six years ago."

"What happened to his mother?"

TJ came back over dripping wet. "She left me and daddy when I was three months old. She went to California and never came back. I didn't have mommy until this summer and now I have the best mommy in the world."

"That you do, my boy," David said.

"TJ, honey, you are dripping everywhere."

"Oh, that's fine," Gwen said.

"Can I go down the slide?"

"Not tonight. We have to get going."

"I'll tell you what," David said. "the next time you come over here, you can go down that slide as many times as you'd like."

"Really?"

"Yes."

"Honey, please go change."

"Ok, mommy."

Without thinking, TJ walked away from us and took off his bathing suit and ran naked into their building. "I'm so sorry," I said.

Both David and Gwen were laughing. "No, that's fine."

"Where do you live?"

"The Jackson Estate."

"The place that is turning into a bed and breakfast?" Gwen asked.

"Yes, ma'am, one in the same."

"How long have you had it?"

"My parents bought it when my brother, sister and I were kids. I purchased it from my parents last year, and it's my dream to turn it into a B&B."

TJ came back dressed. He climbed on my lap. I brushed his hair back and kissed his head. He closed his eyes and within seconds he was sleeping.

"Well, I think we should get going. Thank you for having us over for dinner. That was the best barbeque I've had."

David took TJ from me. He carried him out to the truck and put him in his car seat.

"Isn't he a little big for this?" he asked.

"It goes by weight, and Mr. TJ is under weight, so he doesn't have a choice."

"It has been a pleasure working with you and also meeting TJ. If it is ok with you, I'd like him to call me Uncle Dave or David."

"That would be nice," I said.

"Do you have plans for tomorrow?"

"I'm having dinner with my parents before they leave to go back to Key West."

"If you would like, I like you to join Gwen, Hayley and I tomorrow on our boat. Your parents are more than welcome to join us."

"Yes, I think they'd like that. What time tomorrow?"

"We will leave for Daytona at eight thirty."

"That will be great. Where would you like us to meet you?"

"If it's ok with you, we will come to your house and leave from there."

"Yes, that is fine."

"Drive safe," he said kissing me on the cheek.

They arrived at eight the next morning. We were all up. Mom was excited to meet someone I was building a house for. TJ opened the door when they knocked. They came into the lobby/living room. "Wow!" Gwen said. "How many rooms does it have?"

"It has ten full bedrooms with bathrooms upstairs and a front apartment built-in with four bedrooms, three and half bath. Once I decide on the initial opening day for the B&B, we will move into the front apartment."

"And are there bathrooms downstairs?"

"Yes, of course," I said. "There are six bathrooms downstairs."

"May I use one?"

"Yes," I said with a smile. "Right this way."

Addison came into the room with breakfast sausages, bacon, scrambled eggs, pancakes, crepes, and waffles. Plus, she made lunch for us to bring with us.

I gave them a tour of the house and then we got into their SUV and headed to Daytona. While David drove, I texted Patrick to see if maybe he could join us. He texted me back telling me to tell him when we got there. I did. He responded with he could. I asked David if that would be ok and he said of course. Patrick joined us at the harbor with Trinity who came to meet with a friend. David put the boat in the water, and then we all boarded. Once we were about five miles out, David cut the engine and prepared the fishing rods. Patrick, David, dad, and TJ fished. I went and laid out with mom, Trinity, and Gwen on the bow.

"This is very nice," mom said. "Thank you."

"Oh, thank you for coming."

"What is Hayley doing?"

"She's down below reading."

I fell asleep on the boat. "We should cover her," Gwen said. She stood up and went and got a light sheet. She placed it over my back and legs. "Where does she fall in the line of your children?"

"She is my youngest. I wasn't expecting twins. The doctor kept telling me that I was having another boy. When I went into labor with them, I told the doctor that something wasn't right. After Jamie was born, I felt Kenny drop in the birth cannel. Eight minutes after, I welcomed Jamie, Kenny was born."

"Wow!" Gwen said. "What did you do?"

"My son Parker was three when the girls were born, and we still had his crib. Plus, we had bought new things for the baby. So, we had two cribs. We didn't have anything for girls, so my mother went out and went shopping right away."

"Did you have them together in the same room?"

"We did, but there was so much space that it seemed like they were separated."

"Is Jamie an architect too?"

"No, she is into music. She has a band and they travel, but now she is pregnant with her first child, so she is home now."

"And does Parker have children?"

"He does. He has five children. Three boys and two girls. Kenny has always treated them like they were her own children."

"Has things changed with them since she adopted TJ?"

"No. Not really. Kenny has always wanted to have children, but there was an incident when she was a teenager and she cannot bear her own children. So ever since Michael was born, it was hard to tell who his mother was because whenever Kenny was around him, she never put him down, then our sweet Kate was born, and Addison, my daughter-in-law, thought that Kenny wouldn't want to come around as much. Nope. My Kenny was there even more. Addison had a rough pregnancy with Carter and was on bed rest for the last four months. Kenny moved in to take care of Michael and Kate. When Carter was born, and both he and Addison had to stay in the hospital for almost two weeks, Kenny helped Parker out and brought the kids to her house, so Parker could come and go without the two kids crying and carrying on."

"That was so nice of her. What about with the other two."

"Tyson was born at home. Addison had gotten up at four in the morning sweating profusely, so she went into the bathtub. Parker had left for work already and Kenny was there with them. Addison called to Kenny and said she was having the baby. Kenny delivered Tyson. And our baby Beth was breach, so Addison was in the hospital and a C-section was done."

"Is Kenny close to Beth?"

"As much as she can be. Beth is three now. Beth is Beth," Roberta said. "She's not close to anyone. She gets along with Tyson, but for just so long. But Kenny tries."

"How come she goes by Kenny?"

"Todd started that when they were babies. He called Jamie James and Kennedy Kenny, and it stuck. When they first started school, they had them listed as boys because Todd called them James and Kenny when we registered them. I had to go to the school and speak to the principal quite a few times to get it changed."

"Do they get along?"

"Oh, yes. They have a great relationship. They speak to each other almost every day. They are as different as night and day, but together they are a whole unit and it's beautiful. I love that most about them."

"Did they fight when they were kids?"

"No. Jamie was always into music and making music and writing tunes down, and Kenny was into just about everything else. She was extremely creative, and into athletics. Parker was an athlete as well. So, I had my boy, my girly girl, and my very sparky tomboy. Kenny was lightning as a child. She would be here one second doing something and gone over there in the next doing something totally different. That's just the way she's always been."

Trinity didn't get into the conversation. She was happy to be there with them. She soaked in the stories that mom told Gwen.

When we went back to the harbor, I was still sleeping. TJ had fallen asleep in Patrick's arms and he too was still sleeping. David came over and lifted me into his arms. He carried me off the boat. His breath touched my skin and I startled awake. He stopped and carefully held onto me as I struggled and fought. He spoke softly to me. "Remember where you are and what we did today. We are in Daytona. I took you and your family out on my boat today. You fell asleep on the boat. You are safe. Patrick and TJ are right ahead of us. Your parents are behind us." I calmed down. "I'm not putting you down yet because this ground is too hot, and you don't have shoes on."

"I'm...I'm sorry," I said.

"How long have you been dealing with PTSD?"

"Sin...since I wa...was a teenager."

When we got to a shady area, he put me down and I bolted from sight. "Is she ok?" Gwen asked.

Mom came up behind them. "That's the way Kenny is sometimes. Sudden movements or waking up startled sets her off. And then she stutters."

"TJ is like that," Trinity said.

"That's PTSD," Gwen said. "Did you see where she went?"

Patrick came over with TJ still asleep in his arms. "Where is Kenny?"

"She had one of her episodes," mom said.

"What? Where did she go?"

"I didn't see," mom said honestly.

"Why don't we all just stay calm," David said.

I ran down the beach. I was running hard, looking over my shoulder until I ran out of breath. I bent over to catch my breath looking between to my legs to see if anyone was following me. When I calmed down enough to realize that I was alone from the group and no one was coming after me, I started to walk back.

In the meantime, they had pulled the boat out of the water, they had all rinsed off and changed into clean clothes, and TJ had woken from his nap. "Daddy, where is mommy?"

"She needed a minute alone, buddy."

"But, where is she?"

"I'm not sure."

"Did she leave?" He began to panic. "Mommy left. Mommy left. She left without saying goodbye?" He was hyperventilating and starting to cry and then he screamed out as loud as he could, "MOMMY! MOMMY!"

David, Gwen, Hayley, Trinity, and mom looked at him. He went and stood on the hood of the truck looking for me. "MOMMY!" he yelled.

I heard him screaming for me. I ran as fast as could to find them. He was screaming crying and non-consolable when I got to him. I scooped him up in my arms and cried right along with him. "I'm here," I whispered. "I'm here. I'm sorry that you got scared. I'm right here."

He calmed down after ten or fifteen minutes.

Gwen had watched the entire thing as did mom, dad, David, Patrick, and Trinity. Patrick didn't question where I had gone. Mom had tears in her eyes that now escaped them and ran down her checks. I was holding TJ tight in my arms. I finally brought him down to the ground but didn't let go of him. We crumpled together to the ground and held tight to each other. I was protecting him as he clung ever so tight to me.

It started to rain. Patrick finally spoke to both us. "Kenny, TJ, it's raining. Come. Let's get out of the rain."

I loosened my grip on TJ and he stood up and took Patrick's hand. Mom, dad, Gwen, Trinity, Patrick and TJ ran to get out of the pouring rain. David stayed right there with me. He touched my shoulder gently and I jumped. "Take your time," he said. "When you are ready, we will get out of the rain."

"I can't stand up," I said.

"Can I pick you up?"

I nodded my head in the pouring rain. He reached under my arms and pulled me to my feet. Then he took my weight on him and led me out of the rain. "I'm sorry you had to see this," I said.

"In a way, I'm glad I did."

I looked at him. "Why?"

"Gwen and I deal with people who suffer from PTSD."

"I don't," I said.

"Kennedy darling, you do."

I leaned my head against him. "I'm sorry," I repeated a few times.

We took cover where the others were. I bore my own weight now and walked to a table and sat by myself. TJ started to come over to me, but Gwen stopped him. "Your mommy needs a minute sweetheart."

"Ok," TJ said.

Patrick looked at me. "Should I go to her?"

"Yes," Gwen said.

Patrick walked over to me. He sat next to me. I turned and wrapped my arms around him. "I'm sorry." I said to him.

"For what, honey?"

"Pat, sometimes I can't control my reactions when I'm touched. Oh, God, did I scare TJ?"

"No. How can that scare him when he reacts the same way sometimes?"

I looked at him. "Is it because of me?"

"God no," he said. "It started when he was a baby."

"I wish I would have known about him before this summer. Why did you keep him a secret?"

"Because I wanted to keep him sheltered from getting hurt from anyone else."

"He has so much love in his heart."

"I know he does," Patrick kissed me on lips. "Are you ok now?"

"Yeah," I said. "I'm sorry," I said one more time and then got up. I walked over to group and hugged my mom first. Then dad, Trinity, Gwen and David and last I hugged TJ. I picked him up and squished him with hugs.

"Are you ok now, mommy?"

"Yes, Turner, I'm ok. I'm sorry if I scared you."

"I was scared for you, mommy."

Hayley met up with her friends, so she wasn't going to drive back with us, which meant that there was room in the SUV for Trinity.

The drive back to Orlando, I was quiet. David let Patrick drive home. He and dad were sitting up front talking. Mom and Trinity sat in the row behind them, and Gwen, TJ, David and I sat in the back. TJ sat on Gwen's lap. He was showing her how to play one of his video games. David sat next to me and he noticed how I squeezed close to the wall of the SUV. He had his phone out, where he kept notes of my behavior the whole way home. I had my earphones on and my music turned up a bit louder than it should have been, but I wanted to drown everything out. I didn't want to be in this vehicle with all of them right now. I was humiliated by my own actions and at this moment, I was struggling to deal with it.

"DADDY!" TJ called out. "I have to pee."

"Wow, that was timing," dad said.

"We are pulling into the next rest stop. It's coming up. We will be there in a few minutes, Buddy."

I noticed we came to a stop. "Why are we stopping," I said louder than needed because of my music blasting in my ears.

David reached over and pulled the cord out of the phone socket. "Your son has to go to the bathroom."

"Oh. I'll take him," I said.

When the doors opened and I could get out, I bolted from the SUV. I picked TJ up and walked into the rest stop. We went right into the family bathroom. I turned away when he was going to the bathroom. When he was done, I reminded him to wash his hands. "Stand there and don't turn around," I said to him. I too went to the bathroom.

"Don't forget to wash your hands," he said.

"Funny guy," I said to him.

"Can we eat something?" he asked.

"Let's go see what daddy says ok."

"Ok, mommy."

We walked out of the bathroom and went back outside. David was pumping gas. Gwen now watched me. I went over to Patrick. "TJ is hungry."

"I think we all are," mom said. "Are you?"

"I didn't notice," I said.

Gwen walked over. "David wants to know if you want to stop to eat somewhere."

"Yes," mom and Trinity said together.

We all got back in the SUV. Now David was driving, so TJ sat in the middle section with Patrick and dad. Mom, Trinity, and I sat in the back. Gwen was up front with David. I didn't notice that she was still watching me. She and David spoke quietly in the front seat. "She's lethargic," Gwen said. "She holds her arms squeezed into her body. She has her head pressed hard against the side of the vehicle. It almost appears as if she is punishing herself for something. She's been in this state for more than two hours now," she said.

"David, I'm really hungry," TJ said to him.

"I know, baby. We are going to stop in just a few minutes."

Mom had said something to me; I didn't hear her. She touched my arm and I nearly jumped out of my skin. Trinity told mom to get up and they traded places. Trinity must have sensed something because she took me in her arms and held me as I convulsed. She kicked the seat in front of her. Patrick and dad turned and looked. She pressed her index finger to her lips. "Tell David to pull over," she mouthed. Dad turned back around and leaned forward and told David. "When is the last time she was like this?"

"Fifteen years ago," mom said with tears in her eyes.

"Kenny, try to focus on my eyes," Trinity said. "I know it's hard, and I know this hurts. Just breath, honey. It's ok." Trinity was gently stroking my head and my hair as she spoke me. She could feel the tension inside my body climbing as it took control over me.

David pulled into the parking lot where the restaurant was. "TJ, why don't you go inside and get us a table with your grandparents."

TJ nodded and got out of the SUV. Mom and dad went in with him. Gwen went into her bag and took out a syringe and vile of medication. She filed the syringe and came over to where David had me lying on the backseat. I had my fists clenched tightly and my arms were locked with bent elbows, so my fists were near my face. My head was resting on Trinity's lap.

"We need to roll her on her side. This is going to go in the back of her thigh," Gwen said.

I was groaning in pain. My head was back. I closed my eyes as everything in my body went stiff. David got a rubber bite plate and though it was fight, he got into my mouth, so that I wouldn't bite my tongue. Then he and Patrick got me on my side. Patrick undid my jeans. Then he worked them down so that Gwen could give me the shot, though everything was stiff and hurt like hell, I fought. I was kicking to try to get them away. Patrick took a firm hold of my legs. I tried to scream, but with the bite plate in my mouth, the sound was muffled. Tears streamed from my eyes. Gwen managed to give me in the injection. Five minutes after she gave it to me, I was now limp on the backseat.

"What the hell caused that?"

"Your wife suffers from PTSD. Sometimes it only takes something to trigger it. Today on the boat started it. Then her body went through the flashbacks, and what we just witnessed, it went through the whole experience," David said. "The convulsions, the tension, everything locking up, the fighting and thrashing."

I started to come around. I took the bite plate out of my mouth. Patrick took me in his arms and just cradled me. "Did TJ see this?" I asked.

"No," Patrick said.

"I'm ok," I said after a few more minutes.

We went into the restaurant. Everyone at the table made like nothing had happened. I went into the bathroom and threw up. Though it's a gross thing to do, I felt so much better. I washed my face and rinsed my mouth and then went back out and sat down at the table. I smiled at mom and whispered a thank you to Trinity. Then the waitress came over. We all ordered. Eating that first bite, I felt a wave of nausea, but it soon passed.

"Mommy, can I play my game?"

I looked at his less than half eaten dinner. "Why aren't you eating?"

"I don't know."

"Do you like it?"

"Not really? It's too spicy."

I called the waitress over. "Hi, can we please get something else for my son?"

"Yes, ma'am, of course. What would you like, sweetheart?" she asked.

"Can I please have macaroni and cheese?"

"Yes."

"Thank you," TJ said.

The waitress took his plate away and realized her mistake when she got a whiff of the pepper. "I am so sorry," she said to me. "I brought your son the wrong plate."

"That's ok," I said to her. "You can leave it. I'll eat it."

"Are you sure?"

"Yes," I said.

Between dad, Patrick, David and I, we devoured TJ's order of chicken tenders, broccoli, and the spiciest French fries any of us have ever had. The waitress brought out TJ's macaroni and cheese. It was then that we had noticed that he had climbed on mom's lap and was sound asleep.

"We will take that to go," I said to the waitress. "Thank you."

"Again. I'm sorry about his first order."

"Mistakes are made," I said. "It's ok."

Trinity paid for our dinner. When we were leaving, I took TJ from mom. I cradled him in my arms. "I'm so blessed," I said.

"What honey?" mom asked.

"I'm so blessed to be married to such a wonderful man and to have this beautiful child in my life."

"I have felt blessed just getting to really know you, Kenny," Trinity said.

We went and got into the SUV. We were now only about a half hour or forty-five minutes away from home. David drove. I was now finally back to my normal self. When we got to the house, Patrick took TJ in the house. I jammed my hands in my back pockets as mom, dad, and Trinity climbed out of the SUV and thanked David and Gwen for such a nice day. When they were inside the house with the door closed, I turned to both David and Gwen and put my arms around both of their shoulders. "Thank you for a beautiful day out on the water. And thank you both for taking care of me."

"How often do you have attacks like that?" Gwen asked now that we were alone.

"The last one I had was eight years ago on an airplane."

"Was it as bad as this?"

I stepped back and lowered my head. "I blacked out with that one."

"What triggered it?"

"I was on a flight to Ireland for research. I had fallen into a deep sleep on the flight. The stewardess was walking up and down the aisle and noticed I was shivering. She covered me with a blanket. I was in such a deep sleep; I hadn't felt her cover me. I slept most of the flight. My seat was leaning back. She came over and touched my arm gently and I jumped out of my seat. The man sitting next to me grabbed me because the fasten your seatbelt sign was on because we were descending. I had jerked free of him and then he stood up and pushed me down into my seat. He raised my seat to the up-right position and that was when my body went completely rigid. I remember the two men seated behind us, reached, and took hold me to keep me in the seat. Then the convulsions started and my body was jerking and thrashing. The man behind us, threw his seatbelt off and literally grabbed me under the arms and lifted me up. My head was back on the back of seat and then everything went dark.

"When I came to, I was laying on a cot in the Dublin airport. The three men that had assisted me were there. I was fine the rest of the trip. On the flight back, I didn't sleep."

"Have you spoken to anyone about the trauma?"

"You mean someone professional?"

"Yes," Gwen said.

I kind of laughed. "No."

"Why not?"

"Because that's admitting that something is wrong with me," I said to David.

"PTSD is nothing to be ashamed about."

"That's not what I'm ashamed about," I said.

"Well, let's do this. Why don't we set up an appointment for you to come to the house?" Gwen said.

"When would you want to do this?"

"How about tomorrow in the mid-morning? Let's say ten or ten thirty."

"Yes, that will work," I said.

A car pulled up in the driveway. It was Storm. She got out of the car and came running over and hugged and kissed me. "How are you?"

"I'm good."

"I hope you don't mind that Patrick called me to take him to Daytona for his truck."

"Of course not," I said to Storm. "He's in the house."

She ran into the house. She came out moments later. "Hey, would it be ok if I took TJ with us and I'll bring him home tomorrow?"

"Yeah, that's ok," I said. "Just don't forget his doggy and his blanket."

David and Gwen left before Patrick came outside with TJ. "Hey, we are going to take him with us to get my truck."

"Yeah, of course," I said. "Love you. See you tomorrow."

"I'll be back at the end of the week, but Storm will bring TJ back tomorrow."

"Ok." I said.

Patrick seemed to be reading my mind. "This has nothing to do with what happened today," he said.

"Tomorrow my parents are leaving to go home," I stated.

TJ realized that he would not be staying with Patrick and he started to cry. "I don't want to go," he said. "I changed my mind. I want to stay with mommy. I don't want to go," he cried from inside Storm's car. "MOMMY!"

I looked at the car and ran to him. I flung the back door open and reached in. I unbuckled his seatbelt and lifted him from the car. "Shh. It's ok," I said to him. "It's ok."

"I want to stay with mommy," TJ cried when Patrick came over.

"Yes. Yes," Patrick said. "But I have to go get my truck and go back for a meeting."

I put TJ down and he bolted to the house. I apologized to Storm.

"No. That's ok. Kids know what they want," she said. "Can I come by tomorrow though?"

"You are always invited," I said.

Storm left with Patrick. I went into the house. I found everyone in the kitchen. Mom came to me. "How are you?" She wrapped me in her arms. "Your father and I are going to stay a bit longer."

"I'm exhausted," I said.

"Do you know what causes you or your body to go into total shock?" Trinity asked.

I lowered my head and ran my hand through my hair. I put my head down on the table for a second. "TJ, I want you to go upstairs and please get ready for bed."

"Ok, mommy. Can I come back downstairs?"

"Yes, of course."

With him out of the room, I looked at my parents and Trinity. "I'm sorry that all of you had to see that today. But please. I don't want it brought up in front of the six-year-old. I know that I scared all of you today, and for that I am truly sorry."

"Kenny, you need to talk to someone about what happened."

"Mom, what happened today was a fluke thing. It hasn't happened in eight years."

"You had a seizure."

"No, ma'am, I didn't. I had a convulsion."

"It's the same thing," mom said.

"No, Roberta, it isn't."

TJ came downstairs with his ratty doggy and his blanket. "Can I sit and watch TV in the living room?"

"Yes," I said. "But please come here first." He came over to me and I scooped him up in my arms and snuggled with him for a few minutes. "You are truly the best thing that has happened to me," I told him. "I love you." I put him down. He hugged Trinity, mom and dad. Then he came back over to me and hugged me.

"I love you too, mommy." With that he left the room.

CHAPTER TWENTY-FIVE

The next morning, after a restless night's sleep, I got up and showered and dressed nice in a pair of dress slacks and a pin striped shirt. I went downstairs to find that Addison had arrived. I went to her and dropped myself into her embrace. "Are you ok?" I shook my head against her shoulder. "Where are you going?"

"I have an appointment."

"What's wrong?"

"Something happened yesterday," I said to her.

Mom and dad came in the kitchen. "Good morning," mom said cheerfully.

"Good morning," Addison answered.

"Morning," I said.

"Not a good morning?" Dad asked.

"No, sir, not really."

"Where are you going?"

"I have an appointment and then I have to stop by the office for an hour or two. Storm is coming to spend time with TJ, so you are free to do whatever you are going to do or have planned."

TJ came into the kitchen. "Hi," he said to everyone. He was still in his pajamas. He looked at me. "Where are you going?"

"I have an appointment this morning."

"TJ, would you like to help me make waffles?"

"YEAH!" he said with that bright smile that I loved.

Trinity came into the kitchen. I looked at her. "Where is your car?"

"It's in Daytona. I drove there two days ago with one of my friends and he will bring it back when he comes."

"Would you like to stay here or if you'd like I can drive you home."

"If you don't mind."

"Not at all," I said.

"Please eat something before you go," Addison said.

I took a slice of toast and ate it leaving the crust. Mom looked at it and smiled.

"What?" I asked.

"You've done that since you were a child," mom said.

"Mommy, would you like my first ever waffle?"

"I'll take a bite and then why don't you eat it."

"Aunt Addy said that we are going to make more."

Addison looked down at him and then took him in her arms and hugged him. "Did I do something wrong?"

"No, sweet boy, you didn't," Addison said. "You called me Aunt Addy."

"Is that ok?"

"Yes, TJ, that is great. Thank you."

Storm came into the kitchen. "Good morning," she said. Everyone responded with good morning back to her. "Trinity, your friend will be returning tonight with your car," she said.

"Thank you."

Trinity and I left. Once in the car, I looked at her. "What?" she asked.

"Nothing."

"Ask it," she said.

"Ask what?"

"Kennedy!"

"What, mom," I said to her.

"Ask what you are going to ask?"

"Who is he? What is his name? How long have you been seeing him? Where did you meet him?"

"Kennedy!" she laughed. "You don't miss much."

"No, ma'am," I said. "So?"

"His name is Steffen. We have been seeing each other for a little less than a month. I met him at the casino. He works in restaurant management."

"Good for you," I said to her.

"Please don't tell Patrick. I want to see how far it goes first."

"No, ma'am, I won't say anything."

"Where are you going in your nice slacks? I know how you dress for the office and this isn't how you usually dress to go into work."

"I'm meeting with David and Gwen at their house."

"Why?"

"She's some kind of specialist. Or they are some kind of specialists dealing with PTSD."

"Would you mind if I tagged along?"

"No," I said.

"You called me mom before."

"Yes," I said.

"Won't that piss off your mother?"

"I didn't do it in front of my mother. But I don't think it will. Besides, I call my mother mommy."

"How are you today?"

"I'm exhausted."

"Did you sleep well?"

"No."

"Did you sleep at all?"

"A little bit."

I pulled up at David's condo and parked the car where I parked the other night. Then we got out and went into the building. We went to the woman behind the counter. "Hi, I am here to see David and Gwen Bruno."

"Are they expecting you?"

"Yes, ma'am," I said.

She called up to them. Then she looked at me. "Go on up, Kenny. They are waiting."

"Thank you."

We walked over to the elevator. I pushed the button. When it opened, we stepped in. I pushed the button for PH: Pent House. When it got there, we stepped out into their living room.

"You brought back up," David said to me with a smile. Then he kissed me on the cheek. "How are you today, darling?"

"Thoroughly exhausted," I replied.

"Hi, Trinity," David said and kissed her on the cheek as well. "Please come in."

We followed him to a room that I hadn't seen the other day. It was dimly lit. There were pillows on the floor. Gwen was already in the room. "Hi, sweetheart," she said to me. "Hello, Trinity."

"Hi," I answered looking around the room.

"Please don't get nervous," she said.

"Too late for that," I said.

"I can stay in another room if you'd like," Trinity said. "I brought a book with me and I have some phone calling to make."

David took her out on the balcony. She sat down at the rod iron table. "The kitchen is right here as you can see. Help yourself to anything you'd like."

"Thank you, David," Trinity said.

David left the door to the balcony wide open. Then he went into the refrigerator taking out a bottle of water. Then he came back to the room, where I was still standing where he left me. "This is a safe place," he said. "Please relax," he said holding out the water bottle. "Would you like some water?"

"Nah, I'm good. Where do you want me to go?"

"How about let's just sit here on the floor together."

I sat down closest to the door. Gwen was taking notes. David repeated, "This is a safe place. Please come a little closer." I scooted in about an inch. "Let's start by just talking. How are you today?"

"I told you I'm exhausted."

"Yes, but Gwen didn't hear that," David said. "What is your favorite color?"

"Indigo."

"When is your birthday?"

"September twentieth."

"What year were you born?"

"Nineteen seventy-eight."

"Do you think your life is complete?"

I didn't answer him.

"Kenny," he said. "Do you think your life is complete?" I shook my head. "I need you to answer out loud."

"No."

"Why don't you think it's complete?"

"Because I'm broken," I said.

"Why are you broken?"

I dropped my head. "I can't do this," I said. I got up quickly and ran for the elevator. David came after me. He touched my arm and I went into defense mood. I went to hit him, but he caught my wrist and turned my body into him so that my back was against his chest with his arm around my chest holding my left arm across my chest. "No," I said. Trinity came into the condo. I was struggling and jerking and trying to pull away from him. My head was just below his chin. Gwen came into the room hearing the commotion. "Let me go."

"Settle down," he said.

"Go to hell," I said. I pulled my head forward and he seemed to know that I was going to throw it back against his chest and collar bone. He brought his other hand up and cupped my head. "NO!" I screamed.

"I'm not going to hurt you," he said. "Close your eyes and listen to my voice."

"Please let me go."

He felt my body start to go rigid under his grasp. Trinity was watching it as was Gwen. "Honey," Gwen said.

"I feel it, Gwen," he said. "Kenny, loosen your body. Stop fighting."

I managed to get my wrist free and I started to fight to get out of his hold. He moved his hands and now bear hugged me and he lifted me off my feet. "God please don't rape me."

"What?" he asked.

Then I passed out in his embrace. My head dropped forward. He looked at Trinity. "Was she raped?"

"I'm not sure. Roberta talks about an incident that happened when she was sixteen or seventeen. I know that she had gone out to a party for her graduation from high school and that Jamie didn't go with her. They were seventeen then. Yes, there was an incident when she was seventeen. I know that she was found beaten up and battered pretty badly and naked on the side of the Turnpike."

Gwen went on the computer and looked it up. She found the article. "Jesus, David," she said. By now David had me in his arms as if I were a small child. My head dropped back, and I was limp. Trinity came and lifted my head to his shoulder. She held it. "This was my first case," Gwen said. "She wouldn't speak to me when I went to see her in the hospital. The guy had done a real number on her. He had raped her repeatedly."

"Has she ever gotten over it?" David asked.

"No," Trinity said. "God I've been friends with Roberta since before our kids were born. I watched Kenny and Jamie grow up. Kenny was such a diverse kid. She was into everything. She swam, ran track, played basketball, soccer, and tennis. She took violin lessons. She was such a tomboy. She built a tree house. She was always building things and tinkering with things. When she was in high school, it was her design that had won to be displayed at the elementary school. When she found out that it was going to a permanent structure, she built it sturdy enough to withstand the weather and so that it would always be there.

"Then they graduated. Their graduation party happened right after they graduated and it was over early, so the girls asked if they could go out for the evening. Jamie went to a music party and Kenny went out with other people."

"Did she know the guy?"

"No," both Gwen and Trinity said.

"He saw that she was drunk and offered to drive her home," Trinity said.

"But he didn't," Gwen said. "Instead he drove her to a wooded area off the Turnpike, where she must have fought to get away from him, but she couldn't fight. I remember that there were drugs in her system. Her parents swore up and down that she didn't do drugs."

I started to come to. Once again, I struggled to get away from David. David sat on the floor with me between his legs and he was holding me. "Let me go," I said.

"You need to settle down."

"I need to get the fuck out of here," I said.

He took my wrists in his hands and crossed my arms over my chest. I was kicking and thrashing with my legs. He brought his legs over mine and pressed my legs down. I continued to jerk to try to get free. "Settle down."

"FUCK YOU!"

He leaned back against the wall. "Kennedy, settle down," he said.

I struggled and jerked against him for almost a half hour. Sweat poured from my body. I had bit my lip and it was bleeding.

"She's bleeding," Trinity said.

David released me. I retreated to the far side of the room away from them and curled into a ball. Gwen had gone to get a warm washcloth for my lip. She came back into the room and came to me with the towel. I screamed. She backed off. Trinity took it and came to me. "Kenny, you're bleeding, sweetheart." It was then that she noticed that I had soaked through my shirt. It was drenched in sweat. I was shivering and sweating all at once. She reached out and touched my forehead. "She's burning up with fever." I melted into her touch, rolling on my side, shivering with my teeth chattering. "I'm not leaving you."

"We need to get her out of those clothes," Gwen said. "We need to get her fever down."

This time when David took me in his arms, I didn't fight him. He brought me into the bathroom. Trinity undid the buttons on my shirt. She took my shirt off me and gasped seeing the scars. They took my pants off me. There were more scars on my thighs. I stood up with my own power and put my arms around David's neck and then just collapsed in his arms. He lifted me up and stood with me. Gwen took pictures of the scars on my shoulders and my back. David carried me to the guest room and put me down on the bed. With me now on my back, Gwen took pictures of stomach and thighs. Trinity just looked.

"I can go to her house and get clothes for her," Trinity said.

"I'll go," Gwen said. "You told her that you weren't going to leave her." With that Gwen left the room, grabbed her purse and her keys, and left the condo.

Trinity sat on the bed with me and took me in her arms. David covered me with the blanket. Then he pulled a chair close to the bed. "Has she dated?"

"She's never let anyone close to her until Patrick asked her to marry him."

"Does anyone know about the scars?"

"I'm sure her parents do. I don't know if she's ever mentioned how she got them."

"It looks like it was done with a knife," David said. "When she goes swimming, does she wear a bathing suit?"

"No," Trinity said.

Trinity rubbed her hand over my bare shoulder. She felt the knots and blemishes in my skin. "No, don't touch them," I said softly. "God. I'm so tired."

"It's ok. Go to sleep," Trinity said.

"Don't leave me."

"No, angel, I won't leave you."

"I'm not an angel," I mumbled.

I gave into sleep. While I slept, David measured the scars. Most of them were small, but some of them were long and deep. "She must have pulled away and the knife cut her," he said. "Did they ever catch the guy that did this to her?"

"No. She couldn't identify him." Trinity moved my hair away from face and saw there were scars on my head behind my right ear. "God, what the fuck did he do to her?"

Gwen drove to the house. Addison was there alone cooking. Gwen told her what happened, and Addison turned the stove off, took everything off the heat. Ran upstairs and got me clothes and then went with Gwen to her condo.

When they got back, I was sweat profusely. Trinity's clothes were wet, but she had stayed with me. She looked up when Gwen and Addison came in the room. "Did you give her anything?"

"No. Not since yesterday."

"What did you give her yesterday?" Addison asked.

"A muscle relaxer because her body was stiff," Gwen said.

Addison could feel the heat radiating from my body. "We have to cool her down. And this isn't going to pretty."

"What do you mean?" Trinity asked.

"There's going to be a lot of screaming," Addison said.

"How do you know this?"

"Because I am the one person she has trusted over the years."

"You knew about the scars?"

Addison looked at Trinity. "You didn't?"

"After the attack, I blamed her," Trinity stated honestly. "I would meet Roberta away from the house."

"Why?" David asked.

"After it first happened, she stayed up in her room for about a month. She couldn't stand to have anything touch her. Not human touch, not clothing. I thought Roberta was babying her. I didn't know that he had done this to her.

"When she went to school and met Patrick, who finally came to live with me, I told him to stay away from her. However, they worked on projects and as long as she wasn't touched by anyone, she was fine. They had been doing a project that kept them up for days," Trinity reminisced. "They had to cover all the details of a building. Kenny is good with envisioning how the finish project is before it is even done. She was the lead on this project. Everyone had decided to call it quits for the night. I had six grown men sleeping on the floor in my living room. But she was awake. She had gone over all the details and I came into my kitchen. Whether she didn't hear me or whatever, when I touched her shoulder, she spun around so quickly and then ran from the house. I live fifteen miles from her house. I never knew why she ran home."

"Because the night she was raped, she couldn't," Addison said.

I groaned in pain. "It's ok. We are going to take care of you," Trinity said.

David uncovered me. He lifted me up. I again started to kick and punch. Addison came over. "It's ok," she said. "Your safe, Kenny. I promise you you are safe." I settled a bit. "Do you have a swimming pool?" Addison asked.

"Yes."

"We should take her there."

"Why?" Gwen asked.

"It's more room," Addison said. "Again, this isn't going to pretty. If you don't want to see her go animal like or if you see what happens to her and you are going to use it against her, then don't help, but if we don't get her fever down soon…"

"No one is going to use it against her," David said.

Addison looked at Trinity. "She's the wife to my only son and the mother to my only grandchild, and besides, I have put her through enough this summer as well. I want to help her. I need her to know that she can trust me." Trinity said. "And I have helped to break one of her fevers before. I am in on this."

David carried me down to the pool. No one else in the condo was around.

"TJ gets like this too," Trinity said. "It's been better since Kenny came into his life, but he reacts similar to this when he has a fever."

Trinity and Addison went into the pool. David carried me into the pool. The second the water touched my skin, I screamed. The fight that I put on in the water was massive. The warm cool water against my skin had me fighting to get out of the water.

"Not the water," I kept saying. "Not the water."

They kept me in the water for a few minutes. I screamed and fought like Addison had said. Like a lion in a cage. And then my fever broke, and the struggle was over. I collapsed into the water. David lifted me facing him into his arms. My head rested on his shoulder. My limbs hung in front of him. They brought me upstairs. Trinity and Addison dressed me. Gwen changed the bedding. David came into the bathroom where I was and lifted me again. He carried me to the bed, where I slept for the next two hours.

They were in the kitchen. Gwen had given them clothes to wear and they had changed. David had changed before while they were dressing me. He now stood halfway to the kitchen and halfway to the room where I was sleeping.

"They never caught the guy?" he asked.

"No," Addison said.

"Some of those scars needed stitches," Gwen commented.

"Yeah. The rape had been extremely violent. I have been with Parker since we were in middle school. We were studying together when Roberta called and told us at first that Ken was missing. That she had not come home from the party. It took only seconds for Parker and I to stop what we were doing and throw stuff together and go home. We both feel guilty because we had driven past the truck on the side of the road of the Turnpike on the way home, but we didn't see a body.

"The police were called and then hours later, she was found beaten and naked on the side of the rode. The paramedics had come, and they went to take to her to the hospital; though her body was weak, severally bruised, and bloody, she fought until she couldn't. They took blood and found drugs in her system. But some of those cuts were too deep for them to leave them to heal by themselves, so they had to tranquilizer her. When the nurse came to give her the shot, she fought like hell on earth to get away. It took ten people to hold her down. She was a skinny kid, but she was athletic, and she could fight and hold her own with the best of them, but a part of her died that night.

"We didn't see a change in her until she held Michael. She functioned and went to school, but she was a loner. In a way she still is. She lets the kids close to her. She must know where people are and what is around her at all times. And just within the last couple of years, she lets me, and Parker and James hug her."

"I know that she's not good with being held," Trinity said.

David left their conversation and came and sat in the room with me. He had retrieved a book from their bedroom and now sat in an oversized chair in the room. My cell phone rang from another room. I heard it and groaned and turned the other way and just gave into sleeping.

Meanwhile in the kitchen, Trinity, Gwen and Addison still carried on their conversation. "How is she with Patrick?" Gwen asked.

"She allows him to touch her," Trinity said. "She always has. Even when they were in school together. He could put his arm around her, and she was ok with that."

"It always seemed that Patrick was the only man she ever trusted," Addison said.

I woke up on my own. I turned and saw David sitting there. He looked up from his book. "I'll get you another architect to do your house."

"What?"

"No, I will. No questions asked."

"But that's not what I want," David said.

"I can't be your architecture."

"Why not?"

"Because of what you saw in the last two days. I… I don't allow people to see that. I'm sorry that you and your wife and your daughter saw me like this."

"Are you embarrassed?"

"Yes."

"Are you ashamed?"

"Yes."

"Why?"

He moved closer when we were speaking and now, he sat on edge of the bed.

"I'll get Adam to do the work that you want."

"Kenny, I want you to do it," he said. "You have nothing to be embarrassed about or ashamed of."

"I can't deal with you knowing that I have scars on my body."

"That was from a vicious attack."

"Yes," I said.

"Gwen and I can help you work through it," he said. "Tell me what do you want to do right now."

"Give you a hug, but everything inside of me is telling me to run."

"Why don't we try the hug?"

I got on my knees and reached out to him, but then retreated to the far side of the bed. "That's ok," he said.

I heard voices in the kitchen. "Who is here?"

"Gwen, Trinity and someone named Addison."

"Addy is here?"

"Yes," he said.

I got up and ran to find her. Seeing her in the kitchen, I ran right to her and into her arms. Addison stood four inches taller than me. She wrapped me in her arms. "Thank you for being here." She kissed me head and rubbed my back. Gwen and David both saw me tense up, but I was comfortable in the arms of my sister –in-law.

"Are you ok?"

I nodded against her chest. "Will you take me home?"

"Yes, of course."

When I was ready, I let go of Addison and turned my back to everyone to wipe away the tears. Then I walked over to Trinity, who was sitting at the table. I hugged her. "Thank you," I whispered to her.

"Can I give you a hug?"

I went down on my knees next to her on the chair and leaned into her. She put her arms around me gently and kissed the top of my head. "You are such a wonderful woman and my son and grandson need you in their lives and I need you in my life," she said with tears in her eyes. "I'm so so sorry for judging you and your behavior after you graduated high school. God, I wish your mother would have told me about the scars."

"Mommy and dad don't know."

"What?" I heard from everyone standing in that room.

"How could they not know?"

"I wouldn't let them see me after if it happened. I stayed to myself. I stayed in my room until I could go stay on campus for college. I had gone to the person in charge of housing at school and told them I needed my own room. I couldn't have a roommate. When I did have to have a roommate, I'd stay with Patrick in his room even when he had a girlfriend."

I got up. Gwen handed me a glass of tea. "You need to drink something, and you need to eat."

"I told David that I will gladly get you another architect to do your house."

"What?" she asked stunned. "No. We don't want that."

I sat at their table and lowered my head to the table covering my head with my hands. Gwen came and sat next to me. "What will we have to do to keep you as our architect?" She put her hand on my head.

"This is why I stay away and don't let people get close to me."

"Is that a way to live?" Gwen asked.

"It's a way to survive," I said

"Honey, you aren't alone," David said. "You have an illness and it can be dealt with if you let it."

"I don't want to be scared of my own shadow anymore."

TJ was spending the whole entire day with Storm. She took him to the movies and out for lunch. She took him to the mall and to play in the arcade. She sat him at a table in the arcade and told him that she would be right back. She had to go to the bathroom and when she came back, he was gone. She frantically went running through the place looking for him. She went to the counter and told the staff that she had lost TJ. Three of them went looking for him with her. One of the guys looked under the table where they were sitting and saw TJ pressed up against the wall under the table. "Hey, buddy, what are you doing under there?"

"Is it ok to come out now?"

"Yeah," the young man said taking TJ's hand and coaxing him out from under the table. Once he was out from under the table, Storm picked him up.

"What were you doing under there?"

"Hiding."

"From what?"

"My shadow."

She thanked the staff for their help. Then she brought TJ out to the car. She put him in the car and then she got into the car and brought him to the house. Parker was there now with the kids.

"Mommy still isn't home," he said.

"I'm sure she will be home soon."

"If you would let us," Gwen said. "We can help you, Kenny."

"We want you to be the one overseeing the house for us," David said.

"I'll stay on as your architect," I said. "I'll be in touch."

"Your mother invited us for dinner tomorrow night," Gwen said.

"I'll see you then," I said.

With that Trinity, Addison and I stepped into the elevator and went downstairs to my truck. I climbed into the driver's seat of the truck. Addison got into the back and Trinity was seated next to me in the passenger's seat. I drove us to the house.

When we went into the house, TJ came running full force at me. I caught him in midair and hugged him tight. I kissed him and then put him down. "How was your day with Aunt Storm?"

"It was fun," he said.

"So glad to hear that."

I looked at my phone. "Oh, shit, I missed my one o'clock meeting."

I went into my office and closed the door. I called Henry in Tokyo. "Hi, I'm sorry I missed your call. How are the projects going there?"

"Fabulous," he said. "Those two that you sent really did know and understand the project. It's nearly ninety percent done, so I sent them back to you. I sent you pictures of their work and your collaboration."

"Thank you, Henry."

"Listen I'll be in Orlando with my family at Thanksgiving time. Hopefully, we can get together then and toast your marriage to Patrick."

"And to our child," I said.

"You have a child?"

"Seems as if my husband came with a built-in child. He's six and absolutely the love of my life."

"That's great to hear. I'll be in touch within the next couple of weeks."

"Sounds great. Bye."

I called Lynn and Kara. "Hi, can you please come to the house?" I gave them both my address. Then I went to find Addison. "Can you make one of your specialties for dinner tonight?"

"Yes of course."

"Parker is here right?"

"Yes."

"With the kids?"

"They are playing in the playroom."

"Thank you."

I went into the playroom and crept up behind Beth who was coloring. I reached around her and lifted her. She shrieked with laughter. "Don't make me come in there," Addison called out from the kitchen. Then she heard Carter shriek with laughter. Then Tyson, followed by Kate. She came in the playroom with a wooden spoon. "What is going on in here?" I was behind the door. The kids were watching with sheer excitement as I reached around Addison and lifted her off her feet. She shrieked and the kids laughed. Parker came running into the room.

"What happened?"

"Aunt Kenny," Beth laughed. "Aunt Kenny is so funny."

"I'll give her funny," Addison said.

"Aunt Addy, can Beth and Tyson go swimming with us?" TJ asked.

She looked at Parker. "I'll be out there. I'm fixing the basketball hoop."

"What's wrong with the basketball hoop?" I asked.

"We flew a drone through it," Michael said with a laugh.

"And the net caught fire," Cater chimed in.

"But I was the responsible one and got the hose," Kate said.

"And I got to play fireman," Tyson said.

"Well, as long as you worked together," I said.

"I was playing with my princesses," Beth said.

"We are having guests for dinner," I said.

"David and Gwen?"

"No, honey, they are coming tomorrow night to have dinner with us."

"Can Aunt Storm take us to the movies?"

"If she wants to." I looked at Storm. "Did something happen?"

TJ looked down at his feet. "No," he said. I picked him up and sat him on the counter in front of me.

"TJ," I said. "Did something happen today?"

He reached for me and put his head on my shoulder and cried. "I got scared."

"Why? What happened? Tell mommy and Aunt Storm what scared you."

"I'm scared of my shadow," he cried.

"What?"

"When do I stop being scared of my own shadow?"

"When you realize that it can never hurt you," I said to him.

"But it can, mommy."

"No, sweet boy, your shadow is a reflection of the light or the sun. Your shadow can either be bigger than you or smaller than you, but it can never hurt you. It can't touch you, it can't harm you, and it only exists because of the light."

"He hid under the table in the arcade. I had to go to the bathroom, and he didn't want to go with me. When I came back from the bathroom, I couldn't find him."

"Am I in trouble?" TJ cried.

"You can't be in trouble for getting scared. I can't punish you for hiding under a table today. Did you answer Aunt Storm when she called your name?"

"Yes, but it's really loud in there," he said.

"How long were you separated?"

"It felt like an eternity, but it was about ten minutes or so."

"Aunt Storm is taking us to the movies?" Kate asked. "Oh, is that ok to call you that?"

"Yes, of course," she said hugging Kate. "So, when do you start school?"

"On Monday," Carter said pouting.

"You're not happy to be starting the third grade?" Storm said to him.

"No."

"Why not?"

"He got kicked out of second grade last year," Tyson said.

"TYSON DOUGLAS!" Addison said.

"Well, he did," Tyson said.

"It will be a better school year this year," Storm said.

"Yeah," Carter said.

"Wait! So, do we have to go bed early tonight?" TJ asked.

"No," I said. "After my dinner party, we are all going to stay up and watch movies and eat candy and popcorn."

The kids all celebrated.

"Me too! Me too," Beth said.

"Yes, you can be here too," I said to her picking her up and kissing her cheek. Beth shrieked with happiness. "I not left out."

"No, baby girl, you're not left out," I said.

Ivy called. I answered the phone. "Hello."

"Hi. I'm concerned about my mom," she said. "Her car is here, but she isn't here."

"She is here with me," I said. "Would you like to speak to her?"

"Yes, if that's ok."

"Yep. Hold on."

I handed Trinity my phone. "Hello, darling," Trinity said to Ivy. "Yes, I'm fine. No. I went to Daytona with a friend a few days ago, but he needed to stay an extra day. Kenny was there with her friends, so I caught a ride home with her."

"Are you ok?"

"Yes."

"Is she?"

"Yes."

"Mom, why don't you invite her over here for dinner?" I said gripping Trinity's shoulders for a brief second. Trinity did. She invited Ivy and Bruce over for dinner.

"So, here's the deal," Storm said to me. "I'm going to take the kids to the store and let them pick three movies together and that is what we will be watching tonight."

"That sounds like a plan. You can take my truck. It has the car seats locked and loaded."

"Thanks," she said.

She took the kids to the store. With the older kids with her, she had a great time with all of them. Three movies became six movies. They bought four tubs of popcorn, loads of candy including Twisslers, Peanut Butter Cups in all sizes, and M&Ms in all varieties, Sno Caps, and then an array of the Gummy candies. When they were finished, you would swear that they were shopping for Halloween candy. The last thing they got was Rice Crispy treats.

Addison made a beautiful dinner. We formally set the dining room table. I helped with that. Addison was quite impressed as she watched me set the table. "Where did you learn that?"

"What?" I asked.

"How to formally set a table?"

"I took an educate class in college. We had to learn all napkin folding, place settings and the whole nine yards."

"Are you ok?" she asked coming over and feeling my head. "You're a little warm."

"I'm ok," I said.

"Are you drained from what happened today?"

"I'm…I'm good."

"I worry about you."

"I know you do, and I appreciate that more than you will ever know. I'm so grateful to have you in my life. You are one person, who I have always trusted."

There was a knock on the door. I went to answer it. Lynn and Kara stood there. "Please come into the Jackson Estate," I said.

"This is your home?" Lynn asked.

"It is."

"Can I offer you a glass of wine," Addison said.

"Yes, thank you," Lynn said.

"Is Patrick joining us too?"

"No, he's in Daytona wrapping up a project there," I said. "Let me give you the full tour."

I led them upstairs first and showed them the bedrooms and then the apartment. "When the B&B finally opens, Patrick, TJ and I will move in here," I said.

"When it opens, are you leaving the firm?"

"Not in the least," I said.

We came downstairs and I showed them the game room, the library, the two conference rooms, and then we moved outside to the backyard. The garden was finished, and the new fountains were working.

"When did you buy this place?"

"My parents bought it when I was young. My brother, sister and I grew up in this house. I bought my parents out of it a year ago. The newest add on is the gym. As you can see, there is a full-size track, tennis courts, basketball courts, a racket ball court as well. There are horses in the stables. There is a full riding course for them. My niece and nephews ride BMX bikes, there is full course for them to ride on as well. Along with a skate park, that is also new.

"The people, who stay here, will get three cooked meals a day all exclusive. There are swimming pools, and diving pools. There is everything to offer them."

We went back into the house.

"Did you ask us to come here, to fire us?" Lynn asked.

"Not at all," I answered. "I invited you over to congratulate both of you on a job well done in Tokyo. I spoke with Henry today and I saw the images. I can't promote either of you because you are already high up on the totem pole; so I decided to invite both of you to dinner at my house tonight and also to give you both this," I said handing them each an envelope with twenty thousand dollars in it. "You will get the rest of the money as promised when the job is one hundred percent done, open and running."

"Oh, my god, Kenny. Thank you," Kara said. "Thank you so much."

"You're welcome."

Lynn was taken back. She held tight to the envelope in her hands. Then she finally mustard out, "Thank you so much."

"You are welcome."

Storm came back with the kids. "Hey, guys, I want you to meet two of my co-workers," I said. "Lynn and Kara, these are my nephews Michael, Carter, and Tyson and my beautiful nieces Kate and Beth."

"Nice to meet you," the kids said together.

"And this is Patrick's best friend Storm and she is also TJ's Godmother."

"Please go clean-up for dinner," Addison said to them.

"Do we have to dress nice?" Carter asked.

"Don't you have to dress nice every night for dinner?" Addison asked.

"Yes, ma'am," he said.

They went upstairs and changed for dinner. Then they all six came downstairs. Just as we were getting ready to sit down for dinner, Ivy and Bruce showed up. "Kara and Lynn, this is my mother-in-law Trinity. Her daughter Ivy and Ivy's friend Bruce," I said. "Trinity, Ivy and Bruce these are two of Patrick's and my co-workers, Kara and Lynn.

"Oh, our chef for the night and always here at Jackson Estate is my sister-in-law and one of my best friends, Addison."

With the introductions complete now, we all sat down at the table.

"Ow, mommy made Beef Wellington," Kate said.

Lynn smiled at Kate's reaction. "So, what is like having a chef as a mom?" Lynn asked.

"School lunches are never boring," Michael said.

We had a fabulous dinner. Addison had out done herself yet again. After dinner, I extended the invitation for Lynn and Kara to stay and watch movies with us. They both obliged. We didn't go into the living room to watch the movies, but into the theater to watch it. "Oh, my God," Kara said. "This is incredible."

Mom and dad came home from wherever they were. Addison offered them Beef Wellington, and all though they had eaten dinner, dad did not object. Mom came in the theater with us. Dad followed a short time later. We put a movie in, and all settled into the plushy cozy seats. TJ came and sat next to me. I took him on my lap. The first movie we watched was animated and extremely funny. TJ curled up on my lap. I loved having him like this. I felt so safe and secure with a six-year-old draped on me.

Patrick came home and searched the house for us. We had just put the second movie in. Beth and Tyson were sleeping. Lynn and Kara had left before the end of the first movie. The rest of us lounged in the built-in theater. Storm was sitting next to me.

"I took TJ to the movies, yet we could have stayed here and watched movies here?"

"I can't show new movies here."

"Oh."

Patrick came into the theater. He came over to me. Storm took TJ, who was just about asleep. He startled but relaxed again in Storm's arms. I stood up and Patrick took me in his arms. "Are you ok?" he asked. I nodded into his shoulder. "Come with me please."

We left the room. I closed the doors behind us. We went into the kitchen. We didn't know that Mom had come and was now standing in the living room.

"Please talk to me and tell me what happened."

"David said that he and Gwen work with people who suffer from PTSD. I was driving your mom home and she asked if she could come with me. So, we went to the condo. He has this room that is dark and probably cozy, but I don't and can't do either. He asked me to sit on the floor and I did. Your mom was somewhere else in the condo. Gwen was taking notes."

I sat down at the table and putting my head down on the table ran my hands through my hair; I sat up straight and looked at Patrick. "It seemed like eternity, but it was probably only seconds maybe minutes."

"What seemed that way?" mom asked coming into the room.

I sat up straighter. I looked at her. My shirt had fallen in a way for my shoulder to be exposed. Mom walked over and touched my shoulder.

"What is that? What's wrong with you skin?" She tore open my button-down shirt. "Oh, my god. I heard of this," mom said. "It's cutting right? You're a cutter."

"No," I said.

"Then explain this now or I'm getting your father."

"I've had these scars for twenty-one years."

"What? No. How wouldn't dad and I know?"

"I hid them from you."

"How far down do they go?"

"Wait a minute. I told you about the scars in The Keys," I said. "Whether you choose to accept this or not has nothing to do with me. I told you about them. You refer to the rape as an incident. Why don't we call what it is? I was raped. I got drunk and thought everyone was honest, so I got into a truck with a guy, who I thought was going to bring me home.

"I've been suffering since it happened," I said. "You pretended that I was sick and that I would get over it. So today, I went to try to deal with it. Except I couldn't. Yesterday, on the boat or when we got off the boat and I reacted the way I did, what did you think?

"Patrick probably thought that he married and got involved with a lunatic. I saw the embarrassment on his face. I saw your face. I watched dad look the other way. Hell, dad hasn't even said two words to me since it happened. I have flashbacks. I suffer from triggers. I have super anxiety attacks that I try my damndist to hide. I am humiliated that it happened in front of clients yesterday. It's hard to admit that I have a problem, but I don't want to be afraid to be touched or hugged or loved.

"When Patrick asked me to marry him, I was so afraid of how I was going to react to him. I have loved you for the longest time. But I don't know how I will be at night when we are lying in bed. Intimacy scares the ever-loving shit out of me, but I don't want to lose you." I looked at him. "I thought last night when you left that you weren't going to come home."

"Kennedy," he said in a low voice.

"Well, it true. I didn't think you were going to come back. Originally, you were leaving with TJ. I felt my heart drop watching him get into Storm's car and then you got in. You told me you would see at the end of the week, but you didn't kiss me goodbye. And when he started to cry that he wanted to stay with me, I felt joy. The way he jumped in my arms and hugged me when I opened the car door. Then when he ran in the house, I felt safe. But with you, I didn't know if you would come back and hand me divorce papers or what. I am sure that your mom would love that. She has never thought I was good enough.

"I know that she and my mom have been friends all of their lives. She was here all the time having coffee with mom and playing tennis with mom, but then after I was raped, she stopped coming around the house. She would meet mom out of the house. I'm not idiot. I saw it. Dad stopped asking me to help him with things. Jamie left for college before I did. She didn't know what to say to me. Addy stayed. Addy was here every day. When I wanted to just stay upstairs hidden my room for the rest of my life, Addy made me come out of my room."

She now stood in the doorway of the kitchen. Dad was behind her. I went on with what I was saying.

"The first time Addy got me out of my room, it was only over the thresh hold. She had lifted me up and carried me out of my room. I had grabbed a hold of the door."

Dad saw the scars. It was the first time that he had seen them. "What is that from?" he asked.

I lowered my head. He came over. With an open hand, he touched my shoulder. I tried not to flinch, but I did. His other hand was in his pocket, where he had a pocketknife. He took it out of his pocket. Stepping back, he opened it and looked at it. Then he looked at me. He put the open knife on the table and put his hands on my shoulders and pulled me into a hug. "Kennedy," he said. With my shirt open still, he looked down my back and saw the notches of scars down my back. He took my head in his hand; he felt the uneven skin under his fingers. He pushed my hair back away from my ear and saw that there were scars there too. He kissed the top of my head.

When dad let me go, Addison was standing close.

"Did you fight today?" dad asked.

"Yeah," I said.

"When did you fight?"

"When he was holding me."

"Honey, what he and Gwen do, I think it will work for you," dad said. "If you fight every time but once, then that is an improvement. Don't be embarrassed or ashamed by your reactions. You do whatever you have to do and when they are done working with you, you will be different. You are such a love and you need to be loved.

"And I think that you need to bring TJ for treatment too," dad said. "It's been a strain on him not having a mother in his life and then getting close to you this summer and whenever he loses site of you, he has a super anxiety attack. He becomes completely frantic."

The next day, without contacting them, I went to the condo. I went in and saw the person behind the desk. He called up and then told me I could go. I got into the elevator and went upstairs. When I stepped off the elevator, Gwen took me in her arms and hugged me. "How are you today?"

"I'm ok," I said. "I want to continue to try what we were working on yesterday," I said to her. "But it may take a while."

"As long as it takes," David said. "Are you ok?"

"I'm…"

"You can leave it at that," he said. "Can I give you a hug?"

"Yeah."

He hugged me briefly and then let me go. Then he took me by the arm. The three of us went into the same room as yesterday. Today, Gwen sat with me on the floor. We worked on mediating. I closed my eyes and when she thought I was relaxed enough; she reached around me and took hold of me. I jerked and tried to pull away. "Open your eyes," David said. I did, but I was still struggling. When she released me, I jumped up and ran for the elevator. David: like yesterday, came after me. He caught a hold of me and again turned me so that my back was again his chest. I was kicking, thrashing, and jerking to get away from him, but he didn't let me go. Sweat and tears ran from my body. He brought me down to the floor and held me just a bit tighter. "Let it out," he said. I fought longer and then I screamed out and went limp in his arms. "How long did that last?" he asked Gwen.

"About twenty minutes," Gwen said.

He continued to hold me. He rubbed his hand over my arm. He felt me twitch and then I was fighting again. This went on for almost an hour. I was soaking wet. I had managed to get away from him. I now lay on the floor about five feet away from him breathing hard. I went to get up but couldn't. My legs were gel. He came over and squatted down next to me.

"I'm going to lift you up," he said. I nodded. He reached under me taking my weight and lifting me to my feet.

"That was good," Gwen said.

I looked at her. "How was that good?"

"Fighting is a great sign. It shows that you aren't weak. Now we have to work on where you can be touched and can tolerate it."

"Are you still coming over for dinner?"

"Yes," Gwen said. "Do you want to take a shower?"

"Can I swim in the pool?"

"Sure."

I went swimming for about twenty minutes. Then I went back upstairs and changed my clothes.

"Are you ok to drive?"

"Yes, Gwen, thank you. I'm good."

"Can you come tomorrow about the same time?"

"I have to take TJ to orientation for school tomorrow. But I can come over afterwards."

"Bring TJ. He can swim and go down the slide," David said.

"What time is dinner?" Gwen asked.

"Six."

I drove home. When I got there, I noticed that Parker was unloading the moving truck next door. I ran over. "Hey, you're moving in?"

"Yeah. They said they wanted to be out before the kids start school this year." He looked at me. "How are you?"

"I'm…"

He came over and put his arm around my shoulders. "Dad said that you're going for treatment."

"Yeah."

"How is it going?"

"It's fucking torture."

"What?" He looked at me. "What kind of treatment is it?"

"It's hold therapy."

"What?"

I helped him move a box off the truck. We took it in the house. I explained it to him the best I could.

"How is it going?"

"Gwen said it's going good, but I don't know."

"How is your body reacting to it?"

"I go into complete fight mood," I said. "We did it for like an hour and half today because he waits until I can't fight anymore before he lets me go."

"You fought for an hour and half?"

"Yeah. Pretty much."

"Are you sweating when he lets you go?"

"Beyond that. I'm drenched."

"Make sure you are replenishing your fluids," he said.

"Yeah, I am."

"And eat two bananas."

"Why?"

"So, you don't stiffen up. How often are you going to go this?"

"I don't know. I guess maybe until his house is built. They are coming over for dinner tonight, so you will meet them."

"Ok."

"Thanks, Park."

I helped him with another couple of boxes from the truck. We went upstairs. "Which room is Beth's?"

"The one next to the master."

"Are you ready to set her bedroom stuff up?"

"No. We are going to paint and then set it up."

"What does she want?"

"She wants her room to look the beast's castle."

"Can I do it?"

"Yeah. But when do you have time?"

"I have the time. What does Tyson want?"

"Spider-Man of course."

"And Carter?"

"He wants his room to be space, but not Star Wars. Kate wants musical notes, and Michael just wants a teenager's room."

I pulled out my phone and called Margot, Jenna, Drake, who worked with us occasionally, and I called Lennox. He came over first.

"Hey, what's up?" he asked.

"Can you help paint?"

"Yeah," he said. "You know your nose is bleeding," he said to me.

"What? Shit!"

"Ok, stay calm," he said. He put his index finger and his thumb together and then he squeezed the bridge of my nose. My nose stopped bleeding. "All better," he said.

"Thanks."

The crew showed up. "Ok, here's the deal. We all are going to design and paint the kid's rooms. I'm doing the youngest, who is Beth. She wants her room to be Beauty and the Beast. The castle. Tyson wants Spider-Man with the spider webs, and he wants NYC to be in it. Carter wants space."

"You mean like outer space," Drake asked.

"Yes. He obsessed. Lennox is doing Kate's room. And Michael wants a teenage room. He's starting middle school."

"What are the school colors?"

"Blue and silver," Parker and I said together.

"So, what about blue on one wall, silver on the other and then pin stripes?" Jenna said.

"That sounds nice," Parker said.

"And what about the master?" Margot asked.

We all went into the master bedroom. The room was grey. "Addison likes the color."

"Ok," Margot said. "I brought my daughter and son with me," she said.

I looked at her. "You have kids?"

"Yeah," she said. "Two. Twins. Casey is my girl and Matthew."

"How old are they?"

"Fifteen. They are starting high school this year."

"Mom, we are fourteen," Casey said.

"Casey and Matt, this is my boss Kenny."

"Nice to meet you," I said to them.

"I brought my boys too," Jenna said.

I knew that Jenna had boys. They were fifteen and sixteen. "Tyler and John, right?"

"Yeah," they said.

The kids went downstairs and painted. Casey found the can of a brownish grey color and without asking she went into the kitchen and painted one wall in this tone. Addison walked into the house to see teenagers working hard. She went into the kitchen. Casey smiled at her with a mouth full of braces. "Wow," Addison said.

"What?"

"I was thinking how I was ever going to love this kitchen and you did it."

"What?" she asked again.

"Where is Kenny?"

"She's upstairs."

"Thank you."

"I'm Casey," she said.

"Thank you, Casey. I'm Addison."

"Yeah, I know. We had our basketball banquet in your restaurant last year. Also, I was the one that led you and your son Michael on the middle school tour."

"Yes," Addison said. "How was your summer?"

"Good. My brother and I went to go visit family up north in Tennessee. We had a great time. Our dad lives there."

When they were done talking, Addison came upstairs. I had built a scaffold and was painting the ceiling of Beth's room. Addison came and found me. She looked up when she came in. "Holy crap," she said. I stopped painting. I looked at her. "She's going to love this. You are going to have stop soon. It's nearing six. You have company coming for dinner."

"I'll just finish this and then stop for now."

"This is incredible."

"And it's only paint," I said.

Addison went into Carter's room which was on the same side as Beth's room. She walked into it to see black walls. And then Drake turned off the lights and his room glowed in the dark with white specks everywhere and then he plugged in the projector and outer space came to life in his room. "Wow," she said. "You can paint the ceiling if you'd like."

"Thank you," Drake said. "I'll come back tomorrow and finish it."

"How is it glowing in the dark?"

"It's in the paint," Drake said.

Everyone left except for Margot. "Can I stay a little while longer?" she asked.

"Yeah," I said, "when you are done, come over with the kids and have dinner."

"Thanks."

I ran next door and went upstairs to shower and change. "Hey, where have you been?" Patrick asked me.

"When I got back from David and Gwen's, I saw the moving truck next door, so I went and helped Parker. Then I started working on Beth's room."

"I'm free tomorrow after orientation. I can help. What are you doing?"

I told him what the kids all wanted.

"Wow. Why didn't you call me?"

"Because I know that you and your mom took TJ out for lunch today."

"How are you?"

"I'm good," I said.

Patrick noticed that I was calmer than I had been in days. "Were you painting?"

"I was. Why?"

"It relaxes you."

I didn't respond to that. I went downstairs barefoot. TJ was on the couch playing video games. "Hi, baby," I said to him. "Turn that down ok."

He lowered the TV and then bounced off the couch. "Mommy!" he said running to me. I caught hold of him and lifted him into my arms. "I missed you today."

"I missed you too."

He put his head on my shoulder. I walked with him in the kitchen. Just then David, Gwen and Hayley came into the house. The table was set, and Addison had the dinner prepared. "Where are mom and dad?" I asked.

"They went for a walk," Addison said.

They came back in the house moments later. I greeted David and Gwen. Hayley took TJ. TJ showed her the game room. They were playing darts. We had appetizers in the kitchen before dinner. At seven we sat down and had the feast that Addison had made. Everything was melt in your mouth delicious. After dinner, we went out on the screened in porch and had coffee. Dad spoke to David about the treatment.

"It's a process," David said. "One that she will overcome."

Dad looked at me. "She's my youngest," he said aloud. "I mean I know that she and James are twins, but Kenny is the youngest. She was so spirited when she was a kid. And then that spark died. I catch sight of it every once in a while, but never for long. I miss that about her. I saw the scars last night. I never knew about them. They cover a large majority of her body. Has she mentioned them yet to you?"

"We haven't gotten to the talking about it yet," he said.

CHAPTER TWENTY-SIX

It was my first school orientation since I was in college. I was a little nervous and it wasn't even my orientation. TJ was starting a new school. He would be going to Deerwood Elementary school with Tyson, Carter, and Kate. Kate was receiving her safety patrol belt and schedule and her first homework assignment before the start of the school year. Kate would be in two classes for the gifted program. Carter met his teacher, who was a man, Mr. Gills. Addison went with Tyson to meet his teacher. She was a young new teacher with a thick braid down her back.

"Are you Tyson?"

"Yes, ma'am," he said.

The other kids in the class turned around and looked at him.

"I'm Miss Leyland," she said.

Patrick and I were with TJ. We walked into the first-grade class. Samantha Heyward sat behind the desk. She looked up seeing us walk in. "Hi," she said. She came over and hugged me. "Hi, TJ," she said.

"Hi," he said all shy.

"Hi, Patrick."

"Hi, Samantha."

Other kids started to trickle into the classroom with their parents. A little girl with bright red hair clung to her father's leg. He allowed it to happen and spoke to her softly. When all fifteen kids were in the classroom, Samantha addressed them. "Good morning, girls and boys," she started. "I am Mrs. Heyward and I am new to this school. Please come in and find your name tag and then pick a desk."

All the kids went up to her desk and found their names. TJ picked a desk in the middle.

"Mommy, that's the desk that I wanted," a little boy with brown hair said. "I always sit in the middle."

"You can have it," TJ said and moved to another desk.

"New kids have to sit on the side," a girl with blond hair and glasses said.

TJ moved again.

TJ picked a desk farthest away from everyone. I went over to him. "What are you doing all the way over here?"

"They don't like me," he said.

"Listen kiddo, you are only new for a day, right?"

"Yeah," he said.

Samantha watched. She made notes where all the kids went first. She watched TJ give up a desk twice and then put himself off to the side. She also made note of who started off not to be nice. "As this is only orientation, things will most likely change in the coming weeks. However, I have made packets for everyone and I want you to take them home with you. I need them all back by next Friday," she said

Orientation lasted two hours. The kids played games together. When it was over, TJ came running to me. Another boy went racing to his mom and jumped in her arms. TJ jumped into my arms. "I'm very proud of you," I said to him.

"Will you bring me on Monday?"

"Yes, of course," I said.

Tyson was right down the hall from TJ. Tyson came running out of the class. "I get out of school at noon every day," he said.

"I know you do," I said.

Carter came and found us with Parker coming behind him with a stack of books and workbooks. Kate came over with a pile of books and workbooks too.

Miss Leyland came out of the classroom. She saw all of us gathered in the open hallway. "Tyson forgot his packets," she said. Addison looked at Tyson and then accepted the packets from his teacher.

"And it starts," Addison said with a smile.

"Is he your youngest?"

"No. We have a three old daughter, who is in preschool."

"It was so nice meeting you Tyson," she said to him.

"It was nice meeting you too. See you on Monday."

"I have homework," Kate said.

"Me too," Carter said.

"Me too," TJ said.

"And so does Tyson," Addison said looking at the packets that she held in her hand.

"So why don't we do this," I said. "Why don't we go get Michael from his orientation and then go out for lunch, and then you can do some work while your mom prepares dinner and if you need any help, we will be in the house to help you.

"You don't have to do everything, but we can get a jump start on it."

We went and got Michael, who came out smiling. "Can I try out for the soccer team and basketball team?" he asked.

"Yes," Parker said.

"Then can you come with me to talk to the coaches, dad? Please."

"Yes."

"Can we go to mom's restaurant for lunch?" Michael asked.

"Yes," Addison said.

"I'll go with him and we will meet you there," Parker said.

"Oh, and can I join band?" Michael asked.

"Michael, did you get your books?"

"Yes, mom," he said with a bright smile.

"Do you have assignments to do?"

"Yes, but I thought I could do that at Aunt Kenny's in the conference room like last school year."

"Yes, of course you can," Addison and I said together.

Michael went over and hugged Kate, Carter, and Tyson. TJ was standing off to the side. Michael went to him. "What's wrong?"

"I don't know anyone," he said.

"I know," Michael said. "I'm in a new school too this year, but it's going to be ok."

"Are you sure?"

"Hell yeah, I'm sure, TJ. I promise you; you are going to fit in before the end of the day on Monday."

"Ok," TJ said.

Parker went with Michael into the school to talk to the coaches and to fill out paperwork for him to try out for soccer and basketball and he also filled out paperwork for band. Michael was able to pick his instrument. He chose the violin. The music teacher smiled as she signed it out to him. "Make sure you bring it on Monday."

"Yes, ma'am, I will. Thank you."

Michael showed Parker his schedule. He was in advanced English, history, science, reading, and math. Then he was in physical education, music, and junior ROTC.

"When did you sign up for this one?" Parker said to him pointing to the junior ROTC course.

"They said it was starting this school year and that they were only taking a handful of kids from each grade. I put my name into a raffle and I guess I was picked. It's before school starts. We will get our clothes on Monday and then dress out on Tuesday. But can we try to get them before we leave today?"

"Yeah, let's go see."

The middle school had a bookstore in it. Parker and Michael went in and purchased the gym uniform and the ROTC uniforms and the shoes to go with it. "Thank you, dad," Michael said as they now walked to the car.

The junior ROTC trainer went into the bookstore and inquired which student had just purchased the whole entire uniform and training gear. "The boy's name is Michael Jackson."

"What? Are you serious?"

"Yes," the lady said. "His name is Michael Jackson. He is eleven years old."

"Thank you. Can you tell me what he just bought?"

"He bought the two pairs of shorts and t-shirts, the pair of cargo pants in khaki, the lightweight boots, and the required duffle bag. He also bought his clothes for P.E.," she said.

We met at the restaurant. My phone rang just as we walked in. "Hello."

"Hi," David said.

"Oh, crap. I was supposed to come to your house."

"No, that's ok. You are busy with the kids. I was calling to see if we can do a session at your house on Monday."

"Yes, that would be ok," I said. "But we will have to do it before noon. Beth and Tyson get done with school at noon and they come to the house."

"We can do that," David said. "Have a great weekend and we will see you on Monday."

"Thank you. You too."

We had lunch at the restaurant and then went home with the kids. Their room was set up and I had special places for TJ and Tyson to do their work. With crayons laid out, and markers, and pens and pencils, the kids went into the room together. The five of them sat down wherever they wanted and started their early assignment homework.

I was in the room with them and none of them even noticed. Tyson sat and colored and changed crayons often. He flipped through the first of three packets. The packet was ten pages of coloring, but only coloring certain things and with certain colors. He finished the first packet and moved right on to the second packet. His tongue came out of the left side of his mouth. He was concentrating. Michael looked up from his work and took a picture of his youngest brother sitting with the rest of the kids in a study hall. Tyson zipped through the packets like it was nothing. "Is there more," he asked when he was done. Michael looked at his agenda book.

"You have to write your full name five times on the fat lined paper."

Carter got up and went to the trays where I had paper in various colors and styles. He grabbed a few pieces for him and came back to the table. He put it in front of him and Tyson did the work. "You also have to write the alphabet and the numbers to twenty. You have to leave a finger's space between them each time," Carter explained to him. Tyson did it.

Carter went through his packets as well. He did the math section first, and then the reading, followed by the essay. He wrote about his summer vacation and didn't leave anything out. And then he did his history lesson, which finished his packets.

Kate had all of her books open. She was working diligently on a little bit of everything as was Michael. Their study habits were crazy to me, but they got the work done.

And then there was TJ, who stood up and had his one leg bent leaning on the chair and this is how he worked. He was the exact smaller version of Patrick, who would stand with his left leg bent at the knee on the chair behind him as he stood at the drafting table. TJ worked through the packet.

"Guys, it's time for a snack," I said.

"What?" TJ asked. "We get a snack?"

"Yeah, baby, you get a snack."

"Can we eat in here while we work?"

"No," Carter said. "Snack is in the kitchen."

"Leave everything where it is and like it is and come in the kitchen please."

They all did. They left their stuff and came into the kitchen, where there were fruits, vegetables with ranch dressing, and mini brownies.

"How much do you have left to do?" I asked.

"I have three pages left in my packet," TJ said.

"I'm done with my stuff," Tyson said.

"I'm almost done with my stuff," Carter said. "Well, I'm going to check my work."

"I'm like halfway through," Kate and Michael said together.

"Ok, so Tyson, I want you to go into the room and clean up your workstation please," I said.

He got up from the table and went into the room. He put his stuff in his folder and then put it in his backpack and left the bag hanging on his chair. Then he came back.

A car pulled up out front. Samantha got out of the car and came up the walk quickly. She knocked on the door. Michael opened it for her. "Please come in," he said. "Everyone is in the kitchen."

"Thank you, Michael."

Samantha came into the kitchen. "Hi," she said.

"Hi."

"I didn't look at TJ's file until after you left. He's going to need a little more work than the other kids to make sure he is on task for first grade," she said.

"Ok. What does he have to do?"

She handed me the kindergarten workbook and the first grade workbook. "He needs to do as much as he can before Monday in both books. And if I can get his packet back on Monday morning as well that will help."

"Sure," I said.

"I know that doesn't seem fair, and he's not the only one who has to do this, so please don't think that."

"No," Patrick said. "I get it. No one knows what he is capable of in this school. I went there several times this summer to find out if he needed to do anything before starting school, and I was told repeatedly that he is on task."

TJ had gone to the bathroom and now came in the kitchen. "Oh, hi Mrs. Heyward." He looked at the books on the counter between the three of us. "Who are those for?"

"You, honey," I said.

"Oh, cool. Can I see them?" I handed them to him. He didn't seem to mind the K on the one book and the 1 on the other. "I'm done with my snack; can I go back in the room."

"As soon as Michael or Kate is ready to go back in there," I said.

"I'm almost ready," Kate said sticking a pretzel in her mouth.

"Carter, you can go back in the room when you are ready and Michael the same," I said.

The four kids left the room. Tyson went to go find Parker. Samantha looked at me. "You have a study room in the house for the kids?"

"I do. I told you on the cruise that I home schooled Carter for three-month last school year."

"Can I see it?"

"No," Patrick said. "Maybe some other time. When the kids aren't busy doing pre-school work and pre homework assignments."

Carter came out of the room fifteen minutes later. "Aunt Kenny, I put all my stuff away in my backpack and left it hanging on the chair."

"Ok, sweetheart."

"Can I go play?"

"Yes."

TJ stood finishing his packet. When he was done, he put it in his folder and pushed it aside. Kate scrutinized his work. He did everything right. He answered everything right. She showed it to Michael. Michael brought it to Patrick and me. "We didn't help him on anything," he said.

"What is he doing now?"

"He's working on the K booklet."

He didn't complain or anything. It was mature for him, but he knew that he had to do it and he just did. By the time six o'clock rolled around and we were getting ready for dinner, he was more than halfway done with the K book. Patrick went and got him for dinner. "Daddy, can I finish both books today, so that we can have fun over the weekend?"

"That decision is up to mommy. But let's discuss it after dinner."

"What are we having?"

"Aunt Addison made her special…"

"MEATBALLS!" TJ squealed. He ran to Addison and wrapped his arms around her waist. "Thank you," he said. "And thank you for the snack."

"That was your mom's doing. Not mine," she said. She looked at Kate and Michael. "Where are you in your homework assignments?"

"I have history to do and take the quiz and then science and the quiz," Michael said. "Oh, I was looking at Kate's schedule. Did you know that she is taking music in the middle school before school?"

"What?" Kate asked.

"Your music class is in the middle school in the morning before you start school."

"But it will be dark then when I'm going to school," she said with concern in her voice.

"Well, you won't be alone," Michael said. "I was accepted into the junior ROTC class, so I have that before school as well. When we finish our classes, I could walk you over to the elementary school if you'd like."

"Yeah," she said.

We ate dinner. The whole family. Mom and dad, Jamie and Lennox, Parker, Addison and the five kids, and Patrick, TJ and me. The fourteen of us sat in the kitchen sharing laughs. After dinner, everyone helped clean up and in no time the kitchen was clean. Mom decided that we would all go into the theater and watch another one of the movies that the kids had picked. So that is what we did. We settled in to watch movies.

At nine, Addison and Parker left to go their old house. Patrick told TJ to go up and get ready for bed, but he didn't have to go bed yet and he could come back down once his teeth were brushed and he was in his pajamas. TJ went upstairs, took a shower, brushed his teeth, and got into his pajamas. He came downstairs. He slipped into the conference room where his books were, and he continued to work on the K book assignments. I came into the conference room. "What are you doing?"

"I wanted to finish the one book," he said. He had been working since about four thirty on the new assignments. "I just have a little left, mommy," he said.

Patrick and I moved what we were doing into the conference room. TJ had worked on a packet of thirty pages, which was the first thing he was given this morning at orientation and now he finished the skills book for K. "Can I start the other book?"

"Not now," I said.

"But I like being busy."

"I know that. But now we are all going to bed. Look. Daddy is tired and I'm tired and you need to get some sleep. I'm very proud of you," I said to him. "Come on. Let's go upstairs." I picked him up and we turned out all of the lights. Locked the front door and set the alarm. By the time I reached the first step with TJ in my arms, he was sleeping with his head on my shoulder and his arms and legs wrapped around me. I put him down in his bed. Then I climbed into bed with Patrick. "I want to slap Samantha," I said. "She's been working at the school for more than two weeks now. She knew that she had TJ in the class."

"He has our work ethics," Patrick said. "He stands like you do when you work."

"What?" I said.

"He does. He's picked up so many traits from you this summer."

"Patrick, you stand like that when you are working."

"Then I guess we both do," he said. "I hope it won't be a problem for him in school to stand and do the work."

"And that packet was crazy. It will be interesting to see how the other kids do."

"He's always been a smart kid."

"He has a super intelligent father," I said.

"And now an extremely thorough and accurate mother."

"The best of both worlds," we said together. I kissed Patrick. He kissed me. He put his hands on my back and I didn't flinch when he touched me. I breathed out a deep long breath. "Are you ok?" he asked.

"Yes," I said.

"Do you want to continue?"

"Yes."

He kissed me deeper and then he had me on my back. He was almost on top of me. I stopped for second and closed my eyes. Patrick went on his side and took me in his arms. "It's ok," he whispered.

"It's not. I'm sorry."

"We are working on it," he said kissing my cheek. "I love you so much and much much more," he said to me.

"I love you too. I want to satisfy you without being afraid."

"I know you do. But until we are in the apartment in the front of the house, we can't do much with a six-year-old sleeping in bed in the same room as us."

We laughed together. "I love you," I said to him and closed my eyes.

When I woke up the next morning, Patrick was snoring lightly next to me. I got up out of bed and went into the bathroom. I came out quickly because TJ wasn't in his bed and it wasn't even six in the morning yet. I stepped in a pair of shoes and ran downstairs. He wasn't on the couch watching TV. I saw the lights on in the office. There he was standing there at the table working. "Hi," I said to him. "What time did you get up?"

He looked at the clock on the wall. "At five fifteen."

"Why didn't you go back to bed?"

"Because I want to get this done and still be able to have fun before school starts on Monday. Besides this is fun stuff," he said.

"Are you hungry?"

"No. I ate a couple of meatballs," he said with that little devious smile. "Was that ok?"

"Sure," I said. "I'm going to be right over here if you need help."

"Ok," he said.

I looked to see what he was doing. He was connecting the dots in pencil just like the instructions said. When he was done with that, he moved on to tracing and then finishing the pictures. He knew his fruits: banana, apples, oranges, pineapples, blue berries, grapes, and peaches. "Is a peach a plum?"

"No."

"What's the difference?"

"Come. I'll show you real quick," I said taking his hand and bringing him in the kitchen. Addison had bought both fruits yesterday. "Ok hold out both of your hands." He did. I placed the peach in his left hand and the plum in his right hand. "Tell me how they are different."

"The peach is in my left hand, right?"

"Yes," I said.

"It's fuzzy. The plum in my right hand isn't fuzzy. Oh," he said realizing. "Thanks, mommy." He ran back into the conference room.

Patrick woke up and came to find both of us. "Hey," he said coming into the conference room. "Why is everyone up?"

"There is work to be done, daddy."

"You're right," he said. "How are you doing?"

"Fine."

"Do you need help with anything?"

"No, thank you. Mommy just helped me tell the difference between a peach and plum."

"Wait!" Patrick said. "They aren't the same?"

I looked at him. He looked at me and then he looked at TJ. "What makes them different smarty pants?"

"Daddy, a peach is fuzzy like your face when you don't shave, and a plum is smooth like mommy's skin is all the time."

"What an analogy," I said.

"A what?" TJ asked.

"A comparison," Patrick answered him.

TJ finished a little before noon with the first-grade book. Patrick took the book and looked over the material. He had just done a year's worth of schoolwork within hours. When he was done, we decided to take him out.

"Is that what first grade is going to be like?"

"Yes," I said to him.

We took him the Bok Tower Garden. He was so excited to be back there. We showed Patrick everything. "And the garden was built first, right mommy?"

"Yes," I said.

"And then the owner had the house built," TJ told Patrick. We stayed there all day. We went into the bell tower. "This stands the same height as the lighthouse," TJ said. "I love it here." He looked at me. "Mommy, you should bring David and Gwen here."

"Where?" I asked him.

"To this place."

"David doesn't need any more ideas when it comes to his house," I said. "But you can't say that I said that."

"I won't," TJ said.

Patrick and I were both thinking that TJ was going to be bored in his first-grade class. Patrick and I spoke alone when TJ was at the park going up and down the slides nonstop. "So, our little man did a whole first grade workbook within less than a day," Patrick said. "He is going to be bored out of his mind in first grade. And I looked over his work, he didn't do anything wrong. Not a math problem, not filing in the blanks, nothing. Last year, they kept telling me that he was lazy. He's not lazy, he's brilliant. He gets the work and does it. Other kids would complain about it and fuss and carry on, but not TJ or any of the other four kids that are in school."

"Beth is in school too," I said.

"Oh, yes. I forgot."

"Her teacher called Addison to ask who is coloring in the pictures she is given."

"Why?"

"Because she knows her colors, and she can color inside the lines. She writes her name too. But she is the youngest with everyone else in school around her, so she picks up on things."

"You're selling yourself short," Patrick said.

"How is that?"

"You work with all the kids including Beth," he said kissing me on the cheek. "I wish I'd had known you as a child."

"What? Why?"

"To have seen you when you were Beth's age, or Tyson's age, or at TJ's age. You must have been the cutest littlest thing."

"I was small until I was in fifth grade. Then it seemed I went to bed small and woke up a foot and half taller and then I didn't stop growing until I reached six feet tall. I think I have been this height since eighth or ninth grade. I'll show you pictures when we are home."

Monday morning, Addison brought the kids to the house, where their backpacks still hung on their chairs. Michael and Kate got their bags and Parker drove them to school. Michael didn't dress out for ROTC, but he had the clothes. The teacher took the whole class, which consisted of fifty kids to the bookstore to buy their uniforms. When they all had everything, he brought them out to the soccer fields and had the kids run laps. When it was over, Michael went to the music classroom and met Kate. "Are you ready for your first day of fifth grade?"

"Yeah," she said.

"Look. If you need me, I'm right across the street from you."

"I know," Kate said.

"Then what's wrong?"

"I'm going to miss having lunch with you every day."

"I'll miss that too, Katie Bug, but I'm still going to be there when we sit down to study every day."

"I wasn't supposed to do the whole packet and all of the assignments that I was given."

"So, you're ahead. That's great."

"Yeah," she said hugging him.

A girl noticed Michael talking so sweetly to Kate. She smiled at him when they went by. The first bell rang. Michael walked Kate across the street and then came running back for his first period class a combination of home room and his advanced English class.

"Mr. Jackson, you are late," the teacher said. "Care to explain?"

"Can I tell you after class?"

"You can tell me in detention."

"Yes, ma'am," he said. Michael did the work that was given to him. The teacher handed him a detention slip for after school. He put it in his pocket and went to his next class.

By lunch time the teacher had heard that his younger sister was taking a class at the middle school in the morning and that he walked her across the street, so that she would get there safely. The teacher found him in the cafeteria. "I need to talk to you, Mr. Jackson," she said. Michael got up from the table ever so politely and walked over to the teacher. "Is it true that your younger sister is taking a music class here in the morning?"

"Yes, ma'am" he said.

"And did you walk her across the street to the elementary school?"

"Yes, ma'am."

"Can you please give me your detention slip?" Michael took it out of his pocket and the teacher ripped it up. "Why didn't you tell me that this morning?"

"Because I didn't want my classmates to laugh at me for walking my sister to school," he said. "We both have a class before school even starts in the morning. I just wanted to make sure that she got there safely. I can ask my mom to come get her from now on. I'm sorry, Mrs. Baker. I didn't want you to think that I was disrespectful this morning either."

"It's ok," she said.

The bell rang. He didn't get to eat his lunch, but he packed up all of his things and walked to his next class. Walking into his advanced reading class, he once again had Mrs. Baker. He sat down in a desk and didn't say anything.

"I want all of you to take a copy of The Outsiders and read it thoroughly and then write a book report on the entire book by the end of next week. Here is a packet that goes along with the book that you will have to answer as you go along in the book and that will aid you with your reports. If you finish it before the due date, please hand it in when it is complete."

Other kids griped and groaned. Michael took his copy of the book and started reading.

"Oh, look! A nerd," one of the kids teased.

"Hey! None of that."

When class was over, Michael approached Mrs. Baker. "What if I finished the assignments that we were given at orientation? Can I hand it in?"

"Yes," she said.

"Do you get all the assignments because your the homeroom teacher?"

"Yes," she said.

He bent down and went into his backpack. He took out all of the assignments and handed them into her. "Thank you," he said. "See you tomorrow." He zipped his backpack and zipped off to his math class.

Meanwhile, at the elementary school, Tyson's first day flew by. They were learning and reviewing colors. Tyson knew the information, but only raised his hand a few times to answer. Before he left for the day, he handed his teacher the packets of assignments.

"You did it already?"

"Yes," he said.

"But it's not due until Friday."

"My mommy and daddy make us sit down and do the assignments right away because when we are done, we get to help mommy cook," he said.

"Well, thank you," she said.

Addison was right there waiting for him. Miss Leyland approached her. "Hi. Tyson handed in his packets of work."

"Yes," Addison said.

"I'm glad that he got everything done, but it wasn't necessary to get it all done before school started."

"Tyson is my youngest boy, and has two brothers that sore with schoolwork, so when he's given something to do, he does it correctly the first time. A lot of that has to do with my sister-in-law watching him ever since he was a baby. She is very efficient in everything that she does that it has worn off on all of my children. Those packets may be hard for other kids to sit and do, but not for Tyson.

"You should have seen the work that his cousin was given to do for today. If you want to talk about dedication and persistence. We teach the kids good work ethics."

"Yes, I see that," Miss Leyland said. "Thank you."

Addison took Tyson and went to pick up Beth then she came back to the house.

David and Gwen had showed up at the house at eight thirty with a third person. His name is Lewis. He works with Gwen in her office. We had gone into the playroom, where I moved all the furniture. Gwen had put mats down on the floor. "We are going to do something new today," she started. "I want you to lay on your back and close your eyes," she said. I sat on the mat and then laid back. I closed my eyes. Gwen took hold my wrists and brought them up above my head. Lewis took hold of my ankles keeping them together. I was already starting to struggle. "It's ok," Gwen said. "You are safe."

David came on the mat with us. My shirt was tucked into my jeans. He pulled my shirt out. "No. No. No. Please. No."

"It's ok. We aren't going to hurt you."

My stomach quivered under his hand. My breathing had heightened. Sweat started to trickle off my body. I started to try to pull my arms and legs free, but Gwen was holding super tight on my wrists that she had them pinned to the mat above my head. And Lewis was holding my ankles. I was hyperventilating. I opened my eyes and David saw them rolling back. "Let her go," he said. "Let her go." My body went rigid. Everything constricted. My head went up and back on the mat. It was the only thing that was elevated. David slid his hand under my neck and just cupped my head. My hands were balled tight into locked fists. David rolled me on side; put his knees behind my back and was supporting me. "Don't fight it," he said. "I know it hurts, but let it happen. Gwen, put the bite plate in her mouth." Gwen got it in. It pushed my tongue back. After ten minutes, my body subsided. I now lay in front of David breathing hard, but shallow. David took me and sat me up. I leaned hard against him.

"I...I... can...can't ddd...do,,,"

"It's ok," he said. He put his arms around me, and I started to scream and somewhere deep within me the fighter came back. I was pulling and jerking with all my might to get away from him, but he continued to hold me. I put my head back against his shoulder trying to push him off using my head. "Stop. Stop," he said. "You're going to hurt yourself."

"FUCK YOU!" I yelled. "LET ME GO!"

"I'm not going to hurt you."

"THAT'S WHAT HE SAID."

David moved his hand and I screamed again. He held me for a long time, and I fought to get to away from him the whole time until I blacked out.

"Lights out," Lewis said as I fell limp in David's arms. My whole body crumpled into him.

"SHIT!" David yelled. "That's not what I wanted to do."

After a while I came to. "Slow movements," David said.

"Go to hell."

"I know that you don't think that I or we are helping you, but we need to know how your body is going to react to situations. You are doing well, Kenny. When did he tell you, he wasn't going to hurt you?"

"What?"

"You said that is what he said after I said I wasn't going to hurt you. When did he tell you that?"

I got up and went and sat with my back pressed against the wall. "When he tied my hands up on the bar in his truck," I said looking down at the floor.

"What do you remember about him?" Lewis asked.

"He haunts my dreams," I said just loud enough to be heard.

"Tell us," Gwen said.

"He had blond hair to his shoulders. He has green eyes. I don't know," I said.

"That's ok," Gwen said.

"Did he have any tattoos?" Lewis asked.

"Yeah," I said.

"Can you stand up?" David asked.

I shook my head.

"Can I come get you?"

I nodded. David lifted me up. He touched my left bare shoulder and I went into fight mode. David pulled me away from the wall and brought me into the middle room where the mats were. I fought hard this time.

"That's good. Keep fighting," David said.

"GOD! I'M TIRED OF THIS!"

"Then start talking."

"What?"

"Talk about it. Have you spoken about it to other people than to Addison, who doesn't know the whole story," David said. "Come on. I can take whatever you give."

"David, she's fading," Gwen said. "Hold her."

I went limp in his arms. My head flopped back. Gwen came over. David put me on the mat. I laid there weak. I felt weak and broken. I fought to try to get up. David lifted me. He picked me up and brought me over to the oversized chair. He sat down and held me in his arms.

"You need to cry," Gwen said. "Have you cried?"

"No," I said softly. "I'm sorry."

"Don't apologize," David said.

"Why are you sorry?" Gwen asked.

"Because I let it happen."

"Tell me how you let it happen."

"It's my fault," I said.

"No," David said.

"I let him take me."

"You let him take you where?"

"It's all fragments."

"Don't be afraid to talk about it," David said.

"I have to go."

"Where?"

I got up from his lap. I went outside in the backyard and I ran around the track for the next hour.

Addison offered them lunch before she went to go pick up the kids. "You've stirred a boiling pot," she said. "Now you have to find a way to fix it. She is going to lose weight because she'll stop eating and sleeping. She's already starting to retreat and withdraw."

I came in dripping with sweat. "Are you ok?" Addison asked me. Without looking at her, I nodded. "I need to hear words coming from you," Addison said. "Are you ok, dammit?"

"I don't know," I said.

"What bothers you the most?"

"The scars," I said. "I have to change. Excuse me please."

I went upstairs and took a shower. I sobbed in the shower. Alone. Away from everyone. In private. Hidden. Safe. I didn't hear that anyone had come into the room. "Kenny!" David said. "Are you ok?"

"Yeah," I said.

I turned the water off to the shower. The towel was on the counter, so I opened the shower door and stood there naked and dripping in front of him. "This is what you want to see right?"

"You have a beautiful body."

"Don't."

"You do," he said.

"I have a marred scars up and down my body that is gross to touch."

He handed me my towel. "I know that you think that you aren't doing well with the hold therapy, but you are."

"How is that? I can't relax."

"It will come."

"Before I go crazy?"

"You aren't crazy or going crazy. And let me tell you something. I'd rather deal with a fighter like you."

"What do you mean?"

"Kenny, do you know how easy it to give in?"

"No."

I got dressed with my back to him to now. I put on jeans and was putting on my t-shirt when he stopped me. "What?"

"Are there pictures of this when it first happened?"

"Yeah."

"Do you have them?"

"They are in the bank in the safety deposit box."

"Can we go to the bank and get them?"

"We will have to go tomorrow. The bank is in north Orlando."

We went downstairs. We went into the kitchen. Mom was there. "Hi," I said.

"Hi. I think your father and I are going to move back up here."

"Oh. Ok."

"I thought you'd be a little more excited."

"Sorry. It's been a long day and the day isn't even half over. Would you move back in here?"

"No. We are looking at the cottage."

"Really. It needs work."

"I know, but your father loves it."

"After I get TJ from school, let's go look at it."

Gwen looked at me. "We are going to go. Would you want to try it again?"

"Yes."

"Where?"

"Here. If that is ok?"

"That is fine. We will see you tomorrow morning."

"Without Lewis?"

"Yes," Gwen said.

"Thank you," I said to them both. I gave them each a quick hug.

Mom waited till they left. "Are you paying them to torment you and torture you?"

"What?"

"You heard me," mom said. "What are they doing to you? You look beaten and drained."

"Maybe you forget what it's like to have a six year old."

"No."

"Well, I didn't get to go through the baby stages. It was instant five now six-year-old and I love every minute of it, but I'm tired. He doesn't sleep well. I don't sleep well, so together we don't sleep well.

"Where is dad?"

"He's golfing."

"Oh, how nice," I said. "Want to go with me to pick TJ up from school?"

Meanwhile, when I was going through hold therapy, TJ was in school. He liked Mrs. Heyward. He had handed in the packets and the two books that she had brought over. He had learned that the little red head's name is Cassidy. They played together at recess. They sat together at lunch. TJ also met two boys, who he played with at recess. Royce and Braxton.

Samantha had given them writing assignments to do in class. TJ read it with a smile. *Write a page paper on what you did this summer* was the assignment. TJ began to write.

WHAT I DID THIS SUMMER
BYE TJ Alexander
Age: 6
First Grade: Mrs. Heyward

**This summer has been different from any
other summer I've ever had. First, my dad and**

I went to New York. Because his work plan got cancelled we got see the whole entire city. Just him and me.

He brought me to Kennedy Jackson's house, and I met her for the first time ever. I could not help it. I jumped into her arms when I saw her. She was going to watch me and keep me with her for eight weeks this summer. Dad had to go away on business.

Kenny took us: Tyson, Carter, and Michael, and me to incredble places in Florda. We went t Bok Tower Garden, Pounce de Leon Inlet Lighthouse, Two Tales Ranch, The Keys, Sea World, Kennedy Space Center, the kort house. She married daddy and then became my mommy. It was the best summer ever. And we went on a cruise too.

I was adopted and my family became complete. I got a mommy. Kenny became my mommy.

"Mrs. Heyward, can we draw pictures?" TJ asked.

"Yes, you can," she said.

TJ drew the bell tower, the lighthouse, the elephants, a turtle, a shark, the courthouse, and a cruise ship and a space ship.

"Mrs. Heyward," Cassidy said.

"Yes."

"Look at his paper."

His drawings didn't look like a first graders drawings. He drew things like they were. Mrs. Heyward came over. She looked at his paper. "That's ok," she said. "Keep working."

The last thing TJ drew on his paper was me.

When I arrived, TJ wasn't in the pickup line. I parked the truck. Mom waited and I ran into the school. I walked to his classroom. He was sitting at his desk. I knocked on the door. Samantha looked and waved for me to come in. "Hi. Is there a problem?"

"The students were to write what they did this summer and draw pictures if they wanted to. Here is TJ's."

I looked at it to see a masterpiece. "Oh my god. This is so good. This is great, TJ."

"His grammar is accurate. He misspelled four words in the whole thing. He's not like any child I've ever had," she said. "His drawings are stunning."

"Well, he does have two architects as parents," I said. "Can I keep this?"

"Yes," she said.

"Can he go?"

"Yes."

"Come on, baby," I said to him.

My cell phone buzzed. "Hello."

"Can you get Kate and Carter please?"

"Yes."

"Thank you."

I took TJ's backpack.

"TJ, you know that you aren't in trouble," Samantha said.

"What? Why would he be in trouble?"

"He's not. I asked him to stay, so that you would come in and get him. He is such a great kid. Is what he wrote true?"

I looked at it. "Every word of it," I said with a smile.

"See you tomorrow."

"Yeah," TJ said. "Bye."

Carter was in the front of school looking for Addison. "Mommy's not here."

"Hey, Carter, I'm taking you and Kate home today."

He threw himself at me crying. "Is mommy ok?"

"Yes," I said. "Mommy is fine."

Kate seeing Carter crying came running over. "What's wrong?"

"Nothing. I'm taking you guys home."

"I have to stay till the last bell rings."

"I know. We will wait, Princess."

I took the boys to car. "Hi, grandma," they said together.

"Why the tears from both of you?" mom asked.

"She asked us to write what we did this summer and I asked if we could draw pictures and then I had to stay till mommy came and got me," TJ cried.

"TJ, you aren't in trouble. You did a good thing. Not a bad thing," I said.

"And why are you crying?" mom asked Carter.

"I have so much homework and it's only the first day."

Carter's teacher saw me taking him. He came running over. "Wait a minute," he said. "You aren't his mother."

"I'm his Aunt Kenny."

"Oh, we heard about you today," he said. "Carter, why are you crying?"

"It's a lot of homework."

Mr. Gills told us that he gives the homework packets at the beginning of the week and that it is due on Friday. I thanked him as Kate ran over and jumped into the truck. "Hi, Mr. Gills."

"Hi, Kate," he said.

I brought the kids home. Carter came running into the house. Addison was in the kitchen. He ran to her and jumped in her arms. "What happened?"

"You didn't come pick us up," he said.

"I know. I'm sorry."

"Why?"

"Well because I wanted your favorite cookies waiting for you when you got home from school, but I was distracted when Beth put a marble up her nose and the cookies burned."

"Beth put a marble up her nose?" Kate asked. "Is it still there?"

"No."

"Damn."

"Kate!"

"That would have been cool to see," Kate said.

"No. It definitely wasn't cool to see," Addison said.

"Well, I'm going to go do homework," Kate said. "Love you, mom."

Carter and TJ went in with her. The three of them sat down at the table, opened their backpacks, and took out their work.

Addison and I were in the kitchen. "I'm going to run to the store. I'll be back in a little bit," I said. I told TJ that Addison was in the kitchen and that mom was sitting right there in the room with them reading a book. I ran to the craft store. "Hi, I need to get this matted and framed please."

"What color do you want the mat to be?"

"Blue."

"Do you want this laminated first?"

"No, but can I please get three copies made of this?"

"Yes."

"I want all of them framed the same way."

They were framed. I waited. Then I went back to the house. I went into the garage and got a hammer and nails. I hung it on the wall proudly.

Carter, who had cried over the amount of homework he had to do on this first day of school, finished the packet before dinner that evening.

Kate was working on her stuff. And TJ was finishing his. He had written his spelling words three times each. He had colored a picture of fish. He connected the dots and colored it in. All three of them finished their work that was due at the end of the first week.

When we sat down for dinner, TJ looked up at the wall and saw his essay framed. Patrick looked at it. "Wow, did you do that?"

"Yeah," TJ said.

"Oh, my god that is so good."

Parker came in with Michael just as we sat down for dinner.

"How was school?"

"It was good," Michael said to Addison. "I made the soccer team. I have practice every day from three till four thirty."

It was decided that the kids were going to stay at my house because their old house was full of packed up boxes. After dinner, Michael and Kate went into the conference room and worked on their stuff.

Before Addison left, Beth, Tyson and Carter were already in bed sleeping. "I want Kate upstairs by nine o'clock and Michael by ten," she said.

The kids were really good. They listened to their mother. When Michael came upstairs, Kate snuggled into him as he started to read The Outsiders out loud. Kate was sleeping in no time. I went and checked on the kids before going to bed. Michael was still awake. "Hey, lights out," I said to him.

"Five more minutes?"

"No. You have to get up at six in the morning and we have to leave a six forty-five. Lights out."

"Good night," Michael said.

"Good night."

By the time Friday rolled in, none of the kids had homework to do, so we all decided to throw a party. And on Sunday, Parker, Addison, and the kids would be moving into their new house right next door. I couldn't wait for Beth to see her room. All of us including Patrick had worked diligently in their house. Beth had her princess room with her princess canopy bed. Tyson had his Spider-Man room. Carter's room was outer space with the space station on the ceiling of his room. Kate's room was all musical: music notes, musical instruments, and musical quotes lined her walls. And Michael's room was the teenage room he asked for. Addison and Parker's room had vines with the kids' names on them above the headboard of the bed. We had put their furniture together and set it up in their rooms.

But first was the party on Saturday. The kids invited whoever they wanted. I had extended the invitations to Samantha, to Heather Leyland, to Milo Gills, and Kate's two teachers, Brenda Hanson and Jill Maxwell. I wasn't surprised that they came. I was happy that they came. TJ invited his whole class. Out of fifteen kids, only Cassidy, Royce and Braxton showed up. He was happy for the kids that showed, but I knew he was disappointed. There were toddlers from Beth' preschool class, young kids from the elementary school and a sprinkle of teenagers from the middle school. Michael invited his ROTC classmates, but not all fifty of them showed up. I had invited David, Gwen, and Hayley to come as well as everyone from work. The whole family was together as well.

There were kids everywhere. Some were swimming. Some were playing basketball. Some were in the house snacking on food. There were adults everywhere as well. The party was from one to six. By five, the party had died down to about twenty-five people.

"TJ, who are your friends?" Storm asked.

"Hi, Aunt Storm, this is Cassidy, Braxton, and Royce."

"Hi," all three kids said.

"Hi."

"Is your real name Storm?" Cassidy asked.

"Yep," she said.

"Why?"

Her mom had just come to get her. "Cassidy!" she said. "I'm sorry."

"No, that's ok. She's adorable."

"Hi, I'm Summer."

"Nice to meet you. I am Storm. And this handsome little fella is my nephew and Godson, TJ."

"Yes, I know who he is," she said.

"Want to meet my mom?"

"Yes," she said.

"MOMMY!"

I looked up from the conversation I was having. "Excuse me a moment please." I walked over to where he was.

"Mommy, this is Summer. She's Cassidy's mom."

"Hi, I'm Kenny," I said.

"I heard all about you this week. It's very nice meeting you. Thank you for inviting Cassidy."

"That was totally TJ's doing."

"Well, we have to get going. See you on Monday."

"Bye," the kids said to each other. Then without any word from the adults they hugged each other.

"Looks like when we were kids," Patrick said to Storm.

Braxton's dad came for him and he took Royce with them.

Some of the teenagers were still at the house. "Do you have any movies?"

"Yeah," Michael said. "My Aunt has tons of movies." He came over to me and asked if they could go into the theater. I said they could, but they had to watch something the younger kids could watch too. "My Aunt said we could. I have to ask my brothers and sister if they want to join us."

"Yeah, that's cool," a girl said.

Kate and Carter went in the theater. They watched Spider-Man. Tyson went in there after the movie started. He found Michael, who took him on his lap. Tyson leaned back against Michael's chest. Before the movie ended, Tyson was sleeping on Michael.

"How old is he?" the girl asked.

"He just turned five. My little cousin just turned six on the same day as this guy."

"Where is he?"

"He's probably with my Aunt Kenny."

"Her name is Kenny?"

"It's Kennedy, but she has gone by Kenny since she was a kid. My Aunt Jamie goes by James at times."

"Neat," she said. "Thanks for inviting me."

"Yeah, sure,"

I came in the theater. The movie had just ended. "Michael or Kate, have you seen TJ?" They both said no. Carter got up. I hadn't seen him sitting there. "Do you know where TJ is?"

"No, but I'll help you look for him," he said.

We searched the house. The last place I went into was my office and there he was sound asleep curled on one of the chairs. I went over and scooped him up in my arms. He stirred and opened his eyes. "Mommy," he said.

"Yeah, baby," I said.

"I couldn't find the others."

"It's ok."

"Is Michael in trouble?" Carter asked.

"No, of course not. Why would he be?"

"No reason."

"I was tired, but I was afraid to go upstairs by myself."

"It's ok," I said to TJ.

I carried him into the kitchen, where now there were just a handful of people. Samantha was still there as was Heather and Milo.

"Who's this little guy?" Milo asked.

"This is TJ. He is in my class this year. He's a bright young man."

"As is Tyson. If there were an advanced kindergarten class, he would be the head of it," Heather said.

Tyson came into the kitchen. "I'm hungry."

Heather laughed. "I think he starts saying that at about nine o'clock in the morning."

Addison looked at him. "Please make good choices right now," she said to him.

"But I didn't eat, mommy."

"What?"

"He didn't," Carter said. "Aunt Kenny got the bounce house and until we watched Spider-Man, Ty was in the bounce house."

Parker came in. "Is Tyson in the house?"

"Yes, daddy," he said.

"Oh, good. I was afraid he was still bouncing away in the bounce house."

David and Gwen were still there, but Hayley had left hours ago. David watched me as I held TJ in front of me. His head was pressed into my shoulder. I leaned up against the counter and stayed involved in the conversation.

"So how old is?" Heather asked.

"He's six," I replied.

"How did he get so lucky to get a mom like you?"

I looked at her. "What's that?"

"He's lucky to have a mother who still holds him."

"Thank you," I said. "But I'm the lucky one. I hit the pot of gold at that far end of the rainbow when I got him."

Gwen smiled. David just kept observing.

"Aunt Kenny?" Kate said.

"Yeah."

"Would it be alright if we watched another movie?"

"Yes. Just something that all the younger kids can see too."

"Yes, ma'am," she said. "Thank you."

"So, you just have the one child?" Heather asked.

"No," Addison said. "She has six as do the rest of us until the baby is born. We all share the load of parenting in this family. I think that is why our kids are the way that they are. They are never alone. There is always an adult around. Whether it is me and Parker, Kenny, and Patrick, and now James and Lennox. We don't leave our kids with babysitters. And now that Kenny married Patrick, we have Storm here too."

TJ had his legs wrapped around my waist and now they dropped. I lifted him gently back to my shoulder.

"He's a runner," Samantha said. "He's by far the fastest kid in my class. If I have to have someone go to the office, I send him. He goes, delivers the message, and comes right back." She looked up and saw the framed paper that he did.

"I remember you used to be like that in school," she said to me. "You outran any boy until we were in the seventh grade. Do you still run?"

"I do."

"Hey, do you remember that party after graduation?" she asked. I lowered my eyes. "Did Romeo Quin get you home safe that night?"

"Excuse me please. I'm going to go put him to bed."

Gwen pulled out her phone. She walked out of the room. She called Lewis. "We have a name of the man," she said. "I need a background check ran right now. His name is Romeo Quin. Run it and call me back."

I was upstairs in our room. Patrick came up. "Are you ok?"

"I'm ok."

"What are you thinking?"

"I don't what to think."

"Are you coming back downstairs?"

"Yeah."

By the time everyone had left the house for the evening and we were tidying up from the party, Romeo Quin had been arrested. When the police went into his house with a search warrant, they found my driver's licenses from when I was kid. They found my high school jacket, my high school ring, my graduation cap, my tassel, and the necklace that mom and dad gave me as my graduation gift. His mementos from that brutal night twenty-one years ago. He had taken pictures of me before, during, and after that night. His house displayed the crime and the torture he had put through that night. The police came to the house and informed me that he had been arrested. "Would you be able to identify him?" one officer asked.

"Yes."

"Can you tell us of any distinguishing marks that you remember?"

"His left eye has a scar above it, but it's below his eyebrow. It looks like squiggle mark. Under his chin, there is a scar that goes from one side to the other."

Earlier in the week, David had gone with me to the bank in northern Orlando. In the safety deposit box, I had things from that night. "Can you please come with us to the station?"

"Yes," I said.

"Do you want me to go?" Patrick, Addison, and mom asked.

"Yeah," I said.

At the police station, we were brought into a room. "No one can say anything. The only one who can speak is Kennedy," the captain said. "There will be five men in the line-up in the other room. They can't see you. Whenever, you are ready, please let us know."

I lowered my head and took a few deep breaths. Then I looked up. "I'm ready," I said. They opened the blinds in the room that we were in. I stepped closer to the window. "Number three," I said. I properly identified him.

Samantha was at the police station too. She knew him. She knew who he was. She didn't know what he had done to me. They brought her into the room. They had moved him to the fifth position and she identified him without hesitation.

I was in a daze. I couldn't hear anything at the moment. Mom touched my arm. I looked at her. "You could identify him?" mom asked.

"Yes. He has haunted my dreams for more than half my life."

"But why didn't you tell anyone."

"I did, but I didn't know his name. I didn't think we were ever going to find him."

"Did he go to school with you?"

"No. He's older."

Samantha came over to me. "I'm so sorry," she began.

"I'm so grateful."

"What?" she asked.

"I never knew his name. He was just some guy at the party, who offered to drive me home."

"But he didn't," she said.

"No. No, he didn't."

The police had put up the pictures of the scene on the monitors. There was a picture of me wearing a skirt and bright orange tank top and my high school jacket. A jacket that I had from my freshman year of high school. A jacket that I wore everywhere I went. Whether I wore it, or it was wrapped around my waist, I always had it. That picture was from the party that night. The next image was of me drunk in his truck. Before he had taken out the knife. Then there were images of me with my hands tied above my head, no jacket, my tank top ripped open exposing my breasts, and then the first notched cut with the knife to my left shoulder. When he was done there were hundreds of them all over my body. And then there were the ones that needed stitches. The deep cut to the back of my shoulder from when I had gotten the door open and tried to get away.

"It's hard to believe that girl was me," I said looking at them. "You can see her spirit was taken out of her that night," I said about myself but from another perspective.

The next picture to come up of me was me all bloody when the police and the medics had shown up. I just about winced looking at it. With black and blues covering a majority of my body, cuts, stab wounds, and welts too.

"I'm sorry. I didn't mean for those to go up," an officer said. "Are you ok?"

"Never better," I said. "Can I go home?'

"Yes."

"So, what happens now?"

"He will be processed and there will be an arraignment on Monday morning, and it will go from there."

"Thank you."

CHAPTER TWENTY-SEVEN

That night when we went home, I curled up in Patrick's arms and I slept like I hadn't slept in my life. I didn't flinch when his fingers touched my scars. I slept soundly and secure. For the first time in twenty-one years, I could put my head down on the pillow without fear and anxiety. When Patrick woke up in the morning, I was sleeping pressed against him. I hadn't retreated away from him like I had most nights this summer. When he rolled slightly on his back, my relaxed body drifted with his. And without waking up, I moved so that I was now laying with my head on his bare chest. My arm was bent on his chest with my hand gently laying on his shoulder. When he put his hand on my back, he thought that I would jerk or jump but I didn't. Instead I moved in even closer to him. I tucked my chin and breathed out on his chest. Patrick cupped my head with his hand and closed his eyes falling back to sleep.

I slept till nine o'clock in the morning. I hadn't slept that long since I was in high school. When I woke up, I was still in Patrick's arms. I reached up and kissed him. He opened his eyes. "How are you?"

"Safe," I said. "Thank you."

"You are most welcome," he responded.

"What's the plan for today?"

"Park, Addy and the kids are moving in next door today."

"And when is Jamie and Lennox moving in?"

"I don't know yet." The phone rang. "Let it go to voice mail."

"How long are your parents staying?"

"Um. I don't know."

We got up and went in the shower together. Then we both dressed in a pair of jeans and a black t-shirt. After that we went downstairs to find our munchkin. He was reading. "Thank you for giving mommy and I quiet time," Patrick said to him. "Are you hungry?"

"Yeah," he said.

"What would you like?" I asked him.

"Pancakes."

I dove on the couch with him. He was laughing. I started to tickle him. He was squealing and laughing. Patrick joined in on the fun. TJ touched my one of scars and pulled his hand back. "How come you have those?"

I pulled him in my arms. "Because someone was very angry…"

"With you?"

"No. With life."

"So, they hurt you?"

"Yeah, baby."

"But you're ok right, mommy?"

"Yes, baby, I'm ok."

We went into the kitchen and I whipped up a batch of pancakes with chocolate chips. We had breakfast together and then Parker called to say that they were coming. "Come on. We have to go next door," I said. "Bring the presents with us ok." We went next door and I let us into the house. The kids hadn't seen the house since they did the first walk through. "Let's put their presents on their beds," I said. We were back downstairs when they came into the house.

"Oh my god," Kate said. "And this is our home?"

"Yes," Parker said.

"It's huge," Michael said.

"Wow!" Tyson said.

Carter kept quiet. I walked over to him. "Are you ok?"

He shrugged. "I guess. It's just hard leaving our home."

"But now you have a new home and right next door to me."

"That's the best part," Michael said. "Are you still going to allow us to come and do homework at your house?"

"Yes, of course," I said.

"Listen," Addison said. "Nothing has changed other than the place that we live. I'm still going to be working at Aunt Kenny's cooking. You are still going to come to Aunt Kenny's before and after school. The only difference is now we don't have to drive to go home. We can come and go home whenever we want."

"Well, as long as there is an adult in the house," Parker added.

Michael and Kate laughed.

"Why don't we go check out your rooms?" Addison said.

We went upstairs with them. Michael's room was the first room off the steps on the right. Kate's room was the first off the steps to the left. We all went into Michael's room first.

"Wow. This is great. Thank you, mom, and dad. I have a teenage room. Thank you."

"You're welcome," they said together.

Then we went into Kate's room. "Oh, my god, this is fantastic," she said. "Oh, wow, look at the quotes. This is so great. Thank you."

Then we went into Carter's room, which was next to Michael's. "It's outer space! Oh, wow! It's outer space. I have a space station on the ceiling of my room. Oh, this is great. This is so awesome." Then I flicked off his lights and the whole room glowed. "Oh, it's like what we saw at the space museum, Aunt Kenny. This is so great. Mom. Dad, look. There are planets on my walls. It's the whole solar system. Oh, thank you so much."

Then we went into Tyson's room. "It's Spider-Man!" he said. When we went into Beth's room, everyone gasped.

"Wow!" Kate said. "Who painted her room?"

"Aunt Kenny," Parker said.

Beth's expression was priceless. She had her hand covering her mouth. "I'm a princess in here," she said.

"Say thank you," Addison said.

"Thank you," she said with a smile. "It's Bell's house over there," she said.

And last we went into Addison and Parker's room. Addison looked at me. "This is stunning. Did you do this?"

"No," I said.

"Who did this?"

"Margot. One of our coworkers."

"It's breath taking," she said.

The kids left us after a few minutes. Then we heard them say, "We have bathrooms in our rooms." Each of their bathrooms was decorated as well. Not like their bedrooms, but they were painted their favorite colors and they had everything that the kids liked. Beth's bathroom was the color of Bell's blue dress; Tyson's bathroom was red and blue with a Spider-Man shower curtain; Carter's bathroom was white with a light projector of earth; Kate's bathroom was pink and purple, but not overdone; and Michael's bathroom was grassy green. They loved them.

Then finally we all came back downstairs. We walked through the living room, their dining room, the great room, where their TV was and on the other wall were pictures of the kids and Addison and Parker. And then we made our way into the kitchen. "Holy crap!" Addison said. "How did you know?" she asked.

"It's like a smaller version of the restaurant," Parker said.

"It's gorgeous," Addison continued. "Who's responsible for this?"

"I am," Patrick said.

"My god. It has everything. It's my dream house."

Parker went out in the garage and found a complete workstation.

"So, there is a built-in generator here in the house. If the electricity is out for more than two minutes, the generator will click on. It is wired for the whole house," Patrick said.

"Thank you," Parker said.

We left them in their new house. Carter was the first to come over. He went into the conference room and was doing schoolwork. Patrick found him in there. "Hey, buddy."

"Hi, Uncle Patrick."

"What are you doing?"

"I said I didn't have homework and then I went on the school's website and saw that I do. Is it ok?"

"Yes, of course," Patrick said to him.

Kate and Michael came over too. "They posted homework assignments,"

Michael said. "And I have to get everything done. I have a soccer game this Friday."

"It's ok. Can you show me the website and how to work it?"

"Sure, Uncle Patrick," Kate said. They pulled up TJ's class and he too had homework posted. Then they pulled up Tyson's. He didn't have homework, or anything posted.

"TJ!" Patrick called. "TJ, come in here please." TJ came into the conference room. "You have homework assignments to do."

"Oh. Ok," he said. "What do I have to do?"

"We have to go to the bookstore, and you have to pick a chapter book and start reading it and then write what it is about."

"Ok."

I was working on David Bruno's layouts again because he wanted final changes made. Patrick took TJ, Kate and Carter to the store. All three of them picked books. Then he brought them back to the house. "Do the easy stuff first and get it over and done with," he told them.

"What time is dinner?"

"Six," he said to Kate.

"Is mommy cooking?"

"No. We are having a barbeque. You kids will be eating with us and your parents are going to have a special night together."

"Are they going to kiss?" Carter asked.

"Probably," Patrick said.

Carter laughed.

The kids sat in the room together and worked on their assignments. Patrick worked in the room with them on his latest project.

Kate checked the middle school website. "Damn. I have homework from there too."

"You'll get it done," Patrick said. "You all have the next two days out of school. You go back on Wednesday. So, you can all work for another hour and then we are all going to prepare dinner tonight."

"We get to help?" TJ asked along with Kate and Michael.

"Yes. You all get to help. Everyone must make something. I'm going to go get Beth. I'll be back in a few minutes."

Patrick went next door. He knocked on the door. Parker opened it. "Hi. I came for the baby."

"Are you sure about this?"

"Absolutely," Patrick said. "The kids are going to be fine. We will keep them over our house tonight and send them home in the morning."

"Call first," Parker said with a laugh.

"Yeah, man. I wouldn't want them walking in on that."

They both laughed. Patrick took Beth and came back to the house. He set her up at her workstation in the room with the other kids. He gave her directions. She was making a picture for their new home. "Make it pretty," he said to her.

When Beth was done working, she brought it over to show Patrick. "It's beautiful, he said.

"Up please."

Patrick picked her up and she curled right up in his lap and closed her eyes. He looked at the clock. It was one thirty. Her nap time. The other kids were working diligently on the assignments as usual. At three o'clock, he stopped everyone. Beth was just waking up from her nap. "Leave your work right where it is," he said. "And come with me. We have to go to the store." He took all six kids to the store with him. They went grocery shopping. He asked each kid what they wanted to contribute to dinner tonight. "Cuppy cakes," Beth said.

"Ok. So, Beth and I will make cuppy cakes," Patrick said. Beth smiled so big. She was proud of herself. Patrick didn't correct her. "Tyson, what are you going to make?"

"I like black beans and rice."

"Oh, very good. We can do that."

"Carter, what's your choice?"

"What kind of barbeque are we having?"

"We are having ribs, chicken, steak and shrimp."

"Can I prepare the shrimps?"

"Yes."

"I'd like to make a tomato salad," TJ said.

"And I want to make vegetables," Kate said.

"This sounds like a great dinner. Michael?"

"Can I help grill the dinner?"

"Sure."

"Can we buy beer? I saw this really cool recipe with beer, but we have to buy a whole chicken too."

"We have beer at the house," Carter said.

"Is it in a can?"

"Oh, no," Carter said looking down. Michael came in front of him.

"Just because you said something and it wasn't exactly correct doesn't mean you have get so upset with yourself," Michael hugged him. "You are a great little brother."

"Come. We have groceries still to buy." Patrick said. He sent each of the kids except for Beth scrambling to get what they came for. He took Beth to get cupcake mix and frosting. She decided on blue cupcakes and yellow frosting and sprinkles. All of the kids met him at the register with their fraction of the list and their fraction of the dinner. "What should it come to?" Patrick asked.

"One hundred and seventy-eight dollars," TJ said, "and change."

"How much change?"

"Eighty-six cents," he said.

The girl at the register rang it up and it was exactly one hundred seventy-eight dollars and eighty-six cents. The kids looked at TJ. "Dude, you're like in first grade. How did you do that?"

"I'm good with numbers," he said with a smile.

"That's freaking awesome," Michael said.

"So, what did everyone spend?" Patrick asked.

"Roughly twenty-six dollars, but if you want to know everyone spent twenty-five dollars and fifty-five cents. So, because it is over fifty you round to the nearest dollar, so twenty-six dollars."

"He should be in like fourth grade," Kate said. "Does Aunt Kenny know that he does that?"

"Nope," TJ said.

"Why not? That rocks," Carter said.

They came back to the house. I was on the phone in my office. Carter came barging in. "I need to talk to you," he said. "Please, Aunt Kenny, I need to talk to you."

"Yeah," I said to the person on the other end of the phone. "Can I ask you to hold on a minute please? No. Not my son. My nephew. Yep. Hold on." I lowered the phone putting the call on mute. "Please tell me what couldn't wait another five minutes for me to get off of the phone?"

"TJ has magical powers! TJ has magical powers! Do you know what TJ can do?"

"What?"

"We were at the grocery store and Uncle Patrick asked all of us what the total cost was going to be for the groceries and TJ told him right down to the penny. It was so cool."

"Wow. I didn't know this. Thank you for telling me."

"CARTER!"

"Well, got to go. Just thought you'd like to know this," he said.

"Hey, Carter," I said before he got to the door. He turned and looked at me. "Thank you for telling me that." He smiled before he tore off out of the room. I went back to my call. I got off the phone an hour later. I went into the kitchen, where it smelled like a restaurant. "What is going on in here?"

"We are all making dinner," Beth said.

"Can I help?"

"Nope," Beth said.

"No? Why can't I help?"

"Cause we are making dinner."

I went up behind her and tickled her. She squealed. I bent and kissed her on the cheek. Patrick came into the kitchen. "Oh, hey," he said. "You can't stay in here. The kids and I are busy."

"Ok," I said and kissed him on the lips.

With Patrick and the kids all being as busy as they were, I didn't know what to do with myself. I went into the theater and put in a movie then curled up on the couch to watch it. I must have fallen asleep because when I opened my eyes, I had six children looking at me.

"Look. She sleeps," Carter said.

"I sleep."

"Not really," TJ said.

"Things make you jump when you sleep," Kate said.

"Yeah, in eleven years, you've never slept well," Michael said.

"You all are so observant," I said to them.

"Dinner is ready."

"It smells delicious."

I went with the kids into the dining room, where the table was set to perfection. "What's the occasion?"

"It's move in Sunday," Tyson said. "Mommy and daddy are staying in the house tonight. We are staying here with you."

"I know you are," I said with a smile.

The dinner was splendid. And then we had the "cuppy" cakes, which were out of this world. When dinner was over, everyone helped clean up and then we went into the theater and settled in for a movie. That night it stormed and with us protected in the interior of the house, we only heard a rumble of thunder here and there. That night we slept in the theater. When Patrick saw that all of the kids were sleeping, he came and cuddled with me. And for the second time in two nights, I slept soundly in his arms.

At three in the morning, a dream sequence started. I was running with Carter on a long track. And then Carter was gone and now I was running by myself. The track went on and on into infinity and then I was being chased down.

I started to jerk in my sleep. Patrick woke up. He looked around and it was just the two of us in the room. The kids had trickled upstairs to their beds. He let me continue to dream in his arms.

The guy chasing me, caught me around the waist. I gasped both in my dream and in my sleep. And then the fight began. I was jerking trying to get away from him. Sweat poured off my body again both in the dream and in sleep. "Jesus Christ," Patrick said. The guy in my dream brought me down to the ground and was now on top of me and I was kicking and trying to push him off. I was doing this in Patrick's arms. "Kennedy," Patrick said softly so as not to scare me. "Kennedy, wake up." I started to talk in my dream. "NO. I don't want to do this. Please. No. I'll go with you, but please don't. NO." and the whole time I was saying this, I was still fighting in Patrick's arms. He was becoming wet from the sweat that was coming from me. "Kenny," he said brushing my hair back. And then I screamed. He took me in his arms and started to rock me. I was still fighting hard.

I started to feel the rocking. I started to calm down slightly. My hair was drenched. My clothes were wet with sweat. "Patrick?"

"Yes, sweetheart, I have you."

"I'm sorry," I said with my eyes still closed.

"For what?"

"Not being the perfect woman. Not being the perfect wife."

"Are you serious?" he asked. I opened my eyes and looked up at him. "You are everything," he said.

"I'm drenched."

"Yeah. Tell me about the dream."

I closed my eyes and put my head against his chest. "I was running with Carter and then I was alone and then someone was chasing me. I was on a track that went on forever. The guy grabbed me around the waist and then had me on the ground and he pinned me down." My voice faded as I fell back to sleep. Though we were both wet, Patrick closed his eyes going back to sleep as well.

In the morning, I went upstairs to check on the kids. They were all sleeping soundly in their beds. TJ was in a heap of his oversized blanket, which was a king size blanket, Trinity had bought for him when he was three. She thought she purchased a twin blanket that had the monster truck Grave Digger enlarged on it and other monster trucks around it. She had given it to him for Christmas when he was three and when he opened it, he snuggled into it, so she didn't want to take it away from him. And now here he was laying sprawled out on his bed with the blanket bunched up underneath him and yet it was coving him as well. I changed my clothes and went back downstairs. Patrick was still sleeping in the theater. I went out in the backyard and went for a run around the track.

CHAPTER TWENTY - EIGHT

We were celebrating our firsts. Our first Halloween. My first Halloween as wife. My first Halloween as mother. It was TJ's first Halloween having a mother. It was our first Halloween together. September was drawing close to the end when TJ came to me and asked me if we could decorate for Halloween. I hadn't really celebrated Halloween since my senior year of high school. I accompanied my nephews and nieces' trick or treating, but I never dressed up. I never decorated the house. So here was a first again.

"Can we make a fun house?" TJ asked me as we sat down for breakfast on his day off from school.

"A fun house?"

"Yeah," he said. "I don't like haunted houses."

"Have you been to them?"

"Yep," he said biting into a bagel. "Have you?"

"Not for a very long time."

"Can we have a party?"

"I'm sure we can," I said.

Patrick came into the kitchen. His hair was sticking up. He had bed head. "Good morning," he said kissing TJ on the head and me on the lips. "What are we discussing?"

"Having a fun house Halloween party," TJ said. "And mommy's never been in a haunted house."

"I didn't say never."

"Did you go in the one that we had at the school?" I shook my head taking a sip of my coffee. "But weren't you a part of the construction of them?"

"Yeah, I was," I said. "but once it was built, I never went inside to see the finished outcome. I did the walk through after it was built to make sure everything was sound, but that my extent.

"TJ says that you take him to haunted houses."

"I do. I have since he was a baby."

"Why?"

"To show him that fear is just an illusion. And that even the dark doesn't have to be scary."

This defied everything I knew since I was a teenager. Fear haunted me and tormented me, and I hadn't slept in the dark since then either. When the lights go out, so does my thinking. Panic sets in. I don't function well in the dark. TJ doesn't either.

"I want to be Grave Digger for Halloween."

"You want to be a grave digger," I teased.

"No, mommy. I want to be Grave Digger the monster truck."

It was then that I realized, I didn't know much about monster trucks. Patrick must have read that on me because he simply took out his cell phone from his pocket and pulled monster trucks up on YOU-tube. I sat at the table with Patrick standing behind me leaning over my shoulder and TJ on my lap and we were watching monster trucks.

"I'd like to go see that sometime," I said.

"Awesome," TJ said. "Mommy likes monster trucks."

"So, what will be in our fun house?" I asked after we watched about an hour of monster trucks.

He rambled off a water gun room, where you have to shoot at targets; a sumo wrestling ring, a dirt bike track, horseback riding, a painting room, where everyone has to paint something that they can bring home, a room for Legos, and end it with a Halloween movie. Anything that wasn't scary he specified. He also wanted multiple bounce houses. We definitely had the room to accommodate all of this.

Later that day, the three of us went to the store to start Halloween shopping. We bought witches, and moving skeletons, we bought spiders and spider webs and bats, and then we found spooky fun stuff, black cats, skeletons of dogs and cats. We bought fake pumpkins. We got ghosts and ghouls, we got light up movable things as well, and a talking broom.

"Oh, mommy, we have to have a pumpkin carving contest," TJ said.

"We can do that," both Patrick and I said together. "That would be fun," I continued.

"Do you carve pumpkins?" TJ asked looking up at me.

"Yes. That I have done. I have done that with Michael since he was a baby and then with the others as they came along."

"When can we carve our first pumpkin together?"

"The closer it gets to Halloween," I said to him.

We went home and started decorating for Halloween. Within the next couple of hours, the house was decorated and it looked like Halloween and autumn had thrown up all over the house. Both the inside and outside were decorated. We had material zombies on the roof of the house. We strung Halloween lights with pumpkins and ghosts on the outside of the house. Patrick made an owl flying from the tree to the top of the house. We decorated both the front and back yard. In the back yard we had a monstrous Halloween blowup in the middle of the track. It was definitely starting to look like the beginning of the holiday seasons.

"When are we opening the B&B?" Patrick asked.

"The first week in January," I answered him not looking up from the computer. "I'd like to get us moved into the front apartment this week or next," I said.

"How are your parents doing?"

"They are fine. They are going to rent out the house in the Keys for eight months and then they will go there for four months during the year."

"Did they buy a house yet?"

"They did."

"Close by here?"

"Ah-huh."

"Across the street or something?"

I laughed. "Not that close," I said. "On the next block. It backs up to Parker and Addy's house, but not ours."

"So, when are they coming?"

"They will be here before Halloween."

"Wait till they see the house," Patrick said. "Did they decorate when you guys were kids?"

"Um yeah," I said a little distracted. "but nothing like this."

"Hey, how come we haven't seen the kids?"

"I don't know," I said.

Just then like magic, Carter came running into the house. "Awesome decorations," he said.

"Thanks."

"But isn't it a little soon?"

"No. October is a less than a week away."

"Yeah. I know. It starts on a Monday."

"It does," Patrick said looking at the calendar. "Where is your mom?"

"She'll be here soon. Can I go into the room and do homework?"

"Yes, of course," I said.

"Thanks."

Our house was still the center for projects and homework. Kate came over with a friend. She introduced us, but neither Patrick nor I heard the girl's name. Tyson came over too and then Michael with five boys from the basketball team. "Hi, Aunt Kenny and Uncle Patrick. Would it be alright if we used the theater to watch game reviews?"

"Yes, that is fine."

"Oh, mom said to tell you that she and dad will be over in a bit. And she said to tell you that she is making dinner."

"Thank you, Michael," I said.

"TJ!" Patrick called. He stumbled into the room. "What are you doing?"

"I was playing a video game."

"Go turn it off and do your homework."

"I did my homework," he said.

"Then we want you to read a book for the next hour."

"Ok," he responded.

"How about you start your history project," I said to him. "You have to make a diorama, and dad and I will help you with it, but I want you to do the research that is going into it."

"I have most of it done."

"It needs be done before it is due because we will be out of town the week it is due."

"Ok."

"And what is it on?"

"The civil war. I picked General Lee."

Having architects as parents was a great experience for him because we knew how to construct things and he loved that.

"Where are we going?"

"When?"

"The week my project is due?"

"Good try. We still aren't telling you."

"Damn!"

"TJ!" Patrick said. He smiled up at him. "Get a book and start reading please."

With all the kids working and the amount of kids we had in the house, the house was still relatively quiet. Kate and her friend had moved from the conference room to the living room where they had their books spread out across the floor and they were laying in the middle of all of it doing their homework.

Patrick and I were painting the apartment. Once again, I called our coworkers and asked for assistance. Dillon, Margot, and Jenna came. Dillon got the pleasure of designing TJ's room, which we told him that he wanted monster trucks. Dillon painted the walls green and brown like a mural of a monster truck track and then there was Grave Digger. TJ had a car bed at Patrick's house and he still wanted that, but with Dillon doing the room, he constructed a monster truck bed that sat in the middle of room. On the walls around the bed there was he dresser and desk with a lamp on it. He also had lockers in room like in Michael's room. So, there was a row of six lockers lined up nice and neatly in the room. And on the third wall was a play table. The room looked spectacular. Dillon did the bathroom blue.

Margot did our room and bathroom. Patrick and my favorite color is blue, so she picked different shades of blue for us. She did the bathroom just by adding accent colors and accessories.

Jenna helped us with the painting and hanging pictures up.

My parents had redone the kitchen in the apartment before they left. It had blue granite counter tops and red oak cabinets. They had also redone the bathrooms. Without their stuff in it, it looked huge. And pretty soon it would have our stuff in it. And look homey for us and not my parents.

With the bedrooms done before the first of October, we were going to spend our first night in the apartment. It would be the first time in my life not sleeping in my bedroom at the far end of the hallway. Addison made us a huge dinner.

"Hey, have you heard from mom and daddy?" Parker asked.

"A few days ago. Why?"

"No, I was just wondering when they were coming here?"

"They will be here within the next few days," a very pregnant Jamie said. "Lennox and I will be moving into our house next weekend."

"Yeah, what was the hold up on that?" Patrick asked.

"The people tried to renege."

"How did that happen?"

"We let our lawyers handle it. We are moving in on Saturday," Jamie said.

"Are you going to have a music room?"

"Yes, Katie Bell," Jamie said.

"Can I come over and use it?"

"Yes," they said together.

"Kate!" Addison said.

Kate lowered her head. "I'm sorry, mommy, I'm just really excited that for first time ever we all will be so close. Are grandma and grandpa going to live on our street too?"

"No," Parker and I said together.

"Where are they going to live?"

"On the next street behind us," Parker said. "Our fences will be the only thing separating us."

"Is grandma going to move closer too, daddy?" TJ asked.

"Not as far as I know. Aunt Ivy lives with grandma and they aren't too far away."

"Yeah, I know."

"So, what's it going to be like in mom and daddy's apartment?"

"I don't know," I said to Parker. "I'll tell you tomorrow."

"Are you going to leave the door open?"

"Yeah. For now," Patrick said.

We ate a fabulous dinner of everyone's favorite things. Meatballs, rice balls, corn bread, honey glazed roasted chicken, ham, turkey, ribs, steaks, and different types of pastas. When we were finished eating, we all cleaned up.

"If you have homework to finish, you know where you need to go," I said. The kids that were here earlier had joined us for dinner. Now they moved a bit more slowly to the conference room, but they all went in there to do their work. By eight thirty, the house was pretty empty except for the middle school kids working with Michael.

"Aunt Kenny, do you mind if we work longer?"

"No, it's ok. Is this project due tomorrow?"

"No. It's due in two weeks."

"What is the project?" Patrick asked.

"Something for our ROTC class."

"Well, if you need help, I'm here. I can help you."

"Thank you, Uncle Patrick."

We went upstairs and TJ saw his room for the first time. "Oh my god! This is great. It's awesome. And my bed is Grave Digger." He went through all of us stuff and all of things were there just like they were at Patrick's house. "But Frosty isn't here," he said.

"Who is Frosty?" I asked. With being so busy, I forgot the dog's name.

"Keep checking," Patrick said. "Because I know for sure that Frosty is here."

He opened the lockers and in the second to last one he pulled out a beaten up well-worn stuffed dog.

"Shower and bed," Patrick said.

"Am I going to be in here alone?"

"In your room?"

"No. In the apartment?"

"No. We are going to be here," I said.

TJ went into the bathroom, where he played in the tub for about twenty minutes. Then he drained it and got out. He put his pajamas on and came to find us. "Why couldn't we stay in your room?" he asked.

"Well, because daddy and I decided that you needed your own room again and that we need to get used to living in here because when we open the Bed and Breakfast this will be our home."

"So, would we have our own Christmas tree?"

"We could," I said, "but we will have a big tree downstairs."

"How do you decorate it?"

"Filled with ornaments and presents underneath."

"TJ, you need to go to bed," Patrick said. "Mrs. Heyward told me that you fell asleep in class again."

"You fell asleep in class?" I asked.

"I kinda did," he said.

"TJ, come on," I said I scooped him up in my arms, which I knew he loved. I carried him into his new room and put him down on the bed.

"Will you read to me?"

"Yes," I said. "What would you like me read?"

"The Wind and Willow."

I got the book from his shelf and came and sat with him on his full-size bed. He climbed under the covers. I read the first two pages and he was sound asleep. I kissed him gently on the cheek and left his room. I left the door open.

"I'm going to go downstairs and see if Michael is still working," I said.

"He came up and said goodbye when you put TJ to bed. They left their things and they are going to come back after school tomorrow."

We went in our room. It was the first time that we had a room that was just ours since our marriage. That night, we made love and fell asleep in each other's arms.

Projects littered the conference room. There were elementary history and science projects, and there was a middle school ROTC project and a history project, and then there was Kate's music project. I found myself staring at it and thinking back to when mom and dad had made all of us take piano lessons as kids though Parker and I gave it up, while Jamie strived in it. Kate was the first one to come to the house. "What do you think?"

"It's amazing."

She wasn't being a snob when she answered. "It really is. It's Amazing Grace," she said with a smile. "Thank you for letting us still do homework here and study here."

"Sure, honey," I said.

"How did TJ do in his bed last night?"

He came downstairs smiling and happy. He came into the conference room and hugged me first and then Kate. "Hello," he said.

"Hi, sweetheart," I said to him.

"Hi," Kate said.

"That is so cool."

Michael came over with Tyson.

"Where is Carter?"

"He has a fever and is complaining of his ears hurting him. Daddy is going to take him to the doctor."

A wharf of deliciousness just swept through the house. We all went into the kitchen, where Addison had made a Frittata for breakfast. Patrick came downstairs followed by Lennox and Jamie.

"Where is your brother?" Addison asked the kids.

"Daddy is taking him to the doctor."

"Why?" She didn't wait for an answer though. She pulled her cell phone out and called Parker, who was in the car driving Carter to the doctor. "What's wrong with Carter?"

"He has a fever and says his ears are hurting him."

"Please let me know."

I drove the kids to the school. TJ brought his project. I carried it for him. Samantha stood outside her classroom. She smiled seeing us coming up the walkway to her classroom. "That looks spectacular," she said. "Do you have the report to go with it?"

"Yes, ma'am," TJ said.

"And the index cards?"

"Yes, ma'am," he said again.

"Ok. Bring it in." She put it in the closest, so that the other kids wouldn't see it yet. I hugged TJ goodbye and went to Carter's teacher, who was just unlocking the door.

"Can I help you?" he asked.

"Yes. I am Carter Jackson's aunt."

"Aunt Kenny," he said. "It's nice to meet you. We met on the first day of school." He came to my house for a party, yet this is how he starts conversations. With nice to meet you. "How can I help you?"

"Can you please give me Carter's work for today? He has a fever and most likely ear infections."

"Yes. I can do that," he said. "Come on in."

He had the kids' desks in sections. There were six desks to a section. So, there were three sections and then there was one desk alone. "Who sits there?"

"That's Carter's seat."

"Why isn't in he in a section?

"Because he is the leader."

"Excuse me?"

"He tells me that he was home schooled last year at the end of the school year by his Aunt Kenny."

"Yes, that is true."

"Well, he is so advanced; however, he missed the cut for the fourth grade by four points."

No that is how brilliant he was. He liked being in school with kids his age. He didn't want to be the youngest kid in fourth grade, so he missed the points on purpose. I loved that about him.

"In January, this class will be joined with fourth graders, so it will be a third-fourth grade split and somehow I think Carter will be even advanced for that class. He is an amazing child. We will miss him while he is out sick."

"Thank you," I said and left his class with his assignments. I was leaving when I saw Tyson's teacher bringing him to the office. I ran over to see what happened. "What's wrong?"

"I lost my first toof," he said. He smiled and sure enough one of his top front teeth was missing.

"I can clean him up if you'd like," I said.

"Thank you," she said. "When you are done, Tyson, meet us at special. We have art today."

He nodded. I took him in the bathroom and washed the blood away from his mouth and chin. "Did it get on you?"

"No. I don't think so," he said. I looked him over to see. "Will you take my toof home for me?"

"Yes."

He handed me the tooth. I put it in a container in my purse and then kissed him goodbye. He ran and met up with his class. I went home and gave Addison his first lost tooth. I gave her Carter's schoolwork assignments as well.

I spent the day on site of where the housing development was going on. I was the only architect for David Bruno's house. The property had been marked out and now walls were starting to go up. The hole for the pool was dug and that was going to be poured in with concrete later today. I walked the inside structure of the house on the first floor. It was going perfectly. At midday after the concrete was poured for the pool, I left. I went to the office to deal with phone calls to Japan yet again. I stayed at the office till two thirty and then left to go get the kids from school. They would have gone to after care for just an hour tops, which we paid for. When I got there, I went in and got the four kids. Kate didn't go to after care, for she was a safety patrol and her patrolling ended at three. I saw her on the playground with a boy. The two of them kissed each other on the lips. Then Kate looked up and saw me. The boy she was kissing wasn't from the elementary school. He was a seventh grader. "Ah, shit," she said. "I have to go."

"See you tomorrow in music class."

"Yeah," she said. "See you tomorrow."

She picked up her backpack and came running over to me. "Hi."

"Hi."

"Am I in trouble?"

"I'm not your mother," I said to her.

"Are you going to tell mommy?"

"No, angel."

"Oh, thank god."

"You are going to tell your mother."

"What? Why?"

"Because angel, you are growing up and your mom needs to know that you are becoming a young adult."

The boys came running. They all got into the car and we went home. As they came into the house, Tyson went running into the kitchen where he made an announcement. "KATE WAS KISSING A BOY!"

Kate came in the kitchen. "TYSON!"

"Were you going to hide that from me?" Addison asked her.

"No, mommy. I was coming in here to ask you if I could talk to you alone, but half pint beat me to it," she said.

"Tyson, go play," Addison said.

"Tyson, homework before play," I said standing in my kitchen.

"Can't I do it later?"

"Nope. Homework is to be done after school. Now go."

"But no one is in there."

"TJ is in there."

"Tyson, now!" Addison said.

He went into the conference room. I grabbed a banana and a bottle of water then left them to talk. I went into my office. My cell phone rang. I looked at it. It was a number I didn't recognize. I answered it anyway. "Hello."

"Hi, is this Kennedy Jackson?"

"It is."

"Hi, I am calling to let you know that Romeo Quin's case will be starting in a month."

"Wow. That is quick," I said. "Is it going to trial?"

"No. He waved a trial jury, so it will be heard in front of a judge."

"And will I be able to testify?"

"Yes, of course. That is why I am calling you. I am calling to arrange a time that we can meet to discuss your case."

"I'm available any day for the rest of the week. Then I am going out of town for a week with my family."

"Can we meet tomorrow afternoon say around three?"

"Yes. Where?"

"Our office is moving, so I will have to get back to you with a location."

"How about the Jackson-Alexander building?" She agreed. I gave her the address for the building and directions. Her name was Olivia.

"Poor Carter has duel ear infections and a throat infection," Parker said to me over the phone. "He has inner and middle ear infections in both ears."

I knew that was painful. I suffered from ear infections all of my life. Parker would be staying home with Carter for the rest of week. He was keeping Beth home too because she said she was sick with Dolly Pox. "Dolly Pox? What is that?"

"It's contagious," Beth said.

"And who has this?"

"My dolly gave it to me. She has purple spots and look I gots it too."

She lifted her shirt and showed Parker her purple spot, which she always has because she has a birth mark.

"Well, you will have to tell mommy about this Dolly Pox and see what mommy says."

Beth grabbed her dolly and came over to my house. She had her shirt off now as she walked into the house. "Beth, where is your shirt?" Addison asked as she ran into the kitchen.

"Mommy, I got Dolly Pox."

"You have what?"

"Dolly Pox. It's contagious."

"What is contagious?" I asked coming into the kitchen.

"Dolly Pox."

"Dolly Pox? Is that that giant purple spot on your dolly?" I asked.

"Yep. I gots to stay home with daddy and Carter."

"Well, don't give it to Carter," I said.

"Don't encourage this," Addison said. "You are going to school."

"NO!" Beth yelled. "I can't. Dolly is sick and so am I." Then she fell on the floor dramatically.

"And how long does Dolly Pox last?" I asked picking Beth up off the floor.

Patrick came in the kitchen. "Oh my god, what happened to Frankie?"

"She has Dolly Pox," Beth said.

"Dolly Pox. Oh, mommy this is contagious," Patrick said playing along. "Dolly Pox last until Friday at three o'clock. So, mommy she will have to stay home from school for the rest of week."

Beth laughed.

"You two stop encouraging her," Addison reprimanded. We laughed. "Fine you can stay home with Carter and Daddy, but even if he can't go to school on Monday, you are going to school."

"Ok, mommy," Beth said. "You're the bestest."

Then she ran out of the kitchen and out of the house and went home.

The next day, I picked TJ up early from school and went to the building with him. "Hey, want to see something that you will really love?"

"Sure," he said.

"How was school today?"

He looked at me. "Mommy, I hate school."

"Why?"

"Because I'm singled out."

"You're what?"

"Mrs. Heyward moved my desk away from the other kids."

"Why?"

"We got in two new kids. A set of twins, but one is a boy and the other is a girl, so she said they can sit next to each other, so she moved my desk and now I don't sit in a group anymore. She says I need extra work. She assigned a lot of homework."

We had been walking into a section of the building that he hadn't seen yet, and he saw the airplane. He stopped talking and stared at it. "What's wrong?"

"Is it real?"

"Yes."

"Does it fly?"

"Not anymore."

"Why not?"

"The engine was removed."

"Is this daddy's?"

"And mine," I said.

"Did you fly it?"

"We did."

"When?"

"A long, long time ago."

"Awesome," he said. "Can I go in it?"

"Yes. I have a meeting, but when I'm done, I still want to hear what Mrs. Heyward said." I was starting to remember why we didn't stay friends over the years. "If you have to use the bathroom, there is a bathroom right over there. It's the blue door."

"Ok. See you later," he said climbing into the airplane.

I walked to my office and cleaned up a bit before Olivia showed up. She showed up at three thirty. "I'm sorry. I forgot it was my day to get my kids from school."

"What grades are they are in?"

"My youngest is in kindergarten and she loves it, my nine-year-old is fourth grade, and he hates school, and the twins just started high school. Do you have kids?"

"Yes. I have a son."

"How old?"

"Six. He is in first grade."

"Where is he right now?"

"Playing in our airplane," I said.

She looked at me. "You have an airplane?"

"Yes. My husband and I built it, flew it, and then bought it when we opened our practice here. We took the engine out before we brought it inside the building."

We discussed the case. Though it made me nervous to talk about, I did, and I got through it. The meeting lasted two hours, so it was five thirty or nearing six when I went looking for TJ. I saw him sitting at one of the patio tables doing his homework. He looked up when I came into the room.

"Are we leaving to go home?"

"Not just yet. Are you ok?"

"Yes," he said.

"Do you want cookies or a snack?"

"No, thanks," he said with a smile.

"I have to make a few phone calls, so I'll come back and get you."

"Ok," he said. I turned to walk out of the room. "Mommy, can I go swimming?"

"Yes."

"Thank you."

I went back in my office and called Tokyo. I was the on the phone for about an hour. Then I went looking for TJ again. He was still at the table doing schoolwork. "Hey, are you ready to go? You and I are going out for dinner. Daddy is in a meeting."

We went to a hibachi restaurant for dinner. TJ loved watching them flip the food up in the air. We both ordered beef and shrimp with noodles. They cooked everything right in front of us. "Can you make it a little darker please?"

"Yes," the chef said.

With the food cooking an extra few minute, I watched TJ and saw a sadness there on his face. After the chef put our food on our plates and walked away, I addressed it. "So, you were telling me that Mrs. Heyward moved you away from the group," I began.

"She did. She said because I'm strong enough to work alone," he said. "I am, but I like sitting with everyone else. But she says that I am behind still. She said I'm not on level with the others."

"Did she move you far from the group?"

"My desk is now in the back of the room away from everyone."

He put food in his mouth just as the tears started to fill in his eyes. Big tears ran down his face.

"I'll take care of it tomorrow. And why did she give you extra work?"

"Because Anna said that I said that the work was too easy. She said that I say that all the time?"

"Do you say that?"

"No, mommy. I don't talk in class. Not since she yelled at me."

"When did she yell at you?"

"Like the third or fourth day of school."

"For what?"

"Because I was talking to Tyson in the lunch line."

"Tyson? Our Tyson?"

He laughed. "Yes, our Tyson. I didn't know how to get to the library, so I asked him because his teacher took them on a tour of the whole school. Mrs. Heyward yelled at me saying I should have learned that last year as a kindergarten and if I wanted to act like a kindergarten, she would send me back there. That day at recess, she sent me to Tyson's class, and I had to stay in there for the rest of the day, while my class got to play for the rest of the day."

I was beyond fuming at this point. "I'll address it tomorrow morning, but for now on if something happens that you don't like or you don't think is right please tell me as soon as it happens, so I can take care of it."

"Are you going to tell daddy?"

Just then Patrick was there at our table. "Tell daddy what?"

TJ burst into tears. "I ha…ha…hate sch…sch…school," he cried.

He went into Patrick's arms sobbing. "We will take care of it tomorrow," Patrick said rubbing his back after hearing the whole story. "Did you know about this?"

"No," I said.

The next morning, we were both at the school with TJ. We were waiting for Mrs. Heyward with the principal with us. When she came down the hallway, she stopped for a second and then continued. "How can I help you?"

"Mrs. Heyward, I was made aware of a situation that needs to be addressed immediately," the principal said. "And either you are going to do it, or I will do it for you."

We went into the classroom and sure enough in the back of the classroom was TJ's desk. The rest of the kids' desks were in the shape of a horseshoe. "Why isn't his desk in this configuration?"

"I put him back there yesterday because he wouldn't stop talking."

"Is this true?" the principal asked.

"Nnn…no, sir," TJ said. "I don't talk to anyone because she yelled me at on the fourth day of school for not knowing where the library is. I asked my younger cousin because his teacher took his class on a tour of the whole school."

Two kids came into the classroom. The principal smiled at them. "Can I talk to the two of you outside?"

"Yes," both kids said together. Both kids went outside with him.

"Does TJ talk in the classroom?"

"No, sir," they both said.

"Mrs. Heyward yelled at him on the fourth day of school for not knowing where the library was. She told him he was acting like a kindergarten and then she sent him to one of the kindergarten classes when she let us play for the rest of the afternoon."

"She is always giving him more work than the rest of us."

"And she doesn't let him play at recess. She is always giving him a book to read."

"Thank you both," the principal said.

Another student came over. Without knowing what was going, he said, "I hope TJ finished all of his homework, so Mrs. Heyward doesn't shake him again. She shook him so hard the last time; he pee peed in his pants."

"What?" the principal said.

"Ah, shit," the kid said. "Nothing."

"No, what did you say?"

"She did," the boy said. "She shook him so hard he wet his pants. She's stuck him in the kindergarten class a few times. She doesn't let him play at recess. And she gives him double or triple the homework."

"Thank you," the principal said. He came back into the classroom. "We are going to get a sub for your class today," he said to her. "And then you and I are going to have a long talk about why I shouldn't fire you."

"We are going to take him home for the rest of the day," I said.

"I don't want him doing any more school/homework for now."

"Ok," Patrick said.

We decided to reward him. We got in the car and we drove north to the Bok Tower. TJ smiled so big. We went and spent the day in the gardens, in the tower and of course on the playground. I had totally forgotten about my meeting with Gwen and David. As we were driving home that evening, my cell phone lit up with text message after text message. I wasn't meeting them about their house, I was meeting them for another hold therapy session. I didn't check my phone until we were home. TJ had fallen asleep during the drive home. When we arrived home, I stepped out of the truck and picked up TJ and carried him into the house and upstairs to the apartment. I put him in bed. I left the door open to the apartment and came back downstairs. David and Gwen both sat on the couch in the living room downstairs.

"Hi," Gwen said. I jumped almost out of my skin. "Addison let us in before she left," she continued. "Did you forget that we had a session today?"

"I did," I said. "Patrick and I were dealing with an issue for TJ at school this morning."

Patrick walked into the house. "Who the hell is here now?" he asked walking into the front door. He saw David and Gwen. "Hi. What's so important it couldn't wait until tomorrow?"

"Kennedy blew off a session today," David said.

"We were dealing with our son being mistreated by his first-grade teacher," Patrick said. "That trumps a session."

"Can we talk?" Gwen asked me.

"Yeah, sure."

We went into my office and I closed the door. "How are you doing?"

"I'm fucking pissed off."

"At me and David?"

"No. At Samantha Heyward. She's been being mean to TJ for the last month and he never said anything."

"When did you find out?"

"Yesterday," I said. "It's one thing to be mean to me or Patrick, but to take it out on a six-year-old, who has such a spark about him."

"Can we meet tomorrow?"

"Yes. Here at nine thirty or ten," I said.

She agreed to ten and then we left my office. I hugged her and David when they left. Then Patrick and I went upstairs to the apartment. We went into our room, where we undressed each other and began to fool around. We made love and then just laid in each other's arms. That night sleep didn't come for me. Patrick finally fell asleep after two in the morning. However hard I tried; I still couldn't fall asleep. It was at times like this that I wished I had a dog to keep me company. Finally, I couldn't lay there any longer. I got up and went downstairs. I sat at my desk with white paper lining the desk. I picked up a pencil and started to creatively draw whatever flowed out of me at this point.

I was still up at five in the morning, so I decided to go running. It was then that it dawned on me that the kids' backpacks weren't in the conference room. With deep concern, I went next door. Michael was up, dressed for school, and eating a Pop Tart for breakfast. "Hi," he said.

"Hi. How come your backpacks aren't in the conference room?"

"Mom made us go home yesterday after school because dad was home with Carter and Beth."

"Oh."

"Are you mad?"

"No. Not at all. Things are going to change now that you are living next door and that's ok."

Carter came in their kitchen dressed and ready for school. "What are you doing?"

"We have a field trip today and I don't want to miss it. Hi, Aunt Kenny!" he said throwing his arms around me.

"Hi, baby," I said. "I've missed your smiling face," I said to him kissing him on the cheek.

Parker came into the kitchen followed by Kate. "I can't believe you didn't finish your homework," Parker said.

"But Jenny has the other half of the project. She said she was going to do it." Kate looked and saw me standing there. "Hi, Aunt Kenny."

"Hi, sweet girl," I said to her.

"I'll finish it now, daddy."

"You're grounded for a week."

"What? Why?"

"Because of your attitude and your smart-ass mouth."

"What? When?"

"We are through, Kate. You are grounded for a week and that's final."

"But when did I have a smart-ass mouth and attitude."

"I heard you and the way you spoke to your mother last night."

"Dad, Kate was rehearsing her lines last night. She wanted to surprise you and mommy. She made it in the middle school play."

"Are you sure?"

"Yes, daddy," Michael said.

Kate sat at the table doing her homework. She opened her laptop fand saw that Jenny hadn't done her part of the assignment. She got upset, but she did the full homework assignment. Addison came in the kitchen. "How is everyone this morning?"

"Daddy grounded me for a week," Kate said.

"Why?"

"It was a misunderstanding," Parker said.

"Hi, Kenny," Addison said.

"Hi."

"Are you ok?"

"Yeah. I couldn't sleep so I went for a run and then I checked the conference room and didn't see the kids' backpacks and I was concerned."

"I had them come home and do their homework here, but that didn't work out so well," Addison said, "so today after school they will be back at your house."

Tyson stumbled into the kitchen. "Good morning," he said.

"Why aren't you dressed for school?"

"I am dressed for school," he said. "It's pajama day."

Carter opened his agenda book and saw that it was pajama day. He nodded his head.

"We have to get to school," Michael said.

"I'll take you," I said to them. I took them to school. They were chatty in the car and it was really nice listening to them go on and on about school and the morning programs.

"ROTC rocks," Michael said. "I've moved up a rank."

"Do they let girls do it?"

"Yeah, of course," Michael said.

"I want to do it next year."

I pulled up at the school. They both kissed me goodbye. They walked into the school together. I went back to the house and took a shower. Addison was there starting breakfast. I walked into the kitchen dressed in blue jeans and a sweatshirt.

"Hi. I missed you yesterday. How is everything?"

"I missed you too," I said. "Everything is ok. I'm nervous about the case."

"Why?"

"Because I will have to tell every detail."

"That should be the easy part." I looked at her. "Honey, you live it every night in your dreams; everywhere you go, you are constantly looking over your shoulder and behind you; when men approach, you hold your breath," she said.

"Wow! I didn't know," I said.

"I'm not trying to make you feel uncomfortable, but it takes a lot for you to be calm and… and you never relax. Your legs shake a mile a minute, you wring your hands." She took me in her arms and hugged me. "Telling the judge, who it is, will be a walk in the park for you and we will be there every minute with you."

"Thank you," I said.

TJ came in the kitchen in his pajamas. "I'm ready for school," he said.

"Ok. Let's go."

Tyson and Carter came into the house with their backpacks.

"Where is daddy?" Addison asked.

"He's home with Beth and her Dolly Pox."

I laughed. "Come, my young men, let's go to school."

"I need a chaperone for my trip today," Carter said.

"I can go," Addison said.

"Really?"

"Yes. I will take the kids to school. Love you," she said to me.

"Love you," the boys said and off they went.

Patrick and I had alone time for the next hour before he had to leave for work and I was working from home today, for David and Gwen were coming over for a therapy session that I wasn't looking forward to. But for the time being, Patrick and I were enjoying making love to each other in the quietness of the house. When we were done, I lay on the bed breathing hard. He got up and went into the shower. After a minute or two, I went into the bathroom and joined him in the shower, where we made love again for the first time in our shower. We showered together when we were done making love, and I left the bathroom first to get dressed. I once again put on blue jeans and a sweatshirt and went downstairs. I prepared Patrick's lunch for him. He left the house at nine thirty. He called me telling me that he was going to Jacksonville and would be back sometime tomorrow. "I know your schedule, my love," I said. "I love you. Drive safe."

"Thanks," he said. "I love you too."

At ten minutes to ten, the Bruno's showed up. I let them in finishing my second cup of coffee for the day. "How are you?" David said.

"I'm good."

"Why are you wearing a sweatshirt?"

"I was cold."

We went upstairs to the apartment. I showed them our room and TJ's room. Then without warning Gwen grabbed me from behind. She had my arms pinned down to my sides and she had me in an extremely firm hold. Right away my whole body reacted. I tried getting my hands on her arms, but where she was holding me, I couldn't master the task. I started moving backwards until I backed us into the wall. I was twisting and trying to turn. I threw my head back and it hit the wall pretty hard. And then I went limp in her arms bringing us both down to the floor. David came out from using the bathroom. "Hey, you started without me."

"She knocked herself out," Gwen said.

"What? How?"

"She threw her head back and it the wall with a thud."

"Jesus, Gwen, why would you start without me?"

"Because she wasn't expecting it," she said.

David lifted me from the floor and Gwen got up. When my head fell back off his arm, I jolted awake and started to flare. "No. No. Stop."

I got away from him this time and I raced downstairs and ran out of my house. He came running after me with Gwen not too far behind him. He caught up to me at the end of the long driveway. He grabbed a hold of me. "No!" I said through gritted teeth. "No. Let me go."

Lennox heard the commotion and came running over. He saw me fighting hard to get away from David. "What the fuck is going on here?" he asked. "Let her go right now."

"It's therapy," Gwen and David said together.

"What the fuck kind of therapy is that?"

"This is going to help her learn how to be affectionate?"

"Are you fucking kidding me? This is going to make her neurotic. Please let her go. Kenny, please stop fighting," Lennox said.

I couldn't though. I fought until I passed out. That's when Lennox approached. He took hold of me and punched David right in the face. "This isn't fucking helping her. She has PTSD you fucking morons."

"I know she does."

"Then how in the hell could you do that to her? It doesn't help. You might as well put a pillowcase over her head and water board her, for it's the same shit that you are doing to her."

"She isn't affectionate."

"Yes, she is, and what the fuck does it matter to you two if she is or isn't?" He changed the position that he had me in and now he carried me into the house. "Addison! Addison, are you here?" He put me down on the couch. David and Gwen came into the house. "Don't touch her," Lennox warned. "Addison!"

"She's not here," David said.

"I am asking you both to leave right now."

"We are treating her," Gwen said.

"She's got a knot on her head. What is that from?"

"She banged her head against the wall."

"How, Gwen?"

"She threw her head back when I was holding her."

Lennox got me to wake up. He spoke to me softly. "Are you ok?"

"Yeah," I said. "My head hurts a little."

"Your friends are leaving."

I wanted to say that they are not my friends and that they are my clients, but I didn't. "No, Lennox, that's ok. Thank you. We have business to discuss about their house. Thank you for your help."

I hugged him and thanked him again for everything. Jamie really did pick a really nice guy this time. Lennox hugged me back and then left the house, but not before telling me and reassuring me that he was RIGHT next door. I laughed a little and then he left.

CHAPTER TWENTY-NINE

Addison had accompanied Carter on his fieldtrip. And she kept hearing from everyone excluding Carter that his Aunt Kenny was so much more fun. Their fieldtrip was to the zoo, which if you'd been to Animal Kingdom this zoo didn't even compare, but it was nice. They fed the giraffes and they went on elephant rides and that was when Carter started to talk about Two Tales the elephant preserve that I had taken them to this summer. Addison listened as she heard him talk about it.

"And they have this huge elephant there that trumpets and all of the elephants listen to her."

"You're stupid," a girl said. "The huge elephants are males."

"No," the tour guide said. "The young man is one hundred percent correct."

"Of course, he is, the stupid dweeb."

"Shelby, that's enough," Mr. Gills said. "One more nasty word and you will go sit on the bus with Holland."

Holland was the bus driver.

"But Mr. Gills, Carter has been kicking me the whole time."

"WHAT?" Carter said. "Mr. Gills that isn't true."

"Shelby, go to the bus."

"But why?"

"For being a bully."

Another chaperon walked her to the bus. Holland was a big, tall man. He looked at her. "Not being nice again?"

"I was. It's that stupid Carter again."

"Now Shelby, you don't want me telling your mother how you misbehaved on the fieldtrip again do you?"

"No, Holland," she said.

"Now go sit down and think about what you have you done."

Mr. Gills went on the bus ten minutes later and retrieved Shelby, who promised she would be good. The kids had lunch and then went to the petting zoo. Shelby started her shenanigans again with Carter. When he was squatting down tying his shoes, Shelby came up behind him and shoved him really hard. Carter fell into the fence with the goats.

"SHELBY!" Addison said.

"WHAT?"

"Why would you do that?"

"DO WHAT?"

Addison rushed to see if Carter was ok. He had skinned his forehead and his knees. He was crying. Mr. Gills came over to see if Carter was ok.

"Mr. Gills. Mr. Gills, I had to do it," she said.

"Why?"

"Because he called me a bitch."

"HE DID NOT!" the rest of the class said.

"I know," Mr. Gills said. He took Shelby by the hand and didn't bring her to the bus this time. Instead he brought her to the zoo's front entrance and had her call her mother to come and pick her up.

"My teacher Mr. Gills says I can't ride the bus back with the class to the school. The class is lying, mommy," she said. "An evil boy named Carter Jackson called me the B word, so I shoved him when he was tying his shoes. He might have fallen into a fence and hurt his head and his knees."

Her mother screamed at her that when she came to pick her up that she was going to get a spanking.

"But mommy because of him I had to sit on the bus for an hour."

"You sat on the bus for ten minutes," Mr. Gills said loud enough for her mother to hear him.

Her mom showed up fifteen minutes later. She pulled up right to the entrance. She threw the car into park and came rushing over to the two of them. She snatched Shelby's hand out of Mr. Gills and Shelby planted her feet firm to the ground as her mother tried to pull her to the car. "Do not play with me," her mother said. "Let's go." But Shelby continued to hold her ground. Her mom turned and picked her up. She threw her over her shoulder carrying her to the car. Shelby kicked the whole time. "Listen little girl, you stop it right now or you can wait until Helen can deal with it." Shelby stopped immediately. She got into her mother's car in the back seat and put her head down.

Mr. Gills came back with the class. They were in the gift shop before they boarded the bus back to school. Each kid bought something. A stuffed animal or a t-shirt with the zoo's name on it. Carter bought something for himself and something for Shelby. He bought her a stuffed elephant and a friendship bracelet. When they arrived back at school, they had twenty minutes left till the final bell rang. All of the kids went into the classroom and gathered their belongings. Carter went to Shelby's desk and put the bag with the stuffed elephant and bracelet in her desk. He moved it so it wouldn't be seen unless you looked in the desk. Addison had just watched him. She hadn't asked questions at the zoo or even now.

"I'm going to go get Ty," she said.

"Ok."

"Want me to meet you here or at the car?"

"At the car," he said.

As Addison walked to Tyson's class, she texted me if I wanted her to get TJ. I texted back thank you and please. She smiled at her phone. She was still looking down at her phone when she bumped into someone. "Oh, I'm sorry," she said.

"Hi, mommy," Kate said.

"Hi, sweet girl, how are you?"

"Good. Can I go to Marianna's house for a little while?"

"I don't know who she is," Addison said.

"She's a safety patrol like me," Kate said with a smile. "We are going to do homework together."

"Kate, I have to cook dinner for everyone and there is an inspector coming to Aunt Kenny's, so can Marianna come over today and you can go there another time?"

"She can come over?"

"Yes, of course."

"Can Max and Elliot come too?"

"Yes."

"Can one of their mom's drive me home?"

"Yes, but make sure you are wearing your seat belt."

"Always, mommy," she said.

Carter was helping Mr. Gills in the classroom when the door opened, and Shelby came in the room with her mom and Helen. "Mr. Gills, I'm sorry for my behavior," she said.

"Remember that I always tell you that actions have consequences."

"Yes," she said.

"You will not be able to go on the next fieldtrip," he said.

"Ok," she said looking very sad. Then she noticed Carter standing there. "I'm sorry if I hurt you today," she said to him.

"I'm ok," he said.

"Get your things and let's go," Helen said to her.

"Yes, ma'am," she said.

Shelby went to her desk to get her homework assignments. "Ow, what's this?" she said pulling out the bag from the zoo. She sat down in her chair and looked in the bag. "Oh," she said. She pulled the stuffed elephant out of the bag. "Look mom," she said. "Someone bought me something. Look, Helen."

"You don't deserve that," Helen said.

"Yes, she does," Carter said. "I told Mr. Gills that it was Brandon who was being mean to Shelby. Brandon kept kicking her and he called her the B word. Brandon should've got in trouble too."

Shelby pulled the bracelet out of the bag. "Oh, I wanted this," she said. "Mr. Gills, do you know who bought these for me?"

There was a note in the bag: *Hope to be your friend. Carter*

"You bought me this?" she asked Carter.

"Yeah. Sorry you got in trouble today." Carter hugged her. "See you tomorrow," he said to her.

Mr. Gills asked her if she was ready for the science fair. Shelby looked at the floor. "I didn't know what to do for it."

Helen went to say something. But Carter cut her off. "Shelby, you can come to my house and we can make something together."

"Can I, mom?"

"Yes," she said.

"My mom went to go meet my little brother."

Carter came and found Addison. "Hi, can Shelby come over so we can work on a science project?"

"Yes," Addison said although she wanted to ask Carter if he was fucking kidding her. "Come on. We have to get home," she said.

Tyson, TJ, and Shelby sat in the back seat of the car. "Carter, call dad and see if he is picking up Beth from school."

"She stayed home, mommy," Tyson said. "Remember her doll has Dolly Pox."

"What is that?" Shelby asked.

"Something she made up so she could stay home."

"What grade is she in?"

"Preschool," the boys said together.

"How did she get away with that?"

"Because she's cute," Carter said.

"Helen says I can only stay home from school if I have a hundred and four fever."

"Is Helen your mom?" Addison asked.

"No. She's my mom's live in girlfriend."

"Do you like her?"

Shelby shrugged.

Addison pulled into my driveway. "You all must stay in the conference room. The inspector is coming. I need all of you to be good and behave yourselves."

"I'm hungry," Shelby said.

"Mom is a great cook," Tyson said. "Mom, you left Kate at school."

Addison laughed. "You just noticed that now?"

"I guess so," he said.

"She's coming home with friends."

A car pulled up behind Addison's and Kate and three other kids came out of the car. Two other girls and boy.

"This is your house?" Max asked. Her long blond hair pulled back in a loose ponytail.

"No. We live next door," Kate said. "This is my Aunt Kenny's house and where all of us kids do homework."

They all came into the house. Addison went right into the kitchen to start preparing dinner. The kids went into the conference room. "What do you want to do for your science project?" Carter asked Shelby.

"The way the ocean waves turn."

"Ok." He said. "You can use my computer to do research."

"Will you help me?"

"Sure."

Carter helped her search the movement of the ocean. "Wait. I'll be right back." Carter ran next door. "DADDY! DADDY!"

"What?" Parker called out from his office. "What's wrong?"

"Could you help me please?"

"I can try."

"We have to do a science project; Shelby, a girl who no one is nice to and she isn't nice to anyone either, and I have to do a project together; we want to do how the ocean waves work."

"When is this due?"

"In two weeks," Carter said.

"Well, go finish your homework and we will start it tonight."

"But Shelby is over Aunt Kenny's now. Please, daddy?"

"Let me find Beth and I'll come over."

"Daddy, Beth is at Aunt Kenny's. She's been there since we came home from school."

Parker piggy backed Carter next door. "I have to take care of something really quick first, but I will be right in."

"Thank you, daddy."

Parker went and found Beth. He took her upstairs and scolded her and spanked her. She was wailing. "Go ahead and cry," he said. "Again, you left the house without saying anything."

Addison hearing her crying came running upstairs. "What happened?" she asked Beth.

"Daddy spanked me."

"PARKER!"

"No, Addison, that is the second time that she has left the house and I thought she was playing with her dolls and she came here. The time before she went to Jamie's house."

"Beth, did you do that?"

"Yes," she said.

"Are you allowed to go outside by yourself?"

"No, but I was hungry."

"So why wouldn't you come tell me that you were hungry?" Parker asked.

She shrugged. "Don't know."

He brought her downstairs and put her in time out. "You stay there," he said putting her on the couch. He took the channel changers with him into the conference room.

The inspector finally came to the house two and half hours late, not that any of us in the house were waiting for him. We had gone on with our original plans. He was a short stocky man with a balding head. He wore glasses on the edge of his nose. His suit was light grey and wrinkly.

"Hi," Beth said to him when he came in the door.

"Hi."

"MOMMY!"

Addison stepped out of the kitchen. "Oh, hi," she said.

"Are you the owner of this house?"

"No."

I came into the room. "No. I am. I am Kennedy Alexander," I said. "You can call me Kenny. Where would you like to start?"

"In the attic," he said.

"Yes, sir," I said. "Before we go would you care for something to drink?"

"No. Thanks," he said.

"Beth, come in the kitchen with me," Addison said. She jumped off the couch and went into the kitchen. She sat on the counter eating chocolate chips. "No! Here," Addison said handing her an apple.

I took the inspector up to the attic, which I had spent the weekend cleaning it of cobwebs and getting it organized. "Will guest be able to come in here?"

"No, sir."

"Then this is fine," he said. "How many residents reside in the house now?"

"Three of us. My husband, my son, and me."

"Do you occupy any of the rooms?"

"No, sir, there is a front apartment and that is where we live."

"Will guests have access to that?"

"No, sir."

"I'd like to see that."

We left the attic and went to the second floor. I showed him our apartment first. "How old is your son?"

"He's six."

"Doesn't he have toys?"

"Yes, sir, of course."

"And where does he get to play?"

"Downstairs where we spend about ninety-five percent of the time. There is a playroom down there for games and also for the kids. My five nephews and nieces just about live in my house."

"Do they live here?"

"No, sir, their house is next door."

He checked the faucets and the showers and the bathtubs. He checked the sturdiness of the counter tops in the kitchen and in the bathrooms. He looked under the bed. In TJ's room while looking under the bed, he pulled out a stuffed dog and placed it on TJ's neatly made bed.

"Will you have a staff?"

"Yes. I already do. They worked for my parents and when I purchased the house from my parents, I gained all of them in the process."

"Does that include a cleaning staff?"

"Yes, sir."

"Does the staff reside here at your house?"

"Yes, sir, but not in the main house where the Bed and Breakfast will be."

"So, you have a separate dwelling?"

"A few, sir. There is the barn with the tack rooms, where some of the men stay to take care of the horses. Then there are six cabins and a new building, where the gym is."

"Will the guests have access to the cabins?"

"No, sir."

"Do you have access to the cabins?"

"Yes. My brother Parker and I do."

"Do you keep them up to date?"

"Yes, sir."

We went to the far end of the hall, where my bedroom used to be. All the doors were open. The rooms were all different colors with different accents. "Is there a common bathroom?"

"No, sir. Every room has its own private bathroom with a shower and tub."

He went into the bathroom and checked everything again.

"How many bedrooms are there?"

"There are ten bedrooms."

We went into all of them. Then we worked our way downstairs. "Is there an elevator?"

"Yes, sir."

We stepped into the elevator and took it down and back up and down again. "How often do you use the elevator?"

"Sometimes every day. Sometimes every other day."

We went to the front of the house and he checked every door and window just like he had done upstairs. Then he saw the kids working in the conference room. "What is this room?"

"From eight in the morning to one thirty it is a regular conference room. And from two thirty till nine o'clock it's the kids' study hall."

Michael just came in from school. He was really sweaty. He put his backpack down in the room. Kissed his brothers and sister and then left the room. He ran to the house and showered and changed and then came back with wet hair and no shoes on. He slipped into the room with the others and started his homework.

We continued all around the inside of house until we finally came to the kitchen. Addison was just wrapping up finishing dinner. "Will you be serving dinner to your guests?"

"Yes, sir," we both said.

"Go ahead, Addison," I said.

"We will service the three basic meals of breakfast from six to eleven, lunch from noon until two and dinner from five to eight," she said. "Everything is homemade. Everything is fresh."

"Will they get an option or menu to choose from?"

"Yes and no," Addison said. "I will post the night before what will be served the following day, the guest will have the option to change if they want to, but mostly I will cook a variety of breakfast foods, and lunches and then it will be two dinner options," she said.

He looked out the back door. "Oh, what a yard," he commented.

"Would you like to see it, sir?" I asked.

"I would, but because I was late today, I'll have to come back. Are you available tomorrow?"

"Yes, sir," I said.

TJ came into the kitchen. "Tomorrow is my first fieldtrip, mommy."

"What time will you get back from school?"

"I will be here at three, sir."

"I'll come promptly at four."

"Thank you, sir."

He was two hours late and it took him two hours just to inspect the inside of the house. When he left, I poured myself a shot glass of Fire Ball.

"What did he say?"

"About the inspection?"

"Yeah," Addison said.

"Nothing yet. He asked questions in every room. He asked will the guests go in the attic to which I answered no. Will the guests go in the cabins? No. He asked about the elevator. He was impressed with the playroom and the toy selections and game choices. He liked the library. He asked why the kids didn't do their homework in the library."

"Because we can't see them in there."

"That's what I said," I said with a smile.

"Where is Patrick?"

"He is St. Augustine or Jacksonville until next Wednesday."

"For what?"

"He designed a new law firm's building and it's in progress, so he had to go."

"DINNER!" Addison called. Everyone came into the kitchen even the kids' friends that were at the house. Shelby looked around.

"Who are you?" I asked her.

"I'm Shelby," she said. "Thank you for having me over."

"Yep," I said. I didn't even know this child was in my house.

"Mom, can I take my dinner in the conference room, so I can continue working on my homework?" Michael asked.

"It's not my house, sweetheart. But I'd prefer you have dinner in here with everyone else."

"Yes, ma'am," he said.

He sat down at the table. We ate dinner. Then the kids helped clean up and they went back to do their homework. An hour later there was a knock on the door. Kate, who had just finished her homework, went to the door. "Hi."

"My daughter is here," she said.

"Please come in. I'm Kate. Carter's sister."

"Hi, Kate. Did you go on the fieldtrip today too?"

"No. I'm in fifth grade. The fieldtrip today was for the third and fourth graders."

"Is Shelby ready?"

"You can come in and see," Kate said. "They are in here."

I came into the living room. "Hi, can I help you?"

"Hi, I'm Nadine. My daughter Shelby is here."

"Yes, of course," I said. "You can go in and see her."

Shelby looked up when her mom came in the room. She jumped up and started packing up her things quickly. "Shelby, its ok," her mom said. "Are you ready to go?"

"Yes."

"What are you working on?"

"The science project," she said. "But we can go. I have to go to the bathroom."

"I'll show you where it is," Carter said. Carter left his stuff sitting on the table and walked with Shelby out of the room and to the nearest bathroom, which was the second door in the hallway. "Here you go," he said opening the door for her.

Shelby went into the bathroom and came out a few minutes later. Then she ran into the room and grabbed her stuff. "We should go," she said.

"This is great," Nadine said.

"Mommy we don't want to piss off Helen," she said.

"Who is Helen?" Parker asked. "I'm Parker. Carter's dad."

"Nice to meet you," Nadine said "I'm Nadine."

"You have a very polite daughter."

Nadine looked at Shelby and smiled. "Thank you. That's nice to hear."

"Can she come back tomorrow so we can continue working on this?" Carter asked.

"Yes."

"Who is Helen?"

"Mommy's girlfriend," Shelby said with a lowered head and under her breath.

"Well, come on, Shells, let's go."

"Are you going to yell at your daughter?"

"No," Nadine said.

"She saves that for Helen."

"Well, let's go."

Shelby went with her mom. Carter followed her out to say goodbye. When he came back in the house, Addison was waiting for him. "I am very proud of you," Addison said to him.

"Why?"

"Because she was outright mean to you and without anyone telling you to you bought her a present and then you asked her to come over. You are an extremely nice young man."

"Oh, mommy, it was nothing."

"No, baby. It's something."

The next morning, I drove the kids to the school. I saw Shelby being dropped off not by Nadine, but by another woman. "Now don't you dare act up in school today or there will be a price to pay. Your mother will pick you up. Bye!" and she drove off. Carter waited for her. When she walked closer, he went to her and put his arm around her shoulders. I watched as this young girl melted into him. Carter turned and waved goodbye to me. Then he stopped.

"Aunt Kenny! Wait!"

I walked over to him. "What's wrong?"

"Shelby doesn't have lunch."

"What time do you go for lunch?"

"Eleven thirty," they said together.

"I'll call your mom because I'm going on TJ's fieldtrip."

"Where are they going?"

"To Extreme World," I said.

"Damn," both kids said.

"What?"

"They are going to have soooooo much fun," Shelby said.

They walked away and went to class. I called Addison. "Can you bring a lunch to the school for Shelby please?"

"Yeah. What time?"

"They go to lunch at eleven thirty."

At eight fifteen, the first graders and second graders came to the parking lot where the buses were waiting. I was given a sheet of paper with six children's name on it: TJ, Atkin, Cassidy, Royce, Braxton and Victoria. I had my group sit together. When we arrived at Extreme World my mouth almost dropped open. The place was huge with go carts, trampolines, batting cages, an IMAX screen, and a full arcade. Extreme World was every kid's dream. This place offered everything. Skee ball, basketball toss, bowling, and miniature golf.

My six kids were the only group that was able to do everything. I had sat them each down and asked what they wanted to do. The six of them wanted to do everything. "Ok, its nine o'clock, and we are here till one o'clock, so let's go do as much as we can."

"Are you going to do it with us?"

"Hell yeah," I said. "I've never been here, so I want to have fun too."

TJ hugged me and then they all hugged me.

"Who has to go the bathroom? Let's do that first."

The boys went into the boys' bathroom and I went in the bathroom with the girls. We all finished about the same time and then we were on a day of adventure. An announcement was made that a movie was going to be seen on the IMAX screen at ten. We listened to what movie was going to be shown and as a group the kids decided they would rather skip the movie.

"If you want to see movies, you can come to my house. We have a theater inside the house."

"You're full of shit," Atkin said.

"Atkin!" I reprimanded. "And no, he is not full of shit. He is accurate. We do have a theater inside our house."

"Awesome!" he said.

"He does. I've seen it," Cassidy said.

And we were off to the trampolines. With shoes off and socks left on, we all got on the trampolines and started jumping and bouncing everywhere. We played trampoline dodge ball and trampoline basketball. We played for forty minutes and then we moved on. Then we went to the go carts. There was a slight line, but we waited our turn and then we went. When we were done with the go carts, we saw the remote-control sail boats. There wasn't a line for that because the other chaperones had their kids and groups watching the ninety-eight-minute animated movie. Once they were in there where the IMAX screen was, they couldn't leave until the movie was completely over. Poor kids.

By the time the movie had ended, my group was indulging in lunch followed by cookies. Then we visited the bathroom again and went on for more fun. By twelve we were in the arcade, where I played with every one of the kids in the group. I shot water guns with Atkin, I did a dance game with Cassidy, I played three rounds of skee ball with Braxton, I did a roller coaster virtual ride with Victoria twice, I played toss basketball with Royce, and I played homerun slugger in the batting cage with TJ. And the last two things we all did together was bowling and then we ended on the trampolines.

When we climbed back on the bus, the six in my group sat in their seats. They put their head against the seat, and they were sleeping before the bus even pulled out of the parking lot. The other kids were rowdy and loud and talking about everything they missed out on.

"What did your group miss out on?"

"Nothing," I said. "Oh, we didn't see the movie."

"Wait?" a dad said. "We didn't have to see the movie?"

"No, that was an option," Mrs. Heyward said.

"Dammit. I wish I would have known that."

"We did try to encourage that all of the children stay together," she said looking at me.

"My group of six stuck together," I said.

Getting back to the school, I woke the kids up gently. They all collected their things and climbed off the bus. I picked TJ up. "Thank you, Mrs. Alexander," the kids said.

"The next fieldtrip, I want to be in his group," a lot of the kids in TJ's class said.

I walked to the front office to sign TJ out of school a few minutes early.

"No, he has to come back to the classroom," Samantha said.

I looked at him with his head pressed into my shoulder and knew that he was sleeping. I walked to the classroom. The five others that I had in the group today were shuffling their things around.

"What are you doing?" Samantha asked them.

"We want him to be part of our group," Atkin said. "It's not fair that he has to sit all by himself."

"He doesn't."

"He does until we work in groups," Victoria said. "No one else has to sit by themselves. Not even Jason, who never stops talking all day long."

"Thank you, Victoria," she said. "Ok, that is fine. We can move the desks around tomorrow."

"No," Braxton said. "We need to do it now, so you won't forget like last time."

I glared at her. I wanted to bitch slap her right here right now. Messing with me is one thing. Messing with my child is a whole other world. She saw me looking at her. "Your homework assignment is…"

"Homework!" the kids complained.

"Please listen," she said. "Your homework assignment tonight is for you tell your parents all about the trip. Have a good evening. I'll see you all tomorrow."

I waited for the kids to leave and then I looked at her. "I thought this bullshit of singling my son out was over. Now why is his desk moved away from the other kids?"

"Honestly, it was a simple mistake."

"If it happens again, Sam, I'll have him pulled from your classroom.

Listen you want to be mad at me for me having your friend locked up is one thing, but don't you dare take it out on my son."

"Is that what you think? You think I'm mad at you because you are having Romeo prosecuted?"

"Well, aren't you?"

"No. Not at all. I feel guilty for not mentioning his name years ago."

"You didn't know that that had happened to me. Please stop singling TJ out. All he wants to do is fit in. He had to change schools this school year. Everything is new for him. A new home, a new school, and a new mom. Just having a mom is new for him. He's a wonderful little boy, who has been through quite a bit in his young life."

Tyson wandered down the hall. "Excuse me a minute." I went running to the door. "Tyson!"

"Mommy called the school and said her car is dead."

"I'm here. Go find Carter and Kate and I'll meet you by the office."

"What does it mean that the car is dead?"

"Just that it won't start," I said.

Carter said running up to meet Tyson. "Sorry, I'm late getting here to you."

Shelby was with Carter.

"I need to finish something really quick."

"The inspector is coming at four," Shelby reminded me.

"Thank you," I said to her. "I'll only be a minute."

I walked back into the classroom. I hugged Samantha. "Tomorrow's a new start," I said to her. "See you later."

I got the kids to the car, and now we waited for Kate. She came walking to the car with a smile on her face. "Hi. Where's mom?"

"The car's dead," Tyson cried.

"That's not a big deal," I said.

"Are we going to have to bury…"

"No! Tyson, sweetheart, it probably needs a new battery," I said. "The car is fine."

Within ten minutes we were home. TJ was still sleeping. Lennox saw me pull me. He came running to see if I needed help. He saw TJ sleeping. "Big day?"

"Huge. His first fieldtrip as a first grader."

"Awe. Did you go?"

"You bet I did. I had five other kids with him, and my group of kids did everything."

"Where did you go?" Kate asked.

"Extreme World."

"Ah, man," she said. "That's so not fair."

"Listen. I'll take you there on your next day off if your parents say I can."

"What did you do?"

"We did everything."

"How?" Carter asked.

"We skipped the movie. So, we had five straight hours of just play and play we did. I loved it."

"You played with them?"

"Hell yes," I said.

Shelby laughed.

We went into the house. Lennox carried TJ. Tyson ran to find Addison. "MOMMY!" he cried.

"Oh, what's wrong?" she asked picking him up.

I came into the kitchen. "The car is dead," I said.

"What?"

"That's what they told the kids."

Michael came racing into the house a half hour earlier than usual. "Mommy!"

"I'm in the kitchen," she said.

"Are you ok?"

"Yes. Of course."

"I got a message from school that you were driving the car and that it died."

"The car is fine," Addison said. "I am fine. I couldn't come pick you up because the inspector called and said he was coming early, so I didn't want to leave the house, and no one would be here if he came. I called the schools and told them I wouldn't be able to pick you up and that you should go with Aunt Kenny."

"That's not the message that we got."

Shelby looked at Addison. "They called over the loudspeaker and said to please tell Tyson, Carter, and Kate Jackson that their mother's car is dead and she won't be able to come get them."

Addison looked at her three elementary school kids, who were all three nodding their heads. "I'm sorry that happened," she said.

"It's homework and project time," I said.

"Thank you for lunch today, Mrs. Jackson."

"You're welcome."

The kids went into the conference room.

At five minutes to four the inspector came. I looked at Addison. "He's early," I laughed as I went to greet him. He came through the house and we went out in the back yard. I showed him everything. Last I showed him the barn.

"And people stay out here?"

"They do, but they have their choice to stay in one of the cabins."

"Could we go see them again?"

"Yes."

I brought him to the row of cabins. We went into each one of them. They were fully furnished, they had everything that was needed, a kitchen, two bathrooms: one with a tub and the other with a shower, flat screen televisions in the main common room and one in each bedroom. Each cabin was a two bedroom.

"What are they made out of?"

"Cement," I said.

"But it looks like a wood cabin."

"Yes, sir, but they are concrete. They have air conditioning and heat for the winter. They have running water and cable and internet hook up."

He said that he would have to go back to the office and process the whole inspection and that he would let me know within the next two weeks if anything needed to be done before we can open as a B&B.

CHAPTER THIRTY

And October began. During the second week of October, I went to court for my case against Romeo Quin. It wasn't a trial in front of jurors. It was a judge; it was his legal team a woman and man defense attorneys and him and it was me and my legal team: I had four active prosecutors handling my case.

He was cocky and arrogant. "Honey," he said looking in my direction. "I can barely remember what the fuck I had for breakfast and you want me to remember the things I did…" he said. He didn't say that he may have done. He said did. "twenty some fucking years ago."

"That's quite enough," the judge said. "You may not speak to Ms. Jackson personally. Is that clear?"

"Yeah. Yeah."

"Defense call your witness."

"We call Mr. Romeo Quin to the stand, your honor."

He got up from his seat at the table and pushed his chair back so far that it fell over with a hard thud to the floor. I nearly jumped out of my skin.

"On the night of June twelfth nineteen ninety-six, did you attend a high school graduation party?"

"Yeah. I may have."

"How old were you in ninety-six?"

"I was what nineteen or twenty. No. I was twenty-one by then," he said.

"Was there underage drinking going on?"

"You could bet your life," he said.

"Please answer yes or no."

"Oh. I thought I did. Yes." He hissed out.

"And how old was Ms. Jackson at that time?"

"Eighteen."

I tapped my lawyer. "I was seventeen," I told her.

"Excuse me, your honor. My client was a minor at the time. She was seventeen."

"Oh, yeah. Right. Right. Her birthday is September twentieth. Happy belated birthday," he said.

"Mr. Quin, I warned you not to speak directly to Ms. Jackson."

He turned to the judge and looked right at her. "Judgy person, I don't understand why I am here. And why she is lying about her name."

"What do you think her name is?"

"Jamie Jackson. I would go to parties back then and I'd see this beautiful tease of a girl, who played the most exceptional music I'd ever heard. She would play and my heart would melt. She told me that she would go out with me, but then when I asked her, she laughed at me and called me names."

"Objection, your honor."

"On what grounds?"

"My client's name is Kennedy Jackson not Jamie Jackson."

"No. That's Jamie. Why is she lying?"

The judge looked at me. "Stand up, Ms. Jackson." I did. "Please state your name for the record?"

"Kennedy Rose Jackson Alexander," I said. "I go by Kenny."

"And how is Jamie Jackson related to you?"

"She is my twin sister, your honor."

"Is she here with you today?"

"Yes, ma'am."

"Where is she?"

"I'm here, your honor," Jamie said standing up.

"Wow! Wait a fucking minute," Romeo said. "There's two of them."

"Watch your language."

"I'm sorry. But there are two of them."

"Apparently so," said the judge.

"Why would you want to hurt Jamie Jackson?"

"Because she made me look like a fucking fool."

"What did I just tell you?" the judge reprimanded Romeo.

"Sorry, your judginess."

"So, what did you do to who you thought was Jamie?" the judge asked.

"She was drunk. I offered to give her a ride home."

"And did you drive her home?" the judge asked.

He laughed a sinister laugh. "No, I did not. I took her out to a wooded area. She had fallen asleep in my truck and her skirt was hiked up a bit, so I started to fool around with her," he said. "Then she came around when I was inside of her and she started to scream, but she needed to be taught that you don't tease men like that. I pulled my knife out to make her shut up, but she began to fight, so I ran my knife along her shoulder blade."

Tears welled in my eyes. "Ms. Jackson, do you need a minute?"

My voice cracked when I said no.

My parents and my whole family were sitting behind me in the pews. I heard mom gasp as he went on to describe the vulgar things he did to me.

"And then I put the blade of the knife pressed it into her skin and when she would scream or fight to get away from me, I flick the knife away and make little cuts in her skin."

"How many times did you do this?" the judge asked.

"Hundreds. Maybe even more."

The judge looked at me. My eyes were red from fighting hard to hold back the tears. "I'm going to call a recess for fifteen minutes. Ms. Jackson, could I see you please in my chambers? You don't have to answer me. Just please come with me."

I stood up and my legs felt like Jell-O. Her court deputy came and put his arm around me. I flinched so big. "Are you ok?" he asked. I shook my head. "Can you walk with me?" Again, I shook my head.

Patrick came over. "I'm her husband. Where does she have to go?" He said lifting me into his arms. I put my face into his shoulder. "It's ok," he said. "I have you." He carried me to the judge's chambers.

"Oh, my are you, all right?" she asked. My voice quivered when I said yes. "And who are you, sir?"

"I'm her husband. Patrick Alexander."

"Are you ok with my deputy being in the room?"

"Yes," I said. "Patrick, you can put me down. Thank you." I said to him. "I love you."

"I love you too."

Patrick was told to wait outside. "Do you still have the marks on your body?"

"Yes, ma'am," I said.

"Can you show me?"

"Yes, ma'am."

"How far down do the marks go?"

"The scars go from the back of my head or from behind my ears to my mid-thigh."

"Show me what you feel comfortable showing me."

I pulled my shirt out of my trousers. I unbuttoned my shirt and opened it. She came around the desk. I took my shirt completely off. Her deputy, who was behind me sucked in air as he looked away from me. "What is it?" she asked.

"See for yourself,"

"Please turn around," she said.

As I turned around, I lowered my head. "Jesus!" she said. She touched my scarred up back and I flinched taking a step forward into her deputy's arms. "Can I feel this?" she asked.

"Yes, ma'am." I said. I looked up at her deputy. "Can you just…"

He put his hands on my sides and steadied me. I lowered my head again. She touched the long-puffed scars down my back. She touched the notches of skin. "Are you ok?"

"Yes."

"With your hands, show me how far down this goes?" I put my fingers just below my mid-thigh. "You can put your shirt back on."

I did. I buttoned it and then turned away from both of them and undid my trousers to tuck my shirt back in.

"Can I ask you something?" she asked. I turned and looked at her and then looked at the ground. "When you go out, what do you wear?"

"Long sleeve shirts and pants mostly. I do wear shorts, but I only wear long shorts when I do wear shorts."

"How many people have seen the scars?"

"My mom just recently. My sister Jamie, my sister-in-law Addison, my brother Parker, my husband and our six-year-old son, Turner James, who we call TJ; and my three nephews, and two nieces. And just recently Patrick's mom, his sister, and his best friend. Plus three of my clients, your honor."

"Do you go the beach?"

"Yes."

"Do you ever wear a bathing suit?"

"No. I haven't worn a bathing suit since I was in high school."

"How do you feel about the marks on your body?"

"I'm ashamed of them."

"Did he rape you?"

"Yes."

"How many times?"

Her deputy stepped closer when I wavered. "I don't know for sure."

"More than once?" I nodded my head. "More than twice?" I nodded again.

"Ok. I want you to stay in here while I finish questioning Mr. Quin. You can sit or lay on my couch if you'd like and I'll be back in a little while."

"Thank you," I mustered to say.

She went back with her court deputy. Patrick followed them back into the court room. "Let's continue," she said. "How long did you keep her in the vehicle?"

"Long enough to do her roughly five, six or seven times. One time for each time she laughed at me."

"So about how long?"

"It was morning when I dumped her bloody body on the side of the road and took off," he said.

"How did you leave her?"

"Naked and bleeding."

"What was she wearing that night?"

"An orange skirt and pink tank top or it could have been the other way around. She had her high school jacket on, her school or class ring, a necklace with a cross. Her skin was so smooth. And I made that bitch pay for making me look stupid and making me look like a fool."

"How do you feel now knowing that she isn't Jamie?"

"Well, hell if I'd known that there were two of them, I would have done it to both of those hurdy turdy bitches."

"Did you ever ask her her name?"

"No. For what reason? She needed to pay the price for making me feel and look like a jack ass," Romeo said.

"You are under arrest," she said.

"For what?" he asked.

"Put this man in cuffs and take him away."

"Well, if you are going to arrest me, then sentence me now bitch," he said.

He was put into hand cuffs.

"What did you do with her belongs?"

"I kept them," he said.

"What did you keep?"

"Her jacket, her ring, her necklace, her shoes."

"What did you do with her clothes?"

"I threw them out with her," he said with a grin.

"I'm sentencing you to life. No chance of getting out. No chance of parole."

"I'd do the same thing to you too, bitch."

She came back into her chamber. Patrick came in with her. I was curled up in ball on the couch. She sat on the edge of her desk as Patrick came to the couch and squatted down next to me. When he touched my shoulder, I jumped. She watched my reaction. "Is she always like this?"

Patrick turned and looked at her. "Yes. She never relaxes. She's always jumpy except when she is with our son. Two therapists have been working on a new technique where one of them holds her. It is upsetting to see. She fights and jerks to get away. My brother-in-law Lennox was present when they were having a session with her at our house and when she got away from them; she took off running out of her house. David caught her before she ran in the street, and Lennox said he could hear her screaming. I was out of town when it happened. She constantly looks over her shoulder."

"How long have you known her?"

"We went to under grad and graduate school together. So, I've known her since was eighteen years old."

"Was it before or after the incident?"

"After. My mother knew her before the incident."

"I'd like to talk to her parents and your mother. She can stay in here."

She pulled another deputy to go with her to talk to mom and dad and Trinity. "What was she like before this?" she asked.

"She was a ball of energy," dad said. "She did so many things that it was hard to keep up with her. She loved being hugged and kissed by her mother and I and by her brother and sister."

"And after that?"

"She barely wanted to be around anyone. Before she left for college, she stayed in her room. She covered her body from head to toe," mom said.

"It could be close to a hundred degrees," Trinity said, "and she would be in blue jeans and a long sleeve shirt."

"Has she changed at all?"

"Just recently. This summer," mom said.

"And when was that?"

"When she met my son," Patrick said. "He was five at time and though Kenny and I have worked together since we started the business, she wasn't aware that I had had a son five now six years ago."

"Where is the boy's mother?"

"My ex-wife left TJ and I when he was only three months old. I've been a single parent with my mom's assistance until this summer when I married Kenny and she adopted my son the day we were married."

"When was that?"

"June twenty-eighth. Kennedy is the only mother he has ever known. I dated, but I never let anyone meet him because I didn't want him to get hurt. He met Kenny in the beginning of June. She was going to take him on vacation with her and her nephews this summer because I had to go away for work. We had talked about it, and I asked her to marry me and she said yes."

"I noticed your rings. They are significantly different," she said. "Where did you get them from?"

"It's from a project that we did together in architect school," Patrick said looking down at his hand. "We made them to go on the top of a building that we designed and made. The Circle Crown," he said. "The professor kept the building as we kept our rings."

I had come out of her office with the deputy. When I saw Patrick, I didn't care who he was with at the time, I ran right for him and right into his arms. He embraced me as I cried.

"You will never have to worry about Mr. Quin again," she said. "He's in prison for the rest of his life. I am so sorry that you went through this horrific experience. Is there anything you'd like?"

"What do you mean?" I asked.

"For the damages that were done to you."

"I don't know," I said. "I never thought about it."

"What did you think?"

"That no one would ever love me," I said.

"Have you dated?"

"Yes."

"Were you ever in a relationship?"

"Nothing ever serious," I responded.

"This is a personal question, but just something I need to know. Did you have sex after it happened?"

"Occasionally over the years, but I would never let the guy look at me or my body. And afterwards, I'd never see the guy again."

"Your choice or theirs?"

"Mine. I was too ashamed to let them see me after it happened. I would get out before I had to explain anything to anyone. But with Patrick, it was so different. I loved him since the first time I saw him. I wasn't afraid to show my body to him or my son, who saw my back one day this summer while I was changing my shirt and he noticed the scars on my back. He felt them when he hugged me. He seemed to be ok with them and for the first time in twenty-one years, I was almost ok with them too," I said.

"Have you ever inquired about plastic surgery?"

"No."

"Is there a reason?"

"I didn't want, and I don't want people looking at my body. The scars cover a large majority of my body."

When we finished, everyone was like where do you want to go? Do you want to go out for a late lunch? Do you want to go out for dinner later? What about drinks and toasting to Romeo Quin going to jail for the rest of his life? At the moment, I didn't want to do any of those things. I wanted to go home and to be with Patrick and TJ.

"Can we get TJ from school?"

"It's already five o'clock," Patrick said.

"Who has TJ?"

"Storm. She's at the house with him."

"Ok," I said.

We went to the house. When we got there, and TJ saw the car, he came running out to greet us. He ran right at me and I scooped him in my arms and just held onto him. Patrick hugged the both of us. Storm came outside. "How did it go?"

"He's in jail or prison for the rest of his life."

"He was given a life sentence?" she asked almost in shock.

"Yes," Patrick said. He stepped away from me and TJ and pulled her to the side. "He described the things that he did to her that were gruesome and yet he did it with pride and a smile on his face. He described the birthmark that she has on her inner left thigh."

Jamie and Lennox just got home. I walked over with TJ. I put him down and hugged Jamie. "I am so sorry," she said crying.

"Did you remember him?"

"Yeah," she said. "I had met him when we were fourteen. He was older and said he was in a band and that he was looking for a singer. A group of us went to go see him. Mom took us to where he was playing. He sucked," she said. "He played the guitar and he was awful.

"As I started getting more and more into the party scene and playing at people's parties, I would see him around. When we were sixteen, he asked me out and I said no. He was relentless. He'd show up everywhere. Even at school. I told Mr. Browning about him and that he was stalking me. Browning took care of it. Two weeks before we graduated, I played at the club house for some girl's sweet sixteen. Anyway, he was there, and he asked me out again and I laughed at him and told him to keep dreaming.

"Kenny, I'm so sorry," she said hugging me again.

"Stop. You didn't know. I didn't know who the hell he was."

"Would you, Patrick and this cute little munchkin want to come over for dinner?"

"Yeah," TJ said. "What are we having?"

"Aunt Jamie's secret," she said hugging him.

CHAPTER THIRTY - ONE

Well this was definitely a first for Jamie. She hadn't had her own place yet until now. I didn't know how Jamie's cooking was. As TJ and I walked back to the house, he looked up at me. "Are you ok now, mommy?"

"I am ok, TJ."

"Can you tell me what happened?"

I turned to him and picked him. I walked into the backyard with him and we sat on the wooden swing. "I know that you have heard drips and drabs of things that happened to me a long time ago."

"Yes," he said. "A man told you that he would bring you home and that he hurt you really bad and that is why you have the scars on your body."

"Yes. Well, for a long time I didn't know who this man was. And this year, at the party that we had for all of you kids, I learned the man's name. Today, as you know, we all went to court and I was supposed to talk to the judge about what happened."

"Did you do that?"

"No, baby. I didn't have to."

"Why not?"

"Because he went up in front of the judge and he was asked questions, and he told everything that he did to me."

"Did it make you sad?"

"Yes."

"And where is this man?"

"He's in jail."

"Mommy, why couldn't Aunt Storm help you find this man?"

"What baby?"

"Well, isn't that what Aunt Storm does? Doesn't she find people that are hard to find?"

"Yeah, honey, that's what Aunt Storm does, but I didn't know his name. And yes, Aunt Storm did help me as did you and daddy."

"How did she do that?"

"She kept us safe. Just like she made sure that you were safe with me this summer. She didn't know me. That is why she followed us to make sure that you were well taken care of. She does a wonderful job at what she does."

"So this man can never hurt you again?"

"No."

My cell phone rang. It was Lennox. "Hello."

"Hi, Jamie is in labor," he said. "We are having a baby!"

"Sure. She always gets out of cooking," I said with laughter in my voice. He laughed too. "We will meet you at the hospital."

Just as we were leaving a car pulled into the driveway. It was mom and dad. "Where are you going?"

"James is in labor," I said.

"Why didn't she call me?" mom asked.

"She might have," dad said. "You've been on the phone with your mother since we left the courthouse."

"How are my grandparents?"

"They are coming home from England for Christmas."

"Grandma's mom is alive?" TJ asked.

"Yep," I said.

"Is she nice?"

"No," mom and I said together, and we laughed.

We all went to the hospital. Jamie was in labor for three hours and then the baby was born. She gave birth to a five-pound eleven-ounce baby boy. Six minutes later, she gave birth to a five-pound six-ounce baby girl.

They named their daughter Jordan Rose and their son Delaney John. They were born on October twelfth at twenty hundred hours, which is eight in the evening.

"We weren't expecting twins," Jamie said.

"Neither was mom," I said as mom said, "Neither was I."

They both came out screaming. Delaney was born with not a single hair on his head, while Jordan was born with a head full of flaming red hair. When they were put together on Jamie, they both settled down. TJ watched from outside with the rest of the kids. I turned to see him get down off the bench and sit down. I walked out of the room. "Hey, buddy, what's up?" He jumped up in my arms and he was crying. I walked down the hall with him. He had his legs wrapped around me. I didn't have to ask him what was wrong. I knew what he was going to say. "It's ok," I said to him. "I know what you are you thinking, and all is I can say is she must have been a complete bitch not to love you." He looked at me. "No, Turner, I mean it. Renee must have been the biggest bitch not to see the love that you are. I mean, hell, I saw it the second I saw you. And I haven't wanted to put you down since that day. I know that you are six and you are a growing boy, but I just want to hold you in my arms forever. She was wrong not to see that in you. You are a wonderful little boy and I am so grateful to have you as my son. Not my adopted son and not my stepson, but my son. I treasure you and your father.

"You know what I couldn't wait to do today when the court case ended?"

"No. What?"

"I couldn't wait to get home and hug you."

He hugged me again and kissed me on the cheek. "I love you, mommy."

"I love you too, baby."

We walked back over to the others. Patrick came out of the bathroom. He had taken Tyson and Carter in there. "There is no such thing as a potty monster," he was saying.

"What?" TJ said. "There's a potty monster?"

"No. It's not real. It's a book. It wasn't meant to scare kids, but that's what it does."

"Uncle Patrick, it was dark in the bathroom."

"I know, Tyson."

"I gots scared."

"I know. It's ok."

I laughed. Patrick looked at TJ and then in the window where Jamie was with the babies. Then he looked back at TJ. He ran his hand through his hair. "I'm sorry, buddy," he said.

"It's ok, daddy. Mommy told me."

He looked at me. "Later," I mouthed to him. He nodded. "Why don't we take this bunch to get something to eat?"

"Yeah!"

Lennox came out. "Jamie wants to see you," he said to me.

I put TJ down and walked into the room. I kissed Jamie on the cheek. "Congratulations," I said to them. "Are you doing ok?"

"Yeah," she said. "We missed our birthday this year."

"I haven't celebrated my birthday in years," I said to her. "I gave you a gift and a card and a bottle of wine."

"I know," she said. "But when I come home, we are going to celebrate."

"Sure," I said.

"We have to get another crib. And another car seat, another everything." The doctor came in. "How is it that you…we all missed that I was carrying twins?"

"The ultrasounds always showed one."

"Were they together?"

"Yes," the doctor said.

"What do you want the bedding to be to for Jordan?" I asked.

"God. I don't even know. We never looked at girl stuff."

Addison came into the room. "If you would like, Parker and I will give you Beth's crib and stroller. It's a two baby stroller because Tyson was still little when we had Beth."

"Thank you."

Jamie started to doze off with the babies on her, so we left. We left her with Lennox in the room. He climbed up on the bed with her and snuggled up to her and the babies.

The rest of us took the kids out for dinner. After that, Parker went home with Patrick and TJ and the kids while Addison and I went shopping for the twins. I bought a car seat that matched the one for Delaney. Together Addison and I picked bedding for Jordan. Delaney's bedding was

Oceania Aqua/Blue with sea life on it including a whale and an octopus. Jamie had received the whole set. For Jordan Rose, Addison and I both picked Disney Baby Little Mermaid Sea Princess. The color schemes were close. When we were done, we went a bit crazy with the outfits for her.

By the time Jamie and Lennox were ready to bring the twins home the next day, Addison and I had gone in with Patrick and Parker and built the crib. We had another dresser added to the room. A second changing station for her. We had made up the room for the both of them. Then the four of us went to the hospital to help them out. Mom and dad were there. We brought the extra car seat with us and installed it in the car for them. Between Patrick and Parker, the car seats were in there for the duration. When we went up to see them, we brought the carrier with us. A carrier decked out in girly shades of blue. When Jamie saw us coming with the stuff, she started to cry.

"Hi, what did you do?" she asked.

"We made accommodations and provisions," Addison said.

"What?" a tired Lennox asked.

"Let's just say that the babies' room is ready," I said. I went to Jamie and showed her pictures of the room.

"When did you do this?"

"Last night," Parker said. "Congratulations."

"Now you guys can take it easy and not have to worry about going crazy to get things for this adorable little girl here," Patrick said. "I remember before Renee had TJ how excited I was to set up his room. I couldn't wait to see him and hold him."

"Did she hold him?" Jamie asked.

"Never. She never held him, she never smelled that precious baby sent, and she never changed his diapers. She only carried him for nine months and then she was done with him and moved on from him and from us."

"When did she leave?"

"He was just three months old."

"Did she tell you she was leaving?"

"She had told me that she was going to go see her mother. I asked if she was going to bring TJ with her. She had turned and looked at me and asked me why she would do that. What would be the point? I told her if she left not to come back, but by then I knew she wasn't coming back."

"Why didn't you just tell TJ she was gone?" Lennox asked.

"He already knew that much," Patrick said.

"Do you miss her?" Addison asked.

"No. Not one single day."

"Do you have pictures of her?"

"Not anymore," he said. "What would be the point," he said

The nurse came in with the wheelchair. Jamie got into it. The babies were put into the carriers. Lennox took Delaney and Jamie took Jordan. We all came downstairs together. It was decided that Patrick would drive their vehicle home for them. Upon getting to the house, there were balloons tied to the mailbox. We went into their house; where there were now quadruple the amount of diapers that were there yesterday. Their house was a one-story house with five bedrooms three and half bathrooms and a bathroom in back of the house with a shower by the pool. Their kitchen was nice size not much smaller than my kitchen.

When they came in with the twins, mom and dad were there. "Was this what it was like when you had us?"

"No," mom and dad said together.

"You didn't get to come home together," mom said. "And we had a three-year-old at home. We brought you home first. Kenny had to stay awhile longer in the hospital. When we brought Kenny home, Parker went and sat on the couch and we gave him Kenny on his left and you on his right, and the three of you fell asleep together.

"Parker was in pre-school at that time, so I would be home with the two of you until one o'clock, when the little bus would bring Parker home. The two of you slept when he came home. I would have him take a bath before coming close to you both and then he would sit on the couch with the two of you and you would all sleep."

"Who walked first out of the two of us?"

"Kenny did," dad said. "But you crawled first, and you spoke first."

Parker came in. "Mom and dad thought that Kenny might have been deaf."

I looked at them. "What? I've never heard that. Why would you have thought that?"

"You didn't speak until you were about twenty-three months old. You were almost two."

"The doctor's cleaned a huge blockage out of your ears," Parker said.

"Yes, it's true," dad confirmed. "We took all three of you to the doctor for your checkups. Your mom told the doctor that you still weren't talking and that she thought you may have been deaf. He called in a specialist and when he looked into your ears, he saw a huge build up. He put a solution into your ears and then with an instrument he sucked out the huge build up that you had in both ears. Within a week after that you were talking. You called Parker Parky."

We stayed a little while and then we went to the house. We finished decorating for the Halloween party. We were having a fun house, so we made it fun.

"When is the bounce house coming?" TJ asked.

"The bounce houses will come on the twenty-eight."

"When should I give out the invitations?"

"Definitely on Monday," Patrick said.

"Can we carve a pumpkin?"

"Yes," I said. "Hey, do you want to take a ride with me?"

"Where are we going?" he asked.

"I have to go see David and Gwen." Patrick looked at me. "No, it's ok," I mouthed to him. "Do you want to come?"

"Yeah," he said.

"Come on. Let's go."

"When you get back, we will watch movies?" Patrick said.

"Oh, I thought you could come too."

"Sure. Let me change really quick."

He ran upstairs to the apartment and changed. He put on a pair of blue jeans and a green shirt. He grabbed a jacket for TJ before coming back downstairs. We all three got into my truck and I drove to their apartment building. "TJ, I built this," he said.

"Really?"

"Yes."

"Did mommy help you?"

"Yeah, except she didn't know she was helping me build this."

I looked at him. "What?"

"It's when we first started the firm and you were super busy and hardly sleeping."

"That hasn't changed," I said with laughter in my voice.

"Nope," TJ said.

I reached back and tickled him. "Well, I had asked you to look over the blue prints and the next thing I knew; you changed the front entrance, and you flipped the layout to have the parking lot in the front of building and not in the back. You designed the pools. You made it so that elevator opens up to the apartments, so they wouldn't have to walk down corridors to get their apartment. I over saw construction, but you did the plans."

"Yeah, that sounds like me," I said with a smile.

We went upstairs. David greeted us when we came out of the elevator. He picked TJ up and hugged him and tossed him the air a few times before putting him down. He man hugged Patrick. And then he hugged me. "How are you doing?"

"I'm good," I said. "I…we came here to tell you that your house will be ready on December first."

"Oh, wow."

"You can move in any time after that. I will bring you your keys in a few weeks."

"Hi," Gwen said.

"Hi."

TJ ran up to her and hugged her. Patrick hugged her as well. She walked over to David and I. "How are you?"

"I'm ok," I said her.

"Can I speak to you alone a minute?"

I walked with her into the mediation room. She closed the door for the first time. Then she sat at the desk in the room. "I am so sorry for the last time we had a session," she said.

"It's ok."

"I feel so bad. I want to be friends with you. I want to be able to talk to you and you talk freely to me, but I feel that I have ruined that."

"Gwen, I freak out at times when I'm held. And you and David have seen me freak out a lot. I tried to control it, but I couldn't. Just from the way you grabbed me and the way you moved, I felt my whole-body surge and it scared the shit out of me.

"It doesn't mean that we aren't going to talk. I'm still finishing your house. I'm still going to see you and David. It just will never be for another session."

"I truly am sorry."

"Let it go," I said. I hugged her. She hugged me back. Then we left the room. When we went back into their family room, David was talking about a defense class. "What's that?" I asked.

"We were talking about a defense class that I think that you and TJ should take," David said. "It teaches techniques that I think would be good for both of you to know."

"When is that?"

"They start after Halloween."

"We are having a Halloween Fun House party," TJ said. "Want to come?"

Both David and Gwen looked at me. I nodded. "Yes, we would love to come," Gwen said.

"Would you like to stay for dinner?" David asked.

We stayed for dinner. He made barbeque again. It was out of this world. After dinner, we got ready to go. "What are you doing for the rest of the evening?"

"We are going to watch movies at the house."

"In the theater?" Gwen asked.

"Yeah," Patrick said. Being nice he asked if they wanted to join us. When we left their house, the five of us went back to our house.

Just as we got home, the twenty-five foot blow up dragon came to life on the front lawn. TJ cheered from the back seat. "IT'S ALIVE!" TJ said all excited. A few seconds later another blow up giant black cat came to life. YAY!" he said watching the cat. We had a total of seven blow ups coming up the front walk. A ghost, a tree with a ghost, pumpkins and an owl in the tree, a few pumpkins, and right off the front porch, there stood a skeleton boy. TJ was so excited. By the end, TJ was jumping up and down he was so thrilled.

We went into the house, and we were greeted with a dancing broom. TJ laughed. "This doesn't scare him?" Gwen asked.

"No. He's always loved Halloween," Patrick said.

We went into the theater, where Patrick had installed a popcorn maker.

He turned it on while we all decided what movie we wanted to watch. "Lassie," TJ and I said together.

"Lassie it is then."

I reached into my pocket, took out my phone, and called Addison. "Hey," I said when she answered the phone. "I am just calling to see if you all would care to come over and join us for Friday the thirteenth movie night. We are watching Lassie." Within the next ten minutes, the kids came over. Carter sat by himself for the first time. After a while, I got up and went over to him. "What's going on?"

With tears in his eyes, he looked at me. "I miss you," he said. "You're not going to go trick or treating with us this year."

"Why not?" I asked. "Am I grounded?"

He looked at me and tried so hard not to smile. "Aunt Kenny!"

"Carter, of course I am going trick or treating with all of you. We just have two newcomers that's all. I told you that nothing is going to change, and I meant every single word of it. I am still here and now the cool thing is I am now right next door."

"But now you are in the apartment."

"Baby, it's still in the house. And the front door to the apartment is always opened. And if it's not, it won't be locked. You just turn the handle and come right in. Carter, I'm right here."

He cried and I took him in my arms. "I've had you all my life. I miss you. I miss the adventures." I rocked him in my arms even though he is eight. We watched the movie. Within a half hour, he was sound asleep. I gently put him down on the seat and went back and sat with Patrick.

"Is everything ok?"

"Yeah," I said. "He's having I miss you issues."

Michael came and sat next to me. "You've been a little distant," he said. Then he put his head on my shoulder and started to cry. "We miss you. You usually go to all of our school events and you haven't come to anything yet." My heart sank. "You said things would never change, but they have and we miss you."

"I'll make it up to all of you. I promise you."

Tyson came over and climbed right up on Patrick's lap. "The damn scary part is coming up," he said and put his head against Patrick's chest. He put his little arms around Patrick's neck. Patrick wrapped his arms around Tyson. Tyson didn't make it to what he thought was the scary part of the movie. He was sound asleep. Beth had gone and sat on Gwen's lap when they came. She was still wide eyed. When the movie ended, she stood up and turned and looked at me. "What's next, Aunt Kenny?"

I smiled and laughed. "What would you like to watch?"

"Frozen!"

With the boys sleeping, except for TJ, who went along with anything, we watched Frozen. Beth climbed right back up on Gwen. "Ow this is my favorite part," she said throughout most of the movie.

Patrick had been watching Kate. She had been busy on her phone texting the whole time. "Kate!" he whispered. Kate looked up and looked at him. He motioned for her to come to him. She got up and came and sat down next to him. "Who is it you are talking to?"

"My friend Gunner."

"Is he in the fifth grade with you?"

"Uncle Patrick?"

"Kate!"

"No. He's from the middle school."

"What grade is he in?"

"Seventh," she said.

"No," he said.

"No, what?"

"No," he said again. "Give me your phone."

She handed him her phone and he viewed all the texts between them. "Does he know that you are in fifth grade?"

"No. He thinks I'm in middle school."

"Tell him you want to meet him tomorrow at the mall and I will take you and if I don't like the way things look, I will tell him that you are in fifth grade. Is that clear?"

"Yes, sir," she said.

"Does your mother know this?"

"No, sir."

"Kate!" he said. "Tell him about tomorrow and then say good night."

"Yes, sir," she said.

Kate looked at me. "Uncle Patrick is handling this one sweetheart," I said to her.

"Yes, ma'am," she said. She sent the text and he agreed to meet her at noon in the food court. And then Patrick took her phone. He put his arm around her shoulders and hugged her the best he could not to disturb Tyson.

"We should get going," Gwen said halfway through Frozen.

"No," Beth said. "Please stay and watch till the end?"

"Is that ok," she asked me.

"Yes, of course."

They stayed till the end of the movie. We had put the kids to bed upstairs. Beth, TJ and Kate were still awake. Beth walked outside with us when Gwen and David were leaving. We never saw her climb into the vehicle. They left and we assumed that she ran home. Gwen and David never realized that she was in their SUV until they pulled into their parking lot. By then a storm that had been looming in the distance had moved in and the lightning scared her and she screamed. Both Gwen and David jumped at the sound of screaming child in their SUV. "What the hell?" David said.

"LIGHTNING!" Beth cried and scrambled into Gwen's arms trembling. They ran into the building. Once they were upstairs in their apartment, Gwen called me.

"Hi, I just wanted to let you know that we have a stow away here with us."

"What?"

"Beth climbed into the backseat."

"Shit!" I said. "I'll come get her."

"No. Don't get on the road. It is bad weather. We will bring her home first thing in the morning."

"Are you sure you don't mind?"

"No, not at all," Gwen said. "It's been so much fun being with all of you tonight and having Beth sit on my lap all night watching movies. She's adorable."

"She's something for sure," I said. "Adorable. I'm not so sure of right now."

The thunderstorm kept on all night long. Beth had kept Gwen up most of the night. Finally falling asleep in Gwen's arms at five in the morning; Gwen was sitting on the couch with her and she too fell asleep.

Hayley had woken up at eight in the morning and came into the family room. Seeing her mother sleeping on the couch with a toddler in her arms, made her grow concerned. Hayley went and found David, who was in the kitchen reading the morning paper on his iPad and having a cup of coffee.

"Who is the baby in mom's arms?"

"That is Kenny's niece Beth."

"Why is she here?"

"We were at Kenny's last night watching movies with all of them, and this little spit fire climbed into the SUV with no one knowing. We found out last night when we got home, and lightnig struck and she started screaming."

"Oh my god, dad. Does her family know?"

"Yes, of course," he said.

"Why didn't they come get her?"

"It stormed until about an hour ago."

"It stormed?" she asked.

"Yes, most of the night," he said. "I don't know when they fell asleep. Beth was really scared."

"She's cute. How old is she?"

"Three."

Beth slept in Gwen's arms till ten. Then she woke up. "I have to go pee pee." Gwen got up and took her to the bathroom.

"Come on. Let me take you home."

"Hungry," she said.

"What would you like?"

"Pancakes please."

David had made pancakes earlier and had them waiting. Beth ate three big pancakes. Then she went and sat on the couch, closed her eyes, and went back to sleep. Instead of Gwen coming back to the house, I went there to get Beth also because I had the car seat in my truck. When I got there, Beth was sleeping.

"Are you just going to take her?"

"No," I said. "I'm going to wake her up. She will be very upset if she didn't get to say goodbye. Beth, honey, wake up." After three tries, she opened her eyes. "Hi, honey, we have to go home now. Say goodbye to Gwen and David."

Beth got up and went running to Gwen. "Will you come again?" she asked.

"Yes."

She hugged Gwen and said thank you and then she hugged David. Seeing Hayley, she went to her and hugged her too. "Bye. Bye," she said.

"Bye. Thank you," I said. I left with Beth.

When I got home, Patrick was leaving with Kate, who looked so grown up at nine. She wore a pair of black jeans and an off the shoulder shirt. Patrick didn't invade. He picked a table quite a bit away, but where he could still see her and everything that she did. Gunner was there early. He appeared to be by himself. He was a bit tall at five ten. His brown hair was long to his shoulders and it was wavy. He wore wired rim glasses and a mouth full of braces. His jean shorts were long in length. When he saw Kate, he hugged her. He kissed her on the cheek. "Hi," he said.

"Hi."

"What did you do last night?"

"Watched movies at my aunt and uncle's house."

"What did you watch?"

"Lassie and Frozen."

"Aren't those kid movies?"

"Well, I am kid," she said.

"You're like eleven right?"

"No," she said.

"How old are you?"

Kate played with her hair. "I'm nine," she said.

"You're what? Are you even in middle school?"

"Kind of," she said.

"How are you kind of in middle school?"

"I'm in the music program at the middle school."

"What the hell grade are you?"

"I'm in fifth grade," she said.

"How? You are you nine?"

"I'm advanced. I've been in advanced classes. I got to skip third grade. Can we still hang out?"

"I don't know," he said.

"Why? Don't you like me?" she asked defensively.

"Yeah, I like you, but you are same age as my little brother," he said. "He's in third grade."

"So is my little brother. Well, one of my little brothers."

"How many brothers do you have?"

"I have three. Michael is in sixth grade."

"Wait! Michael Jackson is your brother?"

"Yes. Why?" again she was defensive.

"No. No reason. He's a cool kid. He's in my math class. Are you all advanced?"

"Yeah, except for my three-year-old sister," Kate laughed. "My youngest brother is in kindergarten and they want to put him in first grade, but my mom and dad said he has to stay where he is. He just turned five before school started. My brother Carter is in the advanced third/fourth grade split class."

"So there are five of you?"

"Yeah."

"Where are you in the group?"

"Second oldest," she said. "I'll be ten on Halloween."

"So you are a witchy kid?"

"Yeah, I guess. I'm a Halloween baby."

"What are you doing for Halloween?"

"We all go trick or treating. It will be Beth's first year getting to go. But my aunt and uncle are hosting a Halloween party."

"Oh, cool," he said. "Do you want to walk around a bit?" he asked.

"I need to ask my uncle. He's right over there."

"Where are your mom and dad?"

"They are home."

Parker had come to the mall with Carter and Michael to buy Michael new cleats for school, and Carter needed a new pair of sneakers. They came into the food court and Parker immediately saw Kate sitting at a table with a boy kicking her feet. Michael ran over first. "Hey, Gunner, what are you doing here?"

"Just hanging out with your sister."

"She's awesome with music," Michael said. "Are you in her music class?"

"No. I saw her at school a few weeks ago and we texted each other."

Michael made a face. Gunner looked at him. "What?"

"Dude, she's in the fifth grade."

"Yeah, man, I know."

"She's only nine," he said sticking up for her.

"Again, man, I know."

"But you're like what? Thirteen? Fourteen?"

He laughed. "No, man, I'm twelve."

Carter came running over. "Hi, Kate. Beth is in trouble," he said.

"How much trouble can a three-year-old get in?"

"She went home with Gwen and David last night without anyone knowing."

"What?" Kate looked up at Parker and ran over to him to give him a hug. "Hi, daddy."

"Please tell me how you got here?"

"Uncle Patrick brought me. He's right over there. Is that ok, daddy?"

"Yes," Parker said. "Go back over with your friend. Is he in fifth grade?"

"No."

"What grade is he in?"

"Don't freak out," she said. "He's twelve."

"I didn't ask how old he is. I asked what grade he is in?"

"Seventh," she said.

Patrick walked over. "Kate, go back over with your friend." He pulled Parker aside. "Don't do what you are planning on doing," he said.

"What the fuck would you know? Your child is five."

"TJ is six, you jerk. I have been watching them together. It is innocent."

"He's in the seventh grade."

"He's a twelve-year-old boy," Patrick said. "And Kate will be ten at the end of the month. What is the big deal?"

"He has raging hormones."

"And she is one of the smartest kids that I know," Patrick said. "She is a good girl."

"What do you do for fun?" Kate asked him.

"My dad and I make soap box cars and race them."

"Oh, wow. I want to come see that," she said.

"Well, I have to get going," he said to her. "It was really nice hanging out with you today. Maybe we can do it again sometime."

"Would you like to come to our Halloween party on the twenty-ninth?"

"Yeah, sure," he said. "Where is it?"

"At the Jackson Estate."

"What? No way," he said all excited. "My mom and dad said that that place is turning into a bed and breakfast."

"Yeah, it is. My aunt owns it."

"Yeah, I'll come. Can I bring my little brother?"

"Yeah, sure," she said. "Thank you for the drink and the cookie."

"Yeah, sure," he said. He kissed her on the cheek and hugged her goodbye. When he walked past Parker and Patrick he waved hi. "Mr. Jackson," he said, "you have a real cool daughter. She's a great girl. Thank you for letting us hang out today."

"How come you are leaving?"

"Oh, my dad and I are building our newest soap box car. He's a police officer, so he should be home when I get there."

"How did you get here?" Patrick asked.

"I rode my bike."

"Want a ride home?"

"Oh, no thank you. I'm not allowed to take rides from strangers."

The Halloween Fun House party started at one o'clock on the twenty-ninth. The whole elementary school was invited including all the teachers and the principal and vice principal. Michael invited his friends and their families. Kate invited her middle school friends. Her friends from fifth grade were already invited. Beth's preschool class was invited as well.

We literally had kids all over the place. In the bounce houses, upstairs in the bedrooms, which were set up like cars on a train and they had to find clues to advance to the next room. All the kids that came received a gift after doing the train adventure, which Patrick and Lennox were in charge of. The last car had a scaredy cat that jumped out at the kids and everyone screamed. That's when the kids got glow stick necklaces and bracelets that they could use on Halloween.

Every kid was dressed up for Halloween, so we had a costume contest for each grade. With the different stations, there was something for everyone to do. As kids came in the kitchen to get drinks, we heard them say, "This is the best Halloween party ever." We heard it repeatedly. Not one kid wasn't enjoying themselves.

The party really got kicking when Lennox started up the fly tank. Every kid got to do it. And with the amount of kids that were at the party, Lennox kept track. Jamie had come over with the babies. Her band had flown in. They would be surprising her in a few days telling her the news that they all had moved here to be close to her. It came out in the family room when her violinist saw her and wrapped her arms around Jamie. "We all moved here," she said.

"What? Really?"

"Yeah. Why wouldn't we. You are here and we are your band mates. SURPRISE!" she said. Jamie hugged her again. "Whose house is this?"

"This is my childhood house, but my sister owns it."

"It's a great house and what a great party."

Jamie met with Kate, and now with Jamie's band and the stage that Lennox and Patrick had built, they went out there and without warning, Kate started to play the keyboard with Jamie backing her up on guitar, her violinist picking it up a few notes into it. Then Kate belted out a song and everyone stopped what they were doing and went racing over to see her.

"I can't see, Katie," Beth cried. David picked her up and sat her high on his shoulders. "Thank you," she said. Kate and Jamie sang together, and they sounded like one voice.

Patrick came and stood next to me. He put his hand on the back of my head and played with my hair. "Did you ever want to do that?"

"Sing?"

"Yes."

"Hell no."

"Mommy sings very well," TJ said coming and standing in front of me. I put my hands on his shoulders.

"How would you know?"

He looked up at me, "You sing to me when I can't sleep."

"Watch your cousin," I said.

Gwen wandered over to us. "Where did she learn to sing like that?"

"She was singing before she spoke," I said. "James was like that too."

They did three more sets and then they were done. Jamie hugged Kate. Kate was beaming. Gunner walked up to her and kissed her on the cheek.

The party ended at seven that evening. After all of the kids left, we went into the bounce house and bounced with our kids. We had a great time. We bounced until the men came to collect them. I paid them and thanked them for their service.

"TJ, go upstairs and take a shower please," I said.

Tuesday, October thirty-first. It's my first Halloween as wife and mother. I quickly learned Patrick and TJ's tradition when TJ came in our room and came in our bed at five in the morning. Patrick put on The Great Pumpkin. We watched it twice. Then we got up and did a scavenger hunt for Halloween candy.

"Mommy, what do you usually do on Halloween morning?"

"Ah," I said. "Well, I wish Kate a happy birthday and then I go to their school and do the in-school trick or treating with them. And then I usually go to work."

"Are you going to work today?"

"No. Daddy and I took the day off."

"Oh, awesome," he said.

"Come on. Let's get you into your costume."

He had decided to go as a cowboy for school and the monster truck for trick or treating tonight. We went downstairs and had breakfast with Addison and the kids. Then we went to the school. As in the past, there was a Halloween assembly first, followed by class to class trick or treating and then back in the cafeteria for lunch with all the kids. After lunch, I was asked to come up. TJ, Tyson, Carter, and Kate cheered. TJ looked at Carter. "What is mommy doing?"

"She reads a Halloween story to us," he said.

TJ sat on Patrick's lap. "This is so exciting," he said.

"I know," Patrick said.

I picked the book before walking to edge of the stage and sitting on it. I showed the kids the cover of the book and they all cheered. I opened the book about Casper and I started to read to them. I saw Michael standing in the back of the cafeteria. He crept closer and closer until he was sitting on the floor with his brothers and sister. Tyson came and sat in his lap. Kate leaned against him. When I finished reading about Casper's adventures, the kids asked if I could read another. "Clifford!" a little girl called out. I looked at the principal, who nodded. And why wouldn't he? I was making his day and the teachers' day a walk in the park. After reading Clifford, the kids went back to their classes. Patrick and I went with TJ. Patrick noticed that his desk though it was with the kids was pushed to the side.

"What's up with that?" he asked me.

"TJ stands while he does his works, so he needs a little more room."

"I'll talk to him about that."

"Patrick, no," I said. "He's fine."

"Boys and girls why don't we show your parents what we have been working on?" All the kids went up to Mrs. Heyward's desk. She handed out their projects of ghosts made on construction paper, pumpkins made on paper plates, and scaredy cats made of paper bags.

"Look at his," someone said about TJ's. "Why was he given more supplies to work with?" a father said.

"Dad!" a little boy said.

"All of the kids were given the same opportunity," Samantha said.

"And why does he get to stand while my kid has to sit?" a mother said.

"Mom!" a girl said.

"The children are allowed to do whatever they like as long as their work gets done."

TJ came over to me and buried his head in my stomach. "Can we go home now?"

"Yeah, baby," I said. I lifted him up in my arms. He put his head on my shoulder and started to cry.

"Wow! You made him cry. He's really creative and he tried to help others with their projects, but they didn't want his help," Cassidy said. "He gets picked on enough by kids in this class. Why? Because he is new? My mommy says that you are only new for a day. They just don't want to give him a chance because he is smart."

"Thank you, Cassidy," Samantha said.

Patrick looked at TJ. "Kids pick on you?"

"Yeah," he said not lifting his head from my shoulder.

"Wow. I thought things would be different in this school. I heard this was such a great school with great kids," he said. "What's wrong with him that you don't like?"

"He can't play baseball," a boy said. "He throws like a girl."

"Enough of that Jonah," Samantha said.

"He says yes ma'am and no ma'am," another boy said. "Who talks like that?"

"And he cries," a girl said. "He cries like a baby."

"Donavan!" Samantha said.

"Wait, Donny, didn't you cry on the fieldtrip?" Cassidy asked.

"Shut up, Cassidy!"

"He's the best friend I have ever had," Braxton said.

"Yeah," Cassidy and Royce agreed.

Some of the kids' parents were shocked. Others just nodded their heads.

"He's seven and he cries," Jonah said.

"He's six," I said.

We left right after that. TJ was sleeping in my arms. Addison came out of Tyson's class with him. He was all wound up. Addison saw the tears on TJ's face. "What happened?"

"Most of the kids in his class literally just made fun of him in front of their parents."

"Well, then we know who not to invite to the next party," Addison said.

"Can I go on the swings?"

"No. We are going home."

"Can I go swimming?"

"We will see," she said.

"Can I run around for a few minutes?"

"No. We are going home."

Samantha came out of the classroom. "I am so sorry," she said to us.

"Is it like that every day?" Patrick asked.

"No," she said.

"His whole entire class was invited to the party on Sunday. Hell! The whole school was invited to that party.

"And to hear that he gets teased for throwing a baseball."

"Let's just go," I said. "We have stuff to do before we go tonight."

We went home. TJ slept on the couch, where I put him. Addison prepared dinner for us. We were having an early dinner and then we were all going trick or treating. By five thirty all of the kids were in their costumes. A half hour later, we were out of the house and on a mission to hit every house in the neighborhood. By nine o'clock and three bathroom stops later, we had completed our mission.

"Can I eat some of my candy?"

"We have to check it first," I said.

"For what?" TJ asked.

"If it's not completely wrapped up, it's going in the garbage," Patrick said.

November first, TJ stayed home from school. He went into the office with Patrick and I. He stayed busy building something that he wouldn't let us see until the end of the day. We went through our day. At noon I was starving, so I went to get him. "TJ, it's time to eat."

"Mommy, you can't come in here," he said.

"I'm not, baby. Let's go get something to eat please."

"Where are we going to go?"

"Wherever you want to go," Patrick said.

The three of us left the building and we went out to eat. "When can we go back to Daytona?" TJ asked.

"You know that we go there the day after Thanksgiving," Patrick said.

"But would mommy come too?"

"Would I come to what?" I asked returning from the bathroom.

"It's just that we go to Daytona the Friday after Thanksgiving," Patrick said to me. "What is your tradition?"

"I don't have one."

"What do you do for Thanksgiving?"

"We all cook something and then we go either to Addison and Parker's or they come to my house. James has spent Thanksgiving away ever since we graduated high school, so this is the first year that she will be home. And mom and dad are now back up here, so they will be here."

"Do you do anything the day or weekend after Thanksgiving?"

"No."

"So, can we go?" TJ asked.

"Yes. That would be nice."

When we finished for the day, Patrick came into my office and kissed me. I stood up and kissed him back. I put my arms around his neck and he put his arms around my back. We squished together, which deepened the kiss. We didn't realize that we had an audience. TJ stood outside the door of my office staring at us. When he giggled, we both pulled away. I turned my head away from him and quickly wiped my mouth. "What were you doin'?" he asked.

"It's called kissing," Patrick said.

"But you had your tongue in mommy's mouth. And she had she's in yours."

"It's hers," I corrected him. "Not she's."

"Ok," he said. "And she had hers in yours," he said.

"Yep. That's how adults kiss," Patrick said.

"Ew! That's gross."

"You won't think that way when you are older."

"Can I kiss a girl like that?"

"NO!" we both said together.

"Are you done with your creation?" I asked.

"Yes, mommy. Come see, daddy."

We went with him to see what he had been doing all day long. I had taken my camera. And when we went into an unused office, there on the tabletop stood our house made with logs and blocks.

"TJ!" I said.

"Did I do something wrong?"

"My god no," I said. "This is our house," I said to him taking a picture of it. "This is great."

"Do I have to take it down?"

"No," Patrick said. Patrick took a sheet of blank paper and wrote: PLEASE DON'T TOUCH." He folded the paper in half and stood it up like a triangle on the table. He called Margot. "Hey, are you still here?"

"Yeah," she said.

"Can you come to room eight please?"

"Yep. On my way." Margot came to the office. "Wow! Who did that?"

"I did," TJ said.

"Could you treat this?"

"Sure," she said to Patrick.

"Can you, Dillon, and Jenna mount this?" I asked.

"Yes, of course," she said. "How much of it do you want?"

"The whole thing," Patrick said. "Once you are done with it, can you bring it to the house for us please? I think I know just the right spot for this."

We left them to take care of it and we went home.

CHAPTER THIRTY - TWO

The month of November flew by. Pretty soon we were at the week before Thanksgiving. The Bruno's home was almost complete, and I was going to give them their keys. As I pulled into their apartment complex, a chill ran through my body. I just took it as it had finally started cooling off and it was in the upper forties this morning and I had left the house without a coat. I ran into the building. I went up to their floor and stepped into their apartment. David came over and gave me a hug. I hugged him back. "How are you?"

"Fine," he said.

"Where is Gwen?"

"She's in the mediation room. Come on in there," he said. Still with an arm around me, he led me into the room. Gwen gave me a hug and while she was hugging me, David injected something into my thigh. I wilted in her arms. David lifted me and put me in a chair. He then tied me into it. When I started to come out of whatever he gave me, he back handed me so hard across the face that my teeth vibrated in my mouth. He smacked three more times just as hard.

"You're related to Quin," I said.

"He's my son," David said pulling my head back by my hair. I cried out for the first time.

"Hey, come on!" Gwen said. "You said nothing of roughing her up or hurting her."

David let go of my hair and I brought my head back to the neutral position and then he smacked me again this time harder. I cried out again.

Lennox was always trying new things with his phone and with technology. He had put GPS on my phone and now he was playing with it to see if it worked and to see if he could locate me. He not only located me, but he opened the new camera app that he had installed on my phone and he saw that I was sitting in a room and that I was tied up. Within minutes he had gone to the police station and showed them what he was seeing on my phone. He had seen David shake me by the shoulders.

"Does this have sound?"

"Yes."

"On her end or yours?"

"On mine, but it will pick up sounds from where she is."

"And why did you design this app?"

"To help find people who go missing," he said.

"Why did you have him arrested?"

"You were there in the court room," I said.

"I don't believe you. I don't believe Romeo is capable of doing what you said."

"He fucking branded me," I said. David hit me again. This time catching the corner of my nose. Blood raced to the surface and trickled out of the hole he made.

"Tell me what he did to you?"

"He gave me the date rape pill; he told me that he would drive me home. He put me in his truck and drove to a wooded area. When I tried to get out of the truck, he tied me up. He ripped my close off of me and he rape..." David smacked me hard on my right cheek. "FUCK! Please stop hitting me."

He spread his legs and came right across my lap. He pulled my shirt out of my pants. I began to twist and jerk in the chair. "Oh, god no. Please. Please don't do this. What the fuck is wrong with you. I thought you were a nice guy."

"Romeo is gone."

"What?"

"They found him last night in his cell."

"I had nothing to do with that."

He undid my belt. "FUCK!" I screamed again. He yanked my belt out of my pants loops. The buckle caught me under the chin and made a gash. Blood dripped on my shirt. He stood up and violently undid my pants.

The swat team had the building surrounded. They gained access to their floor from the roof and now entered their apartment by lifting the sliding glass door off of the track. They came into the apartment with guns drawn. They threw tear gas in the room before they rushed the room. They apprehended David, Gwen and Hayley before they got me. I had passed out from the tear gas. When I opened my eyes, someone was standing behind me holding my head and an oxygen mask on my face. I tried to jerk away.

"No," a woman's soothing voice said. "Don't fight. I'm not going to hurt you. We must wait for a special team to come to get you out of the chair. What is your name?"

"Kennedy Alexander. I go by Kenny."

A man came in with welding tools. I jerked trying to free myself.

"No. No. Don't do that. The more you move, the tighter your restraints get."

"C...c...can I...I... I ca...ca...call my..."

I dropped my head angrily because now I was stuttering.

"Who do you want to call?"

"P...p..."

"Your dad?"

I shook my head.

The man with the welding tools turned on the torch and I let out an ear-piercing scream. The woman cop took my head and put it against her stomach. She covered my face with hands. She brought her head to mine. "It's going to be ok. You need to stay still ok." I shivered in her arms. "Hey, can we get a blanket?"

"No," the guy with the torch said. "It could catch fire."

It took them an hour and half to get me out of the chair. Once I was freed from the ties, I remained in the chair. My shirt was ripped open, my jeans were undone. My face was bloody and red from being smacked so many times.

"I WANT TO SEE MY WIFE!"

"P...p...pat...pat..."

"Is there someone named Pat?" she asked.

Patrick came in the room. I didn't look at him. "Ken?" I lowered my eyes to the ground and tried to pull my shirt in front me as much as I could. "Kennedy?" I lowered my whole head this time. He came close to me.

"Sir, don't get upset by her reactions."

"Ken?" He squatted down in front of me and I fell into his arms.

"P...p...p..."

"Shh. It's ok. I'm here. I got you." He lifted me into his arms. I curled up making my six-foot frame as small as I possibly could. "Can someone please give me a blanket to put around my wife?"

"Yes, sir," the woman officer said. "We need to take her to the hospital and have her checked out."

"Can I bring her?"

"No, sir, we need to bring her."

"P...p..."

"Why can't she speak?"

"She has been through something completely traumatizing."

"So tell me how to explain this to our six year old son."

He carried me downstairs to the awaiting ambulance. When he put me down on the gurney, I started to scream and kick my legs. "We need to sedate her," the head medic said. "Hold her down." It took six police officers, and three medics, and Patrick to hold me down while the medic injected me with the sedative. I screamed until I blacked out.

I didn't remember the ambulance ride to the hospital. Once in the hospital, I was handcuffed to the bed. I was checked out thoroughly. "Was she raped?"

"I don't know," the woman officer said. "Her pants were undone, but from how she was tied into the chair, I don't think she was."

Lennox had come to the hospital. "No, she wasn't raped. She was smacked repeatedly in the face. Every time she wiggled or moved, whatever held her in that chair would get tighter."

"Do we know why this happened?"

"A man that tortured her twenty-one years ago and finally went to jail for what he did to her, was found in his cell last night. David and Gwen Bruno are Romeo Quins' parents."

"How is that?"

"Romeo's name is Romeo Quin Bruno."

"How do you know this?"

"Because I'm a federal agent," he said.

Patrick came out of the room. "Please tell me why my wife is handcuffed to a bed right now?"

Lennox stood there looking at me. "Put a goddamn blanket over her." When the nurse came in with the blanket, he snatched it from her and covered me with it. I didn't move. He looked at my battered face. "I'm sorry, Ken," he said. "I found out too late."

Patrick's phone rang. "Hello."

"Daddy, mommy didn't come get me from school."

"Can you get a ride from Aunt Addison?"

"No. She had to take Kate to the dentist and they all went with her."

"I'll be right there," Patrick said.

"But where is mommy?"

"She's in a meeting, buddy. I'm on my way." Patrick left the hospital and went to the school to get TJ. He called Trinity on his way. "Where are you?"

"Home. Why?"

"Something happened to Kenny and I need you to stay with TJ."

"Is she ok?"

"I don't know."

"What happened?"

"I don't know all the details. She's in the hospital."

"Oh my god. Do her parents know?"

"I don't know," Patrick said.

"Where are you now?"

"I'm getting TJ from school."

"Was she in an accident?"

"No, mom, she was fucking tortured for hours this morning. She was tied so tight in a chair that she couldn't move when she was cut free. The police had me put her on a gurney and they had to sedate her to take her to the hospital and she hasn't woken up. And she is struggling to speak. She couldn't say my name. When they gave her the injection to sedate her, she screamed bloody murder until the medicine took affect and she blacked out.

"And now they have her handcuffed to the bed, but she is completely out of it. And everything was going so well. For the first time ever, she was looking forward to the holidays and then this happens."

Meanwhile while TJ waited in the office for Patrick the news was on. TJ saw Patrick carrying me out of David and Gwen's apartment. He watched as Patrick put me down on the gurney and then how ten men and women held me down while I was given something. Tears seeped from his eyes.

"What's wrong?" the lady waiting with him asked.

"That's my mommy. MOMMY!" he cried.

Patrick parked the car and came running into the school. "What happened to mommy?"

"She's ok."

"She's not ok. You carried her from David and Gwen's. I saw you. I saw you put her down and then ten people holding her. I want mommy."

"Mommy isn't well right now," Patrick said.

"Please, daddy. I want mommy. I want mommy."

"Ok. I'll take you to see mommy." Patrick called Trinity. "Please meet me at the hospital. TJ saw it on the goddamn news. I'm taking him to see Kenny."

When he got back with TJ, Lennox had had the cuffs removed. Lennox had them put me in scrubs, so that I wasn't exposed anymore and now a woman officer sat in a chair guarding the room. I was still out of it. Lennox sat by the bed. The medical examiner was just finishing up. "She has suffered severe trauma," she said. "I was able to reattach the skin on her chin. It will be minimal scarring."

"When will she wake up?"

"She could be out a few more hours. She has a saline drip and we are giving her antibiotics as well."

"Thank you," Lennox said. "I appreciate you coming and examining her."

I woke up at eight that evening. When I opened my eyes, I didn't know where I was and panic set in. Lennox was still there with me. I looked at him. He got up from the chair. "Hi, how are you?"

"Nnn.nnn.nnned wat…"

He poured me a glass of water and gave it to me. I drank the whole thing and then closed my eyes for a minute.

"How long did they have me?" I asked with my teeth gritted together.

"A few hours. What do you remember?"

"Everything," I said opening my eyes and looking at him.

"Why were you there?"

"I brought them their keys for their new house." I drank more water.

"Tell me what happened after you got there."

"When I parked the truck, I got a chill," I said. "I went into the building and upstairs. Everything seemed normal. David hugged me. He took me in to see Gwen. She hugged me. Then he gave me something and when I came to, I was tied tight in a chair.

"I want to see Patrick. Is he here?"

"Yes."

Patrick came into the room. "Hey," he said softly. I slowly looked at him. "How are you?"

"I'm ok," I managed to say. I reached for him and he came on the bed. I put my head on his broad shoulder. He put his arms around me, and I fell asleep.

When I woke up, I was in my own bed at the house. TJ sat quietly on the chair in our room. He was reading a book. I opened my eyes and saw him sitting there. "Hi, baby," I said to him. I watched the tears fill in his eyes. "I'm sorry I couldn't pick you up from school. Are you mad at me?" He shook his head and the first of the tears ran down his face. "Want to come here?" He climbed up on the bed. "I promise you that I am ok," I said to him as I took him in my arms. He let out the sob that he was trying so hard to hold back. "Why are you crying?"

"I thought he was so nice."

"I know, honey, I did too."

"Did he hurt you bad, mommy?"

"No."

He ducked his head under my chin and cried a hardy cry. I took him in my arms and held him. "Ok. No more tears," I said. "We have to go downstairs and start looking through the cookbook."

"Why? Isn't Aunt Addy cooking?"

"Yeah, she is, but mommy's tradition is that everybody has to make something."

We went downstairs. Everyone was downstairs. Mom came rushing towards me. Before I was completely down the stairs, she grabbed me and pulled me into a hug. After everyone hugged me except for Beth, I gained my balance. I saw her sitting on the couch pouting. I walked over then sat next to her. "Are you ok?" I asked her.

"I thinked they were nice," she said.

"I know, baby," I said to her.

"I'm so mad."

"Why are you mad?"

"Because all I want to do is punch her in the nose."

"Me too," I said.

Tyson came and sat next to me. "Did he hurt you?"

"Come on guys," Addison said. "Leave Aunt Kenny alone."

"No, it's ok. Let them ask now," I said. "No, he didn't hurt me that bad," I said.

"But we saw Uncle Patrick carrying you."

"What?" I asked. I hadn't seen the news or even heard the news. Just then the local news came on and there I was being carried out of their apartment building and put on the gurney and then being held down. I heard myself screaming. "My god," I said. "And you all saw that?" I asked. They nodded.

"He hurt you bad enough to make you scream," Michael said.

"Shut it off," I said.

"Why did they all hold you like that?" Carter asked.

I stood up and faced all of them. "Ok, I will tell you all what happened." I didn't sit when I told them all what had happened. When I was done, and I assured them that I was fine, and I was. I was shaken up, but telling myself and the family that I was fine, was helping me believe that I really was.

We never made it in the kitchen to look up recipes. We all went into the theater and sat together. Jamie sat close to me as did Parker and mom and dad. TJ sat on my lap. The kids sat as close as they could get to me. Addison sat behind me never taking her hands off my shoulders. Patrick made his way over and he sat on the same seat as me. I rested my head against his shoulder. He brought his hand around me and he touched my chin. I winced. "I'm fine," I said.

"Sorry," he whispered.

"It's ok. I'm fine.

We watched movies all night long. We all wound up sleeping in the theater that night.

Through the weekend, TJ, Patrick, and I raked through the recipe books trying to figure out what we would make for Thanksgiving. "When will we make it, mommy?"

"On Wednesday," I answered.

"What did you used to make with your mom as a kid?" Patrick asked.

I laughed. "I wasn't ever allowed in this kitchen when I was growing up."

"Why is that?"

"Because I…"

Mom and dad came into the kitchen. "Because she ate everything," mom said with laughter in her voice.

"Were you chubby?" Patrick asked.

"Not a day in my life," I said.

"She was the human disposal," dad chimed in.

"Kind of like our son," I said to Patrick.

"She ate raw garlic once on a dare," Addison said coming into the kitchen. She kissed me on the cheek. "How is your chin?"

"Fine," I said.

"You need to treat it again," she said.

"Yeah. Yeah. I know."

"Do you need help doing it?" she asked.

I gripped the counter and nodded. Mom and dad took TJ out of the room. We went upstairs. I layed on the bed. Patrick sat next to me. I put my head back and closed my eyes super tight. Addison retrieved the ointment from the bathroom. She came to the bed and sat on the other side of me. "Talk to me, Ken," she said.

"About what?" I asked through gritted teeth.

"Tell me about the first time you saw Patrick," she said looking at Patrick.

"You know the story," I said still gritting my teeth.

"Yeah, I know. Hey did you ever tell Patrick about the time that you hit that grand slam?"

"No," I said.

"You hit a grand slam?"

"Yeah," I said.

"When?"

"When I was thirteen. I was in middle school. I wanted to play baseball. The coach was new, so I signed up putting down Kenny Jackson, so he assumed that I was a boy. The boys on the team were cool with me trying out and they even helped me out hiding my long hair for weeks. I made it through tryouts and he never realized."

Addison was waiting until I was relaxed, so she let me go on and on with my story.

"We were losing eight to six in the bottom of the seventh with bases loaded. I got up to bat and mom and dad were there. Dad stands up and says really loud that's my girl as I cracked the shit…" Addison applied the ointment. I drove my head back into the pillow wincing and crying.

"I know it hurts, sweetheart. I'm sorry."

"I cracked," I said with a low voice, "the shit out of the ball and it sored through the air and over the fence. When I ran into home plate the coach took my hat off and my hair fell out. He was stunned that eight weeks had gone by and he had no idea that he had a girl on the team."

We had finally decided on our Thanksgiving recipe that we would make as a family. Chocolate Pumpkin brownies with homemade pumpkin ice cream. We were making homemade brownies as well, not from a box. We had gone to the store together to gather all of the ingredients that we needed to make everything. We had kept all of the kids home for the week of Thanksgiving so that they wouldn't be bombarded with questions about me.

My five nieces and nephews were in the house all that week. They watched movie after movie. On Wednesday, Addison finally made them come home to help her prepare what they were contributing to the meal besides what Addison would be cooking in the morning at my house.

Addison had run back over to the house to apply the ointment, which by Wednesday I was getting better with and I could now stand and let her put it on. Patrick still couldn't do it, and I was ok with that. When she was done and I was done groaning and kicking the bathroom door, we went back downstairs. She kissed me and ran out the door. "You smell like bacon," I called after her.

"Shut up!" she called back. "Love you."

"I love you too."

When I came back in the kitchen, Patrick and TJ had started with the ingredients to make the ice cream. I walked up behind TJ and bent over him smelling his hair and then kissing him on the head.

"Daddy, mommy smelled me again."

"Well when she tells you that you are stinky then you have to take a shower."

I laughed so hard. As TJ said, "DADDY!"

"Yeah, Daddy," I said. "But TJ, you are taking a shower tonight no matter what."

"Ok, mommy," he said. "Can we start decorating for Christmas?"

"Not yet," Patrick and I said together.

We finished making the brownies and the ice cream by nine that even. TJ yawned. "No, young man, you cannot go to bed without a shower." Patrick put the ice cream in the freezer and the brownies on the stove covered with a clean dish towel. I carried TJ upstairs and supervised his shower. When he was done and dried off, I handed him his pajamas. He put the pants on with no shirt and then he reached for me. I lifted him into my arms. He put his head on my shoulder and before I walked into his room with him, he was sleeping.

So we had made chocolate pumpkin brownies with pumpkin ice cream. Addison, Parker, and the kids made bacon wrapped cornbread. Jamie and Lennox made a beautiful fruit salad which they put into a dried carved out pumpkin. Mom and dad made pumpkin cider. Trinity made a stuffing casserole with Ivy.

Thanksgiving morning, with the Macy's Day Parade playing on every TV downstairs, Addison came over to start the dinner. She stuffed one turkey with stuffing and stuck it in the oven, then she prepared a turducken, which is a turkey stuffed with a duck stuffed with a chicken. She made a separate plain stuffing that didn't go into the turkeys. She was boiling potatoes for the mashed potatoes and gravy. She prepared the green beans for green bean casserole.

"Are you going to make rice?" TJ asked.

"What, baby?"

"Are you going to make rice?"

"For what?"

"We have rice with gravy for Thanksgiving," he said.

"Yes, I will make rice."

Mom made her special deviled eggs that were topped with well-cooked breakfast sausage and bacon.

By the time everyone arrived that wasn't immediate family there was more than enough food to feed a small army. We didn't have a kids table set up, so everyone sat together. Jamie and Lennox held the twins. Everything went so nice. With all the food that was there, when we were done eating, there wasn't much food left. Everything was delicious. The house was filled with chatter.

Mom said that she was going shopping tomorrow with James and Addison. She asked me if I wanted to go.

"No, thank you," I said.

"She says the same thing every year," Jamie said. "What are you doing tomorrow?"

"We are going to Daytona for a family get away," I said.

"Oh, how nice," mom said.

"You are still doing that?" Trinity said.

"Yes, mom," Patrick said. "It's a tradition."

"But it isn't Kenny's tradition," Trinity said.

"Just the fact that Kenny is leaving the house and getting out this year, is a bonus," Parker said.

"Please drop it," I said.

Before everyone left, we toasted one more time to a very Happy Thanksgiving.

The trip to Daytona was fun. It was just the three of us. We went into the ocean, we fished, the played in the sand, at the park, and in the water. We rode our bikes. We danced together. At the end of the day on Friday, I sat between Patrick's legs and TJ sat between my legs. Patrick had his arms around me. We ignored in coming phone calls for the day and just stayed together. It was so nice.

That night with TJ sleeping soundly in his bed, Patrick and I were intimate. We kissed, we made love, and we just stayed wrapped in each other's arms. In the morning, before Patrick and TJ woke up, I took a shower and got dressed. I went out on the balcony watching the sunrise. I watched the sky turn pinkish orange with purple hues in the distance. I had remembered laying in the woods the morning I was found and seeing a similar sky. I had remembered thinking how in the hell did I ever let this happen. How did I let myself be tortured this brutally? I hadn't head Patrick come out on the balcony. As he touched my shoulder, I jolted forward.

"I'm sorry," we said together.

I stood up and faced him. "They have to know everything that their son did," I said.

"Did you sleep?"

"Yeah," I said. "But Patrick, they have to know."

"You would want to face them again?"

"I have to so I can finally start getting my life back."

"When do you want to do this?"

"As soon as possible," I answered him.

I saw TJ looking at us. I motioned for him to come. He came out on the balcony and I grabbed him and scooped him in my arms. He shrieked with laughter. I lifted him closer to me and bent my head to his stomach putting my mouth on him before I blew out a breath. He giggled and laughed. "Again," he said. I did a few more times. Every time he giggled then laughed.

"Get dressed ok."

"Yeah. Why?"

"Because I'm starving," I said.

"Can we have pizza?"

"What? For breakfast?" Patrick and I said together. "No."

TJ ran into the room and showered with the door opened and then got dressed. We went downstairs. It was still early. There was a waffle house in walking distance, so we walked there. We both held TJ's hands. We ordered breakfast: a kid's plate for TJ, Patrick ordered scrambled eggs with waffles and I ordered waffles with sausage. It was the same as the kid's plate with an added piece of sausage.

When we got back to the hotel, we gathered our stuff. We brought everything downstairs and left it with the concierge while we went to do the lighthouse. "Do you think it changed?"

"No," I said to TJ.

"But could it have?"

"In what way?" Patrick asked.

"Maybe they painted it."

"Maybe they did." They didn't.

"Will it always be red?"

"I think so."

"Why?"

"Because they want lighthouses to be seen," I said to him. "Let's say you and daddy are out to sea and you have lost your way and you start looking around. Don't you think you are going to spot something that first stands so high, and second stands out?"

"Yeah," he said.

"Would you go in that direction?"

"Nope," he said.

I lifted him up and held him like he was an airplane before I took a little nibble in his side, which of course had him laughing. "And why wouldn't you go in that direction?"

"I'd follow the dolphins."

"Oh, daddy, you'd be lost at sea for a long long time," I said laughing to Patrick.

"But mommy would be the hero," TJ said. "Mommy would come find us."

"Yes, I would," I said to him.

"That's because she loves us," Patrick said.

"Nope," TJ said. "It's because we make her whole."

"TJ, stop a second," I said. We all stopped. I got down on my knees in front of him and pulled him into a hug. "I love you so much."

"I love you too, mommy."

I stood up with him in my arms and Patrick joined in on the hug. "It's a TJ sandwich," Patrick said.

TJ laughed. "No, daddy. You just had breakfast. It's too early for lunch."

"Oh, all right." Patrick pulled back a little and then came back to the hug and he gently caught TJ's shoulder with his teeth.

We went up in the light house. It was a cold November morning. I stood leaning against Patrick with TJ leaning against me. We stood there for a long time like that. "TJ, are you cold?"

"No, mommy."

"Where was it that he first called you mommy?" Patrick asked.

"At the Tower," I said. "We were in the garden and he came running over and said mommy and then ran away. Then he thought that he upset me, so he was crying. I went and found him and just held him. I love holding him. I never want to put him down."

When we went home, we started decorating for Christmas. We went to the store buying new lights for outside of the house. After returning home, we hung them. TJ plugged in the blow-ups cheering as they came to life on the front yard. We put up four artificial Christmas trees the biggest and grandest one being in the family room. The one in the game room had Matchbox cars track around it. The one in the library had a train under it. The one in the conference room where the kids did their homework had wrapped empty boxes under it. And the one in the family room had a tree skirt under it with a light up church but was essentially empty under it.

"Is that where Santa will leave the presents?"

"Yes," Patrick and I said together.

"Can we put a tree in the apartment?"

"Sure we can. We will have to go visit Santa so you can tell him what you want. Do you want to write him a letter that we can we leave with him, so he won't forget?"

"Yeah," TJ said excitedly.

Dear Santa,

My name is TJ Alexander. I'm six. I have been a good boy this year. So good that I got a mommy. 😊

I want a puppy for Chwistmass, and games, and new caws to wace awound the tree, and a dwawing book.

The games I want are Mind Cwaft for my new Xbox, the hot wheels video game.

I want Legos and the fwissbee ball. And I want a new Gwavediggy truck, and monsturs twucks.

Love to Mrs. Claus.

Love, TJ

I read TJ's letter to Santa. Although I understood everything that he wrote, I was a little surprised to see how he spelled some of the words. Trinity was at the house. I showed it to her. "He wrote the letter w where the r's should go."

"He's dyslexic you know," she said.

"No, I didn't know," I said. "I've seen his writing for school, and he doesn't usually write like this."

"He's been through a lot."

"What the hell does that mean?" I asked.

"You all have been through a lot," she said. "When he gets nervous, he resorts back to that."

I didn't show it Patrick right away. I went and found TJ. "Hi, mommy," he said.

"Hi, sweetheart. What are you doing?"

"Watching cartoons."

"Can you turn that off a minute?"

He flicked off the TV and looked at me. I held his Christmas letter in my hand. "Am I in twouble?"

"Why would you be in trouble?"

"Did I write too much?"

"No."

Patrick came into the house. "Daddy!" Patrick walked over.

"Oh, you wrote your Christmas letter," he said.

"Yeah."

I handed it to him. Patrick looked at it. "What was going on when you were writing this letter?" he asked.

"Nothing."

"No, something happened."

"How do you know?" TJ asked.

"You misspelled some words here," he said. "You changed all the r's to w's. Did you get nervous about something?"

"You can tell us," I said.

He lowered his head. "I heard mommy on the phone with someone. She wants to see David and Gwen." Then he started to cry. "They hurt mommy real bad. They are bad people."

"TJ," I said. "I'm sorry that you heard me on the phone, but yes, I am going to meet with them."

"Can they hurt you?"

"No."

"Are you sure?"

"Yes. There will be police there to protect me from them."

"But why do you have to go?"

"Well, sweetheart, because they need to hear things and know things."

"And also, mommy needs to know things too," Trinity said coming into the room.

"Are you going to go alone?"

"No."

"Is grandma going with you?"

"I don't know yet who is going with me, but I promise you that I will be fine."

"Can I come?"

"Not this time, sweetheart," I said to him.

Patrick sat with TJ while he rewrote his Christmas letter. I kept the first one. When he was done with it, we took him to the mall and had pictures taken with Santa. First with just him and Santa and then pictures of all of us with Santa.

On Tuesday morning after I dropped TJ and the others off at school, I drove into Orlando and went to the county jail, where David, Gwen and Hayley were being held. I was seeing David first. I went through the metal detector and then I was frisked and patted down three times by three different guards. Finally I was led into a room, where a big thick tall officer stood against the wall. "You sit on this side of the table," he said. "When the prisoner comes in, no touching. Is that clear?"

"Yes, sir," I said.

David was brought it with his hands in cuffs. He sat down at the table. "Hi, how are you?" he asked.

"I'm fine," I said. "I wish I could tell you that I'm sorry for your loss, but I can't."

"Why did you come?"

"Because you need to know everything that Romeo did to me."

"He gave you consensual sex," he said.

"No, not even close. But you knew who I was. That's why you asked for me to build your house, so that you can get to know me, and you could see me. And so that you could see what your son did to me. You wanted to hear it. How he inflicted pain, how he tortured me, how he dumped my bloody naked body in the woods on the side of the road. I was seventeen. I was the same age that Hayley is now.

"Picture her; a beautiful young woman just graduating high school. Going to a party where she's given drinks and drugs by an older guy, who offers her a ride home. However, that ride home never happened. Instead he takes her off the Turnpike in a wooded area, where he ties her up and he has his way with her repeatedly for hours and hours and when she screams, he takes a knife out and presses it to her skin and then flicks away her skin as if erasing her, but it doesn't erase her; instead it mars her skin. He does this over eighty percent of her body before he presses the knife into her back and slices her from shoulder blade down her back repeatedly. And then he rapes her violently one more time before tossing her out of the truck like a piece of trash.

"That is what your son did to me. He striped me naked, he took my ring, my jacket, my necklace, and he kept them all of these years. Every time you went to his house, you probably saw them, yet you never asked how he got them did you?" I took a deep breath. "And then you come into my firm and you see me working and you see the marks that I can't hide and you ask me to build your house and you invite me and my child over your house to get to know us.

"I didn't know your son. I didn't know his name. I learned his name at a school party, which you were at and you heard his name. Why he doesn't have your last, I don't know, and I don't care, but you knew it."

"But why was Hayley arrested?"

"That wasn't up to me," I said.

"She never hurt you."

"Yet," I said. "You couldn't let it go that I don't like to be touched. You fed on the fact that I freak out and in front of my family, you lied saying that you could help me. Were you going to kill me?"

"No."

"Were you going to rape me?"

"No."

"Then why?"

"I wanted to humiliate you and degrade you. I wanted you to hurt."

"I've been hurting for twenty-one years," I said. I got up. The guard stepped closer. I stepped back toward him never taking my eyes off of David. Then I left. Once the door was closed, I leaned against the wall.

"Ma'am, are you ok?"

"Yes," I said.

CHAPTER THIRTY-THREE

We had gone Christmas shopping as a family. All of us together. The first time we went, we didn't buy anything. We all just browsed and looked at things that we might want for Christmas. With mom and dad, Parker and Addison, and Jamie and Lennox, Christmas for them would be easy. A nice housewarming present for their houses.

Michael had shown us clothes and shoes that he wanted. He took Patrick and Lennox in the game store and showed them the video games that he was interested in getting. Kate wanted just about everything in the music store. She wanted a bright pink violin. Patrick bought it for her that day because it was the last one in the store. He called me and told me that he had to go to the house for a few minutes, and he went home to hide the violin putting it high up in the closet out of sight. He had bought her the purple case for the violin as well. When she came and met me, I could see that she was pouting. "Hi, princess, what's wrong?"

"I just know that I'm not going to get what I really and truly want for Christmas," she said.

"And what's that?"

"A pink violin," she said.

"Well, Christmas is coming. You could ask Santa."

"Aunt Kenny, why would I be…"

"Don't finish that sentence."

"I'm growing up," she said.

"And there are four younger ones under you not to a mention the twins when they are old enough."

"But Carmen Sanchez told everyone the truth about…" she stopped because she was watching Beth jumping up and down as she saw Santa. She excused herself and went racing over to her baby sister and lifted her up, so she could see Santa.

"No, Katie, I want to dance with him."

"But he's a little busy right now," she said to Beth.

"But I want to dance with Santie Claus."

Music was playing and Beth threw her arms in the air and she went up on her toes and starting dancing like no one was watching and yet people were. Kate stepped back and started videoing her. She danced until the music stopped. She had brought everything to a halt that Santa rose from his chair and came over to Beth. "What would you like for Christmas," he asked her.

She shrugged. "Will you dance with me?"

And right there at that moment, Santa Claus danced with Beth. He took of her hands and he danced with her. She couldn't stop smiling. She thanked him when it was over, and she ran to Kate. "He danced with me. He danced with me."

"I know. I saw."

Addison had watched with Parker. Beth saw them and she ran not like a toddler, but like a grown girl right to Addison. "Santie danced with me mommy."

"I know, baby," she said picking her up.

Santa had motioned them over. His shift was ending, and the new Santa would be coming in at any minute. Beth had made an impression on him and he wanted to give her something right then and there. Addison and Parker walked over with Beth. "Is this your daughter?" he asked.

"Yes. Our youngest of five," Addison said.

"My name is Beth."

"Hi, Beth," he said.

Tyson came running over with Carter. "Daddy, I have to go," Tyson said.

"Me too," Beth said.

With Parker taking the three of them to the bathroom, Santa revealed himself to Addison. "I have a dance studio. My wife and I teach dance to kids five and up. How old is your daughter?"

"She is three."

"Well, I will make an exception for her. And it will be on me," he said. "Can she start in the new year?"

"Yes," Addison said.

He gave her his card with all the details. "Thank you so much," he said to her. He went back into costume when he saw them coming back and he gave Beth a teddy bear.

"Oh, thank you," she said.

"Thank you," he said to her patting her on the shoulder.

"Bye."

The kids were getting out of school on the twentieth. That day when we took the kids to school, they had parties. Holiday parties and then a special treat happened when the middle schoolers in the music program came to sing for the elementary school. Kate hadn't told anyone that she had a solo. She was called to the stage and given the microphone. Michael had been given permission to come watch. The kids sang Hark the Herald Angles Sing first. And then Kate started their second song with O Holy Night. Her voice carried like an angel's.

"It's hard to believe that she is just a fifth grader," a man said. "I'd pay money to see this child in concert one day."

Kate sang three solos and then she got choked up as they sang their last Christmas song. When it was over, she ran to Addison burying her face in Addison's chest. "What happened?" she asked.

"It's my last Christmas concert here as a student," she cried.

Michael came over and she jumped into his arms. He held her. "It's ok. You get to do this for at least three more years," he said. "I'm so proud of you."

She pulled her head off of his shoulder and looked at him. "You are?"

"My God, Katie," he said. "You're awesome."

She wrapped her arms around him again and then she got down. "Thank you for being here."

When we took the kids home, we all celebrated together. The next few days, we did fun stuff with them. We took them to see snow in Orlando. We took them shopping to buy presents for their parents. Addison took TJ. Surprisingly, we didn't run into each other. When each of the kids had picked something for both parents and everything was paid for, I took them to the arcade. I gave each of them twenty dollars of tokens to go play. After that we went home. Storm was there and she did a craft with the kids. Even with the twins. She had made their footprint and their hand print in ceramic and under it before she baked it, she carved **BABY'S FIRST CHRISTMAS** with their names on it.

"It's mommy's first Christmas being a mommy," TJ said.

"I know, pumpkin," Storm said.

"What can we get her that she will always have to remember?"

"Why don't we go to the store and see what we come up with?"

She took TJ to the store and she had already had TJ's face engraved in a charm. Now on the back, she had engraved from TJ to me, *Mommy's First Christmas 2017*. They picked a nice box to put it in and Storm wrapped it up.

Christmas Eve we all gathered at the house and though we aren't Italian, we had the traditional Italian Fish dinner. Addison didn't cook this meal. Mom did. She was half Italian and she grew up having it for dinner on Christmas Eve and she carried it over to the three of us. The table was decorated so nice. There was shrimp, king crab legs, fried salted cod fish, fried cod fish, scallops, calamari in a marina sauce, and conch in a separate marina sauce. Plus, mom always made conch fritters for us, and there was smoked white fish, which was from dad's side of the family brought to the holiday meal. We all ate dinner and laughed about stories that we were being told.

Once dinner was over, we sat with the fireplace burning, listening to Christmas Carols. At eleven thirty, we all went to Midnight Mass and when we returned home, I read The Night Before Christmas to the kids.

At four in the morning, the presents were brought in and placed around the Christmas tree. We finished the last few things that needed to be assembled. By the time, Patrick and I climbed into bed it was nearing five in the morning. An hour later, TJ and the others started yelling that Santa had come waking up all the adults. We went downstairs and the kids were all gathered by the tree waiting patiently for the adults to come in.

The kids opened their presents first. There were toys everywhere. Beth wanted a doll and all the accessories that came with him. She got the car too. She was so excited. Tyson had asked for Spider-Man things and he was thrilled. Carter had asked for more space things. His biggest gift was a model rocket that we would help him start building over the break. Katie was given a case to keep her music in and a karaoke machine. Michael received new earphones that were wireless. TJ had new cars, a new Grave Digger. There were video games and movies scattered about the floor, yet each kid knew who's were who's.

"Ok, and now for some special presents," I said. "A little something extra that maybe Santa didn't know about."

The kids laughed. Michael wanted to go see a wrestling match, so he was given tickets to go to that. Kate got her new violin and case. Carter was given tickets to go to the space center. He was so excited. Tyson was going to get to spend a day in one of theme parks and get to go on all the roller coasters that he wanted to go on. Beth was given things for her upcoming dance classes.

TJ wasn't expecting anything else. He was thrilled with everything he had received, but he had asked for one more thing in that letter to Santa. I left the room and came back with a box with holes in it. I placed it on the floor gently. "TJ this is for you," I said. He came over and lifted the lid and then he started to cry. "I got a puppy. I got a puppy," he said again.

"Yes, and you can name him anything that you want?"

He took the puppy out of the box and the puppy started licking him and licking him. "I want to name him Jackson," he said.

"That's a great name," Patrick agreed.

After the kids had opened up all of their presents, the adults opened their presents. Jamie opened up the presents for the twins. Addison and Parker opened the gifts from the kids first. I had given mom, Jamie, and Addison a day at the spa.

When I opened the charm and necklace from TJ and Storm, tears rushed in my eyes. I loved all of my presents as well. So did Patrick. I had given him a day to spend with my father, Lennox, and Parker - a day on the golf course.

We ended Christmas day, with a family portrait, but everyone was in it. Whoever was at the house to celebrate the holidays with us was present in the picture.

That night when we went into the apartment, Patrick gave me my gift from him. He handed me a sweater box that was wrapped. I started to unwrap it. TJ came and sat close by. Inside the sweater box, I found another wrapped boxed. I smiled and unwrapped it to find yet another wrapped box. The boxes kept getting smaller and smaller until finally I came to a small box. I unwrapped the last box and opened it to find a ring with a key and a heart. "Because Kennedy "Kenny" Alexander, you are truly the key to my heart. I adore you and I love you."

www.ingramcontent.com/pod-product-compliance
Lightning Source LLC
Chambersburg PA
CBHW031731180726
48283CB00005B/1463